The Life of Captain John Smith

Available from the Simms Initiatives and the University of South Carolina Press

The Army Correspondence of Colonel John Laurens, ed.

As Good as a Comedy and Paddy McGann

Beauchampe

Border Beagles

Carl Werner, 2 vols.

The Cassique of Kiawah

Castle Dismal

Charlemont

The Charleston Book, ed.

Confession

Count Julian

The Damsel of Darien, 2 vols.

Dramas: Norman Maurice, Michael Bonham, and Benedict Arnold

Egeria

Eutaw

The Forayers

The Geography of South Carolina

The Golden Christmas

Guy Rivers

Helen Halsey

Historical and Political Poems (*which includes* Monody, The Vision of Cortes, The Tri-Color, Donna Florida, and Charleston and Her Satirists)

The History of South Carolina

Joscelyn

Katherine Walton

The Letters of William Gilmore Simms, Vol. 1

The Letters of William Gilmore Simms, Vol. 2

The Letters of William Gilmore Simms, Vol. 3

The Letters of William Gilmore Simms, Vol. 4

The Letters of William Gilmore Simms, Vol. 5

The Letters of William Gilmore Simms, Vol. 6 (exp. ed.)

The Life of Captain John Smith

The Life of the Chevalier Bayard

The Life of Francis Marion

The Lily and the Totem

Marie de Berniere

Martin Faber and Other Tales, 2 vols.

Mellichampe

The Partisan

Pelayo, 2 vols.

Poems, Descriptive, Dramatic, Legendary, and Contemplative, 2 vols.

The Remains of Maynard Davis Richardson

Richard Hurdis

Sack and Destruction of the City of Columbia

The Scout

Selections from the Letters and Speeches of the Hon. James H. Hammond, ed.

Simms's Poems Areytos

Social and Political Prose: Slavery in America/Father Abbot

South Carolina in the Revolutionary War

Southward Ho!

Stories and Tales

A Supplement to the Plays of William Shakespeare

Vasconselos

Views and Reviews in American Literature, History and Fiction, 2 vols.

Voltmeier

War Poetry of the South

The Wigwam and the Cabin

Woodcraft

The Yemassee

The Life of Captain John Smith

The Founder of Virginia

William Gilmore Simms

Critical Introduction by Carey Roberts
With a Biographical Overview by David Moltke-Hansen

The University of South Carolina Press

Cloth original published by George F. Cooledge and Brother, 1847
Paperback published by the University of South Carolina Press
Columbia, South Carolina 29208

www.sc.edu/uscpress

Manufactured in the United States of America

25 24 23 22 21 20 19 18 17 16
10 9 8 7 6 5 4 3 2 1

ISBN 978-1-61117-689-6 (pbk)

Published in cooperation with the Simms Initiatives, a project of the University of South Carolina Libraries with the generous support of the Watson-Brown Foundation, and with additional funding by the John Govan Simms Endowment.

William Gilmore Simms: A Biographical Overview

David Moltke-Hansen

Introduction

Harper's Weekly put it succinctly in its July 2, 1870, issue: "In the death of Mr. Simms, on the 11th of June, at Charleston, the country has lost one more of its time-honored band of authors, and the South the most consistent and devoted of her literary sons" (qtd. In Butterworth and Kibler 125–26). Indeed no mid-nineteenth-century writer and editor did more than William Gilmore Simms to frame white southern self-identity and nationalism, shape southern historical consciousness, or foster the South's participation and recognition in the broader American literary culture. No southern writer enjoyed more contemporary esteem and attention, at least after Edgar Allan Poe moved north. Among American romancers (or writers of prose epics), only New Yorker James Fenimore Cooper was as successful by the 1840s. In those same years, Simms was the South's most influential editor of cultural journals. He also was the region's most prolific cultural journalist and poet, publishing an average of one book review and one poem per week for forty-five years.

Before his death Simms saw his national reputation fall along with the Confederacy he had vigorously supported and with the slave regime that many in the North had come to despise. Nevertheless reprints of most of the twenty titles in the selected edition of his works, first published between 1853 and 1860, appeared up until World War I. Thereafter only *The Yemassee*, an early romance about an Indian war in South Carolina, continued in print. The tide began to turn in the 1950s, when five volumes of Simms's letters appeared and a growing number of his works were issued in new editions. Publication in 1992 of the first literary biography, by John C. Guilds, and establishment of the William Gilmore Simms Society and the *Simms Review* the next year at once reflected and fostered this revived interest. Yet not until the 2011 launch of the digital Simms edition of the South Caroliniana Library of the University of South Carolina did scholars of southern, American, and nineteenth-century culture have the prospect of ready access to all of Simms's separately published works. With the University of South Carolina Press's cooperation, readers also will have access to sixty works in paperback editions by the end of 2014. Simms himself never saw nearly so many of his works in print at one time.

Clearly the decline in the critical standing of, and historical attention to, Simms and his oeuvre in the century after his death has reversed in the years since. The last three decades of the twentieth century saw more published on Simms than the previous hundred years (Butterworth and Kibler 126–200; MLA International). The last decade of the twentieth and first decade of the twenty-first centuries saw more dissertations and theses on him (forty-one) than had appeared in all the years before. This is not to say that Simms is yet given the attention directed to some of his contemporaries. For the first decade of the twenty-first century, the Modern Language Association International Bibliography lists roughly four times as many scholarly publications on James Fenimore Cooper, more than ten times as many on Nathaniel Hawthorne, and sixteen times as many on Edgar Allan Poe. Not surprisingly, therefore, Simms is not yet included in most anthologies of American literature, although he is a subject or a source in an expanding and ever more diverse body of scholarship.

To prepare to read Simms, it is important to see his writings in multiple contexts. He rarely wrote about himself outside of his more personal poems and his letters (some fifteen hundred of the many thousands of which survive). Yet he systematically drew on his background, personal experience, and relationships in his work. He also shaped that work through a progressively developed poetics and philosophy of life, history, and art. He did so in the context of his very broad reading of both contemporary and earlier Western literature and in the midst of multiple professional engagements and responsibilities. The richness and variety of these writings and involvements make Simms a key figure for future understanding of the literary culture, issues, and networks in mid-nineteenth-century America.

Background

Simms's family history reflected the dynamics that fueled the spread southward and westward of the populations, plantation economy, and society of the South Atlantic states. Simms's ancestry also reflected the Scots-Irish and English roots of what became identified as southern culture by the 1830s, a generation after the end of most immigration to the region. Two of Simms's grandparents, William and Elisabeth Sims, were Scots-Irish and migrated to South Carolina from Ulster. One, John Singleton, was an American-born son of putatively English immigrants, who had come to South Carolina from Virginia. The fourth, Jane Miller, was daughter of two Scots-Irish and Irish descended people—John Miller, of North and then South Carolina, and Jane Ross. Ross's family also migrated to South Carolina from western Virginia, where members lived cheek by jowl with other Scots-Irish families, who migrated to the Carolinas (White, *Ross*). Simms's father and Uncle James migrated in 1808 from Charleston to Tennessee, then to Mississippi. This was after the bankruptcy of the elder William's business and the deaths of his wife and their other two sons. Following the last of these losses, the elder Simms's hair turned white in a week. To his anguished eyes, Charleston appeared "a place of tombs" (qtd. in Guilds 6, 12).

For the son, however, Charleston was home—so much so that he refused to leave his maternal grandmother and move to Mississippi when his uncle came to get him in 1816. Then the fifth largest and by far the wealthiest city, as well as one of the greatest ports, in America, Charleston was at the peak of its influence (Moltke-Hansen, "Expansion" 25–31; Rogers). Cotton culture on the sea islands to the south, begun in 1790, and rice culture in impounded lowcountry tidal marshes meant that the port was filled not only with sailors of many lands and languages, but also with enslaved people of many African and Creole cultures and speech ways (slaves continued to be imported legally in large numbers until 1808). This street life made vivid the transnational nature of plantation agriculture and the fact that the developing region's dramatically expanding borders "were not just geographic; they also were human, historical, and intellectual" (Moltke-Hansen, "Southern" 19).

Even more important for the future author, the expanding region's borders and nature were taking imaginative shape. The West of the senior William Gilmore Simms and the first Creek War in which he fought, the Revolutionary War of the young Simms's maternal grandfather, the backcountry of many related Scots-Irish settlers, all these became grist for a lonely, energetic boy, who spent as much time with books as he could (Simms, *Letters* 1:161). The possibilities of such settings, incidents, and characters were not confined to history alone. Simms reported that he "used to glow and shiver in turn over 'The Pilgrim's Progress,'" while "Moses' adventures in 'The Vicar of Wakefield' threw [him] into paroxysms of laughter" (Hayne 261–62). Sir Walter Scott's Border and medieval romances and James Fenimore Cooper's Leatherstocking tales also deeply colored his imagination (Simms, *Views* 1:248, and Moltke-Hansen, "Southern" 6–15). As affecting were the ghost stories and Revolutionary War tales of his grandmother and the verses sent, and tales told, by his father.

These diverse tales became reasons to explore—in books, but also on the ground. As a boy, Simms ranged through the city and along the banks of the Ashley River, which fed into Charleston Harbor. He did so in search of scenes of colonial and Revolutionary battles and incidents (*Letters* 1:lxii). He first heard his uncle's and father's many Irish and frontier stories when they visited in Charleston in 1816 and 1818, respectively. He heard more on his trips to Mississippi during the winter of 1824 through the spring of 1825 and again in 1826. The first trip took him through Georgia and Alabama, where he saw elements of the Creek and Cherokee nations. At the time, Simms later reported, he was a boy "cumbered with fragmentary materials of thought, . . . choked by the tangled vines of erroneous speculation, and haunted by passions, which, like so many wolves, lurked, in ready waiting, for their unsuspecting prey" (*Social* 6). When he first got to Mississippi, traveling partly by stage, partly by riverboat, and partly by horse, Simms learned that his father had just come back from "a trip of three hundred miles into the heart of the Indian country" (Trent 15). Later father and son "rode together on horseback to various settlements on the frontier of Alabama and Mississippi" (Guilds 10–11, 17–18). Simms recalled as well "having traveled 150 miles beyond the Mississippi" (Shillingsburg, "Literary Grist" 120). The next year he returned to the Southwest by ship. "During this [second] trip he carried a 'note book.'" There he jotted episodes, encounters, stories heard, characters seen, and descriptions of the landscapes unfolding around him. He also wrote "at least sixteen poems" (Kibler, "First"; Shillingsburg, "Literary Grist" 123).

Simms took a third western trip five years later, writing letters back to the newspaper that by then he was editing (*Letters* 1:10–38). Together these three trips provided materials for his writings over more than forty years. "The first . . . produced mainly short fiction; the second inspired much poetry; . . . the first and third . . . yielded three novels written in the 1830s" (Shillingsburg, "Literary Grist" 119). This was, in part, because of the trips' timing. Sixteen years after the first trip, Simms told students at the University of Alabama that in the interval their world had changed from a howling wilderness into a place of growing civilization (Simms, *Social* 5–6). Had he not gone when he did, he would have been too late to see the frontier. Later travels took him many other places and also provided much grist for his writing. Never again, however, did he experience the frontier firsthand. Furthermore, on these later trips Simms was a practiced professional writer, no longer that boy haunted by passions.

Personal Life

After the ten-year-old boy's momentous refusal to leave Charleston, his grandmother sent Simms for two years to the grammar school taught on the campus and by the faculty of the nearly moribund College of Charleston. By then he already was "versifying the events of the war [of 1812]," just concluded, publishing "doggerel" in the local papers, and learning to read in several languages (*Letters* 1:285). His trip west a decade later helped him decide to pursue both literature and a career in law, but back in Charleston—this despite his father's urging that he stay in Mississippi. Upon his return home, he began to read law and also launched a literary weekly, the *Album,* which ran for a year. He became engaged as well to Anna Malcolm Giles, daughter of a grocer and former state coroner.

A year later the young couple married. This was six months before Simms was admitted to the South Carolina bar, on his twenty-first birthday, not long before he was appointed as a city magistrate. Although living up the Ashley River in the more healthful, less expensive village of Summerville, Simms kept a law office in the city. Shortly after using his maternal inheritance to buy the *City Gazette* at the end of 1829 and moving down to Charleston Neck, just north of the city limits where he had lived as a boy, Simms lost both his father and his maternal grandmother. He also found himself attacked because of his Unionist stance in the Nullification crisis resulting from South Carolina's rejection of a federal tariff. Then, in early 1832, Simms's wife died. Soon after, he took his four-year-old daughter back to Summerville to live and determined to sell his newspaper and leave the state for a literary life in the North.

Fueling his ambition was the correspondence Simms had begun several years earlier with an accountant whom he had published in his *City Gazette* but not yet met—Scots immigrant James Lawson. At the time Lawson, seven years Simms's senior, edited a New York City newspaper and, in addition to writing plays and poetry, was a friend (and, later, informal literary agent) to a wide circle (McHaney, "An Early"). Simms's trip north in the summer of 1832 saw the two begin a lifelong friendship, cemented as they squired ladies about and interacted with Lawson's literary circle. In subsequent years Simms multiplied the number of his friendships, in both the North and the South, making them in some measure a replacement for the family that he had lost. Lawson remained the closest of his northern friends, while James Henry Hammond, a future governor and U.S. senator, became his closest friend in South Carolina.

Late in 1833, after his Summerville house burned, Simms wrote Lawson to say that he was enamored of "a certain fair one" (*Letters* 1:73). Seventeen-year-old Chevillette Eliza Roach was the daughter of "a literary-minded aristocrat of English descent" with two plantations on the banks of the Edisto River in Barnwell District (later County) (Guilds 70). The courtship was protracted, as Simms felt it necessary first to clear debts that friends had bought up on his behalf. He also was determined "to marry no woman" before he was "perfectly independent of her resources, and her friends" (*Letters* 1:78). Therefore he did not propose until the spring of 1836. The nuptials took place seven months later, and as a result, Simms came to call the four thousand acres of Woodlands Plantation, with its seventy slaves, home. It was twenty years, however, before he took over management of the plantation and, then, only in the wake of his father-in-law's final sickness and death. Five years after that, he lost his wife, the mother of fourteen of his fifteen children. Nine of the children Chevillette bore him had already died, devastating Simms repeatedly. Five were still living (three sons and two daughters), as was Simms's daughter by his first marriage, who helped raise the youngest of her siblings. Those remaining children—even Gilly, who fought in the Confederate army—all outlived their father. Gilly and a brother-in-law ran Woodlands after the war, when Simms, though dying of cancer, was earning what he could by writing again for publications in the North and editing one or another South Carolina newspaper.

Career

The trip north in 1832 did not result in Simms moving there. Except during the Civil War, however, he returned almost every year. This was because the contacts he made, and the exposure to literary culture that he enjoyed, helped him define his future as an author. Earlier he had written fiction and criticism as well as journalism, filling the pages of several short-lived cultural journals and his newspaper, but between the ages of nine and twenty-six Simms had focused his literary efforts primarily on poetry. Beginning with his first book of verse in 1825, he had published five small volumes in Charleston. A couple had received positive notice in New York, and in the fall of 1832, J. & J. Harper issued the sixth anonymously from there, *Atalantis: A Story of the Sea.* Coming back the following summer, Simms had in hand for the Harpers a gothic novella, *Martin Faber,* and after his return south, he also would send the manuscript of his first two-volume border romance, *Guy Rivers: A Tale of Georgia.*

The reception of these and the romances and short stories that followed quickly made Simms one of the nation's most successful fictionists. He continued to issue poetry as well—roughly a collection every three years over the thirty-seven years that he worked as a professional author. But this output was dwarfed by the fiction—on average a title every year (counting several serialized works but not counting the many revised editions). Then there were the two dozen separately published orations, histories, and biographies as well as edited collections of documents and dramas and a geography of South Carolina. Add to these the revised editions and the further printings and issues of his own works and it appears that Simms saw a title coming off the presses at the rate of one every three months or so. Making that figure all the more astounding is the fact that, during more than a dozen of those years (the early-to-mid 1840s, the late 1840s-to-early 1850s, and the mid-to-late 1860s), he also was editing a cultural journal or newspaper. Furthermore he contributed reams of reviews and poems, hundreds of op-ed pieces and columns, and dozens of short stories and public addresses, which were never collected and published in volume form.

His career mapped an arc. It ascended meteorically in the 1830s and peaked in the early-to-mid 1840s, before beginning to descend. One reason was the popularity of the historical fiction that Simms began to write. When he left behind the law, his first newspaper, and the Nullification controversy, as well as his sadness, historical fiction was all the rage. Sir Walter Scott had fueled the craze, beginning with the publication of his first Border romance in 1814. He died in September 1832. Seventeen years Simms's senior, James Fenimore Cooper, the closest America had to a Scott at the time, was at the peak of his reputation and success, having started publishing his romances in 1820. Thus the way had been prepared for a writer of Simms's historical imagination and preoccupations. Within five years of his first trip north, moreover, Lawson's (and now his) circle became loosely affiliated with a nationalistic and Democratic group, self-styled Young America, this after Young Italy and similar ethnic, nationalist, European, cultural and political movements (Moltke-Hansen, "Southern"). Edgar Allan Poe and other members gave Simms's first fictions positive, if not uncritical, attention.

By the end of the 1830s, paradoxically, Simms, like Cooper, found his success attracting unauthorized editions of his works because Britain and America did not have an international copyright agreement. Further, in the wake of the panic of 1837, Americans bought fewer books. Simms's response was to diversify his portfolio. He turned to biography and history, including his hugely successful *Life of Francis Marion* (1844). He also returned to the editor's chair, overseeing one and then another cultural journal. These were unlike the ones he had edited in the 1820s: they included contributions by numerous authors, not just those from Charleston, but from the region and also the North. The ambition motivating the journals was to connect and promote Charleston intellectually. Consequently the journals more closely resembled metropolitan quarterly reviews in their offerings.

The mid-1840s saw Simms involved in politics, even serving a term in the South Carolina legislature. By the middle of the Mexican-American War in 1847, he had concluded that the South needed to become an independent nation. Thereafter, although he maintained ties with many in the Young America circle, he no longer promoted his writings as fostering Americanism in literature (*Views*). Instead he increasingly emphasized the ways in which his three romance series — the colonial, the Revolutionary, and the border — were making tangible and meaningful the origins and development of the future southern nation and the sad but inevitable consequences for Native Americans (Watson, *From Nationalism*; compare Nakamura).

Sectional politics colored more and more of Simms's perceptions, speeches, and private communications. The rising tide of abolitionism had him aghast. It also fed his growing sense that his position in American letters was slipping. He returned to editing, and his poetry, which was more often explicitly about the South, became increasingly patriotic in tone. Although his first biographer, William Peterfield Trent, insisted that Simms's declining standing reflected the change in literary fashion from historical romances to realistic novels, Simms in fact wrote more and more as a social realist in the 1850s (Wimsatt, "Realism").

The Civil War consumed Simms. As he wrote Lawson, "Literature, especially poetry, is effectually overwhelmed by the drums, & the cavalry, and the shouting" (*Letters* 4:369–70). He did manage to editorialize often and to rework and finish things long on his desk, including poems, a novel, and a dramatic treatment of Benedict Arnold, the northern traitor in the Revolutionary War. Then, in the wake of the Confederacy's loss and the failure of his vision for the South, he found himself recording the loss in a new newspaper, dealing with the trauma in his poetry, and becoming more existential and psychological in his fictional treatments. Simms's old New York friends tried to help. He did edit and see through publication a volume of Confederate war poetry. Yet it is a measure of his reduced stature that the several new romances he published appeared only in serial form. In part this may have been because he was in a sense competing with himself. Publishers were beginning to reprint volumes out of the selected edition of his writings. Many of Simms's works were available in book form, just not new works.

Associations

As the *Letters* testify, Simms had complex, overlapping networks of friends and colleagues. As a boy and young man, he received the friendship, patronage, and commendation of a variety of well-placed people in Charleston, including Charles Rivers Carroll. It was Carroll with whom he read law, to whom he dedicated his first romance, and after whom he named a son. Both men were Unionists during the Nullification controversy. So were Hugh Swinton Legare (later U.S. attorney general) and the considerably older William Drayton, as well as lawyer and editor Richard Yeadon and Greenville, South Carolina, newspaper editor Benjamin Franklin Perry. Also considerably older was James Wright Simmons, who had joined with Simms to launch the *Southern Literary Gazette* in 1828, when Simms was twenty-two. Through him Simms had direct contact with such British literary figures as Leigh Hunt and Byron (Kibler, *Poetry* 15).

The next group of influential friends and collaborators that Simms acquired were members of the Lawson circle and included such figures as Edwin

Forrest, the Shakespearean actor, and Evert Duyckinck, who published several of Simms's volumes in Wiley and Putnam's series Library of American Books, which he edited. Among the many others were poets and editors William Cullen Bryant and Fitz-Greene Halleck. Simms also made nonliterary friends in New York and Philadelphia, such as John Jacob Bockee and William Hawkins Ferris, the cashier at the U.S. Treasury office in New York who, after the war, helped Simms, Henry Timrod (poet laureate of the Confederacy), and others.

As a Barnwell planter, Simms met a widening circle of South Carolina's leaders and literati. For instance his acquaintance with James Henry Hammond began in the late 1830s and deepened into a friendship in the early 1840s. It was in the early 1840s, too, when he again was editing cultural journals, that Simms became friends with many southern writers. He regarded several of them, including Virginians George Frederick Holmes, Edmund Ruffin, and Nathaniel Beverley Tucker as members, together with Hammond and himself, in a "sacred circle." Uniting the circle were members' devotion to the South and a shared sense of the marginal status and critical importance of the life of the mind in a largely rural and unintellectual region (Faust, *Sacred*). Others of Simms's wide connections in the region did not interact as much with each other, but Simms long corresponded with Maryland novelist and lawyer John Pendleton Kennedy, Irish-born Georgia poet Richard Henry Wilde, Alabama lawyer and writer Alexander Beaufort Meek, and Louisiana historian and assistant attorney general Charles Gayarré, among others. By the 1850s, when Simms once more returned to editing a cultural journal, many of the writers whom he recruited were members of a younger generation. Poets Paul Hamilton Hayne and Henry Timrod were two. Often they and a half dozen others of Simms's and their generations met in John Russell's Charleston Book Shop and adjourned to dinner at Simms's Smith Street home, "dubbed 'The Wigwam'" (*Letters* 1:cxxxvi). Shortly before his death fifteen or so years later, Simms wrote Hayne, "I am rapidly passing from the stage, where you young men are to succeed me" (*Letters* 5:287).

Thought

The welter of Simms's works disguises unities and dynamics of the thought underlying them. From early on Simms was convinced that art ennobles or transforms, as well as gives voice to individuals and societies; therefore it must be cultivated assiduously. Without the potential for high artistic attainment, he insisted, societies are not ready for the independence and regard of free peoples. This is where Simms the historian joined Simms the poet. Societies develop, he argued (using the stadialism of the Scottish historical school), from imitation through self-assertion to achievement and also from savagery through strife to settled agricultural communities and, ultimately, to a hierarchical civilization supporting a rich artistic life. It was the job of the artist to help envision the goal, inspire the pursuit, and inform the process. That process was at once progressive and dialectical. Order, without dynamism, stifled development, as did the obverse—the dominance by ungoverned impulses or uncontrolled license. This was true in the individual, but also in societies as a whole. War was necessary for civilization, but its success was measured in the securities of the home, the center of cultural production and reproduction.

Whether in the public or in the domestic arena, "the true governor, as [Thomas] Carlyle call[ed] him—the king man—" guided rather than impeded the forces of change and progress (Simms, "Guizot's" 122). There were few such men with the capacity to lead. The same was true of nations. Neither all people nor all peoples were equal in either capacity or attainment. That was why Native Americans were overrun and Africans had been enslaved by European peoples in the New World. Indeed, Simms argued, "slavery in all ages has been found the greatest and most admirable agent of Civilization," giving education and examples to less evolved peoples (*Letters* 3:174). The degree to which a people had evolved mattered. That was why, he held, Americans had won independence from the most powerful empire in the world. They had done so through their Revolution, led by an elite that felt correctly its time had come (Simms, "Ellet's" 328). By mid-1847 that also was Simms's judgment for the South: the region had evolved enough to become independent (*Letters* 2:332). The hope inspired and then failed him and the people he sought to lead.

While not all men could rise to the highest rank, they all had the same responsibility at home. There the father was patriarch, protector, and head, while the mother was nurturer, moral instructor, and heart. There, too, children's characters and minds were formed by age twelve ("Ellet's"). Children's upbringing was critical to citizenship, and it was through her sons and the support of her husband, father, and brothers that a woman shaped the public sphere. The culture and character instilled in the child expressed and informed not just the household, but the larger society—the people.

"The history of peoples and their embodiments in institutions, states, and artistic productions—these were the great subjects" in Simms's view (Moltke-Hansen, "Southern" 120). Yet "poets were the only class of philosophers who had recognized" this until his own day, when at last "we now read human histories. We now ask after the affections as well as the ceremonies of society" ("Ellet's" 319–20). Peoples or races—that is, ethnic groups—were not unchanging any more than were their politics and their cultures. They either advanced or were overrun by history. Further, new peoples emerged, and old identities were submerged. The Spanish conquistadors were the creation of centuries of conflict with the Moors: their motivation was the glory of conquest, not the routine of trade or the plow. On the other hand, the English settlements in North America reflected the impulse to transform the wilderness into verdant farms and build society (*Views* 64, 178–85; *Social* 8). The same impulse drove Americans westward in Simms's own day and gave Americans their Manifest Destiny.

To explore these facts of the South's settlement and its place in international conflicts, Simms wrote all together, between 1833 and 1863, two romances set in eighth-century Spain, two set during the Spanish exploration and conquest of the Americas and two during the later English colonization of South Carolina, seven set during the American Revolution, and—depending on how one counts—perhaps eight set on the borders of the nineteenth-century South. After the war he published one more Revolutionary romance and two more that, like it, were set beyond the boundaries of civilization. He also left two unfinished romances, also set beyond society's normal reach. These late works, however, no longer had as their framing justification the cultivation of the South's future and civilization.

White southerners had their independence foreclosed by the war. In his last works, therefore, Simms found himself exploring the psychological, philosophical, and historical impulses that led to the Confederacy's demise and what, in the aftermath, it meant to be a good man and to build for the future, however impoverished. On the first score, he argued that the impulse to idealism behind abolitionism ignored historical realities, becoming inhuman in its consequences. On the latter score, he affirmed responsibility for one's dependents and the virtues of stoicism, as well as a continued commitment to the beauty and truth of art and the impulses to the cultivated life and fields. Therefore, in the face of the burning of his Woodlands home and library in February 1865—during Sherman's march and in the midst of desperate circumstances—he insisted that home, or the ideals and past characterizing its potential, still was at the center of true civilization, but only if elevated by art (*Sense* 8, 17). It was wrong to measure civilization by the getting, spending, and mad dashing, or material progress and utilitarianism, characteristic of both a capitalistic North and also many southerners. These traits he often had attacked even before the war, insisting that "the work of the Imagination, which is the Genius of a race, is only begun when its material progress is supposed to be complete" (*Poetry* 12).

Writings

Simms expressed many of his ideas most personally in letters and most cogently in essays, speeches, and occasional introductions to his books. But he illustrated them most fully in his fiction and poetry. By the time he arrived in New

York in 1832, he had formed many of the core ideals and beliefs that would shape his work. His application of them, however, modified his understanding over time. Growing as a writer and growing in knowledge and experience, he also grew as a thinker.

In his hierarchy of values, poetry came first. It was a prophetic calling as well as evocative of the deeply felt (or, sometimes, the fleeting) and thus testimony to the perdurance and transcendence of the beautiful and the human spirit. Yet, as Simms often ruefully reflected, prose spoke to many more people. That was a principal reason why he turned to writing prose epics or romances. He gave his most concerted consideration of poetry's value and roles in three lectures in Charleston in 1854. Over the prior three years he had given portions of them in Augusta, Georgia, Washington, D.C., and Richmond and Petersburg, Virginia. Entitled *Poetry and the Practical*, they did not see print until 1996, as Simms never found the time to expand them as he wanted. On the other hand, his last address on the same themes, *The Sense of the Beautiful*, was issued soon after he delivered it, also in Charleston.

Many of his important reviews have not yet been gathered, but Simms collected some in 1845–46, and *Views and Reviews in American Literature, History and Fiction* came out in 1846 and 1847 in two "series." Beginning with a consideration of "Americanism" in literature, the first series explored the themes and periods of American history for treatment by the novelist. Simms argued there, and in forewords to several of his romances, that fiction rendered the past more truthfully, interestingly, and tellingly than histories and biographies could because fiction—like poetry—required imagination to look beyond what is not known or expressed. The second series examined additional American writers and what distinguished them, for instance, in their humor.

Despite their early success, Simms's romances, novellas, and stories provoked mixed reviews. Poe eventually concluded that Simms had become "the best novelist which this country has, on the whole, produced" but also insisted that "he should never have written 'The Partisan,' nor 'The Yemassee.'" This was in a review of *Confession*. That novel, like the gothic *Martin Faber*, demonstrated, Poe contended, that Simms's "genius [did] not lie in the outward so much as in the inner world." Yet he nevertheless wrote of Simms's short-story collection *The Wigwam and the Cabin* that "in invention, in vigor, in movement, in the power of exciting interest, and in the artistical management of his themes, he has surpassed, we think, any of his countrymen." Other critics, especially in the genteel and Whiggish Knickerbocker circle, joined Poe in condemning what they considered to be the excessively graphic and vulgar qualities of many characters and scenes, and Simms's prolixity and sententiousness, in his romances (Butterworth and Kibler 64, 50).

The violent realism and earthiness of the romances did not result in realistic novels. Although Simms received early praise for his characterizations (particularly of women), he used the romance formula, with its stereotypic heroes and heroines, predictable themes, and conventional polarities. People were on quests or had lost their way or were fighting long odds or were carrying forward the banner of (and modeling) civilization or were mired in the slough of despond or were resisting all the claims of civilized society and behavior or were pursuing love interests. Deceitfulness, selfishness, and greed opposed honor, high-mindedness, and honesty against the backdrop of the South's development from the earliest days of Spanish exploration to the westward movement in Simms's own youth.

It was only gradually that Simms married the psychological acuity of some of his portraits of the interior struggles of his gothic characters and fiction to the historical romance. Helping him think through how to do so were the biographies he wrote in the mid-1840s, but also the incidents on which he focused particular fictions, such as the murder in *Beauchampe; or, The Kentucky Tragedy* (1842). However incomplete the blending of realism and romanticism or of stereotypical and socially individuated renderings through the 1840s, by the 1850s Simms fundamentally had made the transition to social realism in such works as *Woodcraft* and *The Cassique of Kiawah*. Indeed some scholars have considered *Woodcraft* the first realistic novel in America (Bakker; Wimsatt, "Realism").

In some sense disguising the transition is the fact that Simms also increasingly wrote as a humorist and, in so doing, often rendered his late narratives fabulistically, when not writing social comedy or stories of manners. This dimension of Simms's work was largely hidden, however, until the 1974 publication of *Stories and Tales*, volume 5 in the Centennial Simms edition. There, for the first time, readers had access in print to "Bald-Head Bill Bauldy." There, too, for the first time one could read together that story, "Legend of the Hunter's Camp," and "How Sharp Snaffles Got His Capital and Wife," which was published posthumously in *Harper's Magazine* in October 1870. These and other stories and tales made it clear that Simms was a fecund contributor to southern and American humor.

Humor let Simms take up issues that he could not otherwise address in print and still expect to be well received. He did so both during and after the war. The war also pushed Simms past the emerging fashion of social realism. Having destroyed the familiar, the preoccupation of much realistic fiction, the war made the liminal central (Shillingsburg, "Cub"). While his romances and tales had often explored life on the edge or in extreme circumstances, whether in war or on the frontier or on the verge of madness or in fanciful realms, it had done so against a backdrop of, and with the goal of affirming, social norms and development. In the war's wake that goal seemed absurd. Mythologized memories of a healthy past might nurture a sense of the beautiful but could not help one deal with the present. Thus Simms's conclusion, in a March 1869 letter to Paul Hamilton Hayne: "Let us bury the Past lest it buries us!" (*Letters* 5:214). Fifteen months later he lay dead in the 13 Society Street, Charleston, home of his oldest daughter, with the shell holes in the walls of the bedroom he had shared with several children.

Posthumous Reputation

The twenty years after Simms's death saw him often respectfully treated, first in obituaries, later in memoirs and columns, and also in literary dictionaries and encyclopedias. Yet Charles Richardson's 1887 *American Literature: 1607–1885* proved a harbinger of a shift: Simms, Richardson observed, was "more respected than read," having "won considerable note because he was so sectional" and then having "lost it because he was not sectional enough," although he showed "silly contempt for his Northern betters" (qtd. in Butterworth and Kibler 130). Five years later Trent's biography of Simms appeared. It was the first full-length, scholarly treatment. Its central thesis was that Simms's environment frustrated his abilities: the South was inimical to art and the life of the mind, and Charleston high society's hauteur marginalized Simms despite his talent and character. Trent's second thesis was that Simms's commitment to the romance and his romanticism meant that his works had become largely unreadable in an age of literary realism. Although Vernon Parrington and later scholars recognized Simms's impulses to realism, the two theses long shaped Simms criticism and, indeed, also helped frame study of antebellum southern literature and intellectual life (Parrington 119–30).

A Virginian born in 1862, Trent was a progressive who wanted a New South radically different from the old. He saw his pioneering study of Simms as an opportunity to criticize what the Civil War had made untenable. From his perspective the Old South was not the expanding and rapidly developing environment, with a deep history, that Simms portrayed, but a place where slavery stultified and stunted the growth and progress displayed by the North. Southern—especially South Carolinian—writers occasionally challenged Trent's agenda and conclusions, but those critiques had little impact. Not until after publication of the Simms letters in the 1950s did scholars begin to consider the author in the historical and contemporary contexts that he had rendered in his poetry and fiction. And not until after the centennial of his death did a growing number of scholars, having concluded that southern intellectual history was not an oxymoron, begin to study in detail the culture in which Simms participated and to which he contributed so voluminously and variously.

Some of these scholars also have had agendas: they have wanted to see Simms included in the American literary canon, for instance, or they have wanted to defend the heritage that in their view Trent, and so many others, inappropriately belittled or ignorantly dismissed. More fruitfully, other scholars have begun to reframe the understanding of nineteenth-century American intellectual life by stripping away preconceptions that characterized earlier evaluations of Simms and his contemporaries. They are closely examining the historical record and transatlantic and other contemporary contexts and developments in the process. Although the pursuit of canonical status in a post-canonical age seems quixotic at this point, the explosion of the canon is leading to more varied fare being offered and may, therefore, mean that Simms, once his work is widely available, will be more often anthologized as well as studied. Defensiveness about Simms and the antebellum South may warm the hearts of like-minded people, just as critics of the Old South have been encouraged by shared presuppositions and disdain. Yet dueling cultural ideologies do not advance comity and may only reinforce mutual incomprehensions. Continued, deep research in original sources and the theoretical reframing that Atlantic history, the history of the book, and other perspectives offer—these approaches promise most for further study of Simms, his works, and his world.

Works Cited

For amplified readings by and on Simms and on his world, go to http://simms.library.sc.edu/bibliography.php.

Bakker, Jan. "Simms on the Literary Frontier; or, So Long Miss Ravenel and Hello Captain Porgy: *Woodcraft* Is the First 'Realistic' Novel in America." In *William Gilmore Simms and the American Frontier,* edited by John Caldwell Guilds and Caroline Collins, 64–78. Athens: University of Georgia Press, 1997.

Butterworth, Keen, and James E. Kibler Jr. *William Gilmore Simms: A Definitive Guide.* Boston: G. K. Hall, 1980.

Faust, Drew Gilpin. *A Sacred Circle: The Dilemma of the Intellectual in the Old South, 1840–1860.* Baltimore: Johns Hopkins University Press, 1977.

Guilds, John C. *Simms: A Literary Life.* Fayetteville: University of Arkansas Press, 1992.

Hayne, Paul Hamilton. "Ante-Bellum Charleston." *Southern Bivouac* 1 (October 1885): 257–68.

Kibler, James E. "The First Simms Letters: 'Letters from the West' (1826)." *Southern Literary Journal* 19 (Spring 1987): 81–91.

———. *The Poetry of William Gilmore Simms: An Introduction and Bibliography.* Columbia: Southern Studies Program, University of South Carolina, 1979.

McHaney, Thomas L. "An Early 19th-Century Literary Agent: James Lawson of New York." *Publications of the Bibliographical Society of America* 64 (Spring 1970): 177–92.

Moltke-Hansen, David. "The Expansion of Intellectual Life: A Prospectus." In *Intellectual Life in Antebellum Charleston,* edited by Michael O'Brien and David Moltke-Hansen, 3–44. Knoxville: University of Tennessee Press, 1986.

———. "Southern Literary Horizons in Young America: Imaginative Development of a Regional Geography." *Studies in the Literary Imagination* 42, no. 1 (2009): 1–31.

Nakamura, Masahiro. *Visions of Order in William Gilmore Simms: Southern Conservatism and the Other American Romance.* Columbia: University of South Carolina Press, 2009.

Parrington, Vernon L. *The Romantic Revolution in America, 1800–1860.* Vol. 2 of *Main Currents in American Thought.* New York: Harcourt, Brace and Company, 1927.

Rogers, George C., Jr. *Charleston in the Age of the Pinckneys.* Columbia: University South Carolina Press, 1980.

Shillingsburg, Miriam J. "The Cub of the Panther: A New Frontier." In *William Gilmore Simms and the American Frontier,* edited by John Caldwell Guilds and Caroline Collins, 221–36. Athens: University of Georgia Press, 1997.

———. "Literary Grist: Simms's Trips to Mississippi." *Southern Quarterly* 41, no. 2 (2003): 119–34.

Simms, William Gilmore. *Atalantis: A Story of the Sea: In Three Parts.* New York: J. & J. Harper, 1832.

———. *Beauchampe; or, The Kentucky Tragedy.* 2 vols. Philadelphia: Lea and Blanchard, 1842.

———. *The Cassique of Kiawah: A Colonial Romance.* New York: Redfield, 1859.

———. *Confession; or, The Blind Heart. A Domestic Story.* 2 vols. Philadelphia: Lea and Blanchard, 1841.

———. "Ellet's 'Women of the Revolution.'" *Southern Quarterly Review,* n.s. 1 (July 1850): 314–54.

———. "Guizot's Democracy in France." *Southern Quarterly Review* 15, no.29 (1849): 114–65.

———. *Guy Rivers: A Tale of Georgia.* 2 vols. New York: Harper & Brothers, 1834.

———. *The Letters of William Gilmore Simms.* Edited by Mary C. Simms Oliphant, Alfred Taylor Odell, and T. C. Duncan. 6 vols. Columbia: University of South Carolina Press, 1952–82.

———. *The Life of Francis Marion.* New York: Henry G. Langley, 1844.

———. *Martin Faber, the Story of a Criminal; and Other Tales.* 2 vols. New York: Harper & Brothers, 1837.

———. *Poetry and the Practical.* Edited by James E. Kibler. Fayetteville: University of Arkansas Press, 1996.

———. *The Sense of the Beautiful: An Address . . . before the Charleston County Agricultural and Horticultural Association, May 3, 1870.* Charleston: Charleston County Agricultural and Horticultural Association, 1870.

———. *The Social Principle: The Source of National Permanence. An Oration, Delivered before the Erosophic Society of the University of Alabama . . . December 13, 1842.* Tuscaloosa: Erosophic Society, University of Alabama, 1843.

———. *Stories and Tales.* Vol. 5 of *The Writings of William Gilmore Simms.* Centennial edition; introductions, explanatory notes, and texts established by John Caldwell Guilds. Columbia: University of South Carolina Press, 1974.

———. *Views and Reviews in American Literature, History and Fiction.* 2 vols. New York: Wiley and Putnam, 1845 (1846).

———. *The Wigwam and the Cabin.* 2 vols. New York: Wiley and Putnam, 1845–46.

———. *Woodcraft, or Hawks about the Dovecote: A Story of the South, at the Close of the Revolution.* New York: Redfield, 1854.

Trent, William Peterfield. *William Gilmore Simms.* Boston: Houghton, Mifflin, 1892.

Wakelyn, Jon L. *The Politics of a Literary Man: William Gilmore Simms.* Westport, Conn.: Greenwood Press, 1973.

Watson, Charles S. *From Nationalism to Secessionism: The Changing Fiction of William Gilmore Simms.* Westport, Conn.: Greenwood Press, 1993.

White, William B., Jr. *The Ross-Chesnut-Sutton Family of South Carolina.* Franklin, N.C.: Privately printed, 2002.

Wimsatt, Mary Ann. "Realism and Romance in Simms's Midcentury Fiction." *Southern Literary Journal* 12, no. 2 (1980): 29–48.

Critical Introduction

THE LIFE OF CAPTAIN JOHN SMITH

Carey Roberts

Often portrayed as a sectionalist, a fire-eater, and an intractable defender of southern slavery, William Gilmore Simms held fame in his own day throughout the United States as a writer of historical fiction and prose. Much of his influence came through historical romance. He wrote volumes on colonial America, several more on the Revolutionary era, and tried his hand at virtually every English genre written in the nineteenth century: poetry, drama, humor, short stories, realism, and even detective capers. While popular as a writer of fiction, Simms also gained credibility as an historian, particularly as the writer of essays and biographies. Indeed, Simms's fictional writings may be slowly creeping back into the lexicon of American literature thanks to the efforts of scholarly attention. Yet considerably more attention should be given to Simms the historian in light of the pioneering efforts of historians Sean R. Busick, David Moltke-Hansen, and Jeffery J. Rogers. For modern readers with an interest in American origins and the antebellum understanding of the nation's colonial period, Simms's biography *The Life of Captain John Smith. The Founder of Virginia* is a fitting point of entry.

Simms's importance as an historian rests in how he directed American attention to its own history – away from the ancient world and even further away from relatively recent English history. Indeed, Simms caused Americans to take their own history seriously, understand it in imaginative ways, and ponder the importance of history in both building a nation and tolerating its cultural – and historical – divides. Building upon the works of a number of local historians, biographers, and collections of private papers, Simms taught Americans first, that it was appropriate and selfless to remember their own history and second, that studying the past enriches human happiness beyond merely providing moral examples. For Simms, history could be equally instructive and entertaining, a thought that occurred to few of his contemporaries.

Among early American historians, few equaled Simms in his acumen, attention to detail, dedication to historical documents and oral histories, historical essays, public lectures, and political treatises. Simms may not have produced a magnum opus like George Bancroft's *History of the United States* or a work so endearing as Francis Parkman's *Oregon Trail.* But he shaped the study of American history in countless, tiny ways, by providing works of rugged pioneers, dutiful soldiers, and inspiring heroes. He described his romantic settings with the literary flare of a novelist combined with the details of an historian. Always true to his sources, Simms exercised restraint from entertaining flourishes without smothering his readers in meaningless descriptions. To paraphrase Samuel Clemens's appraisal of James Fennimore Cooper, Simms well knew there was no need to tell his readers about every twig snapping under foot. While he was not alone in popularizing history, Simms played a critical role, if not the most important role, for antebellum Americans.

One key reason, perhaps the most important, for Simms to write his biography of Captain John Smith revolved around the scarcity of Smith's original autobiography. As a mercenary and explorer, John Smith offered no value to Simms's generation. But as the founder of the cradle of America and what was still one of the country's most populous and important states, John Smith held no equal. Furthermore, Smith was not merely the founder of Virginia: after he saved the settlement then abruptly left Jamestown, Smith sailed north to explore new territory. It was Smith who coined the name "New England" to describe the rugged shore of the northern coastline. In many ways, John Smith was the founder of all America, a man of singular importance who saved English colonization in the New World and paved the way for hundreds of thousands of colonists. This is how Simms would characterize the man in his biography.

At one time, learned colonial Americans read Smith's tale, but such was not the case for the Revolutionary generation and that of Simms. Uncovering what time nearly erased was no easy task in the mid-nineteenth century. As with his work on Francis Marion, Simms usually relied upon primary sources rather than popular myths. But in this case, rather than carrying around trunks of personal papers — as he did with other well-known Revolutionary era figures — Simms relied upon what primary sources remained, notably, Smith's rare autobiography.

Simms's biography closely followed Smith's own autobiographical account. At one level, Simms's account did little more than embellish the more charming episodes that Smith himself recounted some two centuries earlier. Simms can be faulted for too closely following Smith's account. No doubt Smith's stories about himself are of dubious authenticity - composed to engineer a legend of himself - rather than offer strictly factual reportage. Simms knew this but still traced Smith from his earliest youth through countless tales of adventure around Europe, Turkey, and North America. He emphasized Smith's own self-described heroic activities, whether fighting American Indians — the "forest monarchs of America" — or exploring the coastline of North America. Details are plentiful in Simms's account, and his attention to such details reflected the well-hewn eye of a master storyteller combined with the care of a trained researcher. He provided personal commentary from the Captain, then interspersed it with Simms's own analysis and reasoning. The commentary itself made *Captain John Smith* a brilliant work of both history and literature. Indeed, the book reads almost like a script for a modern video documentary with Smith's first-hand accounts serving as a formal interview and Simms's narration answering anticipated questions from the "viewer."

At a deeper level, Simms clearly understood Smith's story to be a compelling link between the emerging local history of early nineteenth-century America and a new, national history that Simms hoped to master. In doing so, Simms stumbled upon an incredible, intellectual connection. Scholars have noted the struggle between a pattern of local history writing in post-Revolutionary America and those who wrote national histories strictly from a local perspective. That is to say, early national histories, especially those created in New England, were nothing more than local histories writ large. In time, antebellum historians wrote lengthy, national histories, but pinpointing the leap between local history and genuine national history often eluded even the most serious students of the period. Simms may offer the missing link with his biographies: personal history was the key. Going from the local to the national without the baggage of local prejudice or the chauvinism of viewing one's local community as the epitome of the nation challenged many nineteenth-century historians. Simms, incidentally, is often lumped into such a group. But it was not Simms the historian who realized that biographies of great individuals could be appreciated both for their local characters and stories as well as for their meaning for larger, national audiences.

Simms confronted the problem of uncovering the unknown and remembering the nearly lost. Diligent research might reveal unknown characters and events, but these had meaning primarily as measures of local history. Early Americans had limited scholarly and institutional abilities to transition those things to the country as a whole. But if they could remember in a different way something once known across a wide spectrum of the populace, then a true national history could be told. In effect, Simms the historian practiced the same art as Simms the literary figure. As he wrote in his introduction to the 1856 edition of his short story collection, *The Wigwam and the Cabin*, "to be national in literature, one must needs be sectional" (4). That is, popular figures most important for their local accomplishments — the "founders" of Virginia, for example — contributed to the larger development of the American nation. Honest biography served that purpose; local history did not. Neither did the rising hagiography of national figures such as Mason "Parson" Weems's stories of a young George Washington. Equally unimpressive to Simms were the myriad local histories of New England towns written as if they were microcosms of the nation as a whole.

Not surprising, Simms's publication of *Captain John Smith* connected well with his publication of *The Life of Francis Marion*. In both cases, Simms retraced the steps of pivotal, but under-appreciated, characters in American history. In the language of today's historians, Simms brought attention to not only what was forgotten, but also to what was publicly unknown. Both Smith and Marion were soldiers, together they played indispensable roles in founding America at key stages of its development, and both quickly became the subjects of popular legend. Smith, the "Founder of Jamestown," and Marion, "the Swamp Fox," enjoyed widespread name recognition. But key differences remained, which Simms seemingly wished to correct. Marion became more than a household name in South Carolina; cities and counties were named after him. Indeed, Simms's own father was privy to some of Marion's popularity, as the elder Simms moved to Mississippi and lived in "Marion County," where he eventually died and was buried. John Smith enjoyed little initial popularity, admittedly because he spent scant time in Virginia, leaving behind a soon-to-be starving colony to explore the northern banks of the Atlantic. In fact, without the publication of his popular autobiography, Smith may have been remembered, if at all, as just another adventuresome buccaneer. As Simms remarked when describing Smith's death, "He probably died in obscurity, for none of the facts attending his demise remain to us" (373). While much remained unknown about Smith, much more simply needed to be remembered, as Simms knew.

Such was Simms's task, and it remains the task of all serious historians. They must do more than retell old tales, or chronicle extraordinary events like journalists. This mandate required Simms to convey a compelling story without further fictionalizing Smith's already larger-than-life legend. Here Simms belayed his commitment to solid history by turning to Smith's autobiography, which served as his only principle source. To be sure, Simms deliberately followed a different strategy with Smith than that which he took with Marion. With Marion, the Chevalier Bayard, and even his edited biography of Nathanael Greene, Simms remained dedicated to revealing what nobody knew, thanks largely to the treasure trove of personal correspondence and firsthand accounts he collected about these men.

But why did he refrain from taking a similar tack with Smith? The simple answer may be the best, which is that personal documents of the Captain were beyond Simms's reach on the other side of the Atlantic. Still, he could have written a forward for a reprinted edition of the original autobiography, commemorated a great hero, and quickly cashed in on the popularity of his Marion biography. And, indeed, Simms may have regretted taking on the task of Smith's biography. During the early spring of 1845, he complained to his close friend, James Henry Hammond, about "the pressure of one or two tasks of Biography, which I was ass enough to take upon my shoulders" at a time when he should have relaxed his endeavors (*Letters* 2: 45). A few weeks later, he explained to his literary agent, John Lawson, that his work on Smith proceeded slowly, but assured him that the work would be finished. He confided that "there is nothing in the subject to excite and interest me" (*Letters* 2: 49). Simms often was jaded and anxiety-ridden at the end of a big project, so these objections should not be given too much weight. Yet, we might imagine that the taxes of the writer's efforts were particularly sharp in the case of this biography because of the added irritation of a paucity of sources. Indeed, the bulk of the writing of Captain John Smith, which occurred in 1845, corresponded with a year of events too pressed even for Simms's normally busy schedule. He simultaneously polished off the second volume of his *Views and Reviews in American Literature, History and Fiction*, commenced work on the Huguenots in Florida, and wrote portions of his biography of Chevalier Bayard, all while tending to his wife, who was pregnant with their daughter, Mary Lawson Simms. Yet Simms faced more than plantation chores, household duties, and writing tasks. While finishing the final pages of the Captain Smith biography, Simms lost his fifteen-month-old daughter, Valerie. He continued to write in the face of this tragedy but likely did not finish *Captain John Smith* until early 1846.

Amidst a year of personal tragedy and professional success, Simms also embarked on a new career. In 1845, he stood for election to the Carolina legislature. His subsequent victory in the fall legislative session taxed both his energy and his time. He would have preferred a political appointment from President James K. Polk, perhaps to a distant diplomatic post where he could repose himself to write at leisure and casually fill the duties of office. Lacking the President's favor, he happily accepted a place in the state legislature.

In the meantime, Simms endured a frustrating period of dealing with his publishers. Having just come off one of his most popular books, *The Life of Francis Marion*, Simms gained much needed attention from would-be sellers. Publisher J. and H.G. Langley offered to buy the copyrights to both *Marion* and *Smith* for $1300, which Simms accepted in the late fall of 1846. Alerted to the publisher's troubling financial situation, Simms realized Langley may not fulfill their terms. He sought alternatives and hoped to secure publication for the Smith book before winter set in. When he learned the ailing firm sold the copyrights to another publisher, Simms was outraged. Negotiations among various publishers, Simms, and his literary agent, Lawson, dragged on for months. But he reluctantly agreed to transfer the copyrights to George F. Cooledge and Brother for a slightly lower amount than that promised by Langley, but still a comparatively tidy sum for 1846. It would be March 1847 before Simms's Captain John Smith book was finally published in Cooledge's "Illustrated Library" as *The Life of Captain John Smith. The Founder of Virginia.* The same series also included a republication of Simms's *The Life of Francis Marion* and William Cutter's *The Life of Israel Putnam* (*Letters* 2: 184n, 189, 238-39, 249-50, and 306-07).

Simms repeatedly assured James Lawson that the Captain Smith biography would perform well and gain popularity. As he wrote to Lawson shortly after its publication, "[Captain Smith] has life, spirit, energy ... the essentials" (*Letters* 2: 306-07). While Simms thought highly of the finished product, the book received scant public attention, at least in terms of widespread sales. But there were exceptions. One was the favorable review published in the *Southern Quarterly Review*; the reviewer commended the work "to every generous heart" and praised Simms for "bringing ... into light all the impressive and noble lineaments of his hero." *The Literary World* published a review possibly written by Evert Duyckinck that heaped even greater praise on Simms. The review described the book as "readable," "instructive," and "a fund of good humor." Best of all, the reviewer hailed Simms as a masterful novelist gifted with the historians eye for detail, familiarity with Indian life, and love for his subject (qtd. in *Letters* 2: 272n).

The publication history of *Captain John Smith* sheds little light on Simms's research strategy except to explain that pecuniary interests alone are not sufficient explanations. Yet again, a comparison of *Captain John Smith* and *The Life of Francis Marion* may answer several lingering questions. Simms handled Marion's biography with due diligence to uncovering primary documents. Simms conducted serious academic research, located personal letters, and even interviewed firsthand observers. With John Smith, Simms gathered some additional material, but rarely strayed from the basic narrative laid down in Smith's autobiography. As with his biography of General Nathanael Greene, Simms largely reproduced and slightly edited previous accounts. So, it was Simms's analysis, not research or new stories, that made *Captain John Smith* a powerful historical tome. Given the backdrop of Simms's personal life, his considerable stress under the weight of professional responsibilities, and his budding—but short-lived—political career, it would have been all too easy to patch together random passages of the Smith autobiography to garner fast money. On the contrary, he took extra care, perhaps too much care in the eyes of his associates, in reproducing Captain Smith's story for a new generation that needed to learn more about this important moment in our nation's history and the man who was at its center

Most of Simms's commentary on *Captain John Smith* revolved around publishing concerns, so any explanation of private motives he had for writing the work remains tentative. However, it is quite possible that Simms treated the book as slightly autobiographical. Given that the writing of *Captain John Smith* closely corresponded to his run for office and his new political career, Simms likely found little inspiration from Smith's narrative for the practical concerns for office. At the least, Simms did not view himself as playing the same kind of political role as Smith. For example, Simms portrays Smith as a prototypical, classical hero appropriate for nineteenth-century Romance. As Busick notes, in over sixty instances, Simms labeled Smith a "hero," considered his efforts heroic, or did the same for other characters in the biography (43). Smith was an adventurer, a man of the seas, and an explorer of a new world, all of which contributed to his greatness and played to the romantic heroes favored by Simms's readers. Yet, in his own political career, Simms saw few examples of such heroism, given that American society long progressed away from its founding. Exploration and creating a new "home" required more than the steady, routine deliberation of the local legislator, which in Simms's day could hardly be described as heroic. Dedicated, practical, diplomatic, even strategic might serve to describe the typical nineteenth-century American legislator, much as it illustrated General Nathanael Greene in Simms's biography of the Revolutionary leader. To borrow again from Busick, "Greene's practical brilliance was precisely what was needed to achieve the most wonderful results in the worst of times" (43). But it was not "heroic."

However, in periods of great crisis, such as imperial invasion, those called to defend hearth and home gained Simms's greatest admiration and earned "heroic" dignity. Great legislators, like great generals, served an unparalleled purpose and provided countless examples of model, professional behavior. But they did not inspire human beings in the same way as great heroes. To Simms, Francis Marion gained such respect. It was not by choice of career that Marion raised his gauntlet against the British. It was out of defense of those things that made his life worth living and a willingness to sacrifice everything, including one's life, for the singular purpose of protecting those things that mattered most.

Simms likely saw his task with Smith as particularly urgent, precisely because of its contrast with the current state of the antebellum world. Captain Smith easily highlighted the difference between the founding period of the country's progress with the demands of a settled society. The largely calm, deliberative political scene of a settled society routinely needed to return to first principles. It occasionally needed to resuscitate heroic virtues in order to maintain the progress already achieved. In short, the political progress of a society was neither inevitable nor guaranteed in the long term. To remain civilized, a settled society required more than political habit, procedural regularity, and the slow, steady beat of public festivity. In addition to these things, Simms likely believed a civilized society needed a kind of adventuresome militancy where its members tenaciously cling to their liberty as if their very survival were at stake. They need plenty of Nathanael Greenes in their legislative bodies, but an occasional Smith and Marion proved equally essential. Simms thus followed the common Jeffersonian approach to republican politics. Just as Thomas Jefferson believed every generation must undergo a revolution—meaning to return or revolve—Simms shared the Jeffersonian desire too for each generation to remove the political accretions of time and reconnect to the original principles of their society's origin.

It is, thus, probably no coincidence that in the middle of the 1840s, Simms simultaneously wrote a biography of a "creator" and a "savior" of America, Smith and Marion. It should also be noted that Simms's legislative career closely mirrored his admiration of Marion—a defender of what he knew best, those things he loved, and a person slow to combative resistance. Defending the patrimony of South Carolinians mattered more than creating a new southern nation. Likewise in the late 1840s, Simms's decision to call for South Carolina to secede—the first prominent legislator in antebellum South Carolina to do so—perhaps had most to do with Simms's desire to defend tangible customs of common life instead of fostering abstract, southern nationalism. Perhaps, too, Simms's personal preference for his biography of Marion over Smith reveals a theme all too common among Simms's writings—that people are most often called by duty and custom to defend what historically belongs to oneself. We are seldom the progenitors of those things or the traditions that sustain them. We are rarely a John Smith. But only by remembering the John Smiths of this world—of what was created in a wilderness—do we find the urge to become a Francis Marion.

Works Cited

Busick, Sean R. *A Sober Desire for History: William Gilmore Simms as Historian*. U of South Carolina P, 2005.

Hoobler, Thomas. *Captain John Smith: Jamestown and the Birth of the American Dream.* Wiley, 2007.

Kelso, William. M. *Jamestown: the Buried Truth.* U of Virginia P, 2008.

Moltke-Hansen, David. *William Gilmore Simms's Civil War: Consequences for a Southern Man of Letters.* U of South Carolina P, 2012.

Simms, William Gilmore. *The Letters of William Gilmore Simms.* Ed. Mary C. Simms Oliphant *et al.* 6 vols. Columbia: U of South Carolina P, 1952-2012.

——. *The Life of Captain John Smith. The Founder of Virginia.* New York: George F. Cooledge & Brother, 1847.
——. *The Life of Francis Marion.* Henry G. Langley, 1844.
——. *The Life of Nathanael Greene, Major-General in the Army of the Revolution.* George F. Cooledge and Brother, 1849.
——. *The Wigwam and the Cabin.* New York: Redfield, 1856.

Capt: JOHN SMITH.

THE
LIFE
OF
Capt. John Smith
BY W. GILMORE SIMMS.
NEW YORK.
GEO. F. COOLEDGE. & BROTHER.

THE LIFE

OF

CAPTAIN JOHN SMITH.

THE

FOUNDER OF VIRGINIA.

BY W. GILMORE SIMMS.

AUTHOR OF "LIFE OF MARION," "HISTORY OF SOUTH CAROLINA," ETC.

NEW YORK:

PUBLISHED BY GEO. F. COOLEDGE & BROTHER,

BOOKSELLERS AND PUBLISHERS,

323 PEARL STREET.

S. W. BENEDICT,
STEREOTYPER AND PRINTER, 16 Spruce st.

ADVERTISEMENT.

The works consulted in the preparation of this volume are "The true Travels, Adventures and Observations of Captain John Smith in Europe, Asia, Africke and America," Stith, Beverley, Burke, Purchas, Grahame, Bancroft, Collections of the Massachusetts Historical Society, and the neat and well-written Life of Smith, by Mr. Hilliard, contained in the Library of American Biography. As much of Smith's own language as could be employed has been made use of without scruple, and with little alteration. It has been a favorite part of the plan of the present volume to make the account of the Discovery, Settlement and Progress of Virginia as copious as possible, consistently with the claims of the biography.

TABLE OF CONTENTS.

BOOK I.—CHAPTER I.

CHAPTER II.

CHAPTER III.

CHAPTER IV.

CHAPTER X.

BOOK II.—CHAPTER I.

CHAPTER II.

CHAPTER III.

CHAPTER IV.

CHAPTER V.

CHAPTER IV.

CHAPTER V.

CHAPTER VI.

CHAPTER VII.

CHAPTER VIII.

CHAPTER IX.

CHAPTER III.

CHAPTER IV.

CHAPTER V.

APPENDIX.

THE LIFE

OF

CAPTAIN JOHN SMITH.

BOOK I.—CHAPTER I.

In the long roll or catalogue which the world may exhibit of the great or remarkable men who have distinguished its several epochs and conditions, none have ever so completely ravished the regards of contemporaries as those who have been equally marked by the great and spontaneous readiness of their thoughts, and the resolute activity and eagerness with which they advance to the performance of their actions. In such persons, under peculiar laws of temperament, the blood and the brain work together in the most exquisite unanimity. There is no reluctance of the subordinate to follow the commands of the superior; no failure in the agent properly to conceive, and adequately to carry out, the designs and desires of the principal. The soul responds generously to the dictates of the mind, and no tardy ratiocination, slowly halting in the rear of the will, finally supervenes to reprove the deed when it is too late for its repair, and compel a vain regret for the hasty and unconsidered action. But, on the contrary, the impulses of the blood, and the counsels of the brain, as if twinned together, harmoniously prompt and perform those admirable achievements, which ordinary men regard as the fruits of a sudden instinct, or a happy inspiration. Tried by calm reflection, the process chosen, the labor done, seem to have met the necessity precisely, as if the most deliberate wisdom had sat in judgment upon the event; and yet the performance will have been as prompt as the exigency which provoked it. With persons thus fortunately constituted, deliberation is rather an obstacle than a help to right performance. They seem to conceive and to think more justly while in action than in repose. It is the necessity which provokes the thought. It is the sudden call upon their genius that shows them to be possessed of the endowment. Such are the men who commonly appear to shape and regulate the transition periods in society; to time and to direct its enterprises; to infuse its spirit with eagerness and enthusiasm, and to meet, with the happiest resources and the most unfailing intrepidity, the frequent exigencies which hang about the footsteps of adventure.

Of this class of persons, living in modern periods, and by reason of merits such as these commended to our attention, the name and fortunes of him who is the subject of these pages possess a more than common interest for the American. Capt. John Smith, the real founder of Virginia, is one of the proverbial heroes of British settlement in this western hemisphere. His career will happily illustrate the peculiar sort of character upon which we have thought proper briefly to expatiate. His story is one of those real romances which mock the incidents of ordinary fiction. This we are to gather chiefly from his own narratives, and partly from his contemporaries, by whom his deeds are amply confirmed and put beyond dispute. Of his adventures, which lift into heroic dignity a

Selling his Books and Satchel. PAGE 11.

name so little significant in itself as to be commonly a subject for the vulgar jest, it is enough to say, that they serve to denote the more noble and daring events of a period, distinguished by its spirit, its courage and its passion, for vigorous and stirring performance. It is as one of the master spirits of this period and of modern times, that the subject of our biography challenges the consideration of our people.

JOHN SMITH was born at Willoughby, in the county of Lincolnshire, England, some time in the year 1579. He was descended from an ancient Lancashire family. His father came from the ancient stock of the Smiths of Crudley in that shire; his mother from the Rickards, at Great Heck, Yorkshire. He received his education, such as it was, at the free schools of Louth and Alford. It was, probably, his own fault that his schooling was not better. He was not of a temper to be restrained by schools and tutors. The eager activity of his mind and blood betrayed itself at a very early period. He makes the first exhibition of this activity while at school, and at the early age of thirteen. "Set," even then, according to his own showing, "upon brave adventures," he sold his books and satchel, and was preparing secretly to steal away to sea, when he was arrested by the death of his father. His mother, of whom he does not speak, seems to have died previously. His wandering purpose, arrested by this event, was checked for the moment only. His father left him some little property, which, with himself, was committed to the charge of certain guardians, who provéd quite unfaithful to their trust. They were not disposed to waste his substance upon him, and with shameful cupidity winked at that tendency to vagabondism which his early impatience of restraint seemed to promise. Fortune thus, in lessening his domestic ties and sympathies, seemed to encourage his wandering inclinations. His guardians allowed him much liberty, if they gave him little money. Of the former he soon had enough to enable him to get beyond the sea; but his means were too slender to justify his flight. A little more liberality, at this early period, might have relieved them of all farther annoyance at his hands. Compelled to provide for him at home, they placed him, as an apprentice, with a merchant of Lynn, named Sendall—" the greatest merchant," according to Smith, " of all those parts." But Smith longed for the sea, and Sendall had other uses for him on shore. His apprentice had no taste for these uses, and though his guardians might bind with all the fetters of the law, he was not the lad to reverence such a bondage. The spirit, that already dreamed of doings with the sword, was not to be subdued by indentured parchment. He soon leaped his counter, and never saw his master again until the lapse of eight years rendered it equally unlikely that the latter would recognize or reclaim his fugitive. He thus made himself a freeman with but ten shillings in his pocket. This ten shillings was the liberal allowance of his guardians, " out of his own money," given him, as he tells us, " to get rid of him." His flight from the merchant does not appear to have been withheld from their knowledge. In all probability he fled to them from Sendall, in order to procure the means of getting to sea or passing into foreign countries. These were his favorite ideas. They constituted his passions, and, as the nearest step to their gratification, he found means to enter the service of the sons of the famous Lord Willoughby,* then under tutelage, and about to make the tour of the continent. We are not told in

* "The Right Honorable Peregrine, that generous Lord Willoughby, and famous soldier."—*Smith's Narrative.*

what capacity he attended these young gentlemen—most probably as a page, scarcely as a companion. He was not long in this situation. Within a month or six weeks after entering France, "his service being needless," as he himself tells us, he was dismissed with a liberal allowance of money to take him back to his friends. But such friends as our apprentice had left behind him in London possessed very few attractions. Their bonds were not so very grateful as to move him voluntarily to resume them. He had as yet seen but little of the world. He had but partially gratified the strong curiosity which had carried him abroad. He remembered the ten shillings bounty of his guardians, and the object for which it had been given, and he concluded to linger a while longer in France. He made his way to Paris—a boy of fifteen, without friends or companions—how, he does not tell us, but under what difficulties, doubts and dangers, at that early period in his own life, and that unsettled period in the history of the country, through which he went! This very progress illustrates, in some degree, the courage and daring of his mind. At Paris, he made the acquaintance of a Scottish gentleman, named Hume, in whose eyes he soon found favor. Hume replenished his purse, and becoming interested in his grace, spirit and intelligence, furnished him with letters of introduction, couched in terms of liberal commendation, to his friends in Scotland. The idea, which possessed the mind of this gentleman in behalf of his youthful protegé, sufficiently proves the great hopes which he had formed of his endowments, even at that early period. The object of his advice and letters was to make of him a courtier, to procure for him access to the person, and, if possible, employment in the service of King James, the well-known Scottish Solomon. What was the influence of Hume and his friends at court, it would not now be easy to discover.

Looking to the sequel in the career of Smith, it would prove his patron to have been a man of discernment and sagacity. The design certainly proves that Hume beheld in the boy some foreshowings of the future man. We are prepared to see already that he was no ordinary boy—we see that he at least possessed some of those outward accomplishments which compel the regards of older heads. These accomplishments, whatever they may have been, were all certainly of his own acquisition. They did not come from the free schools of Louth and Alford; they scarcely had their foundation behind the counter of the Lynn merchant, and it does not appear that he was much, if anything, indebted to his parents. They were the fruits of a peculiar original endowment. All that was precious in Smith's education came from his experience.

But Smith was still too much of the wayward boy to follow implicitly the directions of his friend. Though at first honestly resolved to do so, his temper was quite too capricious just at that moment to continue in his purposes. There were too many objects in France for his diversion. His mind was too eager for the novel, too impatient of the staid, too wild, too erratic, to remain long at this period in any one way of thinking. And let us not too seriously censure these exhibitions of caprice. It is curious to observe how frequently, not to say inevitably, they attend the career of the young adventurer who carves out his own fame and fortunes. It is in this way that nature prompts to the necessary acquisitions of the performer. The restlessness of mood which we thus witness, leads to constant discovery. The wandering footstep is associated with the keen eye and the scrutinizing judgment; and the mind finds its strength and volume in this seeming caprice and purposeless misdirection, as the muscle of the child grows from the feverish restlessness of its feeble and uncertain limbs. While we studiously train the young to the steady exercise of their faculties, we must allow, at the same time, for the indulgence of those impulses which cause vigilance, far-sightedness, promptness of decision, and great activity.

Scarcely had Smith got out of the sight of his Scottish benefactor, when he forgot the ambitious purpose which was entertained in his behalf. He forgot Scotland and its pacific monarch in a new impulse to adventure. It is probable that the attractions of courtier life made a less lively impression on his fancy than upon that of Hume. At all events, arrived at Rouen, he finds his money all spent, and listens to other counsellors. The sound of the trumpet stirs his soul with more delightful and powerful sensations. He hears the shouts of the horsemen, and the preparations for war. Instead of Scotland he takes the route to Havre de Grace, where, in his own language, "he first began to learn the life of a soldier." This must have been somewhere between the years 1608 and 1610. What were the lessons he learned, what battles he saw, in what wars or on what side he was engaged, are left wholly to conjecture. The civil wars of the Catholics and Protestants, terminating in the assassination of Henry IV., prevailed about this period. That Smith shared in these conflicts, and on the Protestant side of the question, may reasonably be inferred from all the circumstances. These wars were at an end. Peace in France made that country no longer an attraction to him who had just taken his first lesson in the art of war, and Smith at once passed into the Low Countries—then, and long afterwards, destined to become the great battle-ground for half of Europe. Here he served four years under a Captain Joseph Duxbury. He was probably one of a band of English auxiliaries serving against Spain in the great conflict which finally secured to the Netherlands their independence. Of his own share in this war, and of the position which he held, Smith tells us nothing. Though he wrote much, Smith was not an elegant writer. Though sometimes tedious, he is so more on account of his style and manner of narrative than because of his material. He is never copious, and satisfies himself with barely glancing at events, the details of which, we perceive, would enrich the story and delight the reader. It is only when he arrives at a trust, when he becomes a leader, that he speaks distinctly of himself. Of Smith in the ranks, as one of many, doing nothing more and nothing better than the rest, he is modestly silent. He was still little more than a boy while under Duxbury, could scarcely have had any trust assigned him, and evidently considered himself as barely serving out an apprenticeship. He was more faithful in this than in the service of the Lynn merchant. That he was diligent in his studies, that he took to his art *con amore*, and mastered it quickly and with a rare ability, we have every reason to suppose from his subsequent career. Indeed, but a short time after, we find him boasting of his acquisitions even when silent on the subject of his performances. He tells us with equal pride and modesty that he had mastered all in the martial schools of France and the Netherlands that "his tender years could attain unto." These acquisitions could only have been attained by practice; this practice could only have been found in the actual exigencies of war. These inferences are unavoidable. Still, it is to be wished that his narrative had not been so meagre—that we could have been suffered to see the eager spirit of the boy, and how he bore himself in these preparatory campaigns. We should have been the better prepared to understand the origin of those audacious instances of valor, and those admirable proofs of skill and sagacity, which subsequently became so completely associated with his name.

His apprenticeship to the art of war, as pursued in the Low Countries, was prolonged for three or four years. At the close of this period, in some interval of the service, or possibly in one of his usual caprices, Smith bethought himself of the Scottish letters furnished him by Hume. He suddenly resumed the purpose which he had abandoned at Rouen, and once more determined to proceed to Scotland. He embarks accordingly at Ancusan for Leith. In this voyage he was destined to enjoy a foretaste of that harsh fortune by which his genius was to be schooled, in order to the requisite training for its true performance. The vessel in which he sailed was wrecked. He narrowly escaped drowning only to encounter another equally great danger from a severe fit of sickness, which seized him on the Holy Isle of Northumberland, near Berwick. Here he lay in as much danger "as sickness could endure." As soon as he had sufficiently recruited, he entered Scotland, and delivered the several letters which Hume had given him for his friends. The proverbial hospitality of the Scotch people was not denied to Smith. He had no occasion for complaint on this score. The persons to whom his letters were addressed—"those honest Scots at Kipweth and Broxmouth"—received him with the greatest kindness, but beyond this his mission produced no fruits. It does not appear that he was ever presented to the king. He himself tells us that there "was neither money nor means to make him a courtier." His native independence of character may have been an obstacle, may have rendered impossible, to his spirit, those preliminary servilities which ambition, taking this course, is compelled usually to undergo before it can hope for the attainment of its object. The good sense or the proud stomach of our hero, may have saved him from this sort of degradation; and such it was like to have been, in fawning upon such a monarch as James the First. By a comparison of dates, it is highly probable that this sovereign was now becoming eagerly anxious for the robes of Elizabeth. Her demise followed a few years after, and looking to this event we may reasonably conjecture that bonnie King Jamie had no particular reason to increase his establishment in a country from which at any moment he might have been summoned to depart. What would have been the effect upon Smith's fortunes, and those of England, had the former found his way into favor—in anticipation of Buckingham—had his nobler spirit dictated the enterprises, and stimulated the courage of the kingdom? Imaginative histories, equally instructive and amusing, may sometimes be wrought by the happy intellect, pursuing some such grateful conjecture, upon a single fact assumed, to its probable conclusion, in changing the destiny of kingdoms and in averting the fall of kings. This is one of these subjects.—Smith taken into the family of James, while yet a boy at the Court of Scotland, might, with the vigor of youth, have pursued and carried out the brilliant schemes of Raleigh, then no longer young; and by realizing some of the nobler objects of that great man, while yet he lived, might have yielded a human consolation to his dying moments. The roving passion was strong in both their bosoms, and their career in arms was not unlike. They both received their early lessons of war in France and the Netherlands, fighting for the same behalf, that of the Protestants. We shall see that one at least of the adventurous projects of Raleigh was destined to owe its successful prosecution to the sagacity, the courage and the energy of Smith.

Whatever may have been the cause, our hero was very soon diverted from any thought of pursuing the toils and

the occupations of the courtier; and, possibly with some feelings of chagrin and disappointment with the world, he returned to Willoughby, in Lincolnshire, his place of birth. Here it appears that he lived a great deal in society; but the society even of his early abode, the first sensations of pleasure over, was not calculated to satisfy a mind of his eccentric energies. He describes himself as "glutted with too much company, wherein he took small delight." In moments of exhaustion, from previous excess of toil or enterprise, the spirits of persons of this order flag, and require a degree of repose strictly proportioned to the energy they have displayed in their preceding exertions. To a man like Smith in particular—one who had lived so rapidly, and had already seen so much of the world—there could have been no condition so well calculated to pall upon his tastes as the tame and monotonous movement of daily life in the humdrum quiet of a country town. His blood was naturally fretted by inactivity, and the very presence of a crowd, of a society that was performing nothing, must soon have disgusted a temper which, for so long a period, had enjoyed for its daily food the humors and the excitements of a camp, the variety and the animation of a great city, the dangers of the sea, and the thousand stimulating aspects and avocations of a strange land. His remedy against the apathy into which he was in danger of falling from his intercourse with a society which to him could afford no nourishment, was of a kind to denote the impatience and the independence of his mind. He fled altogether from communion with men, adopting a like resort with many of the bold and eccentric persons of past times, and betook himself to the solitude and shelter of the forests. "In woodie pasture," thus he writes, "invironned with many hundred acres of other woods," he adopted the guise and the manners of a hermit. "Here, by a faire brooke, he built himself a pavillion of boughs, where onely in his clothes he lay." We see in this proceeding the romantic tendencies of his character—that eager, enthusiastic nature, which always yearns for the wild, the strange and the extravagant—disdaining the beaten track, and eagerly striving after a condition and performances from which the ordinary temper shrinks ever in dismay. In this very errantry we may see the germ of that adventurous mood which led him in maturer years across the Atlantic to the fathomless depths of forest in Virginia.

Here, in his "pavillion of boughs," he gave further proofs of the decided character of his genius in the books which he read, and the exercises, strange enough in his hermit life, which he adopted. His "studie was Machiavellie's Arte of Warre" and Marcus Aurelius; his exercise, a good horse with a lance and ring. His moods, errant though they were, did not, it seems, interfere with that self-training, which was certainly the best that he could have chosen for service in his future career. The horse, the lance and the ring brought to him the skill, and show him to have been imbued with the spirit of chivalry. Few of the courtiers of King James are likely to have been as decidedly inclined to such exercises. As a hunter he practised some other of the minor arts of war. His food was chiefly venison of his own taking. He states this fact slily thus: "his food was *thought* to be more of venison than anything else," as if he were troubled with certain misgivings on the subject of the game-laws. His other wants were supplied by a servant, through whose means he still maintained some slight intercourse with the world which he had forsworn.

His library, thus limited to two volumes, and those not of a character to beget the impulse to such an eccentric mode of life as that which he adopted, we are to look for this impulse to the natural constitution of his mind, urged by an ambition which is yet vague in its developments, and taught by a judgment yet in the green of youth, and from the early exercise of his will, equally uncertain in its aim and resolved upon its prosecution. Smith had something of the poet in him, and wrote smooth verses upon occasions, but does not seem to have been much a reader of the poets. His romantic excesses were probably all native, the natural overflow of a mind, vigorous, easily excited, and so full of spontaneous utterance, as necessarily to rush at times beyond the limits of a sober and restraining reason. And yet it is only by a course of reasoning based upon the ordinary habits of the merely social man, that we shall see anything to astonish us or to provoke censure in the hermit seclusion and studies of our hero. The eccentricity of this mode of life soon had the effect of making him notorious; and here we may remark that, in all probability, this was not the most disagreeable result which he anticipated from his present strange career. The mind of Smith, naturally ambitious of distinction, was swelling like that of the Spaniard. He was one of those who crave to live ever in the eyes of men—who entertain a passion, born of impetuous blood, which seeks present distinction and reward for performances, and which works constantly with an appetite for present homage. To such persons the applause of contemporaries is fame, or such a foretaste of it, as to make it certain that they shall attain the object which they seek. He was not displeased when the rustic world around him began to stare at the strange stories which they heard about their neighbor hermit. He found his pleasure, and possibly his profit also, in provoking the wonder of the peasantry. By degrees the fame of our anchorite extended to the wealthier classes, and at length an Italian gentleman, a sort of master of the horse to the Earl of Lincoln, was persuaded to seek out our hermit in his "pavillion of boughs." He did so. He penetrated to the forest den of Smith, and made himself known to him. The visit did not offend our hero, who, in all probability, began to tire of his seclusion. The conversation of the Italian pleased him, and his horsemanship no less. Gradually, at length, as an intimacy grew up between them, Smith was beguiled from his solitude, which he abandoned with his new associate. But the society which he thus acquired did not suffice for the exacting spirit of our adventurer any more than did that of Willoughby. "Long these pleasures conld not content him," and he chafed in his inactivity, as the lion, born for the desert, chafes at the close limits of his cage. Smith was not encaged. He was not to be kept. He was of that hardy nature which yearns for the conflict, and loses the pleasant consciousness of its strength, unless in the absolute enjoyment of the struggle. He probably appeared even to disadvantage in moments of repose and quiet. Be this as it may, in such quiet as that for which his solitude had been surrendered he was not willing to remain. His Italian friend failed to keep him at Tattersall's, and we find him, very soon after, breaking away from this intimacy and from England, once more to seek his fortunes in the Low Countries.

CHAPTER II.

"Thus," says our hero, in his own narrative, "when France and the Netherlands had taught him to ride a horse, and to use his armes, with such rudiments of warre as his tender yeeres in those martial schooles could attaine unto, he was desirous to see more of the world, and to try his fortune against the *Turkes*, both lamenting and repenting to have seene so many Christians slaughter one another." The passage would seem to imply that he had a second time seen service in the Low Countries. Yet of this period and service we have no particulars. It was his period of apprenticeship only, in which fortune afforded him no opportunities of distinction, or his "tender years" made it impossible that he should avail himself of them. He was at this time but nineteen years old, hopeful, sanguine and warmly confiding, as is usually the case with persons of this temperament. He was to incur its usual penalties, and to pay dearly for that caution which experience alone can teach, and which is so important for him who seeks to be a leader among men. We next find him in company with four French gallants, famous rogues it would seem, who flatter his vanity and take advantage of his youth. Nobody is more easily betrayed than the youth having large enthusiasm of character, and a warm faith in what is allotted for his performance. One of these cunning Frenchmen passes himself off upon our hero as a nobleman. The rest are his attendants. It is not difficult to deceive a character such as that of Smith. Vigilant by nature against the enemy, the same nature places no sentinel against the approach of friendship. In this guise, our cunning Frenchmen play their parts to admiration. Our hero yields them his full heart. They persuade him to go with them into France, where they should not only obtain the necessary means for going against the Turks, but letters from certain distinguished persons to the general of the Hungarian army. The pretences were all plausible, the end to be attained of considerable importance. The parties embarked in a small vessel, the captain of which, if not a party to the designs of the Frenchmen, at least was disposed to wink at their proceedings. Smith had money and fine clothes. In these respects they were less liberally provided. He was a youth, very confiding, and might be plucked with safety. It does not seem to have required much skill in the operation. It was on a dark and gloomy night in winter, when they reached the port of St. Valery, in Picardy. Under cover of the night the conspirators, with all their own baggage and that of Smith, were taken ashore by the captain without the knowledge of the other passengers. It was not until the rogues were fully beyond reach that the treacherous shipmaster returned to his vessel. When the robbery was detected it was without present remedy. It is very probable that the captain was a sharer of the spoils. He no doubt commanded one of those coasting luggers of mixed character, to be found at that period in all the maritime countries of Europe, which played according to circumstances the character of the smuggler or of the honest trader. The extreme youth of Smith, and the manner in which he had been stripped of everything, awakened the compassion of the passengers, while the evident treachery of the captain enkindled all their rage. Some of them supplied the present wants of the former. He had been left wholly without clothes, those only which he wore excepted; and with but a single penny in his pocket, was compelled to part with his cloak for the payment of his passage. The indignation against the master of the vessel had nearly led to disastrous consequences. The passengers were kept with difficulty from putting him to death in their fury, and nothing but their ignorance of the ship's management prevented them from running away with her. Fortunately these intemperate counsels did not prevail, and the vessel was relieved of her angry inmates without suffering, except in the fright of the captain, which, we may be allowed to hope, afforded him a proper lesson of prudence, if not of honesty.

In these events our luckless adventurer was not wholly without consolation. He found friends among his new companions. One of these, in particular, who was himself an outlawed man, and might therefore be naturally expected to sympathize with one so young and so friendless, helped him to money, and brought him from place to place to a knowledge of his own friends, by whom he was everywhere hospitably entertained. His story interests the people, who are won by his youth, the frankness of his temper, and the graces of his person; those externals of character and figure which prompted Hume to think of him as a courtier for King James. He meets with kindness and protection finally from lords and ladies, whose names he gives, but whom it is scarcely possible for us to identify, disguised as they are by the antique English spelling of our author. With these persons he might, as he writes, "have recreated himself so longe as he woulde ;" but, as he adds, "such pleasant pleasures suited little with his poore estate and his restlesse spirit, that could never finnde content to receive such noble favours as he could neither deserve nor requite." Accordingly, breaking away from his new friends as he had done from the old, he resumed his wanderings, seemingly without an object beyond the

3

gratification of that restlessness of mood and independence of resolve, which were the prime characteristics of his genius for ever after. In these wanderings he is made to endure much misery and privation. His means are soon exhausted, his stout heart begins to fail him, probably because of the want of food; and, one day, finding himself in a forest, he flings himself, nearly dead with grief and cold, "beside a faire fountaine under a tree," as if resolved to yield to despair and to go no farther. Here he is found by a neighboring farmer, who takes pity on his condition, relieves his wants, and gives him means to resume his journey. And thus he fared, travelling from province to province, and from port to port, following the bent of a wayward inclination, still dissatisfied and vexed with those vague yearnings which naturally troubled the mind of him who has not yet learned to address himself to his legitimate objects. While thus wandering, the fortune which refuses to find him better opportunities, helps to gratify his revenge. Alone, and vagabondizing in Brittany, he accidentally meets in a wood with one of the treacherous Frenchmen who had robbed him of his clothes and money. This fellow was named Cursell. The parties recognized each other at a glance, and under an equal impulse their weapons were bared in the same instant. With an avowed object or enemy before him Smith was decisive always. They had no words. "The piercing injuries" of our hero, in his own language, "had small patience." His superior skill, together with (as we may surely assume) the goodness of his cause, gave him rather an easy victory. He tells of it without any boasting. The fight took place in the presence of several persons, the inhabitants of an old tower standing in the vicinity. In the hearing of these he extorted an ample confession of his guilt from the robber he had overthrown and wounded. But he obtained

Meeting and Conflict with Cursell. PAGE 26.

no further satisfaction. It appears from Cursell's confession that the rogues had quarrelled among themselves for a division of the spoils, that they had fought, and he had been driven away from any participation of it. With this story, and the honorable victory which he had won, Smith was compelled to be satisfied; and leaving the wounded robber to his own conscience and the care of the peasantry before whom he had confessed, he directed his steps to the seat of the Earl of Ployer, whom he had formerly known during the wars in France. By this nobleman and others, his kinsmen, Smith was received with distinction. They took pains to show him the country, "Saint Malo's Mount, Saint Michael, and divers other places in Brittany," and when he was ready to depart, they supplied him with means and sent him on his way rejoicing. Pursuing such a route as would enable him to see the country, and gratify the caprices of his curiosity, he at length made his way to Marseilles, where he took passage in a ship for Italy.

He was destined on this voyage to experience another of those trials, by which it would seem that fortune studies to task the strength, while she confers upon genius the degree of hardihood which is essential for great achievements. The vessel in which Smith sailed was crowded with pilgrims of the Catholic faith, making their way to Rome. She had scarcely put to sea when she was driven by stress of weather into the harbor of Toulon. This mishap, and possibly some indiscretion of his own, drew all eyes particularly upon himself. They discovered that he was the only Protestant on board. He was the Jonah, accordingly, to whom their misfortune was ascribed, and they exercised their own ill-humor, and his patience, by denouncing his religion and his nation, in no measured language, to his teeth. How, with a temper so quick and passionate, he forbore his defiance at this treatment, or that he did forbear, is not told us. The matter was not mended when they resumed the voyage. The bad weather continued, and the vessel was once more compelled to seek the refuge of a port. They cast anchor under the little isle of St. Mary, which lies off Nice, in Savoy. Here the pious Catholics once more gave vent to their indignation at the presence of so pernicious a heretic among them. "They wildly railed on his dreade sovraigne, Queen Elizabeth;" "hourly cursing him not only for a *Hugonoit*, but his nation they swore were all pyrats." In short, concluding "that they never should have faire weather so long as hee was aboard them, their disputations grew to that passion" that at length they cast him into the sea. We are told by one of the authorities, that he used his cudgel soundly among them before they proceeded to this extremity; but the assertion is grossly improbable, allowing anything for his discretion, and his own narrative affords no sanction for the story. That he may have defended himself when they offered to lay hands upon him—that he did defend himself—is probable enough. But that he offered violence in anticipation of this proceeding is highly questionable. Smith, even at this early day, was not without discretion. He was bold enough, but scarcely so rash or so thoughtless as, without help, to rush into conflict with a whole ship-load of angry enemies. That he met their vituperations with responses fashioned in a like style—that he gave them as good as they sent in the way of spiritual doctrine, and berated the pope as savagely as they cursed his "dreade sovraigne, Elizabeth," may be admitted; and in this way he may have precipitated those extremities, which at a later day his prudence would have taught him to avoid. But, whether imprudent or merely unfortunate, the storm still prevailing, he was dismissed by these pious pilgrims to the tender mercies of the deep. Well for him was it that the vessel was so nigh the shore. It was among the accomplishments of his desultory mode of life that he was an able swimmer. His heart did not fail him, nor his limbs. Buffeting the seas manfully, he succeeded in making his way, with little hazard or difficulty, to the dry land on St. Mary's isle. The place was uninhabited, except by a few kine or goats; and here, but for his better fortune, he might have become another Alexander Selkirk, with a temper quite as well prepared as his to make the most of his barren empire. But the very next day he was taken off by a French vessel, which, like his own, had put in to find shelter from the storm. This vessel was commanded by one Captain La Roche, of St. Malo, who proved to be a friend of the Earl of Ployer. When he ascertained the friendship of this nobleman for Smith, he treated him with the utmost kindness and consideration.

To the roving mind of our hero it did not much matter to what quarter of the globe his face was turned, and, well entertained, he made no sort of objection to accompanying his new acquaintance on his voyage. They sailed accordingly to Alexandria, in Egypt. Smith does not tell us in what capacity he went with Captain La Roche, nor whether he participated, except as a looker on, in any of the proceedings of the latter. But he was of an age and a character which must have made him highly useful in any situation, and we may readily conceive that he was not simply "an idle mouth" on the passage. Discharging her freight at Alexandria, they went to Scanderoon, "rather," says Smith, "to see what ships were in the roade than anything else." The truth seems to be that our vessel of Brittany was something more than a merchantman. She could serve a turn at other purposes, and her cruise simply "to see what ships were in the roade" was not a quest of idle curiosity. "Keeping their course by *Cypres* and the coast of Asia, sayling by Rhodes, the *Archipellagans*, Candia and the coast of *Grecia*, and the isle of *Zeffalonia*," they lay-to for a few days, evidently on the watch for prey, between the isle of Corfu and the Cape of Otranto at the entrance of the Adriatic Sea.

Here they did not watch in vain. Their cruise was rewarded by an encounter with a Venetian argosy, richly laden with gold, silks, velvets, tissue, and other rare products of that genius and invention, in which the Venetians were then very much in advance of the age. This encounter enlightens us somewhat in regard to the object of our Frenchman's course, although it is not certain that his quest was a Venetian vessel. It does not appear that war at that time existed between France and the Republic, but this was not necessary to make insecure the rich argosies of the one nation, meeting with a cruiser of the other, where no cognizance of their mutual doings might be had. The suspicious demeanor of our vessel of Brittany startled the fears of the vigilant Venetian. He very imprudently answered the civil salutation of Capt. La Roche with a shot, affording him in all probability the very pretext which he desired. This shot, killing one man on board the Frenchman, brought on a general action. The conflict which followed was exceedingly fierce. Twice in the space of an hour and a half did the French board the Venetian, and twice were they gallantly repelled. A third attempt resulted in the two vessels taking fire. The mutual danger led to their separation. The fire was soon quenched, but not the fury of the assailants. Their rage at being baffled led to more desperate efforts, and these were successful. The Venetian, in a sinking condition, yielded to the captors. They went to work to stop the leaks only that they might be enabled to rifle her of her valuable merchandize. This required twenty-four hours at the least, and Smith tells us that the "silkes, velvets, cloth of gold and tissue, pyastres, chicqueens and sultanies which is gold," of which they despoiled her in that space of time, "was wonderful." Having crammed their own vessel, they cast off the prize, leaving in her as much good merchandize as would have "*fraughted* such another Britaine." The Venetian was four or five hundred tons in burthen, the Frenchman but two hundred. The latter lost fifteen, the former twenty men in the engagement—a sufficient proof of its severity. That Smith took conspicuous part in the fight, with the hearty good will and the stubborn courage of the Englishman, may be inferred from his share of the spoils, which amounted to "five hundred chicqueens (sequins) and a little box," *God-sent him* (that is, we suppose, the immediate spoil of his own right hand) with as many more. The box was probably one of jewels.

Smith, so far as mere pecuniary fortune was concerned, had every reason to be satisfied with this adventure. But he was not satisfied to pursue the career thus handsomely opening before his eyes. He prepares to leave La Roche, and, at his own request, with his sequins and his jewelry, is set on shore in Piedmont. He parts kindly with La Roche, whom he styles "this noble Britaine," and who seems to have treated him with an appreciating and just consideration. His next journey is for Leghorn; and, making the tour of Italy, he meets the friends with whom his first pilgrimage had been made, Lord Willoughby and his brother. He finds them under painful circumstances upon which he does not dilate: "Cruelly wounded in a desperate fray, yet to their exceeding great honour." Yet what had been their experience, compared with his, from the moment of their first separation, when all of them were boys, to that of their present meeting? What a life of adventure had the nobleman of nature led in comparison with the easy fortunes which were theirs—the noblemen of society? What lessons had he learned of courage, and wisdom, and expedient, to serve him in a perilous career, and to secure him future eminence?

Smith visits Rome, where it was "his chance to see Pope Clement the Eighth, with many cardinals, creepe up the holy stayres." From Rome he went to Naples, and other great places, "to satisfie his eye with faire cities, and the kingdome's nobilitie;" and after a very ample tour, the description of which, as contained in his own narrative, is exceedingly bald and valueless, but in which we have reason to suppose that he was pretty well relieved of all his sequins, we find him suddenly awakened to a recollection of the original purpose for which he sailed from France—that of joining the armies of Rodolph of Germany, then waging war against the Turks, under the third Mahomet. From Venice he proceeded to Ragusa, on the Adriatic, where he lingered "some time to see that barren, broken coast of Albania and Dalmatia;" thence to Capo D' Istria, "travelling the maine of poor Slavonia," till he came to Gratz in Styria, the residence of Ferdinand, Archduke of Austria, and afterwards Emperor of Germany. Here he met with an Englishman and an Irish Jesuit, by whom, having made them acquainted with his desires, he was presented to Lord Ebersbaught, Baron Kisell, the Earl of Meldritch, and other persons of distinction in the imperial army. He was soon successful in finding his way to the confidence of these noblemen; and attaching himself to the staff of the latter, who was a colonel of cavalry, proceeded with his regiment soon after to Vienna.

CHAPTER III.

The time at which Smith made his appearance as a volunteer in the armies of Rodolph was particularly favorable to the desires of one having so large an appetite for military achievements. A cruel war had long been raging between the Christian power of Germany and the Grand Seignior. The close of the career of Amurath the Third had been hastened and embittered by disaster. He entailed upon his successor, the third Mahomet, the necessity, or more properly the seeming policy, for continuing the same bloody warfare. The year 1601, at the close of which Smith made his appearance in this new field, had been distinguished by many terrible conflicts, the advantage remaining in some measure with the Turks. They had ravaged Hungary, and taken some of its best fortresses; and Ibrahim Bashaw, with an immense army, had laid siege to Canissia, a place of strength on the borders of Styria, nearly surrounded by deep marshes. The Christian forces undertaking the relief of this place were defeated with great slaughter, and Canissia was finally surrendered. Flushed with this success, the Turks pushed forward to other conquests, and, with a force of twenty thousand men, laid siege to Olympach. The defence of this town was assigned to Lord Ebersbaught, one of the officers of the imperial army, to whom our hero had been introduced at Gratz. In this new acquaintance he had found a willing listener to the narrative of his military career, and to certain suggestions, which might have been original with Smith, for the improvement of the art of war. Something of his views may have been gathered from his reading, more perhaps from his experience, and a good deal from the activity of his mind, which could digest with equal independence the material derived from these twofold sources. Smith's brain seems to have been full to overflowing of strategic matter. He was at once the thinker and the worker: that rare combination of character, as we have said before, by which men of action are distinguished. He was always—to use his own phrase —"trying such conclusions as he projected to undertake." Some of these conclusions, with which he succeeded in impressing Lord Ebersbaught, were, as we shall see hereafter, of considerable service in obtaining advantages over the enemy. That he so readily obtained the ear of this nobleman and others, must be ascribed to an address of peculiar felicity. The English friends who introduced him could scarcely do more for him than say that he had seen service, and had experienced many vicissitudes. As yet he could boast none of the distinction of having been a leader of men. He had served a valuable apprenticeship; it was now for the first time that he was to reap its fruits.

Ebersbaught, in addition to the evident qualifications of the youth, most probably saw that he was ingenuous, that he did not belong to the ordinary class of military adventurers. It was a real passion for glory, and not a thirst after spoil, that brought him at that doubtful juncture into Hungary. Certainly, as we have shown, no moment could have been more unpromising for the imperial forces than that in which our hero joined himself to the regiment of the Earl of Meldritch—the Imperialists, defeated in successive actions, their strong places overthrown, their country ravaged, the Turk growing daily more confident and strong, and Olympach, greatly shattered by the besiegers, cut off from all communication with its friends, and nearly hopeless of succor from without. The forces appointed for its relief, under the Baron Kisell, a general of artillery, were inadequate to the task assigned them, and could give assistance in no other way than by occasionally annoying the besiegers, whenever opportunity offered for preventing them from obtaining supplies, or by cutting off a detachment. It was quite too feeble to attempt any more formidable enterprise against the main body of the besiegers. The regiment of Meldritch formed a part of this command of Kisell, and, as cavalry, was no doubt actively engaged in the business of this campaign, that being of a nature particularly to commend the use of horse. Of Smith's share in this business he tells us little, till we find him serving as a volunteer immediately about the person of the baron. That he had proved useful, and had succeeded in drawing attention to himself, may be inferred from this circumstance. He was about to prove himself more useful still. In the straitened condition of Olympach, Kisell was exceedingly anxious to attempt something in concert with the besieged; but how to effect this simultaneous operation was beyond his ingenuity. Communication with the town had been long since cut off. The Turks in vastly superior force lay between them, and closely watched as was the place, with an army of twenty thousand active and barbarous enemies, who were never known to spare, it was not possible to find a soldier sufficiently daring and reckless to hazard himself in the attempt to pass the *cordon* which their vigilance maintained. In this difficulty Smith came to the relief of his commander. He reminded him that among the numerous schemes of a military character, which he had communicated to Lord Ebersbaught, now in defence of Olympach, there was one of a telegraphic alphabet by which, with signal torches corresponding regularly with the letters of the alphabet, a correspondence might be carried on between persons not too far asunder for properly detecting and discriminating the lights. This scheme of a telegraph, as old as the days of the Greeks and Romans, may have been picked up by Smith in his military readings, but is by no means too intricate for his own unassisted invention. The fortunate circumstance was that he should have communicated it to Lord Ebersbaught among his "projections" and "conclusions," without entertaining any distinct conception of the present emergency, by which its usefulness was to be determined. The hope now entertained was that Lord Ebersbaught would sufficiently remember the suggestion to comprehend the signals. At all events, Smith succeeded in persuading Kisell to try the experiment. Seven miles distant from the town of Olympach stood a mountain of considerable elevation, which seemed to our hero suited for his purposes. To this mountain he conveyed himself with the necessary agents and implements by night. Here he first displayed three signal fires, equidistant from each other. These drew upon him the attention of the garrison, and were at once comprehended by the governor, whose wits, sharpened no doubt by the emergency, found no difficulty in recalling the scheme as related to him by the English adventurer. What was the joy of Smith when he was replied to by three torches from the walls of the town, showing him that his signals were understood! The rest was easy. The lights were then displayed from the mountain in proper order so as to form the successive words, thus—

"On—Thursday—at—night—I—will—charge—on—the—east—at—the—alarm—sally—you."

The answer was immediate—"I will!"—and this matter thus happily adjusted, Smith returned to camp, equally prepared to take part in the conflict, and to attempt further schemes for making it successful. His active genius conceived a plan for remedying the inferior numbers of the troops under Kisell; and by this means to keep in such a state of doubt and uncertainty a large portion of the besieging army, as to prevent them taking much or any part in the battle. The Turks were divided into two bodies, of ten thousand men each. These bodies lay apart, separated by a river. The entire force of Kisell amounted only to ten thousand. To fall suddenly upon one of the Turkish bodies, and to restrain the other, by reason of its own fears, from any attempt to second or assist it, was the desirable object. The river by which they were separated favored the scheme of Smith. This was to prepare some "two or three thousand pieces of match, fastened to divers small lines of an hundred fathom in length, being armed with powder," which "might all be fired and stretched at an instant, before the alarm, upon the plaine of Hysnaburg, supported by two staves at each line's end, and which would thus seem so many musketeers." This scheme, which had for its object to render vigilant the one half of the Turkish army, which it was not intended to assail, in watching the imaginary musketeers, is easily comprehended.

The result was eminently successful. While ten thousand of the Turks, wholly unendangered, were thus placed *hors de combat*, waiting anxiously for the momentary charge from the foe that had no existence except in their fancies, the actual warriors of Kisell, with Smith among them, were penetrating with havoc and slaughter among the ten thousand that lay encamped on the opposite side of the river. The *ruse* was admirably seconded on the part of the garrison. The Turks, bewildered and distracted, ran to and fro, without concert or courage, and offering no effectual opposition, were slaughtered in great numbers. More than a third of the ten thousand thus attacked, were slain or drowned in the attempt to swim the river to their comrades, who, on the other side, maintained such a resolute and watchful front against the imaginary army, as most effectually to discourage its assault.

The result was a triumphant one for the assailants Two thousand picked soldiers were thrown into the garrison, and the Turks, hopeless now of its conquest, retired in disgrace from before its walls. Our hero was not without his recompense for his share in an achievement, the success of which was due so largely to his ingenuity and skill. He received a command of two hundred and fifty horse in the regiment of his friend, the Earl of Meldritch, to say nothing of other honors and rewards.

CHAPTER IV.

A BRIEF interregnum, which seemed like peace, followed the relief of Olympach, to be succeeded by newer and greater preparations for the war. But the soul and intellect of Smith were not at rest. His was not the spirit to which repose is desirable; but, if not absolutely in action, contemplating action with the eye of his imagination, he was perpetually schooling himself for its vicissitudes. Never was mind more observant than his of the progress and condition of the world about him. His narrative, as a volume of travels, would be absolutely worthless to the reader who seeks for anything more than to ascertain the simple fact that the traveller himself had been an observer. Of this there can be no question. The mind of Smith was not given to description, and disdained details. It was of a sort fond of generalization, and taking in at a glance all the vital conditions of its subject. He describes little, but you see that he comprehends. He gives but a few words to the manners and customs of a people, but you see in these words that he conceives and appreciates them. The military eye of our hero is evidently keenly exercised in all the countries that he visits. He comments shrewdly on their forts and garrisons, on their weapons of war, their training, or the ease or difficulty with which their strong places may be overthrown. These notices, sprinkled over all his pages, show the source of that frequent mental provocation by which the resources of his own genius were brought into exercise and development. They show him watchful and shrewd, not easily persuaded by novelty, not easily deceived by show—of a calm, clear mind, a firm spirit, and one which, if it has not survived its youthful enthusiasm, is at least no longer to be deluded by it.

It was in busy study and contemplation that Smith employed the interregnum following the relief of Olympach, and the resumption of the actual events of war. The campaign opened early in the year. The levies of the Turks were prosecuted with unwearied diligence and activity, while, on the other hand, three large bodies of troops were raised by the emperor. One of these was commanded by the Archduke Mathias; one by Ferdinand, Archduke of Styria; and a third by Gonzago, governor of Hungary. The lieutenant of the Archduke Mathias was the Duke Mercury (Mercœur), who led a force of thirty thousand men, ten thousand of whom were French. Smith served in this division, still under the immediate command of the Earl of Meldritch. To Mathias was given the defence of Lower Hungary, and the Duke Mercury began the campaign vigorously by laying siege to Alba Regalis, a strongly fortified town in possession of the Turks, and considered in that day almost impregnable. Here Smith's talents as an engineer were put in requisition; and here we again find him counselling novel inventions in war, by which to obtain unusual advantages. He suggested to the Earl of Meldritch the employment of a sort of shell, which, filled with combustible matter, was discharged from a sling. These were called "Fiery Dragons" by their inventor, who describes them as "round-bellied earthen pots," filled with "hard gunpowder and musket bullets," and covered with a coating of brimstone, pitch, and turpentine. His plan was favorably entertained. He was permitted to try the experiment, which he did successfully. Having first learned from spies and deserters, or prisoners escaped from the town, in what quarters it was usual for great numbers of people to assemble on occasions of alarm, his bombs, or hand-grenades, to the number of forty or fifty, were flung at midnight into the city, directed to those places where the greatest crowds were likely to be brought together. "It was a fearful sight," says Smith, "to see the short flaming course of their flight in the air; but, presently after their fall, the lamentable noise of the miserable slaughtered Turkes was most wonderful to heare." These combustibles had the farther effect of firing the suburbs, "which so troubled the Turkes to quench, that had there beene any means to have assaulted them, they could hardly have resisted the fire and their enemies." The Turks fought bravely, nevertheless, making frequent sallies, and doing very slaughterous deeds whenever they came forth. But valor did not avail them. The place was finally taken by a bold and well executed manœuvre, which gave to the besiegers possession of the city. The bashaw by whom it was defended was faithful to his trust. Desperately fighting, and disputing every inch of ground with the assailants, he drew together a select body of five hundred men before his own palace, resolved in perishing to sell his life dearly. The conflict was a terrible one. The Turks were almost cut to pieces, and the bashaw saved in his own spite by the Earl of Meldritch, who, with his own hands, protected him from the fury of his troops. This city had been in possession of the Moslem for sixty years. They valued it accordingly. An army of sixty thousand men, under Hassan Bashaw, had been sent to its relief at the beginning of the siege, and was rapidly pressing forward when the news of its conquest was received. This did not arrest the march of the Turkish army. The loss of Alba Regalis was a severe stroke, seriously felt at the beginning of the campaign, and a subject of deep mortification with the Turks. Hassan Bashaw was disposed to risk much for its recovery. Pressing forward with all his energy, it was his hope to surprise the army of the Imperialists before they could well repair the breaches in the walls. He was mistaken in this expectation. The Duke Mercury had promptly provided for the defence of the place; and, apprised of the undisciplined and inferior character of the Turkish levies, he adopted the bold determination of marching out with twenty thousand men to meet them. The two armies encountered on the plains of Girke. The battle was joined upon the march, regiment after regiment mingling in the *melée* as they severally came upon the ground. The conflict was obstinate and bloody. If the Moslems lacked discipline there was no deficiency of valor, and valor makes so large an element of successful warfare, that it will not do to overlook or disregard it when estimating the resources of a foe. Besides, the Turks were thrice the number of the Christians. Discipline at length prevailed, after a long and murderous struggle. The skill and practised valor of the forces of Duke Mercury more than supplied the deficiency of number, and with equal courage and bravery effectually baffled that of the foe. The battle closed only with the night, nor was the affair then concluded, since, as it has been said of the British in recent times, the Turk did not know when he was beaten. The affair was destined to be resumed with the beginning of another day.

Smith approved his valor in the conflict, was wounded, and had his horse shot under him. But he was not the warrior to be content with this, and to remain dismounted when there were so many noble steeds running masterless around him. He was soon supplied with the means of renewing his labors in a field, in which his ardent and fearless spirit found so much to delight him. The wound of Smith in this action he calls a sore one. Nothing is said of the part which he took in the final assault when Alba Regalis was carried; yet if we recollect that the last desperate struggle with the governor took place with the troops under the immediate command of the Earl of Meldritch, we have every reason to conclude that our hero had his share in the worst dangers of that bloody conflict.

Night, which separated the combatants on the plains of Girke, left the affair still doubtful. But the Turks thought otherwise. Hassan Bashaw was a brave man, and had the most perfect Moslem faith in the sword and doctrines of Mohammed. Flattering himself that the Christians were wholly in his clutches, he committed the gross military error of detaching twenty thousand of his men, and sending them off to begin the leaguer of that town which he had been marching to relieve. He proposed to finish the affair with Duke Mercury the next day with the forces which remained. Never was general more mistaken. He failed in both his objects. The precautions which the Duke had taken before leaving Alba Regalis, in providing amply for its safety, without regard to his movements or fate, enabled the garrison to beat off and baffle the assailants. The situation of the Duke himself was much more hazardous. With the return of daylight the generals of both armies opened their eyes with an increased respect for each other, and each proceeded to intrench himself where he lay, under sight of his enemy. Thus they lay for two or three days, the precautions of the Imperialists being rather greater than those of the Turks, as was proper to their inferior numbers. By the latter they were frequently taunted with their weakness, and defied to come from behind their trenches. These provocations finally goaded them to the encounter. The Christians were led out by the Rhinegrave, by Culnitz, and Meldritch, in three bodies. The struggle was a short one. The Turks were driven to the cover of their intrenchments, with a loss of six thousand men; the Imperialists forbearing to press their advantage, because of the sudden appearance of a large body of troops, coming from an unexpected quarter. The success thus obtained, while it lessened the Turkish appetite for a renewal of the game, did not increase the courage of the Christians. We are not told of their losses in the two conflicts which had already taken place; nor of the character of that body of men, whose sudden appearance in the midst of the last battle prevented Duke Mercury from pressing his advantage to a final victory. In all probability there were good reasons in his own weakness for this forbearance. Thus intrenched, the two armies lay watching each other for some days more, until at length, growing impatient, or hopeless of any good result from longer delay, Hassan Bashaw broke up his camp, and retired from his trenches; the Imperialists hanging upon his march, and assailing his rear frequently and with success. The Turks fled to Buda, and the Duke divided his army into three parts. One of these divisions, consisting of six thousand men, was given to the Earl of Meldritch, who was sent to assist George Busca against the Transylvanians. With this division went our adventurer, and to its fortunes we must confine our attention. Our notice of the history of the country, as a matter of course, will be confined to such glimpses only as are necessary to a proper comprehension of the part taken by Smith, and the relation to public events in which each occurrence finds him. Transylvania at this period was assailed by very different enemies. Sigismund Bathor, the native prince of the country, was contending with the Emperor of Germany on one hand, and with the Turks on the other, who were the deadly enemies of both. While the latter were the invaders of his land, the former was ambitious of its sovereignty. Meldritch had been sent against Sigismund, but being a native of Transylvania, he preferred serving the native prince to the invader. He was perhaps the more readily persuaded to this, as he found Sigismund already in possession of the best footholds of the country. He did not find it difficult to divert the arms of his followers into the direction which he himself proposed to take; particularly, indeed, as he could urge upon them the better booty to be won from the Turks, than that which could possibly be gleaned from the poor natives, his countrymen. The Emperor had not been a very good paymaster, and this was another argument easily persuading to a change of service. Besides, why fight against Christians, when the Turkish enemies were before them, at once the foes of their country and their faith? A war, too, carried on against these, was a war in favor of both of the Christian princes, though they might be contending in deadly hate against each other. We cannot reproach the Earl of Meldritch and his followers with their change of service. Smith, certainly, had neither moral nor social obligations to adhere to the banner of the Germans. Nay, to have done so, in carrying war into Transylvania, would have been on his part a gross offence against society and morals. His own previous convictions would have denounced him, as he had long since "repented and lamented to have seene so many Christians slaughter one another;" and he had sought the army of the Imperialists, with the express desire to "trie his fortune against the Turkes."

He was still to enjoy the pleasure. Sigismund was very well pleased to obtain the services of a captain so brave and well experienced as Meldritch, and readily consented that he should endeavor to drive the Turks out of his country. It so happened that they held possession of those very portions of Transylvania in which the earl's family estates were situated. His motives were therefore quite as personal as patriotic. He began his career with his wonted vigor.

CHAPTER V.

In the campaign which followed, Smith was employed in a manner which must have afforded him an excellent training for his future career among our North American Indians. The country, in which its operations were to take place, was one equally wild and savage in its natural and social aspects. The greatest trials of strength were to be found in regions which to ordinary courage would have seemed inaccessible. In these regions had the Turks planted their stronghold. They occupied the rocky mountains of Zarham, and ravaged the tributary plains and valleys. Over these wild and stony passes, in regions possessed by herds of bandits and renegades of all descriptions, Turks and Tartars—a people not so much Turks as outlaws—not so much men as savages—the troops of Meldritch must make their way to get at their enemies, and gain possession of his estates. They had to contend with a people practised in guerilla or partisan warfare—a warfare more than all others calculated to draw out the resources of military genius, to stimulate ingenuity and activity, and prompt courage to feats of the greatest audacity. Meldritch knew the country, and was by no means ignorant of its difficulties. He soon brought his troops to an acquaintance with the predatory warriors by whom it was possessed. These were sought and pressed, and with daily and unremitting industry. Gradually, they yielded before his arms, and left him in possession of the plains. They had their cities in the mountains, and to these they retired from before the presence of the foe. To one of these, as utterly impregnable, they ascended when they could no longer find safety below. This was the city of Regall, a place of great natural strength, to which the military art of the day had added suitable fortifications. Regall was full of men, and so placed among the mountains, at one side only accessible, thatnothingbut the most extraordinary perseverance and courage would ever think of subduing it. But these were the very qualities which the Earl of Meldritch brought against it. He had been twenty years a soldier, was full of resources, and had under him no doubt many adventurers who, like Smith, could contribute to his success at the perilous moment by original expedients in arms. He had much at stake in the enterprise, and he approached it cautiously. His examination of Regall, of its approaches, strength and general characteristics, was thorough and satisfactory. He began the siege with the opening of spring. "The earthe no sooner put on her greene habit," says Smith, "than the earl overspread her with his armed troops." Meldritch proceeded as he had begun, with great energy. He strove in the face of a thousand difficulties. His ordnance was to be carried up through narrow passes of the mountains, in which he was liable to capital misfortune at any moment, unless watched by vigilance and the most ready courage. A race of active mountaineers, familiar with the country, and practised in the sort of warfare which it requires, might long succeed in baffling an invader of ten times their numbers. The banditti in possession of the mountain were not prepared to forego the advantages of their position, and every step on the part of the assailants was distinguished by conflicts which were equally obstinate and bloody. But perseverance, which is moral courage of a distinguished order, co-operating with that of ordinary valor, and seconded by experience and skill, succeeded in arraying the force of the Christians on the table of the mountain, and in front of Regall. The defenders of the city, apprised in season of the attempt against that place, had lined its walls with soldiers, and stored it abundantly, as well with provisions as with the munitions and implements of war. Confiding in the strength of the place, their own numbers and courage, and the ample supplies which they possessed for maintaining the siege, they laughed to scorn the attempts of the assailant. The seemingly feeble force brought against them—for the whole army of Meldritch did not exceed eight thousand men—seemed to justify the contempt which they expressed. But they were soon taught another language. Even with this small army he succeeded in all the skirmishes in which they met, and had fully beleaguered them within the walls of Regall before he was joined by the forces of Prince Moyses, nine thousand in number. To him, the chief command was surrendered.

The preparations of the besiegers were now deliberately made. These were to secure them in the position which they had won. It occupied near a month before they were able to intrench themselves fully, and to plant their batteries. The slowness of these proceedings increased the courage of the Turks. They were amused rather than alarmed by that deliberation, which was in truth the strongest proof of their danger. With a blind confidence in their numbers and the strength of their walls, they derided the besiegers with frequent messages of scorn and defiance. One of these messages was of the very character best adapted to provoke the more chivalrous persons in the Christian army, as it mingled the lofty tone and temper of chivalry with the insolence of inflated self-esteem. It roused an individual spirit in the besiegers. It reproached them with their inactivity—said that they grew fat for lack of exercise; and—expressing a fear lest they should suddenly depart from the city without affording any pastime to the ladies thereof,—proposed a defiance from the Lord Turbishaw to any captain having the command of a company. The head of the vanquished, with all that he possessed, was to be at the mercy of the conqueror. The challenge was after the fashion of knightly times, and these had not entirely gone out of the memories of men. The very motive to the offer—"to delight the ladies, who did long to see some courtlike pastime," partook largely of the best spirit of the Middle Ages. There were not wanting numerous brave captains in the Christian army whose hearts bounded to the acceptance of the challenge with the eagerness of the ancient war-steed, stirred suddenly by the onset sounds of the trumpet; and but a single mode was left of deciding upon the champion—that of casting lots for the noble privilege. We need not say that Smith was among the claimants, and that special fortune befriended him. The ballot upon which his name was written was the first to present itself; as if the watchful fate, for ever heedful of her favorite, had snatched for him the golden opportunity for fame.

The preparations for the combat were as great as the anxieties for the issue were lively. A truce was made between the opposing armies, in order to the completion of arrangements for this event; and as both parties possessed a very equal knowledge of the sort of state which should distinguish such proceedings, the affair absolutely recalls very vividly to the mind the great jousts and solemn tournaments which characterized the famous deeds of knighthood, as they were practised a hundred years before. On the day appointed for the combat the Christians were drawn out in battle array, making the most lavish display of banners, trophies, and heraldic insignia; while the ramparts of the town were covered with fair ladies, and men glittering in armor. The Turkish dames in these regions seem not to have shrunk from a display of their persons to the eyes of infidels, as they were compelled to do in the more central cities of their religion. Living on the borders of a Christian land, some of their social habits might naturally enough be modified by familiarity with the customs of their neighbors.

The Turkish challenger, as in duty bound, first made his appearance on the field. A "noise of howboys" announced his coming and his presence. His *entrée* was calculated to rivet the attention, and compel admiration. He was well mounted, and clad in a suit of splendid armor. "On his shoulders were fixed a paire of great wings, compacted of eagle's feathers, within a ridge of silver, richly garnished with gold and precious stones." Three Janizaries attended him; one going before and bearing his lance, the two others walking beside him and conducting his horse to the station which was assigned him. Such was the proud entrance and imposing aspect of the Turkish champion. That of Smith was far less showy. It does not appear that he wore any but his ordinary armor, or that he had any other to wear. We have reason to suppose, however, that he was not regardless of his personal appearance; particularly as he was to fight in the presence of the ladies. That they were pagan dames did not lessen his respect for the sex; and, if the truth were written, he was more than usually solicitous of his toilet on that day. That he donned his best surcoat, that he selected his most showy scarf and plumage, we may conjecture with sufficient safety. But he was no carpet knight. He did not keep the Turkish champion waiting. He rode into the field with a flourish of trumpets, attended by a page bearing his lance,—passed his foe with a courteous salute, and gracefully wheeled into the position which was designated for him. There was no delay. At the sound of the trumpet the combatants rushed into the deadly embrace of the strife, and the encounter was ended with the single shock, and almost as soon as it had begun. So admirably true was the aim, so firm the nerves of the Christian champion, and so well trained his steed, that the lance of Smith penetrated the beaver of the Turk, and passing through his eye into the brain, he fell dead to the ground at the first thrust, without so much as grazing the person of his conqueror. Smith leapt to the ground, unbraced the helmet of his enemy, and finding him lifeless, smote off his head, which he bore away in triumph to the Christian host. The body of Turbishaw was delivered to his friends. The spoils of war necessarily became the property of the victor.

CHAPTER VI.

We may imagine the exultation in the camp of the Christians, and the good auguries of future triumph which were conveyed by so gallant a beginning. The hero was met by the army with a shout of general welcome. In just the same degree was the mortification of the good people of Regall. Sorely did they lament the fall of their champion, and sadly, we may suppose, did the "faire dames" of the city sigh as they thought upon the delightful pastime which was made for them by the Christian, Smith. But the chief mourner in Regall was one Grualgo, the bosom friend of Turbishaw, and a fierce and powerful warrior. In the first paroxysm of his grief and fury he despatched a special message to the conqueror, proposing his own head as the stake for the recovery of his friend's. To make the bait the more tempting to our champion, his horse and armor were also proposed as pledges upon the issue. It need scarcely be said that, flushed with one victory, and having full confidence in his own prowess, Smith was ready to seek the chances for another. The challenge was promptly accepted. Nothing, indeed, could have been more agreeable to our hero. It is true, he had given the head of Turbishaw to Prince Moyses, who had "kindly accepted it," but it cannot be doubted that the prince would gladly risk his prize with the expectation of getting that of Grualgo also for his collection. There were no difficulties in the way of the arrangement, the field was prepared as before, and the ensuing day was appointed for the combat.

The walls of Regall were again covered with spectators.

5*

The fair and the brave once more came forth with mingled feelings of delight, expectation and anxiety—pride, and hope, and apprehension, duly mingling in their bosoms, according to the temper of the individual. Grualgo entered as his friend had done, with a noise of hautboys; Smith, as before, with a flourish of trumpets. The sound of the trumpet gave the signal for the combat. At the first passage the lances of the combatants flew into pieces; but, while the Turk was nearly unhorsed in the encounter, Smith kept his seat as if he had grown to the saddle. The splintered spears were thrown aside, and seizing their pistols, shots were instantly exchanged between the parties. At the first shot Smith was slightly wounded, and Grualgo escaped unhurt. In the second, the latter was less fortunate. His left arm was shattered, and his horse became unmanageable. In this plight he was thrown to the ground, and lay at the mercy of the conqueror. The age was not favorable to much forbearance in such cases, nor had the terms of courtesy between the contending armies been of such a sort as to render the want of pity a reproach to either from the other. Besides, the Turk had staked his head with a full knowledge of all the dangers, and having the fate of Turbishaw before him. Smith had voluntarily subjected himself to the same risk, and this he scarcely would have done, but with a view to his obtaining all the profits of his risk. The conditions of the field seem to have been inevitable, and leaping to the ground, the conqueror smote off the head of Grualgo as effectually as he had done that of Turbishaw. Head, horse and armor remained his trophies. The body, he is careful to tell us, with all its rich apparel, was sent back to the city. Our champion took nothing more than he had a perfect right to take.

These were severe strokes to the defenders of Regall.

We have every reason to suppose that Turbishaw and Grualgo were their very bravest champions. No more challenges were sent from that city. The desire among the Turkish warriors of delighting the ladies of the place with such courtlike pastimes seemed fairly at an end, and the chivalry of both parties was now exercised in daily conflicts of a more general nature. The Turks made frequent sallies, but did not long wait for the skirmishes they provoked. "They would not endure," says Smith, "to any purpose." They had, by this time, tested sufficiently the superior prowess of their assailants, and their sorties had no other object than to divert or retard the operations of the leaguer, of which they may reasonably have begun to be more apprehensive than at the beginning of the campaign. These operations were of a character too slow and tedious for the temper of Smith. The approaches were left to unskilful engineers, and the progress to the consummation of the event was too unpromising to satisfy the impatient and ambitious nature of our champion. Burning for some new occasion for displaying his skill and spirit, he determined to take the initiative in a new attempt to delight and amuse the ladies. "With many incontradictible persuading reasons" "to delude time," Smith obtained leave from his commander to send a message of defiance into the town. It was couched, however, in language of particular courtesy, as being addressed to the ladies of Regall themselves. He begged to assure them that he was not so much enamored of the heads of their servants in his possession, but that he was ready to restore them upon proper terms, and he invited them to send forth some other champion who would risk his own to recover them. Smith concluded by declaring himself willing that his head should accompany the others, if their champion was prepared to take it.

Thus addressed, it became a point of honor with the gallants of Regall that the ladies should not lack a champion. The challenge of the Christian was accepted with sufficient promptness by a brave fellow, whose name in our English orthography does not create the impression of any very formidable personage. How it would look and sound in Turkish costume is beyond our conjecture. Bonny Mulgro—thus written by Smith—was the name of the third champion sent forth from Regall. He came only to add a third to the trophies of our hero. The arrangements were made for the ensuing day.

The combatants entered the field as in the previous instances, and under like auspices—the day fine, and the camp of the Christians, and the entire population of Regall, turning out to behold the issue. But there was one difference in the arrangements which had like to have brought about an important difference in the result. The choice of weapons being with the challenged party, taking counsel from the fate of his predecessors, he declined having anything to do with the lance, of which weapon Smith had shown himself a perfect master. (How much of this mastery did he owe to his practice when playing hermit in the woods of Lincoln?) Bonny Mulgro chose the pistol, the battle-axe, and falchion; in the use of which weapons, particularly in that of the battle-axe, he was more than commonly a proficient. The combat honored his discretion, and had nearly resulted in his victory. At the sound of the trumpet the combatants rapidly darted upon each other, discharging their pistols as they drew nigh. No damage having been done by these weapons, they were thrown aside, and a close and severe combat followed with the battle-axe. For some time the strife was doubtful. Sound strokes were given on both sides, with such hearty good will, and such imperfect defence,

Combat with Boney Mulgro. PAGE 57.

as to leave neither of them scarce sense enough—so Smith tells us—to keep their saddles. At length, however, the Turk succeeded in giving his antagonist a blow so severe as to deprive him of his battle-axe. At the sight of this advantage gained by their champion, the people of Regall set up such a shout as shook their ramparts. This, while it encouraged Bonny Mulgro to do his utmost, may be supposed to have stung his opponent into a full recovery of his senses—never more necessary to him than just at that moment. He did recover them. It was very fortunate for him that he was so efficient a horseman. It was only by the dexterous management of his steed that he succeeded for some time in avoiding the blows hailed upon him by his enemy. Smith is not unwilling to share some of the merit with his horse, whose "readinesse" he eulogizes, while insisting upon his own "judgment and dexterity in such a businesse." It was beyond the expectation of all the spectators—almost beyond the hope of his Christian friends—that our hero, finally, "by God's assistance," not only escaped the hatchet of the Turk, but drawing his falchion, succeeded in running him through the body. This event dismounted him; and though he alighted on his feet, he was not suffered to keep them long. He soon shared the fate of his companions; and Smith, still in possession of his own head, added a third to his former bloody trophies.

CHAPTER VII.

These several victories, the fruit of so much skill, judgment and valor on the part of our champion, had the most inspiriting effect upon the soldiery, and were duly honored by the commander of the Christians. A most imposing pageant took place in his honor. With an escort of six thousand men, the three Turks' heads borne before him on so many spears, preceding the three horses with their panoply, the spoils of the three combats, Smith was conducted to the pavillion and into the presence of the general. Prince Moyses welcomed him with embraces, complimented him as his deeds deserved, bestowed upon him a noble charger richly furnished, a splendid scimetar and belt worth three hundred ducats. Count Meldritch added to these gifts another, which our hero in all probability valued quite as highly as any of the rest. He made him a major in his regiment. Nor were these the only rewards which followed his unwonted and successful chivalry. At a later period Sigismund Bathor, Prince of Transylvania, coming to review the army, and being made aware of his peculiar achievements, distinguished him with the highest personal attentions, gave him his picture set in gold, a pension of three hundred ducats per annum, and crowned all with a patent of nobility. This patent entitled him to a coat of arms, bearing three Turks' heads in a shield, with the motto, " *Vincere est Vivere.**

---

* For this patent and the certificate of the English garter king-at-arms, Sir William Segar, by whom it was admitted and put on record in the Heralds' College, England—see *Appendix.*

But Smith was destined to undergo other perils and vicissitudes, and to make other exhibitions of courage, skill and endurance, before these last mentioned honors were conferred upon him. Regall was yet to be taken, and however keenly its defenders might feel the mortification and loss of three of their favorite champions, their determination to defend the place to the last moment was not a whit lessened by their fate. The works of the besiegers being at length completed for the grand assault, they opened upon the walls of the city with six and twenty pieces of artillery. In the space of fifteen days two breaches were made. These were defended by the Turks with all the earnestness of desperate men in maintenance of their last favorite places of retreat. A general assault at length was commanded, and after a furious conflict, hand to hand, in which the assailants suffered severely, the town was entered by them sword in hand. The surviving defenders fled to the castle or citadel, as the only place of refuge. But this was not to be a place of refuge long. In vain did the little garrison send out a flag of truce, entreating composition with the besiegers. The prayer was rejected with scorn and indignation. The Christians had old massacres to avenge, and the castle, subjected to a like battery with that which had overthrown their ramparts, was taken the next day by storm. Then followed one of those terrible instances of havoc and brutality which, in all similar circumstances, in that and preceding periods, has marked the victory obtained over walled places in the phrenzied and exciting heat of actual conflict. Dreadful was the massacre which ensued. All who could bear arms were put indiscriminately to the sword, their heads cut off and set around the walls upon stakes, such as had been done to the Christian defenders when the place had fallen into the hands of the present victims. Humanity asks without being answered, "What of the fair women, the beautiful and young, whose presence on the walls, at a more exhilarating moment, had stimulated the valor of knighthood, and whose smiles had lighted up the field of chivalry?" The ferocious temper which spared not the submissive warrior, was not likely, in the desperate mood which the sacking of a city demands, to forbear excess and violence to the pleading and the loveliness of his women, particularly when the very faith with which they professed, placing them among the heathen, seemed of itself, in the estimation of that day of bigotry and superstition, to put them out of the pale of humanity. Though our adventurer spares us the melancholy details of this ferocious history, it is to his credit that his language, when he refers to the subject, is that of regret and sympathy. We have no reason to suppose that he ever had occasion to feel remorse for his share in these proceedings, or to reproach himself with deeds which were not performed in the heat of actual conflict, and under all the necessity of self-defence.

The ramparts of Regall being repaired, and his own besieging works overthrown, Prince Moyses manned the place with a strong garrison, and proceeded to other conquests. We need not say that Smith accompanied him. Like successes attended the Christians at Veratio, Solmos and Kupronka. These places also fell by storm, were sacked—the garrison sharing a like fate with the arms-bearing inhabitants of Regall, and the decrepid, the women and children, two thousand in number, being carried into captivity. We are to conjecture for ourselves the sort of experience, busy and bloody, of strife and slaughter, through which our hero passed in this melancholy progress of sacks and sieges. But the heart of the soldier is not necessarily a callous one; and the fervor of actual combat subsiding, the more genial humanities are apt to recover all their sway in the bosom which rather obeys the prompting of an impetuous nature, than the cold and cruel dictates of diseased and vexing passions. Smith's narrative is never allowed to shock our sensibilities. He speaks of the conflict in the spirit of the warrior; but,the strife at rest, he seems to shrink from such details as degrade him from his humanity. It may be urged that he was not ignorant of the final issues of war, and the atrocious practices which usually accompanied it at that period, and in the wild countries in which he waged it; but this will be insisting upon standards of morality which did not belong to his time, and would not properly apply in the case of one so neglected in his youth and training as himself. Besides,he was too much the creature of action, too fond of adventure in fields which tax all the energies of the soul and spirit, to be easily diverted from employments which gave exercise to these, because of the occasional repulsiveness of their conditions. Our object, however, is not to excuse but to represent him justly. A wild time and wild countries demand a prompt and unscrupulous courage. Though Smith laments the horrors of warfare, and speaks always with the gentleness and meekness of that better spirit which sometimes softened the aspects of the feudal ages, he is not to be driven from the profession of arms, because of its occasional massacres. We find him still commanding under Meldritch, though by this time certain political changes in the affairs of Transylvania left him no longer under the same superior. Hitherto, the Prince Sigismund, from whom he had received his honors, had maintained a sufficiently bold front at once against the Turks and the emperor, whose authority he had defied, asserting for himself all the rights of an independent sovereign. But the struggle was too unequal.

The resources of his principality were exhausted in the conflict; and, with the spectacle before his eyes of ravaged fields and wasted territories, the proud spirit of the Prince was humbled within him. Smith gives in a few words a painful description of the condition of the country after the close of this twofold struggle. From being "one of the fruitfullest and strongest countries in those parts," it was become "rather a desert, or the very spectacle of desolation; their fruits and fields overgrowne with weeds, their churches, and battered palaces, and best buildings, as for feare, hid with mosses and ivy: being the very bulwarke and rampire of a greate part of Europe, most fit by all Christians to have been supplyed and maintained, was thus brought to ruine by them it most concerned to support it." But what was the true interest of the country or of Europe to the prerogative of the Emperor? The latter was unyielding, and Sigismund, with a humane regard to the distresses of his people, craved a truce from his invader. This truce led to the desired concessions, which were followed by a partial disbanding of the army under Prince Moyses. Sigismund accepted a munificent pension, and yielding up his perilous sovereignty, retired upon the rank and estate of a private nobleman. But this was an arrangement by no means satisfactory to all the parties. Young hawks must be fed; and soldiers by trade are not the less willing to fight because they are disbanded. Prince Moyses, the lieutenant of Sigismund, declared his resolution never to submit to the Germans; and disobeying the commands of Sigismund—perhaps compelled by his troops to disregard them—he marched against the forces of the Emperor, commanded by one Busca, an Albanian. A few small successes which he obtained were followed by a bloody conflict, in which he was finally defeated, and fled for refuge to the Turks at

Temesvare. His overthrow removed all obstacles to the progress of the Emperor; and it was not difficult to enlist the same soldiers of fortune who had fought for the one in the armies of the opposing Prince. It does not appear that Smith had made cause with Moyses in his insurrectionary and frantic movement against Busca. On the contrary, he seems to have adhered to the fortunes of his more immediate leader, the Earl of Meldritch, and soon found employment with him, as before, in defending the country from the infidel. There was no lack of employment in those days, and in that region, for the warlike man-at-arms. The Turk was no such imbecile as we find him now, to be trodden upon and buffeted with impunity by all his neighbors. There were few of the contiguous nations, indeed, which at that time he did not cause to tremble; and his restless ambition rendered necessary the maintenance of veteran armies everywhere along the frontiers of his empire. Wallachia was then a Turkish province, the people of which revolting against the tyranny of their vaivode or governor, one Jeremias, expelled him from their territory, and called in the assistance of the emperor's forces. These were not slow in coming at the call, and at their presence and with their assistance, a new vaivode was proclaimed in the person of Lord Rodoll. But Jeremias, the governor who had been expelled, having succeeded in assembling a numerous army of forty thousand men, prepared to contest the authority which had succeeded to his own, and to subdue and scourge the revolt among his subjects. Rodoll, unable to contend with such an army, fled at its approach, and took shelter among the Transylvanians. It became necessary to assert the rights of the new vaivode by force of arms, and Busca, anxious to furnish employment to the old regiments of Sigismund, of whose fidelity he seems to have had some doubts, found no difficulty in yielding them for this purpose, to the application of the fugitive. It was thus that Smith, still under the command of his old leader, the Earl of Meldritch, again took the field against his ancient enemy, the Turk. Meldritch led to the support of Rodoll a powerful army of thirty thousand men. This body of troops, well trained, well officered and admirably experienced, was perhaps the most veteran force in Transylvania. This army, penetrating Wallachia, advanced upon the camp of Jeremias, who lay strongly entrenched in the plains of Peteski, awaiting reinforcements from the Crim Tartars. Here the Christians encamped also, watching their enemy, but not daring to assail him in the strong position which he held. Frequent conflicts took place between small parties of the opposing forces, which were chiefly remarkable for the shocking cruelties which they practised. While Rodoll beheaded his prisoners, and flung their gory heads by night into the Turkish trenches, the latter, not to be outdone in brutality, flayed his victims alive, and staked the still warm carcases on huge poles in sight of their infuriated comrades. To seduce Jeremias from his entrenchments, Rodoll fell upon a plan of retreat, which was intended to have all the appearance of a flight. His scheme was well devised, and at a given period, firing the country as he withdrew from his camp, he retired in the night upon the Brinki in seeming precipitation. The *ruse* had the desired effect. The Turks, against the will of their commander, forced him to lead them in pursuit, and while the rear-guard of Rodoll was skirmishing with the advance parties of his enemy, the main body of his army was putting itself in the most favorable position for the reception of the pursuing foe. Smith gives us a lively account of the battle which ensued. His is one of those frank and generous natures which shows no reluctance in declaring the merits as well of friend and enemy. Meldritch and Busendorfe he describes "rather like enraged lions than like men," and fighting the assailants "as if in them only had consisted the victory." Meldritch's horse is slain under him, and the desire of the Turks to make him prisoner, and of his own followers to save him from this peril, makes the battle hottest where he stands. He is remounted, and "it is thought with his owne hands he slew the valiant Zanzàcke, whereupon his troopes retyring, the two proud bashawes, Aladdin and Zezimmus, brought up the front of the body of their battel." The fight becomes desperate and bloody. The bravery and skill of Jeremias, which are highly commended by our hero, leave it for some time doubtful, even with the object of his stratagem obtained, if Rodoll will remain the victor. The conflict is one of individual combats, and becomes a massacre rather than a fight. "There was scarce ground to stand upon," says Smith, "but upon the dead carkasses which, in less than an hower, were so mingled as if each regiment had singled out the other." It is really pleasing to hear him speak of the Turkish champions. "The admired Aladdin," says he, "that day did leave behinde him a glorious name for his valour, whose death many of his enemies did lament after the victorie." "Zezimmus, the bashaw, was taken prisoner, but died presently of his wounds." "Jeremie * * * like a valiant prince in the front of the vantgard, by his example so bravely encouraged his soldiers that Rodoll found no great assurance of the victorie." But the victory finally fell to the Christians. Their veteran experience determined the odds in their favor. The havoc had been immense. The Turks lost their bravest officers, and not less than twenty-five thousand dead of both armies were left upon the field, a bloody proof of the resolute hatred of the opposing legions. Of his own share in this battle,

Smith modestly tells us nothing. His eulogies upon the valorous deeds of others, friend and foe, leave him no room to relate his own. But a struggle so hotly and so closely contested, with regiment grappling regiment over the bodies of slain comrades, is not likely to have been spared the exhibitions of that spirit, skill, strength and courage, which had so often individualized his previous career. We have no doubt that our adventurer did not suffer himself to be outdone, and his own glory obscured, by any Turk or Christian in the two arrays. He did not repose upon the laurels of Regall, but in all probability dyed his sanguinary chaplet trebly red in the havoc of that mortal struggle.

CHAPTER VIII.

Jeremie, the leader of the Turks, after performing prodigies of valor, escaped from the field with some fourteen thousand men, making his way to Moldavia. Lord Rodoll resumed his rule as vaivode in Wallachia; but his fate seemed resolute that he should not hold it long without disturbance. The Turks and Tartars again drew to a head in numbers, and, under the conduct of Jeremie, who had succeeded in uniting the remnant of his forces with other troops in Moldavia, again appeared upon the field. The numbers of his army had been greatly underrated; and Meldritch, laboring under this error, was sent against him with but thirteen thousand men. With an enemy before him numbering nearly forty-five thousand men, Meldritch slowly yielded to a pressure which it would have been madness to resist. He retired towards Rottenton, a strongly garrisoned town of the vaivode, but was terribly harassed by his enemy on the retreat. The skirmishing parties of the two armies were in constant collision, and not without advantage to the Christian army; which, however, still continued its retrograde movement, made momently more and more conscious, by the accumulating presence of the foe, of the tremendous disparity between the two forces. A night march which Meldritch's troops made, with incredible expedition, through a wood, brought them unexpectedly upon two thousand of the Turks laden with plunder. Favored by a thick morning fog, which concealed their approach from the foe, they immediately charged with complete success, slaying many, and taking numerous prisoners. But this success was accompanied by the knowledge, gained from their captives, that their rapidity of march had availed them nothing. They were apprised that Jeremie with his Turks had got in advance of them, and now lay in waiting, guarding the only pass through which they could escape. To support him in his position, the Tartars, twice his number, were approaching at a little distance, conscious of their vast superiority of force, and eager for their prey. The prospect only increased the desperate valor of the Christians. It became necessary to force the passage, if possible, before the junction of the Tartars with the Turkish army under Jeremie; and here, again, the ingenuity of the "English Smith," as he styles himself, was put in requisition for the relief of the beleaguered army. Smith, remembering the excellent success which had followed his experiments of "fiery dragons" and "false musketeers" on previous occasions, conceived the idea of a "pretty stratagem of fireworks," of which he instantly advised his superior. By means of these he proposed to diminish materially the danger and difficulties of fighting his way through such a host as that of Jeremie, in the advantageous position which the latter occupied. Meldritch, who had already seen the excellent skill which our hero possessed in gunpowder, gave ready ear to his suggestions. The plan of Smith was quite simple. Rockets, of a highly explosive and eccentric character, were immediately prepared, and fastened to the ends of their lances; and under cover of the night the passage was attempted. The expedient had all the success which was expected from it. The rockets, two or three hundred in number—"truncks of wild-fire" —at the end of the charging spears, "blazed forth such flames and sparkles, that it so amazed not only their horses but their foot also, that, by the meanes of this flaming encounter, their owne horses turned tailes with such fury, as by their violence overthrew Jeremias and his army, without any losse at all to speak of to Meldritch." The Turks were in fact beaten and driven from the field by this simple stratagem, and the dangerous passage was passed, with hopes of safety renewed among the Christians, having so unexpectedly surmounted the obstacle which had been so much feared. Truly, the English Smith was a valuable companion in a moment of emergency; and it is to be recognized as a sufficient proof of the estimation in which he was held, that he finds his way at pleasure to the private ear of his superior, and his counsel is usually adopted with ready confidence.

But the success of the "pretty stratagem of fireworks" was only temporary. They had discomfited Jeremie, but the Tartar with his forty thousand men lay still in the path. The army of Meldritch was now reduced to eleven thousand only. Pressing forward with this remnant with more speed than prudence, they encountered the enemy in force within three leagues of Rottenton, the fortified city which they aimed to reach. The position in which the two armies encountered was such as to render it impossible to escape the conflict. The alternative for fight was to "be cut to pieces flying."

"Here," says Smith, bitterly, reviewing the danger, "here Busca and the emperor had their desire." His allusion is to the obvious anxiety of the Germans to be rid of auxiliaries, whose very fidelity made them suspected by his enemy and successor, and whose veteran valor he had excellent reason to fear. It is in this place that our adventurer exhibits the glow and ardor of that spirit which was at the bottom of his chivalry. It is here, in his book, that his tones rise, and his voice dilates in the swelling language of the Spaniard. And there is a rude vein of poetry apparent in his narrative at this and other like places, which reminds us of the verses of genuine bards. Thus when he says, "The sunne no sooner displayed his beames than the Tartar his colours," we feel that he is quite as natural, and even more happy in his figure, than Dan Chaucer in the famous line—

> "Uprose the sunne, and uprose Emilie;"

since the pomp and splendor of the image which furnished the comparison is much more appropriate to the gorgeous aspects of battle than to the making of a damsel's toilet.

The terrors and dangers of the approaching conflict do not render our hero indifferent to the beauty and magnificence of the spectacle. "It was a most brave sight," he exclaims, "to see the banners and ensigns streaming in the aire, the glittering of armour, the variety of colours, the motion of plumes, the forests of lances, and the thicknesse of shorter weapons, till the silent expedition of the bloody blast from the murdering ordnance, whose roaring voice is not so soone heard as felt by the aymed-at object, which made among them a most lamentable slaughter."

Delivered up to almost certain destruction by what Smith styles—having reference, we suppose, to the emperor in withholding succor—"a tyrannical and treacherous imposture," "a cowardly calamity," the Christian army prepared for the terrible encounter with the coolness and resolve of veterans. It was "in the valley of Veristhorne, betwixt the river of Altus and the mountain of Rottenton," that "this bloody encounter" took place, "where the most of the dearest friends of the noble Prince Sigismundus perished." The affectionate manner in which Smith speaks of this Prince, and of the followers whose fidelity he had experienced, is very pleasing and honorable. His sense of the beauty of fidelity is another of those traits of chivalry, which are conspicuous equally in the events of his life, and in the narrative which records them. He dwells with more than ordinary minuteness upon this last fatal battle.

Meldritch, always a good captain, made the best possible disposition of his forces. His eleven thousand men were drawn up at the foot of the mountain, and in their front and on their flanks sharp stakes, hardened in the fire and bent against the enemy, were planted in the earth. By digging numerous holes at frequent intervals along the line, it was aimed still farther to lessen the vast superiority which the Tartars possessed in cavalry. The infantry was ranged among the stakes, having orders to retire behind them when they found themselves too severely pressed. All the precautions which were practicable in the condition of their affairs seem to have been taken with deliberate coolness and resolve—the preparations made being of a character to show, that it was the conviction of the Christian commander that the struggle was a final one for life rather than victory—though, in such an issue, the former seems necessarily to imply the other.

It was noon before the armies joined battle: "the sunne" that had risen so gloriously, according to Smith, "for shame did hide himselfe from so monstrous sight of a cowardly calamity." But the calamity, however great, could not suffer from the reproach of cowardice, unless it be charged upon the Tartar forces in regard to their overwhelming numerical superiority. These, *forty thousand* in number, were also arrayed for the struggle with skill and judgment. The battle was begun by Mustapha Bey, who came on, gallantly enough, in the midst of a storm of music from drums, trumpets and hautboys. He was bravely met, and beaten back by the regiments of horse under Nederspolt and Mavazo. His attack was followed up by the bold and headlong onslaught of a Tartar chief named Begolgi, whose advancing squadrons darkened the skies with their multitudinous arrows. The lieutenants, Veltus and Oberwin, struggled under this terrible pressure for more than an hour, yielded finally, and sank agreeably to order behind the stakes which had been planted for their safety against this very emergency. Then followed, heedless of this obstruction, of which hitherto they had seen nothing, the blind rush of the Tartar cavalry. "It was a wonder," says Smith, "to see how horse and man came to the ground."

The disorder was so great among these "mangled troopes," in consequence of this unlooked for disaster, that the Christians, enlivened by new hopes, began to shout for victory ; and, with five or six field-pieces which now played with effect upon the discomfited horsemen, succeeded for a brief space in arresting the assailants. But the hope was illusory. The respite was for an instant only. The Turks soon recovered from their disorder and surprise, and renewed the combat with new legions and a fresher fury. Their reckless onslaught, and swarming multitudes, soon satisfied Meldritch that nothing short of a miracle could save his army, that any hope of victory was idle, and that all that now remained for him to attempt, was to cut his way through the enemy with a select body of his men. With this resolution he drew together his choice troops and his reserve, and gave orders for the desperate charge. The attempt was only in part successful. The passage was made by Meldritch himself and some fourteen hundred horse, who succeeded by swimming in throwing the river Altus between themselves and their pursuers. But heavy was the toll which he had to pay in making that passage. Numbers fell in the flight, and among these many of his bravest officers. Of the sanguinary terrors of that conflict some idea may be gathered from the fact, that of both armies thirty thousand men were left upon the field. Nor did the commons suffer only. Earls and barons, colonels and captains—the brave generals Nederspolt, Veltus, Zarvana, Mavazo, and Bavell—were among the slain; and Smith, with praiseworthy patriotism, does not omit to make a record which he deems honorable to his native land. "Give me leave," says he, "to remember the names of our owne countrymen * * in these exploits, that, as resolutely as the best, in the defence of Christ and his Gospell ended their dayes; as *Baskerfield*, *Hardwicke*, *Thomas Milemer*, *Robert Mollineux*, *Thomas Bishop*, *Francis Compton*, *George Davison*, *Nicholas Williams*, and one *John*, a Scot, did what men could doe; and when they could doe no more left there their bodies, in testimonie of their mindes. Only Ensigne *Carleton* and Sergeant *Robinson* escaped."

Smith himself was left severely wounded, and seemingly dead, among a heap of the slain. His rich armor drew the attention of the conquerors, while his groans, uttered in his unconsciousness, showed him to be still alive. His life was spared in consideration of his ransom. Carefully nursed and tended, his wounds were healed, his strength gradually recovered, and when fit for inspection, he was offered for sale in the slave-markets of Axiopolis. He was bought by the Bashaw Bogall, and sent by him in chains to his "faire mistresse" at Constantinople. "By twentie and twentie, chained by the neckes, they marched in files to this great citie, where they were delivered to their several masters, and he (Smith) to the young *Charatza Tragabigzanda*."

CHAPTER IX.

The Bashaw Bogall, though no hero, was yet ambitious of the fame of one; and, in sending Smith to his mistress, he committed the blunder—to say nothing of the worse offence against morals—of telling her that the captain was a Bohemian nobleman, who had yielded to the vigor of his own right arm in battle. The personal appearance of Smith was in his favor; and his address soon awakened in the fair Charatza a degree of interest which was not allowed to escape his notice. To what extent he availed himself of this discovery, his own modesty forbids us to know. That he won her affections is unquestionable. The story of the wooing, as told in his own narrative, reminds us strongly of that of Othello. The narrative which she had received from Bogall prompted her discourse. She sought him from time to time, and demanded of him the particulars of his overthrow by her lover. When she heard the falsehood of the tale with which the latter had imposed upon her, her indignation against the impostor prepared the way for another sort of feeling for himself. She could speak the Italian language, and as he had travelled in Italy, there was no impediment to their free communication with one another. When he told her that he had never seen Bogall till he had been sold to him in the slave-market of Axiopolis—that he was no Bohemian, but an Englishman, who had succeeded by his prowess to a command in Wallachia—her curiosity and interest increased in the captive. But she did not yield herself implicitly and without proper precaution to his narrative. She tried his veracity by inquiries propos-

Presented as a Slave to the Wife of the Bashaw Bagall. PAGE 74.

ed to other persons—slaves also, we suppose, who could speak the English, French, and Dutch languages—by all of whom the honesty of Smith's assurances was confirmed, and her sympathy with him—Smith calls it "compassion,"—was necessarily strengthened and increased. As she arrived cautiously at her "compassion," so she observed a like degree of caution in giving it utterance. She was not herself sufficiently free to do boldly what she desired; but when she sought the society of her slave she feigned sickness, which enabled her to discard other company for that of the preferred one. She had lonely moments, sad ones, when it pleased her mood to retire to "weepe over the graves;" and we are permitted to fancy, that on such occasions Smith was always nigh to give her lessons in English, or to confirm her practice in Italian. The burial-places among the Moslems are rare and beautiful retreats—frequently garden-spots, filled with singing-birds—and the stately and solemn moods of the people render them highly eligible as places of resort to the contemplative and gentle spirit. Their superstition somewhat increases the security of such places, and the loving as well as the sorrowing heart may thus equally find them useful. It is quite natural that an author should become abrupt at this stage of his narrative. It belongs to him, as a *preux chevalier*, to relate only what is unavoidably necessary to his biography. But he had won her heart, and the discovery, unfortunately, was made by others quite as soon perhaps as by the parties. Charatza is suddenly alarmed lest her mother should sell her favorite. She is not her own mistress, and dares not openly oppose this design. She finds but one way to avert it, and that is by sending him to her brother Timour Bashaw, of Nalbritz, in Cambia, one of the provinces of Tartary. This proceeding satisfies the mother, since her only object was to separate the maiden from the captive in whom she had such a tender interest. But never could choice be more unfortunate. The letter which Charatza wrote to her brother unhappily betrayed to him her secret. She relied too much upon his regard for herself, and did not hesitate to demand from him the best of usage for the prisoner. His sojourn in Tartary was to be temporary only, for the purpose of acquiring the habits and the language of the Turks, and until time should make her mistress of her own person. This last suggestion, which so completely betrayed the nature of the interest which she felt in the captive, awakened all the national bigotry in the bosom of the brother. It provoked a treatment equally prompt and cruel, which the poor Charatza little fancied would befall her favorite. The haughty Bashaw was not prepared to countenance such a connection between his sister and her slave. To degrade the object of her interest was his first movement; and within an hour after his arrival, our adventurer was stripped naked, his head and beard shaven "so bare as his hand," his body clad in undrest skins and haircloth, and a heavy ring of iron, "with a long stalke bowed like a sickle riveted about his neck." The rest of his treatment was of the same description. He was tasked with the vilest labors, in a condition, as he himself expresses it, beyond the endurance of a dog;—a slave, as the last comer, to the whole herd of slaves, hundreds in number, in bonds to this petty tyrant; who, "for all their paines and labours, no more regarded them than a beast."

Smith was an attentive observer, so far as his opportunities would allow, of the peculiarities, the manners, and condition of the country, no matter what were the circumstances in which he found himself. Though his narrative is usually a meagre one, he yet suffers us to see that he notes all things with a shrewd and military eye. We have constant proofs of it in his pages, which are seldom heedful of very nice details. Thus, in his transit from Constantinople to Nalbritz, we have a bird's-eye view of places and objects on the route, though it is not always easy to identify the points which fix his attention, under the names or the orthography which he employs in designating them, with such as are familiar to us now. Nor is it important that we should. A prisoner, closely watched and guarded, is not likely to see much of curious interest in his progress, and ours is a biography, not a book of travels.

He remarks always the face of the country; how the towns lie; what are the approaches by water; how the forts are built, and their apparent strength or weakness; straits, how defended; channels, how obstructed, or how accessible; and sometimes gives us a bit of military history, as applicable to the particular place which attracts his attention. All this he does unobtrusively, and without the slightest pretension.

As a bondsman among the Tartars, he was compelled to notice other things, as well as to perform other duties, which hitherto had received but little of his attention. Several chapters of his memoirs are given to the diet of the Turks; to their slaves; the attire of the Tartars; their religion; modes of warfare; modes of living; feasts; estates; buildings; tributes; laws; justice; slaves; entertainment of embassies; armies and levies; arms; provisions for armies; division of spoil, &c. Where his personal observation fails in regard to these subjects, he pieces it out with materials drawn from books; and in all probability, after coming out of captivity, he read all that he conveniently could in relation to the countries which he had traversed, or in which he had been held in bondage.

His own observations are not favorable to the Mussulmans. Their food disgusts him ; their drink ; their loathsome and filthy habits ; and, as a matter of course, their brutal treatment of the captive. But Smith saw things through the rings of his fetters, and his picture of the people and the country could scarce be other than unfavorable. He certainly takes away, by his description, much of the picturesque in the habits and history of the wandering Tartars. He pays willing tribute to their laws and justice as administered among their own people ; and frankly credits their hardihood of life, their physical constitution, their agility and strength, their horsemanship, their prompt obedience, and their endurance of evil without complaint. The four chapters which he devotes to these subjects, while they prove his good sense, excellent judgment, and vigilant observation, are scarcely of any interest in the present advanced state of our knowledge in regard to the condition of the several countries to which they relate ; to say nothing of the material changes in habit and character which Turk and Tartar have undergone since the period when they were written. They suffice only to show how diligent was his mind, and how patient his watch, that could enable him to see and remember so much while in the irksome bonds, and busy in the degrading labors to which he found himself condemned. How long he remained in these bonds is uncertain. His own narrative is silent on the subject ; but from the period when he was made prisoner to that in which he returned to Transylvania, the interval is something short of one year. An obscure passage in one of his chapters leads to the inference that he may have been something over six months a bondsman with Timour Bashaw. In this period he was without consolation. The sympathies of woman, the blandishments of love, no longer lightened his sorrows.

He heard nothing from the fair Charatza, upon whose affection he built his only hope of delivery from thraldom. She was, in his own words, "sure'y ignorant of his bad usage;" or if not ignorant, she was not permitted to con tinue or to resume an intrigue which so much revolted the pride of her watchful parent, and despotic brother. But though disappointed and wearied with the hope deferred, he did not despond. He did not rely upon the one hope only. He was not the man to wait events when he might shape and give them impulse, and he frequently discussed with his fellow-bondsmen the subject of their condition, and the probabilities in favor of any attempt which might be made for their escape. But these gave him no encouragement. Neither "reason nor possibility" encouraged their attempts. He probably found among them no such spirit as his own; the long period of their slavery having somewhat reconciled them to its severities.

Smith had not reached this condition of resignation, and he was to find the door of his prison-house unfolded at a moment when he least expected it. "God," he exclaims, with that complacency which prompts every adventurous mind—every man of genius, in other words—to consider himself the child of a peculiar destiny: "God, beyond man's expectation or imagination, helpeth his servants when they least thinke of helpe, as it hapned to him." In common speech, an opportunity offered itself at once for escape and vengeance, and his manly courage did not suffer it to pass unemployed. His task, for some time previous, had been to thrash corn at a country-house, more than a league distant from the dwelling of his Tartar lord. To this place the latter frequently came, and on all such occasions Smith was particularly the victim of his ill-usage. The affections of the sister had provoked the antipathies of the brother, and our adventurer was thus made to endure abuses in due proportion to those delights which had soothed him in the first days of his captivity. It was by beating and buffeting her slave,that Timour did justice to the entreaties made in his behalf by the loved and loving Charatza Tragabigzanda. He was destined to repeat this wanton exercise once too frequently for the patience of his captive. On this occasion it so happened that the circumstances were all favorable to the latter. The two were alone together in a spot removed from the other prisoners, remote, indeed, from the observation of all; and when the petty tyrant, in his humor, smote the slave over his task, the ordinary thrashing-flail which he worked with became the ready implement of his defence and vengeance. Stung to fury by the repeated indignities, and counselled by the auspicious circumstances of the occasion, the love of the sister was forgotten in the rage which the brutality of the brother had provoked, and darting upon his tyrant unexpectedly, Smith beat out his brains in an instant.

The deed was done as effectually as suddenly. But this was only the beginning of the game. There was no time to lose, and with the same readiness and resolution as he had shown in slaying his enemy, our hero dressed himself in his garments and threw his carcase out of sight beneath the straw. This done, he filled his knapsack with corn, closed the doors, and mounting the Tartar's horse, which stood in waiting, he pushed with all speed, at a venture, for the solitude of the desert. He knew nothing of the route before him; could not even conjecture what course to pursue to avoid his enemies, and thus wandered wildly forward, not daring to seek information, but rather striving to avoid encounter with all along the road. For three days he wandered thus desperately, and in this miserable manner. But the child of destiny once

Smith kills Timour Bashaw. PAGE 80.

more finds himself the object of a special providence. The power which had favored him thus far seems to have guided his footsteps in a peculiar manner, since the first intimation of his whereabouts and route which he received, was from the sign of the cross! This was a huge guide post set up by the wayside, and shaped like the cross, to indicate the highway to Muscovy, a Christian country. Such a symbol, thus encountered, might well, in the case of a Christian, be regarded as an auspicious augury; and Smith so esteemed it. The God whom he served, had directed his unconscious footsteps to the symbol of his Redeemer's sufferings; and Smith was very far from being unmoved by the unlooked for circumstance. He has previously given himself up to despair, "even as taking leave of this miserable world;"—when "to his dying spirits thus God added some comfort in this melancholy journey, wherein, if he had met any of that vilde generation, they had made him their slave; or knowing the figure engraven in the iron about his necke (as all slaves have), he had beene sent back again to his master." The sign of the cross, at the foot of which he suddenly finds himself, was the sign of his safety, and filled him with new confidence and courage. Now, this emblem was only one of many which, according to Smith's account, are common to the country. It is by such symbols, adapted to the particular nation, that the Mussulmen indicate the people to whose territories their fingers point. Thus, while the cross denotes the route to Muscovy, the "half moone" shows that "to Crym-Tartary; "a blacke man, full of white spots," guides to Persia and the Georgians; and "a picture of the sunne to China." But the naturalness of this discovery did not lessen its religious influence upon him. In this sign, even more certainly than in the case of Constantine, lay the hope of our adventurer. He darted exultingly along the path which it pointed out, and, in dread and tribulation, but still in hope and without disaster, he pursued for sixteen days his solitary journey; arriving at the end of this time at Ecopolis, a garrison of the Russians upon the river Don.

CHAPTER X.

It was the peculiar good fortune of our adventurer in all situations of great emergency and distress, to enlist the sympathies and secure the assistance of individuals of the gentler sex. We have seen the place which he seems to have taken, almost at the first glance, in the affections of the Turkish damsel, the fair Charatza Tragabigzanda; and his arrival at Ecopolis conducts him to the smiles and bounty of another lady, equally Christian in character, and more so by education. This was the lady Callamata, who "largely supplied all his wants." We know nothing more of her than this. Nothing is said in the narrative to awaken a single suspicion of the perfect purity and simplicity of her benevolence. With that respectful and considerate regard for the sex, which invariably marks the bearing of our hero when he approaches them, his language is frank yet unequivocal,—gentle and affectionate, yet always within the limits of a becoming warmth and propriety. "The Good Lady Callamata largely supplied all his wants," is the single phrase which declares his obligations in the text. Subsequently, in his dedication of the "Generall Historie of Virginia, &c.," to the "Illustrious and most noble Princesse, the Lady Francis, Duchesse of Richmond and Lenox," he sums up his general indebtedness to the sex in a single paragraph, for which this may be a place quite as appropriate as any. Apologizing for his presumption in calling an eye "so piercing" and "so glorious" as that of her grace, to view his "poore ragged lines," he is yet encouraged by the recollection of their previous kindness and indulgence. "My comfort is that heretofore honorable and vertuous ladies, and comparable but amongst themselves, have offered me rescue and protection in my greatest dangers. Even in forraine parts I have felt reliefe from that sex. The beauteous Lady Tragabigzanda, when I was a slave to the Turkes, did all she could to secure (succour ?) me. When I overcame the Bashaw of Nalbritz, in Tartaria, the charitable Lady Callamata supplied my necessities. In the utmost of many extremities, that blessed Pokahontas, the great King's daughter of Virginia, oft saved my life. When I escaped the cruelties of Pirats and most furious stormes, a long time alone in a small boat at sea, and driven ashore in France, the good lady, Madam Chanoyes, bountifully assisted me. And so, verily, these my adventures have tasted the same influence from *your* gratious hand, &c."

This is all perfectly unexceptionable, and we do not perceive in this accumulation of references any signs of that complacency which, in the case of such a person, having such a history to unfold, might seem pardonable enough. What is said in regard to the Lady Callamata, does not show her to have been influenced by any feelings less pure and more passionate than that of a human and a Christian sympathy and pity. But some of his eulogists are less forbearing, and make larger assertions when they come to deal in rhyme ; and the good Lady Callamata, who, for aught that we know, may have been an ancient matron, entirely past the period of youthful susceptibility, is described in the same category with the Turkish damsel, who only waited to be her own mistress to become his. One of these poets, who signs himself " R. Braithwaite," writes, in the midst of other doggerel, such lines as the following :

"But what's all this ? Even earth, sea, heaven above,
Tragabigzanda, *Callamata's love*,

> Dear Pocahontas, Madame Shanois, too,
> Who did what love with modesty could do." &c.

We see no reason, and find no authority for the imputation. Smith does no more, in the case of this lady, than acknowledge her bounty to an unfortunate. And this is done with the gentlemanly solicitude of one who is habitually earnest in his deference to the sex. That his personal bearing had its effect upon those, of both sexes, by whom he was favorably entertained, is very likely. That it quickened the pulses of female charity is probable enough. He seems to have been of that class of persons who impress favorably at a glance; was manly and graceful, exceedingly courteous in his bearing, frank in his deportment, and of features at once pleasing and impressive. He finds ready credence when he shows himself, and his narrative is heard. It is not from the Lady Callamata alone that he finds favor at Ecopolis. The governor takes off his irons, treats him so kindly that "he thought himself new risen from death;" and when he is invigorated and prepared to depart, gives him letters of recommendation and the protection of a convoy to Hermanstadt, in Transylvania. His melancholy story of captivity precedes him on his route; and his journey through the wretched and sterile regions which he is compelled to pass, is everywhere soothed by the attention of the people. The grateful heart of our adventurer prompts him to declare, that "in all his life he seldome met with more respect, mirth, content, and entertainment; and not any governor where he came, but gave him somewhat as a present besides his charges." The sympathy of the people was due in some degree to their common liability to a fate such as that from which he had the good fortune to escape. At that period, the wretched country which he traversed was obnoxious to the frequent incursions of the Tartars ; and it was but seldom that the people who were borne into captivity were so fortunate as to be able to return and tell the story. The story of our hero was one, therefore, which found its echo upon the hearth of many a peasant. Yet, says Smith, "it is a wonder [that] any should make warres for them."—"They are countries rather to be pitied than envied." He pauses to describe their hovels, which are like the meanest log-cabins of our frontier; their modes of defence; their weapons ; and the manner in which their roads are constructed ;—all of which indicate the very lowest condition of human civilisation.

Arrived in Transylvania, he had the satisfaction of meeting with many of his old friends and associates, who, knowing his worth and valor, had long lamented him as among the slain on the fatal field near Rottenton. Among these friends were his colonel, Meldritch, and Prince Sigismund. They received him with open arms, and attentions so affectionate and warm, that he professes himself "glutted with content, and neere drowned with joy." It was on this occasion that he received his honors from the hands of Sigismund, and fifteen hundred ducats of gold to repair his losses. "But to see and rejoyce himselfe (after all those encounters) in his native country," he would scarcely have torn himself away from his friends in Transylvania.

The liberality of Sigismund, whom he styles "the mirror of virtue," enabled him to traverse a considerable portion of Germany, France, and Spain ; to linger in their principal cities, and visit all places that seem to promise most gratification to his curiosity. It is probable that while his ducats lasted he found sufficient excitement in the populous cities of Europe ; and felt no great thirst after new adventures. He forgets for a season that he was hurrying home "to rejoyce himself in his native country," and makes a tour which in extent would, even at the present day of steam navigation, do honor to a traveller going abroad for the first time. Satisfied at length, as he himself tells us, with Europe and Asia, and hearing of the wars in Barbary, he suddenly feels an impulse to new adventures in this quarter, which it is not possible for him to withstand. In all probability it has become necessary to replenish his purse. To return to England as destitute as when he left it, scarcely comports with his ambition: and though he tells us nothing of this sort, the suggestion is by no means inconsistent with his own conduct, and with the nature of the individual. He proceeds accordingly to the African coast, where he forms an intimacy with the captain of a French man-of-war, named Merham, who soon became attracted to our adventurer, and appears to have become quite as fond of him as the Lady Callamata. With this person, and twelve others, he goes on an excursion to Morocco, the ancient monuments of which he desired to examine. He gives us, in the space of a couple of chapters, a brief but comprehensive account of the things he saw, and a summary of what he had learned by reading and the reports of others, in relation to the country which he visited. His narrative is enlivened by several traditions and anecdotes gathered in this manner, and characteristic of the country and the people, which, as they do not in any way concern his own fortunes, we forbear to notice. His conclusion, from his inquiry into the politics of the Barbary States, is to have nothing to do with either party in the civil wars by which the country is distracted, and which first drew his attention to its shores. The perfidious character of the natives, "their bloody murthers, rather than warre," only provoke his loathing; and he returns with his Frenchman, Captain

Merham, to the man-of-war, destined, in his own language, "to try some other conclusions at sea."

It is not so certain, in going on board the ship of Merham a second time, that our adventurer proposed to take any decided step with him, or indeed contemplated anything more than a brief visit. His narrative speaks of the visit and invitation as one for the day only; two or three other persons, not of the craft, being the guests also, and with similar invitations. But the welcome of the Frenchman was so warm, and his hospitality so grateful, that whether designedly on his part or not, they linger on board too late to return to the shore that night, and are constrained, not unwillingly we fancy, to take their beds in the vessel. The evening was fair at first and pleasant, but by midnight such a storm arose as to compel our excellent Frenchman to slip his cables, and carry his guests with him to sea. We do not hear that Smith ever complained of any baggage left behind him. Our Frenchman is compelled to run before the wind, and before the parties know where they well are, his ship is at the Canaries. This flight resolves itself into a cruise, and as the storm abated and the seas grew smooth, Merham amused himself and guests by capturing an occasional vessel laden with wine of Teneriffe; thus converting a mishap into a very profitable sort of exercise. In this pursuit, however, his eagerness carried him a thought too far, and pressing all sail to overhaul two strange vessels which had hove in sight, he suddenly finds that he has caught a Tartar, in the shape of two sturdy Spanish men-of-war, far superior in force to his own. But this does not quell the spirit of our Frenchman. Merham, whom Smith calls "an old fox," "seeing himselfe in the lion's pawes," showed a clean pair of heels, but not so clean as to escape altogether the consequences of his temerity.

His chase had been too eager to make escape easy, though he prided himself upon his vessel as a fast sailer. The action became unavoidable, and was one of those fierce and bloody struggles of which naval history in all times affords us so many terrible instances. The Spaniards fell upon the Frenchman with a broadside, and succeeded, after a severe fight of an hour, in boarding him. The danger was imminent, and Merham's ship must have been carried or destroyed but for certain lucky cross-bar shots, and "divers bolts of iron, made for that purpose," which at the fortunate moment drilled such a breach in one of the Spaniards as left her in a sinking condition. Of the consternation which ensued in the injured vessel the Frenchman availed himself so as to disengage his ship from the grapplings of the enemy, and to renew his efforts at escape. But the chase was hotly kept up by one of the Spaniards, and a running fight followed, which lasted from noon till night. By this time the pursuing Spaniard was rejoined by his consort, who had succeeded in repairing her breaches, and the two together continued the chase with pertinacious diligence all night. They succeeded at length in overhauling their enemy a second time, and bringing him again to action within musket shot. On this occasion the stately Don began the affair with unnecessary civility, promising the Frenchman fair quarters if, without giving them farther trouble, he would surrender to the flag of Spain. But Merham had no surrender in him. He knew, as Smith tells us, "well how to use his ordnance," and his answer to this civil soliciting was made by his cannon. The action was thus renewed, and the assailants a second time succeeded in laying the chase aboard. Our Frenchman fought with desperation, but the overwhelming force of the Spaniards enabled them to cover his decks, and to rush aloft in numbers to unsling his mainsail. This he contrived to bring down so suddenly, while they were yet in the rigging, as to place them *hors du combat;* while another party were blown off by the desperate Frenchman, with a part of the deck and the grating. These achievements, while they drove the Spaniards back to their own vessel, left that of Merham on fire. Drawing off to escape this danger, the Spaniards kept playing upon him, seeking his destruction rather than his capture, which the desperate valor of the Frenchman seemed to render impossible;—while on board the latter, to extinguish the flames gave sufficient occupation to all hands. While the danger lasted none could be spared for the scarcely less pressing business of the conflict. The flames were at length extinguished, and this done, Merham renewed the fight with the same spirit as before. It was in vain that his enemies proffered to parley with him—to grant him the best of terms, and admit him to fair quarters. The desperate Frenchman had but one answer, and that was through his cannon. And thus another day was spent, and half the following night, when the fire of the enemy slackened and the distance widened between the combatants. The firm courage and reckless valor of the Frenchman saved him; for at dawn the Spaniards were no longer to be seen. This desperate action is not unlike that of the Serapis and the Bon Homme Richard. Merham must have been a warrior like Paul Jones; and he probably found a worthy lieutenant in our adventurer. Smith modestly forbears saying anything about his own deportment in the action. You would scarce suppose him indeed to have been present, but for his evident familiarity with all its details. He describes at no second-hand. His events are vividly told, as by one who saw them all, and knew their motives and their consequences. His very phraseology has a *sang-*

froid about it which seems to show, not only that he beheld, but that he enjoyed fully the whole terrible affair. From his known character there can be no doubt that he did so, and shared amply in all its dangers. He had always rejoiced in the excitements of war, and the unequal conflict invariably warmed his chivalry. Reasoning from all that we know of his genius and resolution, we need not question that these qualities largely seconded our Frenchman in the admirable and successful defence which enabled him to beat off and baffle his assailants.

BOOK SECOND.

CHAPTER I.

We have now to change the scene in our eventful drama, and to show our hero, after all his perils, once more seated in safety within his native land. He returned to England some time in the year 1604. He was still a very young man to have undergone such vicissitudes and varieties of fortune. Few young men at twenty-five have ever lived through such a trying experience. But this experience had made a man of him indeed. His mind had ripened with his toil, his judgment had become matured in fields of danger, and in the life-conflict with a thousand necessities; and without losing any portion of that energy of character, and enthusiasm of spirit and of temperament, which had forced him upon the paths of enterprise, and made the field of peril grateful to his impulses, he was now better prepared than ever to convert these admirable qualities of courage into useful and efficient agencies for the prosecution of great designs.

It was at a season highly auspicious to the exercise of these endowments that he returned to his native country. The spirit of colonial enterprise which, at a previous period, had been excited beyond the boundaries of reason and prosperity by the successful examples and discoveries of the Portuguese and Spaniards, and which numerous disasters had tended to discourage and subdue, had, under more favoring circumstances received a new impulse to exertion. The first effect upon the English people of the unfolding by Columbus of the ponderous gates of the Atlantic, had been rather injurious than serviceable to the interests of maritime and colonial adventures; and the reign of Queen Elizabeth was distinguished by hopes and passions, founded upon discovery in the new world, such as no exertions in the adventurer, and no resources in nature, could have possibly appeased or realized. It was, in the first place, a subject of mortification to the English that their sovereign had rejected the eminent services of Columbus; and the growing interests of commerce, under the wise and powerful administration of Elizabeth, goaded in especial by their jealousy of the Spaniards, and further stimulated by the recent grand defeat of the "Invincible Armada," enabled them to see, in some degree, how vast had been this sacrifice. The commercial mind of England was not disposed to yield El Dorado entirely to the Spaniard, and this mind, succored by an intellect more daring and perhaps more influential than its own, was soon enabled to diffuse throughout the national heart an intense passion for discovery and colonization in America. The eager eyes of popular desire were opened upon a realm of equal loveliness and treasure, which cupidity and curiosity became equally anxious to explore. The master spirits of the age surrendered themselves to this passion. The voice of the nation seconded the impulse, and the very difficulties which the jealous Spaniard contrived to throw in the way of other empires seeking a similar path with himself, contributed to confirm the wild impressions which had gone into all lands of his miraculous treasures in the new. Romance took possession of the theme and dressed it in her richest habiliments. The sanguine gave their credence, and the sedate and doubtful knew not how to deny. The policy of many among the wise seemed to render denial injudicious, since, in the prosecution of a great work, the argument to the convert must be such as his nature will most readily receive. And yet it is very doubtful if the very wisest among them did not acknowledge as probable the gorgeous fictions narrated of the new world, which the experience of the old had never yet found true. Sir Walter Raleigh himself, a man of not less intellect than ambition, whose character, by the way, bold, sanguine and impulsive, martial in spirit and curious in research, very much resembled that of Smith, though with the advantages of far better training in youth, and more approved associations in manhood ; he, too, was one of those who certainly deceived themselves quite as much as they deceived others, yielding a too willing faith to their own fancies. In his day and that of Queen Elizabeth, the vulgar mind everywhere in Europe was possessed of impressions in regard to America which were worthy only of the fairy empires of Aladdin; and the popular histories of the new continent were better suited to the invention of a quick-witted sultana,* in danger of the bowstring, than the sober speculations of the sage and reverend grey-beards with whom they found such ready credence and respect. Seen through this happy medium it was the land equally of refuge and delight. To the boy-dreamer about Arcadia and the golden age, it offered all that imagination could conjecture and Astræa could supply. To the veteran, grown grey in stratagems and spoils, without having grown strong in their retention, it opened the most easy paths for the attainment of his selfish objects. Freedom from all restraints of law, and conflict only with a people entirely

* Scheherazade, the sultana—see *Introductory Chapter to the Arabian Nights' Entertainments.*

put without its pale and protection, were considerations beyond price to the habitual ruffian, who, in the world itself, found nothing more precious than an oyster which he was permitted to open with his sword; and England, to say nothing of the continent, was filled with "men in buckram" such as these. To the disbanded soldiery of the Low Countries in particular, to which England had sent her full share of discontents and profligates—the prospect of conflict with the native savages in a region where gold had a vegetable period of birth and growth, and was to be had for the gathering, was rather more grateful as the medium for the acquisition of wealth than the wretched drudgery of the ordinary tasks of industry. To the young and fanciful the same wild regions offered the romance of eternal forests, the beauty of strange landscapes, and the foreign charms of a race of dusky and confiding beauties, not to speak of that exquisite twilight pic turesque, which ever paints the far-off and the foreign in the natural landscape. Others again, the enthusiasts in the world of contemplation, longed for the subdued pleasures of a life passed in solitude—a passion, which is so frequently found, in youth, to possess for a season the hearts of those who are equally ambitious and energetic, and who seem in this way to find a necessary repose of the mind before it is bent and strained to its uttermost tension in aiming at objects which call for great decision and endeavor. To another class, religion came with her persuasions also; and her arguments, urged in behalf of the heathen of the strange countries not yet admitted into the fold of Christ, afforded specious pretexts, by which avarice and ambition contrived to deceive their neighbors, and not unfrequently themselves. These various motives, commerce and cupidity, romance, ambition and religion, were still sufficiently influential, in spite of numerous complete defeats, in enterprises of the same description, to bring together many a motley band to whom the forests of America promised full satisfaction for all the desires of their hearts. To these may be added yet another class, of whom Walter Raleigh himself and our own hero, Smith, may be mentioned as sufficient specimens, who loved adventure for its own sake, who never looked to the mere personal rewards, and not often or too closely to the consequences, and who were better pleased to be doing and achieving, even if suffering also, than in the acquisition of the spoils, or even the honors of the achievement.

Smith's arrival in England was singularly opportune, not only as it regarded his own employment, but in relation to the success of the experiment, now once more to be renewed, which had always met before with failure. He brought to the work a degree of courage and experience, of skill and resource, which made him a person of mark wherever he appeared. He was not long in making himself known to those who took most interest in maritime adventure; and indeed his reputation had in some measure preceded him, and prepared the public mind to regard him as one particularly fitted for the exigencies of the time and its peculiar object. That object was scarcely of so vague and deceptive a character as it had been in the previous reign. The actual experience acquired by British mariners in the time of James the First, had furnished a greater body of facts, on the subject of foreign countries,to the nation, than it had possessed during the sway of Elizabeth. The defeat of the Armada was one of the great events to which the English people owe their rapid progress upon the high seas. It taught them an increased confidence in their skill and prowess, the results of which were steadily increasing, under the exercise of their powers, and these powers were mainly exercised in the business of discovery in foreign lands. It may be well, for the better comprehension of our history, to glance briefly at the progress, in this particular, during the reign of Elizabeth. A brief space will suffice for this object. The commercial career of England may be said to have begun in the time of Henry the Seventh, in the maritime labors and discoveries of the Cabots. At that early period it was proposed to plant colonies in the new world. The reign of his successor, though hardly favorable to the commerce of his kingdom, was yet not wholly unmarked by events which showed how certainly mercantile adventure was determined to make itself felt among the great interests of the nation. The blood of the old Northmen was too large a constituent of the stock to be satisfied with the progress upon the seas of other and rival nations, without being desirous of contending with them upon an element which seems really to belong to the genius of the people. Voyages of discovery were undertaken in the time of Henry VIII.; and a spirit sufficiently maritime was shown to awaken the special jealousy of the Spaniard. The statutes of Edward VI. continued to favor this rising and ambitious interest; nor could the bigotry of Mary, who succeeded him—the creature, as she was, of a purely Spanish influence—suffice to check the excited and natural tendencies of the nation. The elevation of Elizabeth gave a new vigor to the efforts of her people in this, as in all other of the interests of the kingdom. Her successful resistance to Spain may be said to have placed England fairly afloat upon the high seas. Her ships penetrated at the same time the waters of the East and West, and were at the same moment in the rivers of Russia, the bays of Newfoundland, and among the Spanish galleons in the harbors of Spanish America. Seeking a northwest passage, the possibility of effecting which had been asserted by Cabot, Frobisher, in a small vessel, made his way to the shores of Labrador; and, by these brilliant illusions, "golden" all, first prompted Elizabeth to an exhibition of royal patronage in an attempt to look for the precious metals in arctic abodes, at the very time Drake was gaining that glory which redeems his name from the charge of piracy by the circumnavigation of the globe. Sir Humphrey Gilbert, the step-brother of Raleigh, shared his passion for discovery, and we may add his fortunes. With more moderate views of the results of adventure, and more rigorous and reasonable aims, he obtained a liberal patent and put to sea in 1579. But the event was failure and mortification. A second attempt was more unfortunate still, and the stout old mariner perished at sea.

Raleigh's experiments followed those of his step-brother, and were scarcely more successful. His vessels, under the Captains Amidas and Barlow, coasted the Carolinas in 1584, penetrated Ocracocke inlet, and formal possession, with the usual ceremonies, was taken of the country; which, in honor of the "Virgin Queen," was called Virginia. On this occasion, however, no settlement was attempted. That was reserved for the ensuing year, when, under the same charter, a colony of one hundred and eight men was confided to Sir Ralph Lane. The settlement was made on the island of Roanoke, and some fruitless explorations were made in the neighboring country. But a single year sufficed for the experiment, when the colonists abandoned their lonely hamlet and returned to England. Fifty men,* left by Sir Richard Grenville, in 1586, in charge of the deserted settlement, were massacred in a little while; their miserable remains alone being found

* Bancroft says fifteen; Smith and others fifty. The latter seems the more probable number.

in and about their ruined habitations, in warning to their successors. But Raleigh was not yet discouraged. A new colony was planted, and this time the solitude and sterility of the wilderness were cheered, in the eyes of our Englishmen, by the presence of woman. But theis did not avail. The history of the colony is a blank. Of its fate we know nothing. But a single authentic fact remains to us; namely, that during its brief existence of little more than a year, one female child was born in the wilderness to the foreign settlers, and received the name of Virginia, after the European name of the country.

Raleigh was a ruined man. He could no longer pursue his enterprises on the strength of his own resources; but still resolute in his experiments, he endeavored to do so by means of companies. Unhappily for himself and his cause, his personal attempts were all made in other latitudes. Had he himself but led his colonists to Virginia, instead of wasting himself in fruitless researches after mines in Guiana, his own fate and that of the colonies in North America might have been far more fortunate. His enterprises seem really to have failed through the miserable incompetency, the want of moderation, prudence, skill or courage, among his agents. But his spirit survived himself!

This disastrous history wonderfully tended to subdue the eagerness of English adventure in colonizing North America. As John Brierton, one of the adventurers of a later day, expresses it, "all hopes of Virginia thus abandoned, it lay dead and obscured from 1590 till this year 1602." Then it was that Bartholomew Gosnold made his way across the Atlantic, and, contenting himself with a cargo of sassafras, returned to England after an absence of four months. This voyage renewed the subject in men's minds of Virginia colonization. A second expedition, consisting of two small vessels, was sent out by private adventurers, under Martin Pring—only a few days after the death of Elizabeth—and this voyage was also comparatively successful, met with no disaster, but made no settlement. Other expeditions followed. The way, still an indirect one (for the direct passage was very gradually attained) became at length fairly opened, the pathway familiar, and moderate successes stimulated anew the passion for maritime adventure, which had been sickened so completely by disaster, and by the failure of all its brilliant anticipations.

Such was the condition of English discovery in America, and such the condition of the popular mind in England, when Smith reached his native country from abroad. We are not told where his French cruiser set him down, nor in what manner he passed from the continent of Europe to Great Britain; but there we find him somewhere in 1604, already busy in urging upon the public the claims of Virginia to colonization, and linking his fortunes with those of Bartholomew Gosnold, Edward Maria Wingfield, Robert Hunt and others. An ample patent was obtained, but nothing more, from James the First, with leave to "deduce a colony into Virginia." Circumstances were in favor of the experiment. The time for American colonization had arrived. The route across the Atlantic was comparatively familiar, and the wild and wondrous character of the enterprise having been taken from it in some degree by the absolute facts of which the public were in possession, secured for it the support of a more steady and solid, though a less imposing countenance. The edge of romance had been somewhat taken from the appetite of adventure, and though the precious metals were still the objects of insane search and speculation, and though the accounts were still extremely exaggerated in all the descriptions of

Virginia, yet there was no longer that wild fancy which taught that the gold was to be had for the gathering, and all was to be smiles, and sunshine, and smooth sailing in the experiment. There was work to be done, and dangers were to be met, and toils endured; and hence the importance of a man like Smith, to whom these were not only familiar but grateful. It required the active parties more than a year of zealous service in England before they could move "certain of the nobility, gentry and marchantes" to entertain their schemes; in other words, furnish the necessary funds for their prosecution—Gosnold, Wingfield, Hunt, Smith and others, being thought to have risked quite enough when they perilled their lives upon the adventure. The letters patent, bearing date April 10th, 1606, were issued to Sir Thomas Gates, Sir George Somers, Richard Hackluyt and their associates. This, the first charter under which the English succeeded in planting a colony in America, was one which was designed to establish a mercantile corporation. It allotted a sufficiently ample territory, extending on the sea-coast of America from the thirty-fourth to the forty-fifth degrees of north latitude, together with all islands within a hundred miles of their shores. This was to be divided between two rival companies,—one of which, however—that in which Smith was a leader—alone succeeded, and to this alone will our attention be directed. The territory actually yielded by the charter to the one company, occupied exclusively "the regions from thirty-four to thirty-eight degrees of North latitude; that is, from Cape Fear to the southern limit of Maryland." The territory was ample, but the charter was one of the narrowest limitations. The selfish monarch granted nothing but a desert waste of forest, with the privilege of peopling and subduing it, reserving to himself all authority. He framed the laws, controlled the appointments, and looked largely to the future revenues. With that morbid jealousy of his sovereign prerogative, which rendered him tyrannical, when nature perhaps only designed that he should be ridiculous, he tenaciously took to himself the labor of devising the whole scheme of the colonial government; and contrived—very happily as he thought, but very unroyally as we may be permitted to think, to say nothing of the blindness and peevishness of the whole proceeding—to withhold from the emigrants themselves every elective franchise, to deny them every attribute of self-government. "They were subjected," to employ the language of a modern historian,* "to the ordinances of a commercial corporation, of which they could not be members; to the dominion of a domestic council, in appointing which they had no voice; to the control of a superior council in England, which had no sympathies with their rights; and, finally, to the arbitrary legislation of their sovereign." This was only so much rare fooling, by which the feeble king endangered the power, in the assertion of which his morbid jealousy kept him in continual and feverish apprehension. The transmission of this miserable quality of jealousy to his unhappy descendants, without his own accompanying love of approbation, was the true secret of all that was vile and wretched in their subsequent career and fate.

But the folly of James did not end here. The names of governor and council, and his instructions how they should proceed, were all carefully sealed up and confided to them in a strong box, not to be opened till after their arrival in Virginia. They were consequently under no authority until that period, and to this circumstance some

* Bancroft.

of the misfortunes which marked their voyage may be ascribed. Their squadron consisted of three small vessels, the largest not exceeding one hundred tons burthen; the whole being under the command of Captain Christopher Newport, an experienced mariner. The colonists were but one hundred and five in number, of whom we learn that forty-eight were *gentlemen*, *twelve* were laborers, *four* were carpenters, *one* was a blacksmith, *one* a bricklayer, *one* a tailor, *one* a mason, *one* a barber, *one* a drummer, *but one* a sailor, *two* were chirurgeons, and there were *four* boys. The exceeding disproportion between the gentlemen and the mechanics and laborers reminds us irresistibly of the limited allowance of bread to sack in the domestic economy of Falstaff. Why gentlemen should be wanted in a wilderness would somewhat puzzle the philosopher; and of those who went on this expedition we have a sufficient glimpse, contained in a single passage of the narrative of William Simons, reported by Smith, who describes "some few of the greatest ranke amongst us as little better than atheists."

CHAPTER II.

THUS motley in the composition of their members, the colonists set sail from Blackwall, on the 19th day of December, 1606—a little more than one hundred years after the discovery of the continent by Cabot. The commencement of their voyage was inauspicious, and its progress was unhappy. They were not suffered for six weeks after anchor had been weighed, by reason of contrary winds, to lose sight of the English coast. In this time our adventurers employed themselves in the most scandalous dissensions, which arose at length to such a height of violence as to task all the best efforts of the more judicious among them to maintain the peace. Mr. Hunt, the preacher, a mild and sensible person, who had actively participated with Smith, Gosnold, and Wingfield, in originating the adventure, now approved himself worthy of the Christian ministry in the activity which he displayed in restoring harmony, or at least the appearance of harmony, among these ungenial spirits. But it was an appearance only, to be thrown aside upon the first new provocation, however slight. The substance of peace was wholly wanting to the company. The elements among them were of too mixed and conflicting character ; and these elements, from the silly commands of the king, that their instructions should not be opened until they had reached Virginia, by leaving them without any recognized authority, left them free to the indulgence of all their capricious moods and impulses. What share Smith had in these troubles and controversies does not appear. We are left only to conjecture from what we know of his claims and character, and from what is subsequently revealed to us of his treatment, that the provocation to their violence, in all probability, came from him. That he was the true man of the expedition was probably very soon apparent to all parties. That he was not the most beloved on this account, is a fair presumption from what we know of the insolence, the insufferable pride and vanity of many of his companions. The account from which we draw our own, at this point of the narrative, is that of William Simons, "Doctour of Divinitie," who was not of the voyage, but who is very likely to have procured his intelligence from Hunt. Simons distinctly ascribes this dissension to envy of, and hostility to Smith, on the part of those "godlesse foes, whose disasterous designes (could they have prevailed) had even then overthrowne the businesse." The history is a common one, and the motive insisted upon is, unhappily, in the weak and vicious state of our depraved humanity, natural enough. The world-man cordially hates the God-man, and will destroy him if he can; and the conflict, for life, and for all lives, is inevitable between them. We can readily conceive how such a man, so taught by experience and all sorts of fortune, should, in their wretched wind-bound and storm-impeded progress to the Canaries, have given provocation in a thousand ways, by his very address and energy and natural command of character, to the herd of conceited gentlemen sent out to seek their fortunes, by whom he found himself surrounded. Easy for such a man, among such men, to stir up the acrid humors, to provoke bile, and bitterness, and wrath. His unquestionable genius, his notorious experience, his noble aspect, his ready decision, these in all probability acquired him a command during the voyage, in place of the sealed authority of King James, to which a peevish vanity would not always be ready to submit. The storm which Preacher

Hunt had partially quieted, burst forth with new violence when the little fleet of Newport reached the Canaries. Here, having matured their schemes, the malcontents seized upon the person of our adventurer and committed him to close custody, under charges equally ridiculous and scandalous, of sedition and treason to the crown– "some of the chiefe (envying his repute) who fained he intended to usurpe the Government, murther the Council, and make himselfe King;"—a truculent conspirator to be sure—and "that his confederats were dispersed in all the three ships, and that divers of his confederats that revealed it would affirme it." Smith seems to have submitted patiently, waiting events, economising his strength and courage, wasting nothing in vain struggles, vexing nobody with vain complaint—but manfully biding his time, and looking calmly to the coming trial. For thirteen weeks such was his condition. Meanwhile, our little fleet proceeded to the West India islands. It had pursued, as we see, the old circuitous route,—the path which the Genoese had first opened with his prows. At Dominica they took in water, carried on a smart trade with the "salvages," and enjoyed a refreshing respite of three weeks on shore; in which it is very possible that our prisoner was not permitted to share. Fortunately, he is one who has ably learned the great lesson of endurance. He waits in his chains with what philosophy he may, while the dominant party regale themselves among the soft airs and the delicious fruits and flowers of the tropics. If he is to be sovereign in Virginia he can very well afford to wait.

At length the voyage is resumed, and our little fleet steered northward, searching for the island of Roanoke. Three days had they passed their reckoning, yet found no land. The discontents increased, and Captain Ratcliffe, of one of the vessels, was urgent with them to abandon the whole expedition and return again to England. Such was the infirmity of purpose, the feebleness of will, and utter worthlessness of resolve among the very "chiefes" who were most hostile to our adventurer. Luckily, while yet they debated, a violent storm which compelled them to hull it all night under bare poles, drove them towards the desired coasts, which they made on the 26th of April, 1607. The Bay of Chesapeake, a word signifying in the Indian dialect "mother of waters,"—a name admirably applied—received the weary and exhausted wayfarers. To the first land which they descried they gave the name of Cape Henry, to the opposite Cape that of Charles; and the point of land which breasted the pleasant harborage in which they dropped their anchors, they called "Comfort," in token of the grateful emotions with which its appearance had filled their bosoms. The beauty of the scene around them sank sensibly into their hearts, softening their moods, and elevating all their fancies. The green plains, with their great trees and wanton foliage, dipping into the very lips of the ocean, now just beginning to flush and brighten in the embrace of spring, were doubly beautiful in the eyes of those so long saddened with only the aspect of the sea. The world of wood and waste, green and fresh, which spread away with hill and dale, crowned with the profuse luxuriance of the unbroken forest, seemed to them to embrace a very paradise, in which they might well delight to plant their homesteads, fully assured that it was under the especial eye of heaven. Smith, in his pleasure at the prospect, speaks fully for the rest. "Within," says he, "is a country that may have the prerogative over the most pleasant places knowne." * * * "Heaven and earth never agreed better to frame a place for man's habitation, were it fully manured and inhabited by industrious people. Here are mountaines, hills, plaines, valleyes, rivers, and brookes, all running most pleasantly into a faire bay, compassed, but for the mouth, with fruitfull and delightsome land."

The land which they had discovered had never been seen by any of them before. Their destination had been the island of Roanoke, distinguished by previous attempts at colonization. The aspect of the region which rose up around them, in all the magnificence of its primeval state, in its unpruned luxuriance and beauty, seemed to promise full satisfaction for all their desires; and, availing themselves of the discretion which had been allowed them, they preferred rather to try the experiment of a colony in this attractive country, than to continue their search after a spot which was really only known to them by disaster. A party of thirty of them went ashore at Cape Henry to "recreate themselves," and received an unexpected lesson of caution—which, however, did not avail them to any great extent—in consequence of the assault of five Indians, who crept upon them from the hills, and though beaten off by the terrors of their muskets, wounded two of the party very severely with their arrows. They were thus warned that, if the country was beautiful, its inhabitants were brave—a lesson too frequently taught by them in long succeeding conflicts to be easily forgotten by those whose fortune it is to possess the pleasant places of their inheritance.

Virginia being now reached, it may be well to see in what manner the British Solomon proposes that the new colony shall be governed. The sealed box of their instructions was accordingly opened on the night of their arrival, and the documents were spread before the colonists. By these it was discovered that the council was to consist of *Edward Maria Wingfield*, *Bartholomew Gosnold*,

John Smith, *Christopher Newport*, *John Radcliffe*, *John Martin*, and *George Kendall*. These were to serve for one year, and to elect their president from among themselves. This is all that concerns us to know of these instructions, and the way that they were disposed of. It does not appear that Smith was present at the opening of the seals. He was still in bonds; still waiting with patience for the coming of his hour.

To select a proper spot for a settlement, our colonists were employed seventeen days. During this period they were busy in the work of exploration. The treasures of the earth and of the deep were searched for with industry. In the latter they groped for oysters, which lay in places as "thick as stones," and the former they found covered with "flowers of divers kinds and colors," and "goodly trees, cedars, cypress, and other kinds," goodly as ever seen by British voyager before and elsewhere. Strawberries, too, refreshed their eyes and lips, "fine and beautiful," four times bigger and better than ours in England." A brave world at first beginning for our discontents. "Pleasant springs issue from the mountains," "the goodliest cornfields ever seen in any country," salute their eyes, and give ample guarantee against famine; and they are refreshed by the fumes of tobacco from the pipes of savages, who give them a more friendly welcome than that which they met from the five creeping scoundrels at Cape Henry. These invite them to their towns of Kecoughtan and Rappahannock, spread their mats for them when they come, feed them with hominy when they hunger, and teach them to smoke a pipe after the repast. "As goodly men" as our Europeans "had ever seen," are these savages; no ways savage, gentle, quite civil indeed; their *werowance*, or chief, coming at their head to meet the strangers, playing on a flute made of a reed, with a crown of deer's hair, colored red, in fashion of a rose, fastened about his knot of hair, and a great plate of copper on the other side of his head, with two long feathers in seeming of a pair of horns placed in the midst of his crown. Scarcely a Christian costume in the eyes of Christians, but not amiss in the thinking of our Virginians. As we are to have much future commerce with this people it may be as well to continue this description, which comes to us from the pen of George Percy, a brother of the Earl of Northumberland, a volunteer in the expedition, who has given us a very interesting narrative to be found in Purchas.

"His body (that of the Werowance) was painted all with crimson, with a chain of beads about his neck; his face painted blue, besprinkled with silver ore, as we thought; his ears all behung with bracelets of pearl, and in either ear a bird's claw through it, beset with fine copper or gold. He entertained us in so modest a proud fashion, as though he had been a prince of civil government:"—as we suspect he was, Mr. Percy, after the fashion of his country. The Indians were armed "with bows and arrows in a most warlike manner, with the swords at their backs beset with sharp stones and pieces of iron, able to cleave a man in sunder."

Penetrating a spacious river, which the Indians called Powhatan, after their king, but which our no less loyal colonists subdued into the James, in honor of him from whom they had received so liberal a charter, and such admirable counsels,—the little fleet of Newport ascended for a space of forty miles from its mouth. Here they fastened their vessels, in six fathoms of water, to trees growing upon the shore, and, landing upon a peninsula on the north side of the river, they fixed upon it as the site of their future settlement. "A verie fit place," says

Smith, "for the erecting of a great citie:" though it seems that there was some difference of opinion among the captains even then upon this subject; and subsequent experience seems to have proved the propriety of the doubt. But here, nevertheless, the majority so willing it, on the 13th day of May, 1607, the axe was buried in the trees, and the first shafts were hewn out for the foundation of the forest city of the Royal James,—henceforward to be called Jamestown. But the foundation of the city was a small and trivial event to that of the great nation which has yet grown from this small beginning: and he whose eye beholds now upon this memorable but neglected spot no trophy more significant than the rents of ruin in the arches of a single tower overgrown with ivy, and the rank forest growth which denotes the mound where sleep the bones of the early settlers, will scarcely be persuaded that he beholds the obscure nest and birth-place, as lowly as that of the sea-fowl which leaves her eggs along the shore, of the great nation whose wing now spreads, or is fast spreading, over the whole vast continent of North America. Such is, nevertheless, the simple and the startling truth! One hundred and ten years have elapsed from the discovery of the country by Sebastian Cabot, and twenty-two since Raleigh first attempted unsuccessfully its colonization. From this memorable movement the tree takes root, in the future shade of which a mighty people are to find shelter, and in the fruits of which a thousand generations are to gather strength and sustenance. Verily, we may not look upon that ruin of a town, that low and lonely remnant of our royal hamlet, on the north side of the river Powhatan, with unconcern and indifference!

CHAPTER III.

The site of their future habitations chosen, the first duty of our council was to appoint a President. Their choice fell upon Mr. Wingfield, by whom the members of the council were sworn to the performance of their duties. From this privilege Smith was especially excluded; the president declaring his reasons for the exclusion in a speech, which we may easily suppose embodied the several charges which had been made against him, of treason and sedition. We can readily understand the propriety, nay, the absolute necessity of excluding from a seat in the government, an individual who stood under such imputations; and though the exclusion was in direct disobedience of that authority under which they acted as a council, yet we are of opinion that it is a vital constituent of every social or political body to be able to determine who shall properly appear among them. It certainly does not seem an injustice—assuming that the members of the council are themselves free from improper agency in the matter—that, while such charges are pending over the head of an associate, they should refuse to grant him an exercise of power which might contribute to the promotion of the dangerous designs which he is supposed to meditate. And we are bound to believe, until the issue is known, that the council consists of honest men, who are only solicitous of what is right. At all events, Smith makes no complaint. You hear no murmurs from his lips. He is cool and resolute, patient as strong men generally are, not anxious about the result, pretty well assured, indeed, what it must be. He knows the persons with whom he has to deal; has sounded their depths already, and is familiar with all their shallows. What is more, he knows himself—his innocence and his resources equally; and steadily maintaining his temper and his calmness, he fortifies himself in the daily increasing confidence and affections of those whose morbid vanities are not mortified by his evident superiority of character.

But though his services are rejected from the council-seat, they are not to be slighted when the toils and perils of the field are to be undertaken. The colony is quite too feeble to forego the vigor of any able-bodied man, and as soon as the work begins we find our adventurer busy with the rest in providing for the security and comfort of the settlement. Trees are to be felled, forts to be raised, wigwams built, and clapboards are to be split for freighting the returning vessels—our patrons at home requiring as rapid return for the outlay as possible. Each man is assigned a labor suited to his capacities; and while some are engaged upon the tents and cabins, some in the forest hewing trees and getting clapboards, others are weaving bushes into a shelter for their homesteads, and others are laying out gardens, and are preparing gins, snares, and nets for the taking of game and fish. In any of these labors we may be sure that Smith would hold his hand with the best. But he is required for other toils; and as soon as things begin to be tolerably secure and comfortable in the settlement, he is despatched with Captain Newport and twenty others on a voyage of exploration up the river of Powhatan. He offers no objection to this service, though nothing is said of his trial, and he is still denied the place in council which his sovereign has assigned him. But Smith is superior to his enemies. He entertains no sulks, has no petty revenges, but conscientiously having the good of the colony at heart, cheerfully goes upon the duty which is assigned him. They ascend the river to the hamlet of Powhatan himself, the great chief of the country, who dwelt near the falls, and just below the present site of Richmond. This prince is described as a "tall, well-proportioned man, with stern countenance, a head somewhat grey, his beard quite thin and insignificant, his limbs straight, his person erect, of an able and hardy frame, equal to any labor, and at the time of making the acquaintance of the English, near sixty years of age." He is the Emperor of all the country surrounding Jamestown for a space of sixty miles—is supposed, out of a population of six or eight thousand, to be able to bring from fifteen hundred to two thousand warriors into the field. Dwells in some state at his royal hamlet of Powhatan, but has numerous residences; is ordinarily attended by a body guard of forty or fifty of the tallest men in his country; and a strict military discipline environs his dwelling-place with guards day and night, who regularly relieve each other, and who neglect or slumber in their watches at peril of a bastinado, not unlike that of the Turkish in its severity. Like the Turk, he has his Hareem, his religion offering no limit to his appetite. When weary of his women, he bestows them upon his favorites. His power seems to have been a pure despotism; though it appears that under particular circumstances his subjects are permitted the rare privilege of grumbling. They exercise this privilege when Smith and Newport visit the emperor at his village. They resent the intrusion of the strangers; but Powhatan, with better policy, quiets their apprehensions while seeking to disguise his own. "They are harmless—they want nothing but a little land." A little land! The poor savages little know how nearly allied to a land's safety and their own is the knowledge of its value. Powhatan treated the English with a lofty courtesy. He was no common man among his tribe. A born sovereign, he extended his domains by conquest, and absorbed the conquered people among his own. He was of an ambitious and fearless nature, but rendered cautious by the usual training of the savage. An object of fear and awe among his subjects, the presence of the whites, among whom he evidently inspired no such sentiments, was ungracious to his eyes; but with the sagacious instincts of a strong mind, he saw at a glance that he had to deal with a superior race, and the weapon which he proposed to employ against them was one the use of which was familiar to his genius—treachery.

Nobody could have been treated with more kindness and courtesy than were Smith and Newport by our Indian Emperor. Indeed, the entertainment which marked their progress among the Indians was one of the warmest hospitality. They were everywhere received with dancing and feasting. The food spread before them consisted of bread and fish, strawberries, mulberries, &c.; in return for which the Indians received the most precious baubles in the shape of bells, beads, pins, needles, and looking-glasses, which made them the happiest of mortals for the time. Powhatan himself furnished them with a guide to explore the river, receiving a warrior as a hostage "in pawn" for the Indian. In this progress Smith exhibits his customary acuteness of remark, and his vigilance of examination into all that met his eyes. He has left us a considerable body of facts, collected on this and subsequent voyages, illustrative of the manners and habits of the Indians; their costume, their religion, their superstitions, their modes of going to war, and all the peculiarities in short which distinguish their condition, and all the facts or traditions which could illustrate their history. These materials, to this day, furnish the ample storehouse for the student seeking a knowledge of the condition of the aborigines of Virginia and the surrounding countries at the period of the English settlement.

Having pursued their voyage of discovery until the river ceased to be penetrable by their prows, our voyagers returned to Jamestown—their return somewhat hurried by something suspicious in the demeanor of certain of the Indians on their route. It may be that Smith and Newport were rendered farther doubtful by the evident incompetency of the president, Wingfield. This man, who is described as a "grovelling merchant of the West of England," seems to have been filled with an insane or idiotic jealousy of his own people, and would not only permit of no martial exercise or display among them, but actually arrested their labor in the erection of the necessary forts for the safety of the colony, so that of this work nothing was done, but what was achieved, almost in his despite, by the extraordinary diligence of one of the captains. A rude fortification in the shape of a half moon, consisting only of the boughs of trees heaped together, offered the only physical obstacle to the savages, who it appears were suffered to come and go at pleasure, their pacific behavior entirely disarming the English of their caution. The result was to be expected. The colonists were suddenly surprised by a force of four hundred Indians, and but for the timely aid afforded by the fire from the shipping they would have been cut off at a blow. Scattered about at their different occupations, some in the woods, some at their gardens, and all unprepared—their very weapons not convenient to their hands—seventeen of them were wounded at the first onset, and one boy was slain. A cross-bar shot from the cannon of the shipping, rending the limbs from the trees above the heads of the Indians, luckily astounded them with a danger of unknown character, and dispersed them for the time, affording the English an opportunity to place themselves under cover, and prepare for their defence. The members of the council were among the sufferers. Most of them were hurt, and the President, Wingfield, was now better persuaded to risk something at the hands of his own people, in order to make the settlement secure against the open enemy. Our chronicles afford us no light on the subject of his apprehensions. It is not said why this overweening jealousy of one another was entertained among the colonists. The fear seems to have mainly lurked among the members of the council, and we are left to conjecture entirely as regards its origin. We have but a single clue to a mystery which seems so difficult of solution; and this occurs to us in the case of Smith. That he was a man of desperate valor, was well known to his associates; that he was a favorite, calculated equally to lead and to persuade among the common people, was sufficiently apparent. It had been found necessary to the success of the settlement that he should be suffered to leave his prison and go forth upon his duties with the rest. Was it the guilty consciousness of the wrong which they had done him, that made them dread to place weapons in the hands of his followers and friends—that would "admit no exercise at armes,"—and even arrested the progress to completion of the very fortress which was meant as a cover against the common enemy, lest, in a passionate mood and in a favorable moment, he should rise suddenly, and take vengeance for his wrongs. In all probability this wretched apprehension was the true secret of the insane jealousy and weakness of the President.

The fort was now palisadoed, the ordnance mounted, the men duly armed and exercised; and it appears not a moment too soon. The first alarm at the discharge of the ordnance being over, the savages came back to the assault, and their attacks were frequent. They watched the progress of the colonists with a degree of hostility that never suffered an opportunity of doing mischief to escape them. They ambushed the forest paths; and the keen eye, and nimble foot, and deadly arrow of the savage, made it a death-peril for the colonists who straggled off without protection from the garrison. "What toyle we had, with so small a power, to guard our workmen a dayes, watch all night, resist our enemies, and effect our businesse,—to relade the ships, cut downe trees, and prepare the ground to plante our corne,"—may be readily conjectured. But the ships were at length laden; and now that they were ready to depart, our President gave Captain Smith a kindly intimation that he should depart with them for England. The council was pleased benignantly to refer him for censure to the council in England under general charges, rather than, by trying him themselves, with the proofs in their possession, endanger his life, destroy his reputation, and make his good name odious to the world.

This was cunningly devised. But they were yet to know the man with whom they had to deal. It was because he valued his good name and his reputation, rather than his life, that he scorned their pretended indulgence, defied them to the proof of his guilt, and demanded his trial on the spot. And now it was, that his patience, his manly bearing, his good conduct, courage, and character, while in bonds and under accusation, produced their full effects. He had grown strong in all opinions. His innocence and the malice of his foes had made themselves apparent to the whole company in the thirteen weeks of his confinement, and the six subsequent weeks in which he had enjoyed comparative liberty. The council did not dare refuse him the trial which he demanded, and the result was a triumphant acquittal. It was something more than an acquittal. It was redress and indemnity. He convicted his enemies of their malice; the persons whom they had endeavored to suborn against him confessing the facts, and accusing the accusers of their subornation. So utterly disproved were the charges which were urged against him, and so notoriously malicious, that he was acquitted by acclamation; and the President, in whom they originated, was condemned to pay two hundred pounds damages—a sum which Smith at once applied to the necessities of the colony. His magnanimity was not to be outdone by their justice. His seat in council was withheld no longer; and this occasion was seized upon by the worthy preacher, Mr. Hunt, with "good doctrine and exhortation," to appease this and other animosities, which had sprung up among his flock. On the ensuing Sabbath they all partook of the communion, in confirmation of the sincerity and Christian character of their reconciliation. Peace was formally made the next day with the Indians; and leaving the colony, consisting of one hundred and four persons, under these pleasant auspices, Newport sailed on the 15th of June for England, promising in twenty weeks to return with fresh supplies.

CHAPTER IV.

The pleasant auspices under which Newport left the colony did not long continue. The colonists began to suffer from the oppressive heats of summer. They were strangers to the climate, and engaged in labors for which no previous training had prepared them. Their food was bad, consisting of wheat and barley, which, having been kept for six months in the hot hold of a ship, was now rather bran than corn, and contained quite as many worms and insects as grains! While the vessels remained, the evil had not been so severely felt. They enjoyed a daily allowance of ship's-biscuit, for which they paid the sailors in "money, saxefras, furres, or *love.*" Their departure cut off this supply. The ships had been the taverns of our colonists. With them went hotel, and brewhouse, and bakery. "Had we beene as free from all sinnes as gluttony and drunkennesse," says our narrative,* with a sad enough sort of humor, "we might have been canonized for saints." The common kettle was all that remained to them, and even of this the individual allowance was inadequate. Half a pint of wheat and as much barley, was as much as the President allowed per day for each. To himself he was much more indulgent. He engrossed for his private use, the "oatmeale, sacke, oyle, *aqua vitæ*, beefe, egges, or what not," liberally forbearing, however,

* Chap. II. of third Book of Smith's Virginia, and evidently in great part from the pen of Smith himself, though signed, "written by *Thomas Studley*, the first cape merchant in Virginia, *Robert Fenton*, *Edward Harrington*, and *I. S.*" Smith (I. S.) probably wrote, and the others signed with him as witnesses.

to touch the contents of the common kettle. "Our drinke was water," says one melancholy humorist, "our lodgings castles in the ayre." Such diet and lodgings, coupled with severe labors, constant and diligent watch, in the oppressive summer climate of that region, were fatal to European health and strength. In a short time after the departure of the ships, so extreme was the suffering that scarcely ten men of the hundred were able to stand. Gosnold died; Smith, Martin, and Radcliffe were all dangerously sick, and so were most of the soldiers. Fifty of them were buried, and those who survived were in danger of starvation. Their provisions, worthless as they had become, were soon consumed; and from June until September they lived only upon sea-crabs and sturgeon. Very good living, too, it will be said, for famishing men; but these they had to snare and take for themselves, almost too feeble, from long sickness, for toils so moderate. But the sea-crabs and sturgeon finally disappeared from the waters, and the terrors of famine returned upon them. At this very time our wretched colonists had reason to apprehend an inroad from the Indians, who during the midsummer had given them a little respite. Even while they suffered from this cruel condition and melancholy prospect, the selfish wretch to whom they had confided the Presidency was secretly meditating his own flight to England in the pinnace, leaving them to their fate. He had probably exhausted his private stores, and was now disposed to fly from the suffering which he had been willing neither to relieve nor share. His treachery was discovered, and so much moved the colonists, in spite of their languor and prostration, that they deposed him and put Radcliffe in his place. This was substantially placing Smith at the head of affairs. Radcliffe was incompetent; "of weak judgment in dangers, and lesse industrie in peace." He was perfectly satisfied that Smith should relieve him of the toils of his office and its responsibilities together. The result of this change was instantly apparent in the improved aspect of affairs. The manhood of Smith's character became conspicuous the moment that he felt his burdens. Still feeble from sickness, not well recovered, he at once addressed himself to his tasks, as vigorously as when he fought the Turks at Regall, and made his way from Nalbritz to Wallachia. When he began his new labors there were no houses to cover the settlers; the tents were rotten, and the cabins worse than useless. The chief men were sick or malcontent, the "rest being in such dispaire, as they would rather starve and rot with idleness than be persuaded to do any thing for their owne reliefe without constraint." With such necessities to encounter, with such materials to work with, Smith, by good words, fair promises, and his own example, succeeded in setting some to build, some to mow, others to bind, and others again to thatch—always, however, tasking himself beyond any of the rest. In this way he managed to provide comfortable dwellings for all but himself, and to give to Jamestown, for the first time, the appearance of a decent hamlet. In these labors he seems to have met with little resistance, if he found but little sympathy and succor. The council, in consequence of the death of Gosnold, the departure of Newport, and the expulsion of Kendall—who had been concerned in the schemes of Wingfield—consisted only of Radcliffe, Martin, and Smith; and of these Radcliffe and Martin were still upon the sick-list, neither of them being very much beloved or very competent. It happened fortunately for the colony that Smith's exertions were seconded by the favorable aspect of the Indians, who, with their usual caprice of character, suddenly laid aside their bows and arrows, and brought supplies of maize, greatly needed, to barter with the Europeans. This supply lasted for some time. Without waiting to see it all consumed, Smith prepared to provide against that event. And here our adventurer takes occasion to meet the complaints of those who were disposed to blame the company in England for sending forth a colony with inadequate provision. The manly sense of justice, which makes so fine an element in his character, strikes the murmur at its root. He tells them they are "ill advised to nourish such ill conceits. * * * The fault in going was our own; what could be thought fitting or necessary we had; but what we should find, or want, or where we should be, we were all ignorant. * * * Supposing to make our passage in two moneths, with victuall to live, and the advantage of the spring to worke, we were at sea five moneths,—where we both spent our victuall and lost the opportunitie of the time and season to plant, by the unskilful presumption of our ignorant transporters, that understood not at all what they undertooke."

This is laying the blame on the right shoulders. The true evil was in the vanity, the worthlessness, and utter selfishness of those to whom so much of the power had been intrusted. Our author proceeds in a general reflection, which, even were it not that of Smith himself—as we believe it to be—is worthy to be preserved in this connection.

"Such actions have, ever since the world's beginning, beene subject to such accidents, and everything of worth is found full of difficulties; but nothing so difficult as to establish a commonwealth, so farre remote from men and meanes, and where men's minds are so untoward as neither doe well themselves nor suffer others."—Truth in itself, but here a history, which accounts for all the mishaps of the colony to the present moment, and makes the merit so much the greater on the part of him by whom all obstacles of untoward minds and inferior means were finally overcome.

A few months have made a surprising alteration in his own and the fortunes of the colonists. His enemies are deposed. The prisoner is taken from his cell and placed at the head of affairs. The spirit of exulting selfishness is humbled into silence—crushed down with conscious humiliation, while it beholds the noble forbearance of him whom it has injured to exult in turn. His revenges are of the kind commanded by Scripture. He heaps fire on the head of his foes, by deeds of manliness and mercy. He interposes for their safety, and with success. They are soon made to see that he alone can be successful, that he is the king-man of the expedition, a sovereign by the appointment of nature. No one looks to Radcliffe or to Martin; Wingfield goes out of sight, remembered only as a poor thieving mercenary, from whom no man has anything to hope. Smith is master. He has compelled the tasks of labor; he has done the work which no man had thought, or perhaps knew how to do before; and now, as he sees the provisions of the Indians running low, he has measured out the allowances, and finds the supply sufficient for only eighteen days—he prepares to go in search of their granaries. He fits out the shallop, takes with him a select crew of seven men, and, with a store of European commodities—hatchets, and beads, and bells, and glasses—he sets forth on a cruise. Ignorant of the Indian language, with seamen who neither know nor love the use of the oar, his men wanting in apparel, and few in number compared with the multitude of savages they must meet—these, he tells us, are impediments in his way, but do not discourage him. Descending the river to its mouth, he reaches the hamlet of Kecoughtan, where Hampton now stands. Here he found the natives too well acquainted with the condition of the colony to treat him with respect. They deride his offers of barter, and taunt his poverty with scraps of bread, tendered for their swords and muskets. The arts of trade are exercised in vain. They regard the fate of the colony as in their hands, and are not to be tempted with the toys and trifles which are spread before them. Courtesy finds nothing but insolence; and the necessities of Smith are such as will not suffer him to return with empty hands. "Though contrary to his commission," he "makes bold to try such conclusions as necessitie inforced." His true commission is to see that the people do not starve, and to this all other commissions must give place. But, though determined to obtain by force what he cannot get by trade, he is yet willing to "do his spiriting gently." He suddenly gives them a volley, directed so as to do no hurt, and then boldly runs his boat upon the shore. At this decisive movement the savages betake them to the woods, and, marching upon the hamlet, Smith finds their houses well stored with maize. It is with difficulty that he can restrain his hungry companions from seizing at once upon the prize; but he is too good a soldier to suppose that his enemy will suffer this. He keeps his men together and prepares them for the assault, which follows almost immediately. The savages, recovered from their panic, to the number of sixty or seventy, painted in a variety of styles and colors equally hideous and fantastic, came darting from the woods in order of battle, timing their movement with songs and dances, after the manner of the ancient Spartans. They brought with them their Okee, or god, a monstrous image made of skins, stuffed with moss, painted like themselves, and decorated with rude and uncouth ornaments. They were well armed with clubs and arrows, bows and targets, and charged the English without hesitation. Smith requites them, still disposed to pity, even where he must chastise, with pistol-shot only. These answer the purpose. The idol is the first, and perhaps the principal victim. It falls into the hands of the whites, while the red men again fly to the shelter of the woods. Some of them are hurt, but none, it would seem, severely. At all events these hurts provoke no anxiety, while all the apprehensions of the tribe are awakened for the fate and captivity of their god. He must be recovered. He has to be ransomed. They understand and comply with the conditions; load the boat of the colonists with maize, and bring them besides a bountiful tribute of venison, turkeys, and wild-fowl. Smith not only restores their *Okee*, but takes them to his friendship and protection. He has shown them that he can be a destroyer: he seeks to show them that he can be a benefactor also. He bestows upon them beads and hatchets, and they celebrate the reconciliation with songs and dances. His return to Jamestown infuses new life into the despairing settlers. But no increase of providence on their part follows his enterprise and industry. Their late miseries teach them no useful lesson. They waste as fast as he supplies, and his voyages require to be frequently repeated. In these voyages he is not only successful in procuring the necessary provisions, but he makes frequent discoveries of new towns and tribes; forms their acquaintance, becomes known and remarked by them in turn, and notes the resources of the country, and the manners, habits, and numbers of the people. The Chickahominy was penetrated in this way, and a trade opened with the people of that river. The tribes of Wanasqueak, of Tappahannock, and of Paspahegh, furnished ample markets. The latter he styles a churlish and treacherous people, jealous of their acquaintance with other tribes, yet not themselves loving them—who set spies upon their movements, and, but for the vigilance of our Captain, would have possessed themselves by stealth of the weapons of the Europeans. Smith travels among them by night and day, is always vigilant, yet never betrays apprehension. He treats them with kindness always, and is entertained in like manner. So anxious do they become to trade, that they will give the grain to him if he will not buy it, and they follow him in their canoes for this purpose. But he must let them hear his musketry, and to oblige them he gives a volley to the wild fowl upon the river, the Indians much fearing and wondering to behold the feathers fly.

Thus indefatigable, our hero is yet doomed to discover that his toil consists in drawing water in a sieve. He toils for the worthless and the ungrateful. The malcontents, now that they have recovered from their illness, have resumed all their evil nature. Wingfield and Kendall engage in a conspiracy, to which they persuade certain of the sailors, to seize upon the pinnace which Smith has kept in order for his domestic enterprises, appropriate the provisions which he has brought, and steal away for England. The conspiracy is fairly a-foot, when it is discovered by one of the mechanics. This man, showing some insubordination, was chidden by the President, whom he defied and assaulted with his smith's implements. For this act the offender is tried by a jury, and sentenced to be hanged. It is only when he is actually upon the gallows that he can be persuaded that he will not be rescued by those comrades whose secret practices have led to his mutiny. When actually assured of his fate, he revealed the secret of the conspiracy. This premature discovery urged the conspirators into instant activity. They seized upon the pinnace, and would have made off, but that Smith turned the guns of the fortress upon them, and forced them to remain where they were, or be sunk in the river. They chose the more prudent course, and the only victim to their insanity was Captain Kendall, the chief conspirator, who was tried by a jury, condemned, and shot to death.*

Here it was Smith's energy again that interposed for the safety of the colony. It was his timely return that baffles the conspiracy, and saves the pinnace. His prompt decision, that, training the guns of the fort upon the conspirators, compels the surrender of their chief, and brings the rest back to their duty, without rendering necessary any lavish sacrifice of life.

The conspiracy is no sooner quieted than our sleepless adventurer embarks upon a new voyage of trade and discovery. His course is up the Chickahominy, which the council desires him to follow to its source. He finds several new towns; finds the store of grain in the country somewhat diminished, but procures a good supply, and returns to Jamestown, just in season to prevent another effort on the part of the malcontents to abandon the colony and return to Europe in the pinnace. But this attempt

* This fact is thus distinctly stated in the narrative of Smith himself, professing to be written by Tho. Watson, Gent., entitled, "A true relation of such occurrences and accidents of noate as hath happened in Virginia since the first planting of that colony," &c. London. 1608. According to Stith, Kendall is slain *in the action;* but this mistake seems to have arisen from the vague manner in which the facts are given in the third book of the "proceedings and accidents," where it is said that he (Smith) "with store of sakre and musket-shot forced them stay, or sink in the river, which action cost the life of Capt. Kendall." In other words, the movement, the seizure of the boat, the overt act of treason, cost him (the chief conspirator) his life.

was after due form of law—a resolution submitted in council, and sustained by Captain Archer and the President; Martin and Smith opposing it. It might have been difficult to arrest this new movement, thus legitimate in form and appealing to the home-sickness of all parties, but for an agreeable change in the circumstances of the colony. The winter was approaching, and had covered the rivers with wild fowl in abundance. Ducks and geese were to be had for the gathering; wild beasts, as fat as they could be eaten, drew near to the settlement, as if seeking to be slain; and the prudence of Smith, his ample provision of the commodities furnished by the Indians—maize, pease, pompions, fish, and poultry—giving assurance of abundance through the winter, did more to quiet the discontents than any argument. Smith knew his countrymen well, and knew through what medium in especial it was required to approach their intellects. "The Spaniard," he himself remarks, "never more greedily desired gold than he victuall, nor his souldiers more to abandon the country than he to keepe it." The living was so good, "that none of our *Tufftaffaty** humorists desired to goe

* This is not a coinage of our author. He has authority for it among the poets. The allusion is to the condition of the velvet habits of our *gentlemen* colonists. These were worn into tufts. The Taffeta or Taffaty had become *tufty*. The word is a compound of Tuft and Taffata. Beaumont and Fletcher write "*Taffaties*, silk grogans, sattins, and velvets are mine." But Donne is more explicit, and applies directly to our case:

> "Sleeveless his jerkin was, and it had been
> Velvet, but 'twas now (*so much ground was seen*)
> Become *tufftaffaty*."

The word not being in common use in Smith's time in England, nor indeed at any time, the effort will not be great to fancy that our Indian trader was a frequent reader of the poets. His prose, indeed, would go far to prove the fact.

for Englande." With returning health and vigor, life in the forests of America, with so much game around them, was a long day of pleasure, and, so long as it lasted, no more discontents or vain repinings after the mother-land were to be apprehended. The riant spirit which now filled their bosoms was that of Jeshurun. Having waxed fat, they kicked. Smith's enterprises, which had saved them from perishing, did not now meet the general expectation. His associates in council reproached him with not having explored the Chickahominy to its sources. This river, it was absurdly fancied, would conduct them into the South sea, then the great object of European discovery. It was in vain that he urged the greater importance to their present objects and necessities of laying in the winter supplies of maize when it could be procured from the Indians, and before the improvident savages became conscious of any scarcity. The river could always wait. He was told that he was slow. He might have answered—"I am sure; and always fast enough for the necessity." But contenting himself with declaring the motives by which he had been governed, in forbearing the contemplated exploration—and with which we are perfectly satisfied—he chose the most effectual mode of silencing the murmurs of the council, by withdrawing himself from sight, and by going upon the proposed expedition.

The winter of 1607, remarkable for an extraordinary frost in Europe, was extremely cold in Virginia; but no seasons seemed to discourage the enterprise of our hero. He penetrated the Chickahominy for fifty miles in his barge, cutting his way through trees where they had fallen across the stream, and pressing on, from point to point, with all the diligence and address which marked his character. At length, the shoals becoming such as to endanger his vessel, he procured a canoe from the Indians, two of whom were engaged as oarsmen. Having put the barge in security, and given express charge to his men not to go ashore, he took with him two of his people, and with the two Indians continued his further voyage in the canoe.

At this place in his narrative Smith deems it necessary to apologize for the extreme risk which he incurred by this proceeding. "Though some wise men," he remarks, "may condemn this too bould attempt of too much indiscretion, yet if they will consider the friendship of the Indians in conducting me, the desolateness of the country, the probabilitie of some lucke, and the malicious judges of my actions at home—as also to have some matters of worth to encourage our adventurers in England—might well have caused any honest minde to have done the like, as well for his own discharge, as for the public good."

These, we may remark, are the suggestions of a very noble mind. It is the probable "lucke" of the colony that moves him to risk his life, and the anxiety to "encourage other colonists from England;"—even the errors of judgment, which we find in this apology, are proofs of a high and generous spirit, superior to the exactions of a petty self. He confides in the friendship of the Indians, which the cowardly and jealous nature will seldom do; and he has "malicious judges at home," whom he would silence and disarm for ever by deeds of courage, which not one of them has the soul to emulate. If the argument of Smith does not wholly prove the correctness of his policy, it proves his own worth and manliness of character—his courage, and the honesty of his ambition. He thinks that his motives might well cause any "honest minde to have done the like." So they might; but "honesty," Captain, is scarcely the sufficient word in this connection! Let it remain, however, as it is written.

Smith had learned many admirable lessons in foreign warfare, but he was yet to learn the subtlety of those tribes whose forests he had begun to subdue. The probability is, that every footstep which he took from the mouth of the Chickahominy was noted by the spies of Powhatan. Whether the two Indians who rowed his boat were faithful to him is quite questionable. He himself was without suspicion, as he was without fear. He ascended the river in the canoe some twenty miles above the spot where his barge was anchored. Here, as the river was cumbered with trees and foliage, though still keeping sufficient depth for his progress, he left the canoe in the charge of the two Englishmen and one of the Indians. The other he took with him, and went ashore "to see the nature of the soil," and to head or cross the tributary branches of the stream. On leaving the canoe, he instructed his followers to keep their matches alight, and to discharge a piece at the first appearance of danger. With these precautions, deeming himself tolerably secure, he passed with his guide into the forests.

A quarter of an hour had not elapsed, after his leaving the canoe, when he was startled by the war-whoop of the savage. No warning matchlock apprised him of the proximity of any enemy, and believing that the two whom he had left with the canoe had been betrayed and murdered by his Indian guide, with the prompt decision of his character, he at once grappled with the Indian, his companion. The stern resolution of our adventurer, with the suddenness of his movement, disarmed the savage and subdued his spirit; and Smith, with his garters, bound the arm of the savage tightly to one of his own; thus preparing to use him as a buckler. He had scarcely taken this precaution, when he felt himself struck with an arrow upon the thigh. This shaft did no hurt, being discharged

Smith surprised by Opechancanough. PAGE 133.

from a respectful distance; but a moment after the vigilant eyes of our hero discovered two other Indians about to draw their bows upon him. He anticipated them by a discharge of his pistol, the effects of which they already knew. This sent them flying for a while, and enabled him to reload his weapon. But they soon returned to the conflict, and Smith, retreating with his face toward them, and his fettered Indian—who proved quite submissive—still as a buckler between their darts and his bosom, slowly aimed to make his way backward to the canoe. But the sudden appearance upon the ground, of Opechancanough, one of their greatest chiefs, at the head of more than two hundred warriors, soon lessened, if it did not utterly destroy his hopes. But Smith was not to be subdued. He knew too much of the barbarian nature to exhibit any apprehensions; and, steadily continuing to retire, answered some twenty or thirty of their arrows with four or five pistol-shots. To approach him closely while possessed of these formidable weapons was no part of the Indian policy, and to do him much hurt at a distance, while he so adroitly interposed their comrade between him and their shafts, was soon discovered to be no easy matter. A conference took place between the parties. Smith was told that his two followers were slain, but that his life would be spared if he would yield himself. But he must have better terms than this. He must be permitted to retire in safety to the boat. He will not deliver up his arms. He will use them, and shoot with them famously, though his Indian buckler-man importunes him not to do so. This conference was carried on with less formal state than is customary on such occasions, as well in barbarous as in Christian countries. It was a sort of running conference—a running fight at the same time; Smith backing regularly as he argued, and drawing his tethered Indian along with him, very awkwardly placed, no doubt, between two fires, and anxious to get away; Opechancanough pressing upon him within treating and fighting distance, unwilling to provoke the pistol, but resolved that the Captain shall not get away. It is difficult to say how long this curious sort of strife could have been maintained, and what would have been its final issue, had not a mishap befallen our adventurer, against which he had made no provision. Retreating still, with face averted from the path which he treads, he walks suddenly into a morass, into which he drags perforce his unwilling companion. This morass alone had protected him from assault in the rear. But he was too busy with his foes in front to think of any other danger, and, up to his waist in bog, he cannot extricate himself without assistance. The hope of escape is at an end. He flings away his pistols, and makes signs of submission; and he who has tasted of the perils of Turkish bondage will now have an opportunity of comparing it with that of the Apalachian.

CHAPTER V.

The misfortune of Smith seems to have been due entirely to the misconduct of his followers, whom he had left behind him in the canoe and barge. Had they not in both cases disobeyed his orders, neither they nor himself would have suffered harm. But, scarcely had he gone from sight, when the people in the barge determined to enjoy their freedom on the land. They, too, in all probability, had some vague notions of coming upon the great river leading from the northeast into the South Sea—the vain desire, built upon gross ignorance, which possessed many of the adventurers in that age; or, seeing at a distance some headland of shining earth, they had brighter fancies of gold and silver ore to be gathered by the bucket. With vague appetites like these, or possibly only with the boyish desire to run and leap among the seemingly quiet woods, they drew nigh to the shore in their barge, and leaving her to the care of fortune, straggled off into the forests. They had not gone far, when they were surprised by Opechancanough, with three hundred warriors. They succeeded in escaping to the barge, and in saving her, though not without great difficulty. One of their number, George Cassen, fell into the hands of the savages, and was made to suffer the miserable penalty of death for all the rest. In the hope to save his life, the captive revealed the secret of Smith's progress into the interior. The secret obtained, the poor wretch was despatched by the most cruel tortures—dismembered limb by limb, and cast into the fire. After this, Opechancanough hurried upon the trail of our adventurer. The men left in the canoe were equally remiss of duty with those in the barge, but paid more heavily for their error. They, too, had left the vessel, had gone ashore, built a fire, and were shot to death while they slept before it. Every step which Smith had taken was then followed, until he fell into the bog, and into their hands. The treacherous morass which enmeshed him, seems to have been one of the numerous swamps from which the river takes its rise. He had, therefore, involuntarily pushed the exploring survey much more deeply than was at all needful in discovering its sources. But he had been no such easy victim as his besotted followers—three of them had he slain in the struggle, and "divers others had he gall'd." His skill and valor, while compelling their fears, commanded their respect and admiration.

These he was careful not to forfeit. Drawn from the morass, cold and nearly frozen, he showed no signs of fear, and behaved with the most intrepid spirit. Brought before Opechancanough, he presented him with the pocket-compass with which he travelled, and showed him the uses of the instrument. Great was the marvel at the play of the needle, which he could see through the glass, but never touch; and when Smith proceeded to explain to him, by mingled sign and speech, its wonderful properties—how it would follow sun, moon, and stars,—indicate his route on earth, and guide him to realms, and continents, and seas, of which our savages now heard for the first time, they were struck with amazement and silent wonder. This toy amused them for an hour, and when it ceased to do so, they fastened the captive to a tree, grouped themselves around him, and placing each an arrow on his bow, they prepared to shoot him. It is probable this was only an experiment upon his courage. He was a Captain—a Werowance or Chief—of whom much curiosity was entertained, and from whom much ransom might be expected. At a signal from their king, their weapons were dropped, and leading him to the fire—where he beheld the body of one of his men, Thomas Emry, stuck full of arrows—they suffered him to warm himself, chafed his limbs, which were nearly frozen, gave him food, and treated him with kindness. He had occasion to remark, that though they fed him bountifully, not one of them would eat with him;—a forbearance which reminds us of the reluctance of the Arabs and other Eastern nations to partake of food with those to whom they intend evil.

He was reserved to grace the triumph of Opechancanough. This sagacious savage was the King or Chief of Pamunkee—is styled one of the brethren of Powhatan; but subsequent narratives—for he made a figure in after events not less distinguished than that of Powhatan—represent him not to have been considered by the Indians a relative of Powhatan in any degree. Indeed, they describe him as being a foreigner, the Prince of a distant people in the southwest, who was adopted into the nation; probably having been taken from his own while yet in his infancy.* He was a man of large stature, of noble presence and extraordinary parts, and a dignity of thought and carriage which might honor the highest places of Christian civilisation. His treatment of Smith while his captive, making due allowance for his own wild training, was creditable to his delicacy and humanity. That his captive should minister to his triumph, was due to the customs of his country; and the practice does not seem to have discredited any of the Roman conquerors. It has policy for its justi-

* See Beverley, Hist. Va., 51, 52; and Burke (Hist. Va.), vol. iii., pages 57–8–9, for an interesting account of the capture of this chieftain, under the English colonial administration of Sir W. Berkeley, and of his brutal assassination while in captivity.

fication, and infuses courage into a people, and strengthens and confirms their patriotism.

The procession which conducted Smith through the Indian towns, was one of rude state and ceremonial. He himself was guarded on either side by a sturdy savage, who kept fast hold upon his wrist. Opechancanough moved midway in the column, and the guns, swords, and pistols, which had been taken, were borne before him. Their approach to a settlement or hamlet was distinguished by the wild songs and dances of the warriors,—their yells of death and victory first bringing out the women and children to behold their spectacle of triumph.

His first resting place in this humiliating progress was at Orapakes, where he was taken to a house and closely guarded by eight warriors. Here he was so well fed, with venison, and other food, that he began to be troubled with misgivings that their purpose was to fatten him for the table. To go to a feast, not to eat but to be eaten, was an event in prospect, not more agreeable to Smith than to Polonius. But this fear was only momentary, and proved to have been groundless. It does not appear anywhere that the North American savage was a cannibal. At Orapakes one of the Indians to whom Smith had made some small present when he first came to Virginia, remembered the gift with gratitude, and brought him his gown, which he seems to have discarded when first assailed by his captors. The gift was a grateful one, as the weather was intensely cold, and his condition was one to demand every possible consolation.

Some delay was made at Orapakes. It was one of the favorite residences of Powhatan, and here it may have been expected to meet him. It is probable that his captors waited here for instructions from their emperor. This detention increased the intimacy between Smith and the savages, of which he contrived to avail himself in getting a letter to Jamestown. In this letter, which was written on the leaf of an old table-book, he wrote his wishes to the people at the fort; described his condition exactly, instructed them to do all that they could to terrify the messengers, who were in fact spies, and upon whose report would depend their decision whether to assault the fort or not—a measure greatly urged by the King of Paspahegh; who sagaciously insisted upon the moment the great *werowance* of the whites was in their power, and his people in consternation, as being particularly suited to the attempt. The letter also counselled certain things to be sent him, of which an inventory was given. His messengers—three in number—took the letter in weather so bitter and cold, with frost and snow, "as in reason were impossible by any naked man to be endured."

But they returned in three days, having faithfully executed their commission. The reports which they brought of the terrors by which the fort was environed, confirming the dreadful accounts of mines, great guns, and engines of such dread, that no proper names for them could be found, determined them to forego the attempt upon the colony; and then it was that the triumphal progress was resumed. But before this could take place, and, indeed, before Smith's dispatches had been written, an incident occurred which had nearly rendered unnecessary any further negotiation.

It appears that, soon after he had reached his present resting-place, he was summoned to the assistance of one of the men whom he had wounded with his pistols. Looked upon as a conqueror—as a great *medicine*, at least —it was taken for granted that he could heal as well as hurt; and nothing seemed to them more natural and proper, than that he should do so where he himself had inflicted the injury. But Smith found the wounded man in the last extremity, and declared frankly he could do nothing for him. Something, he said, might be done, could he procure a certain medicine which he had at Jamestown; and a requisition for this medicine was actually made in the letter which was sent. But the savage dying soon after, his father set upon our adventurer to revenge his death; and would have slain him with his sword, but for the timely interposition of the guard. Baffled in this way, he endeavored to effect his object by shooting at him in his prison, but was again arrested in his designs before any injury had been done. So intense was this wild passion of revenge, which the practice among the savages made justifiable, that, to defeat the purposes of his fury, they were compelled to remove the object of his pursuit and hate to other places of security. This, indeed, is given as one of the reasons for resuming the triumphal progress.

The route of the procession was a circuitous one. The real object seems to have been to gratify the curiosity of as many townships as possible; and possibly the vanity of his captors, before taking him to Werowomoco, where Powhatan at this time resided. First, they carried him among the people who dwelt on the Youghtanund, or Pamunkee river. From the Youghtanund they led him to the Mattaponies, the Piankatanks, the Nantaughtacunds, or the Rappahannock, and the Nominies, on the Potomac river. These rivers being passed, they showed him to numerous other tribes, with names equally barbarous. He was then brought back to the habitation of Opechancanough, at Pamunkee, where a wild and singular species of incantation was destined to take place; the object of which is stated to be to ascertain by magical orgies what had been and were his real purposes towards them. In other words, the priests and conjurors of the nation were disposed to show themselves necessary to its safety, and to avail themselves of a novel circumstance to strengthen those vulgar superstitions by which they lived. For three days they conjured him by the rudest sort of ceremonials. Smeared with oil and paint, begrimed with black and red, garbed in the skins of wild beasts, and shaking their gourd-rattles over head, they danced around him, with shrieks and howlings, from the rising to the setting of the sun;—then fed themselves and him, for neither had been suffered to partake of food while the day lasted; but they took especial care not to eat with him—a circumstance which still serves to keep up in our hero's mind a lively anxiety with regard to their cannibal appetites. Three days were thus spent in these and similar orgies; the details of which could not enlighten, and would scarcely please the reader. These over, he was removed to the dwelling of Opitchapam,* the brother of Powhatan, who afterwards succeeded to the empire. Here he was still well treated, that is, well fed; his imagination, as he tells us in doggerel verse—in which he not unfrequently deals—conjuring up "hydeous dreames," in his waking moments, of "wondrous shapes," "strange bodies," "huge of growth,"

"And of stupendous makes;"

the effects probably of over feeding, an inactive condition of body, and a mind full of active apprehensions. But his spirits do not fail him, nor his courage. His aspect is still such as to command the respect of the savages. They seek to persuade and to intimidate him. They offer him "life, liberty, land, and women," if he will only show them how to get possession of the fort at Jamestown. They exult in the possession of a bag of gunpowder, the qualities of which they know; and which, regarding it as

* Beverley calls him Itopatin.

a seed, they proposed to sow, in hope of future crops, by which to retort the explosive missiles of the pale-faces.

Smith loses no opportunity to impress them with a sense of the superiority of the whites ; of their wondrous resources, and unmentionable powers. He does not undeceive them with regard to the gunpowder, and we may suppose that they sow the crop at the due season in spring. He is equal to all their arts. They bring him one of his pistols, requiring him to discharge it, in order, as he perceives, that they may learn its use. But his subtlety equals theirs. He adroitly breaks the cock of the weapon, which he succeeds in persuading them is accidentally done. They can make nothing of him, and he, if he makes nothing of them, at all events maintains his manhood in their eyes, and assumes the guise of cheerfulness, though grief sits heavy at his heart. At length, after a long delay, which was probably not without its object, the captive is conducted to Werowocomoco,* the residence of Powhatan, and into the presence of that despotic chieftain.

* Called Meronocomoco in the "Discoveries and Accidents," vol. i., c. ii., p. 162, of the octavo edition printed at Richmond, Va.

CHAPTER VI.

We have now reached a period in the career of our hero, the events of which are much more intimately associated with his memory in the minds of men than those of any other in the whole of his long eventful history. Though not more remarkable, perhaps, than many others—not more imposing or impressive than his three single combats with the Turkish champions before Regall—than his captivity and escape from the bondage of the Bashaw of Bogall, bearing with him the blood of that cruel despot, and the tender affections of his gentle sister—yet there is something in the first appearance of the sweet forest damsel, Pocahontas, upon the scene in which Smith is the hero, and nearly the victim, which commends this part of his story, more than any other, to the sympathies and remembrances of our people. It is as the prisoner of Powhatan, the great Indian Emperor of Virginia—as the captive doomed to perish in the hands of savages by a sudden and a cruel death, and rescued at the last moment by the unexpected interposition of the young and tender-hearted child of the fierce old monarch—that our hero fixes the attention of the hearer when his name is but mentioned. We have reached that point in his career upon which the eye inevitably fastens, heedless of every other, when he becomes the subject;—that exquisite episode in the history of the new world, which, appealing equally to the affections and the imagination, has never lost the charm of its original loveliness and freshness, even though a thousand iterations have made it the most familiar of all our forest stories. It is one of those tales which combine several elements of the tender and the tragic—like that of the Grecian daughter—like that of the Roman Virginius; more certainly true than either of these legends, and not less touching and beautiful; which, partaking of similar sources of interest, and appealing equally to the deepest sources of feeling in the heart, the mind treasures up naturally and without an effort, as a chronicle equally dear to its virgin fancies and its sweetest sensibilities.

From the moment that Smith became the prisoner of the savages of Opechancanough, he had every reason to fear the worst. Threatened with assassination by his personal foes, even against the will of those who had him in captivity, there were yet other ominous circumstances which, as he well knew the practices among the Indians, furnished sufficient reason for his fears. They fed him, and refused to eat with him; and he was borne about on a sort of triumphal progress, as a sort of show, from town to town, in order, as it would seem, to the gratification of all eyes, before he should be finally conducted to the stake. The object on every hand of a peculiar curiosity, the condition of our captive was sufficiently humiliating. Brought at length to Werowocomoco, which lay on the north side of Fork river, in Gloucester County, and seems to have been the royal residence for the time, his mind appears somewhat to have yielded to his fatigues, his privations, and not improbably his fears. He conjured up the worst phantoms for his torment; and some of the images that oppressed his imagination may have grown out of the grim and hideous aspects by which he was constantly surrounded. Brought to the residence of Powhatan, he was not immediately conducted into the presence of the Emperor, but remained at some distance in the forest, in order, as it would seem, that sufficient opportunity should be afforded the latter for making his preparations for the reception. This, it appears, was to be an affair of great state and ceremonial. A barbarous sort of pomp had already distinguished his progress through the country, and his reception at the various towns and settlements. It was held necessary that the royal reception should far excel anything of the kind that had yet taken place. Kept in waiting, accordingly, our hero was constantly attended by crowds, who watched and wondered at his every movement. "Grim courtiers," Smith himself styles them, more than two hundred in number, who stood gazing upon him "as he had beene a monster."

At length the signal was received, and the captors and the captive were vouchsafed an audience. Powhatan had completed his preparations. Himself and suite were assembled. The interview seems to have taken place in the open air, among the great trees of the forest; a pleasant space in the woods, which, as we may reasonably conjecture, was usually assigned for similar purposes—for the reception of ambassadors, a seat of judgment, and a place of fatal sacrifice together. Certainly there could not be a more royal saloon. Great pines sent up their gigantic pillars; wide spreading oaks stretched their gnarled and antling branches overhead; and through the umbrageous masses the blue canopy of the sky was visible and hanging over all. Conspicuous in this area, sate, or rather reclined, the Indian Emperor. His seat of state was a sort of bedstead, raised about a foot above the ground, upon which he might either sit or recline at pleasure. Some ten or a dozen mats formed the covering of this rude seat, immediately in front of which a great fire was kept blazing. Upon this couch or throne, half lying, in something like Oriental state, the form of Powhatan was seen between the persons of two young damsels, neither of whom was more than eighteen years of age. These were, in all probability, the favorites of our forest sultan. On either hand, and ranging behind this group, were the warriors and the women who formed the suite of the Emperor. These were sitting or standing in alternate rows, and were all apparelled in such ornaments as they could respectively command. Some had their heads decorated with the white down, and the plumage of native birds. Some wore strings of white beads upon their necks and bosoms. Others were otherwise adorned; and all of them appeared with cheeks, brows and shoulders thickly painted with a brilliant red. But the chief, as the central figure of the group, was Powhatan himself; a man who needed not the foreign aid of ornament to render him conspicuous in any circle. This prince, at the period of which we write, was fully sixty years of age. But time had taken nothing from the intense fire in his eye, and in no respect subdued the erect energies of his ample stature. His aspect was severe and noble. His presence was majestical. His bearing was that of one to whom sway was habitual, and the haughtiness of which seemed not unnatural or improper to one accustomed to frequent conquest. "He wore," says Smith, "such a grave and majestical countenance, as drave me into admiration to see such state in a naked salvage." Yet Powhatan was no naked savage, and the rudeness of his state was by no means inconsistent with its dignity. The "rich chaynes of great pearles," which we are told encircled his neck, and the "great robe, made of rarowcun (racoon) skinnes," which covered his person—their tails all properly disposed and pendant—were no doubt worn with quite as much grace and majesty as the most costly habiliments of civilisation by the potentates of Christendom. Indeed, it is not often that the dignitaries of the civilized world—

the creatures of a capricious art, and an unstable convention—could compare in nobleness of bearing with the lords of the American forest, taught by nature herself, and with limbs rendered free and graceful in spontaneous movement, by the constant exercises of battle and the chase. It is certain, at least, from all accounts, that Powhatan needed quite as little of dress and decoration for the purposes of state as any hereditary prince in Europe. The face, the air, the carriage of the Emperor, seemed fully to justify the unlimited sway which he held over the affections of his people. Whatever might have been the deficiencies of our forest chieftain, it is very sure that the qualities of a noble bearing, lofty demeanor, calm grave intelligence of aspect, and free natural movements were not among them. His grace in the management of ceremonial shows him "to the manner born;" and, subsequently, speaking of him at another interview under less trying circumstances to himself, Smith describes him sitting "uppon a throne at the upper ende of the house, with such a majestie as I cannot expresse, nor yet have often seene, either in pagan or Christian;"—a brief but complete description, to which farther details could give no efficiency.

There was one person in this assembly whom yet we are not permitted to see. This is Pocahontas. That she was present we know from the conspicuous share which she took in the proceedings of the day. But no place has been assigned her at the opening of the scene by any of our narrators. It is very apparent that she was not seen by Smith until the moment when she rushed forward to his rescue; and this exclusion may be easily accounted for. At this period Pocahontas was a child of ten years old. It has been the error to describe her as twelve or thirteen. This is the statement in Stith, Burke, and other writers, but it is without authority. Others have confounded her with one of the two young women who sate at the head and feet of Powhatan; but Smith himself describes them as "young wenches, of 16 or 18 years,"—a phraseology which he never employs where Pocahontas is concerned. In the narrative of Simons in Smith's history, no allusion is given to her age. She is spoken of as the "King's dearest daughter," always respectfully and affectionately, but in no more definite manner. The deficiency is supplied, however, in the narrative entitled a "True Relation," &c.,* purporting to be written by Th. Watson, Gent., but in reality by Smith himself. The internal proofs of this are quite conclusive, even if there were no other. In this narrative we have this description: "*Powhatan, understanding we detained certain salvages, sent his daughter, a childe of tenne years old, which not only for feature, countenance and proportion, much exceedeth any of the rest of his people, but for wit and spirit the only nonpareil of his country, &c.*" That the girl here described was Pocahontas we know elsewhere from the narrative of Simons, who makes full mention of the mission upon which she is sent, the particulars of which we shall reach hereafter.

That a child of ten years old should not be conspicuous

---

* "A true relation of such occurrences and accidents of noate as hath happened in Virginia since the first planting of that collony, which is now resident in the south part thereof, 'till the last returne from thence. Written by Th: Watson, *Gent.*, *one of said collony*, to a worshipfull friend of his in England. London: Printed for John Tappe; and are to be sold at the Grey-hound in Paule's Church-yard, by W. W. 1608." The copy before us is an excellent reprint, made by the publishers of the Southern Literary Messenger, and in connection with that excellent periodical. A preface to this pamphlet, signed L. H., and purporting to be written while Smith is still one of the council in Virginia, asserts him to be the author of it, and ascribes the *alias* to the blunder of a printer.

at such a scene as that to which Smith is conducted, is natural enough. She may have been concealed in one of the troops of damsels that stood behind or beside the couch of her father; she might have been sitting, timidly crouching, on some low rock at his feet. That she was present, and destined to exercise a vital influence upon the events which were to follow, we already know.

The appearance of the captive before the king was welcomed by a shout from all the people. This does not appear to have been an outbreak of exultation. On the contrary, the disposition seems to have been to treat the prisoner with becoming gravity and consideration. A handsome young woman, the Queen of Apamattuck, is commanded to bring him water, in which to wash his hands. Another stands by with a bunch of feathers, a substitute for the towel, with which he dries them. Food is then put before him, and he is instructed to eat, while a long consultation takes place between the Emperor and his chief warriors as to what shall be done with the captive. In this question Smith is quite too deeply interested to give himself entirely to the repast before him. He keeps up a stout heart and a manly countenance; but, to employ some of the lines quoted by the quaint narrator whose statements he adopts,

——"Sure his heart was sad;
For who can pleasant be and rest,
That lives in feare and dread?"

The discussion results unfavorably. His judges decide against him. It is the policy of the savages to destroy him. He is their great enemy. He is the master spirit of the powerful and intrusive strangers. They have already discovered this. They have seen that by his will and energies, great courage and equal discretion, he has kept down the discontents, disarmed the rebellious, and strengthened the feeble among his brethren; and they have sagacity enough to understand how much more easy it will be, in the absence of this one adventurous warrior, to overthrow and root out the white colony which he has planted. It is no brutal passion for blood and murder which prompts their resolution. It is a simple and clear policy, such as has distinguished the decision in like cases of far more civilized, and even Christian communities;—and the award of the council of Powhatan is instant death to the prisoner. He is soon apprised of their decision by their proceedings. Two great stones are brought into the assembly, and laid before the king. "Then as many as could lay hands on him, dragged him to them, and thereon layd his head." "Being ready with their clubs to beate out his braines," it was then that "Pocahontas, the King's dearest daughter," interposed for his safety. It seems that she first strove to move her father by entreaties, but finding these of no avail, she darted to the place of execution, and before she could be prevented, got the head of the captive in her arms, and laying her own upon it, in this way arrested the stroke of the executioner. And this was the action of a child ten years old! We may imagine the exquisite beauty of such a spectacle—the infantine grace, the feminine tenderness, the childish eagerness, mingled with uncertainty and fear, with which she maintained her hold upon the object of her concern and solicitude, until the wild and violent passion of her father had been appeased. This is all that comes to us of the strange, but exquisite dramatic spectacle. Few details are given us. The original narrators from whom we draw are cold and lifeless in their statements. Smith himself says little on the subject; and in the narrative already quoted—that of Watson—especially known as his, it is curious to note that the whole event is omitted, not even

Saved by Pocahontas. PAGE 150.

the slightest allusion being made to Pocahontas. But it is not denied that we may conceive for ourselves the beauty and the terror of this highly tragic scene. Imagination may depict the event in her most glowing colors. The poet and the painter will make it their own. They will show us the sweet child of the forest clasping beneath her arm the head of the pale warrior, while the stroke of death, impending over both, awaits but the nod of the mighty chieftain, whose will is law in all that savage region. They will show us first the rage and fury which fill his eyes as he finds himself baffled by his child, and then the softening indulgence with which he regards that pleading sweetness in her glance which has always had such power over his soul. "She was the King's dearest daughter:"—this is the language of the unaffected and simple chroniclers, and her entreaty prevails for the safety of the prisoner. Her embrace seems to have consecrated from harm the head of the strange intruder. The policy of her nation, their passion for revenge and blood, all yield to the potent humanity which speaks in the heart of that unbaptized daughter of the forest, and the prisoner is freed from his bonds and given to the damsel who has saved him. Henceforth he is her captive. That is the decree of Powhatan. He shall be spared to make her bells and her beads, and to weave, into proper form, her ornaments of copper.

CHAPTER VII.

The effect of this timely interposition of Pocahontas was not limited to the mere saving of our hero's life. The results were highly advantageous in other respects to the colony of the English. It secured for it the tolerance of the Emperor, while it gained for Smith himself the special favor and friendship of the savage. In all probability the superstitious, not less than the human feelings of Powhatan, were touched by the unlooked for interference of his daughter in the bloody scene which he was preparing to enact. Such a boldness at the perilous and precious moment, in a child so young, might well awaken, even in more sophisticated natures, an impression that the act was of providential inspiration—the work of a superior agency. At all events, the benefits were soon apparent. Smith was not only spared, but taken into immediate favor. The Emperor assured him of his friendship, professed to regard him as his own son, and promised him his liberty in a few days. But these favors were coupled with conditions. Powhatan was ambitious of being the possessor of certain of the great guns, of whose terrible powers vague accounts had already reached his ears. The uses of a grindstone were also known to him, and one of these was an object of his desire. To obtain these chattels, he promised his captive the entire country of Capahosick; a territory the limits of which it would perhaps be somewhat difficult at this day to define.

Smith was somewhat cheered by these assurances, and this display of kindness; but he put little faith in the sincerity of the savage monarch. He was conscious himself of a certain degree of practice in his own assurances, and felt but little confidence, accordingly, in what was told him. Their conferences together were very frequent, and on the best footing of amity. What had been told of our hero to Powhatan had evidently impressed him greatly with his ability and courage. All that he had previously related to Opechancanough was now to be repeated; and a thousand questions were asked with regard to the coming and objects of the English, which it required all the prudence and subtlety of Smith to answer, without endangering the friendly relations between the parties. It need not be said that our adventurer made no scruple of suppressing the truth where it served his purpose to do so. He had discovered that the Indians of Powhatan had suffered some injuries from Spanish vessels, and he framed his own story to suit the prejudices of his hearer. His people had been overpowered in a fight with the Spaniards, their enemies, and had sought shelter in the Chesapeake. The story was plausible, and the enmity of both to the Spaniards was the source of a new tie between them. But his exploring voyage in a canoe to the heads of the rivers of the country, suggested a new doubt to Powhatan, and new difficulties to his captive. But to his questions on this head the ready invention of Smith found a prompt answer. A brother had been slain by a people living in the rear of the territories of Powhatan, who were supposed to be the Monacans, his enemies also. The murder of this youth it was his business to revenge. These motives our savage found very good and justifiable, and led Powhatan into a description of his territories and those of his neighbors; how they lay, and how they were watered; what was the number, and what were the habits of the Anchawachucks—whom he assumed to be those by whom Smith's brother had been slain—and the "Pocoughtronacks, a fierce nation, who did eate men." Some of these people were described as carrying "swords like pollaxes," and wearing long hair on the neck, though their crowns were shaven. Beyond the territories of these, Powhatan described yet other tribes, some of whom wore short coats, with sleeves to the elbows, and travelled the seas in ships like those of the English. He had other tales of yet other kingdoms and people—vague outlines which, when we consider the imperfect modes among the savages of estimating time and distance, it would be quite unprofitable to examine or review. Smith, however, drank in his statements with attentive ears. A mighty river was described by Powhatan, having numerous kingdoms on its banks, which might be the Mississippi; the imperfect knowledge of the languages of the parties rendering doubtful between them, even matters the most precise and natural. A clothed people, cities of walled houses, a people having abundance of brass—or gold; these were the wonders which the Indian Emperor related to his European companion, expatiating upon his own and the prowess of his tributaries and rivals. Smith was not to be outdone in wonders. In requital for the geography and history of Apalachia, he bestowed upon Powhatan a comprehensive account of all the wonders of Europe;—the multitude of ships and cities—the thunders of their wars—the glories of their martial array—and the ear-piercing character of drums and trumpets. Our sagacious adventurer knew well in what manner to awaken the admiration, and compel the respect of the dusky chieftain. He took care to impress him with the military powers in the possession of Captain Newport, who was daily expected with supplies from England; and whom, adopting an Indian title, the better to be understood, he called the

Werowance, or Prince, of all the waters of the sea. By this timely suggestion he made it easy sailing for Newport in after days.

These mutual communications greatly increased the intimacy between the parties, though Smith does not seem to have foregone his doubts of the good faith of Powhatan, until he was fairly beyond his power. His detention lasted but a few days, which were naturally demanded by the curiosity of the Indian monarch, and his people. Indeed, less time could scarcely have been yielded to the immense amount of diplomacy which was required between them. So greatly did Powhatan come to admire his European acquaintance in the sequel, that he desired him to forsake the country of Paspahegh, where he had settled, and to come more closely into the immediate neighborhood of Werowocomocco. He promised that the English should lose nothing by it, but that he would supply them with all necessaries—with corn, venison, and all manner of food, and protect them against all enemies, for which he should demand nothing but their labor in finding him in hatchets, and working copper for him according to instructions. Smith gave him good words, and spoke him fairly but evasively. He promised him his great guns, and grindstones, as soon as he should get to Jamestown; and after being treated with a hospitality and kindness, which Smith acknowledges without reserve, he despatched him under the charge of twelve men* on his way to the colony.

* "*Twelve guides*" according to the "Discoveries" and "Accidents." The "True Relation" says *four*, and with such detail that the sentence deserves to be given. "Having, with all the kindness hee could devise, sought to content me, he sent me home with 4 men,—one that usually carried my gowne and knapsack after me, two others loaded with bread, and one to accompany me." Both

But the apprehensions of Smith were not to be lulled into quiet, by all these shows of kindness, and one or more little circumstances, while on the journey, kept him in a state of lively apprehension. He still had his fears that he was to be eaten, and that this was the true secret of all their solicitude in feasting him. He was only to be fattened, and decorated, like a lamb for the slaughter. The distance, in a direct route, from Werowocomocco to Jamestown, was only twelve miles, yet nothing could persuade his guides to advance properly forward. "The Indians trifled away that day, and would not goe to our fort by any persuasions." The first night after leaving Powhatan, they "quartered in the woods," so we are told by one narrative; another, more certainly his own, says, "in certain olde hunting houses of Paspahegh, we lodged all night." "He still expecting (as he had done all this long time of his imprisonment) every houre to be put to one death or other, for all their feasting." But his apprehensions proved groundless. "Almighty God (by his divine providence) had mollified the hearts of those sterne barbarians with compassion." They neither killed nor eat him; but, whatever might have been their motive for the unnecessary delay, "the nexte morning, ere sunrise, we set forward for our fort, where we arrived within an hour."

Here Smith found himself welcomed on every hand with the truest shows of friendship and satisfaction. He

---

narratives may be correct; other Indians may have joined them *en route;* and when we recollect that grindstones, and great guns, were to be carried back by the savages, twelve of them will not be deemed an excessive number for the escort. One would think too, that two men to *carry* the bread alone, would be a rather large proportion to the number which it was to feed, if these were limited to *four*. The point, however, is of no great importance.

was greeted as one from the dead; it was as if the grave had given up its prey; and in his absence, and supposed loss, the colonists, perhaps for the first time, began to feel how necessary he had been to their safety, and the success of the settlement. Things had gone ill during his absence, and there were some few exceptions to the almost universal language of congratulation which hailed his return. Captain Archer, who had been sworn of the council, in his place, and while he was supposed to have perished, was by no means glad to see him; and there were some two or three of his creatures, who suffered him to see that he was much less likely to offend them while he remained with the Indians, than when he came to thwart their progress in the infant settlement. His return was exceedingly opportune. He found a large party of discontents preparing once more to run away with the pinnace, and to break up the colony. Their plans were laid, and the appointed hour had arrived, and all was baffled again by his providential coming. He soon fathomed their schemes, and being rightly advised, with the soldier-like decision that distinguished all his actions, he put the fort and his chosen men in order, so that the mutineers could only succeed in the teeth of "sackre, falcon and musket shot," in getting off with the pinnace. "For the third time," at "the hazzard of his life," Smith "forced them to stay, or sinke."

Finding that they must submit, and that nothing could be effected with such a "master of fence" at his own weapons, they had recourse to subtleties, under the name of law, for the better overthrow of their arch enemy. Having laid their own heads together, and so confounded that of the President, Captain Martin, as for the time to get his sanction to their proceedings, they charged upon Smith the death of the two men, Emry and Robinson, who had been slain by the Indians, at the time of his capture. The Levitical law was applied to the case of our adventurer, and, urging that it was by his fault or practice that they had come by their death, they required that his life should atone for his crime or error. The two persons, for whose lives he was thus required to answer, had fallen victims to their own imprudence, and the neglect of Smith's especial orders. Upon this charge, so very absurd, they built their hopes to take his life, or at all events to depose him from his sway in the colony, and his seat at the council. But Smith was too much of a man and soldier to be caught, and thrown upon his back, by such flimsy subtleties as this. He quickly took such order with these crude colony lawyers, that he laid them by the heels, and had them very soon as prisoners on the high road to England. The timely arrival of Captain Newport enabled him more effectually to triumph over his enemies. Newport saw through their malice, and his support and sympathy served for a time to silence and to subdue all disaffection to that authority which it was in the nature of such a man as Smith to exercise, in every situation of difficulty and distress. The want of food which ensued upon his absence from the colony, had given strength to the objects of the malcontents, none of whom seems to have possessed the ability, the courage, and the skill by which Smith had always before succeeded in procuring the requisite supplies. His failure and captivity served completely to discourage their enterprise. His resolution, and determination to keep the discontents from leaving the colony, were assisted by the news he brought of the favor of Powhatan, and of the abundance of food which might be obtained from that savage chieftain, in this season of his good humor ; and his story of the rescue of his life by Pocahontas, " so revived their dead spirits," as to make almost all of them abandon their fears of famine. They saw in this alliance with the greatest potentate of the country, and in the affection which he and his daughter had conceived for their favorite leader, a guaranty against all the privations of the future; and, as is usual with persons of such condition, were as easily persuaded to the extreme of hope and exultation, as, but a little while before, and with as slender reason, they had been hurried to the verge of despair and mutiny. "Now whether," writes John Smith, though his chapter is claimed to be the production of three others* besides himself, though his hand is clearly legible in every sentence; "Now, whether it had beene better for Captaine *Smith* to have concluded with any of those severall projects, to have abandoned the countrey, with some ten or twelve of them, *who were called the better sort*, and have left Mr. *Hunt* our Preacher, Master *Anthony Gosnell*, a most honest, worthy, and industrious Gentleman, Master *Thomas Wotton*, and some 27 others of his countrymen, to the fury of the savages, famine, and all manner of mischiefes and inconveniences (for they were but fortie in all to keepe possession of this large countrey), or starve himself with them for company, for want of lodging; or for adventuring abroad to make them provision, or by his opposition to preserve the action, and save all their lives (here the four writers dwindle into the first person singular), "I," here Smith speaks out for himself—"I leave all honest men to consider," is the conclusion of the paragraph. Time has saved us the work of consideration. The results have justified the proceedings of our hero. We must not omit to notice his allusion here to the "ten or twelve" called "the better sort." Smith, from the be-

* Written by *Thomas Studley*, the first cape merchant in *Virginia*, *Robert Fenton*, *Edward Harrington*, and *I. S.* (note to Chap. 2, Book 3, of the "*True Travels*."

ginning, complains of the vast disproportion between the workingmen and the gentlemen sent to the colony. The passage which we have just quoted, is evidently meant as argumentative and justificatory, and intended to neutralize the opinions which the representations of these gentlemen in England might provoke at his expense.

Smith did not suffer the commotions and strifes at Jamestown to make him forgetful of his Indian guides, and the promises he had made to Powhatan. Having fed and housed them well, endeavoring as well as he could to impress them equally with his magnificence and hospitality, he called them up on the morning after his return, and placed the great guns and the grindstones before them. The cannon proffered them were two demi-culverins. The weight of a grindstone, of ordinary size, may be imagined. It is needless to say that a single trial of Indian strength upon these formidable masses, soon put out of their heads entirely, the notion that they could be carried upon their shoulders; and their reluctance to make the attempt was greatly increased, when stuffing the bowels of his cannon with a decent load of powder and stones, Smith applied the torch, and allowed them to hear the bellowing thunder, and see the wild lightning which issued from their jaws. And when they saw the effect among the trees of the forest, their great boughs loaded with icicles, torn away by the shot, and tumbling in all directions to the ground, the trusty followers of Powhatan took to their heels, half dead with fear. They could not be persuaded to burden themselves with gifts, as terrible as they were burdensome and weighty. But our adventurer did not send them away with empty hands. He was not ungrateful to Powhatan, still less was he indifferent to the sympathies of the sweet forest damsel to whose warm humanities he was indebted for his life. For her he felt a deep attachment, such, perhaps, as a father might feel for a dear child, as precious to him by reason of her own merits, as by blood. It is one of the vulgar errors of modern times that Pocahontas felt for Smith a different sort of attachment, and it is made his reproach, that he showed himself insensible to her love. This is mere ignorance and absurdity. By his own showing she was but ten years old at this period, and he was near thirty. He speaks of her always as a child—as a dear child; and it is evident he thought her so, and her language for him is that only of veneration. It is an erroneous notion of the requisites of the romantic, to demand that a warmer sentiment than that of father and daughter should spring up between such parties. It is to this notion only, that we owe the charge of ingratitude which has been made against Smith, because of his supposed neglect of her affections. But of this hereafter. Enough that he sent away his Indian guides well satisfied with the commodities substituted for the great guns and the grindstone. Nor does it anywhere appear that Powhatan was any whit less contented with what he received, than his messengers with what they bore.

BOOK THIRD.

CHAPTER I.

The captivity of Smith among the people of Powhatan lasted for nearly seven weeks. Though painfully, this time was not unprofitably spent. Habitually a close observer, he gathered a very large amount of useful knowledge from the Indians; learned to comprehend their modes of thinking and feeling; to trace their motives; to analyze their arts; and to fathom, with great sagacity, their general character. That he mistakes frequently, and misrepresents, is to be expected from his imperfect knowledge of their language, and from the policy of the savage, who is cautious, circumspect, and peculiarly anxious to avoid examination. Smith finds them brave, capable of great endurance, a simple but a shrewd people, and cunning and treacherous, as all inferior people are apt to prove themselves when brought into contact with a superior. If anything, he undervalues them, and withholds a proper acknowledgment of their virtues. He was quite too much the soldier of that period to escape the usual prejudices of the class, and cannot well be expected to think well of a race by whom he expects momently to be eaten—sacrificed to their hideous god, with an unpronounceable name, Quioughquosickee; their Devil, as Dr. Simons writes, but most likely their god of physic. Setting forth with a notion very common at that time in the

European world, that the savages of the unknown regions are generally cannibals, he looks with a jaundiced eye, and with growing suspicion of their objects, even when they are practising the highest virtues of hospitality and society. It is because of prejudices such as these, that the mild European became himself so frequently a savage when he found himself in contact with the wild and wicked inhabitants of the western world. Smith despised the race because of their feebleness and unperformance; and feared and hated them because of their supposed indulgence in habits and practices, from which subsequent experience shows that they were perfectly free. But, in their power, he was sagacious enough to betray none of these prejudices or passions. He could play the politician, when it served his turn, as well as the soldier; and the stroke of death once suspended by the interposition of Pocahontas, he puts forth all the cunning of his right hand, to maintain himself in the position of favor which he has so unexpectedly won. He flattered the pride of Powhatan, and conciliated the stranger chiefs around him. He was soon enabled to observe what were the distinguishing traits of the savage, and to ascertain in what respects they were peculiarly susceptible. To their vanity, which is strong in the Indian bosom, he made judicious appeals; and, while flattering their self-esteem, he contrived very happily to impress them with admiration of his own wonderful resources. To make them feel and respect his importance, without subjecting their own vanity to mortification, might be a matter of some difficulty; but, as his experience proved, it was not an impossible one.

To us, with our better knowledge of the Indians and the country than he could possibly have acquired then, his description of these objects can possess but little value. We refer to them now only to show how vigilant was his observation, and how generally extensive and correct. But the knowledge which he thus obtained was of vast service in his day, to the colony, and of very considerable interest in Europe, in correcting the erroneous impressions which were generally afloat in regard to the American aborigines. To the colony it came at an auspicious juncture, as it occasioned renewed confidence in an enterprise which, in the treaty of amnesty and amity made with Powhatan, seemed to have received the last essential and desirable sanction. Nor did events for some time contradict the sanguine assurances of Smith, and the eager hopes of his people. The Indians seemed all of a sudden to have reformed the usual caprice of their character. The intimacy begun with Powhatan was kept alive by a frequent interchange of good offices between the parties; and the young maiden, Pocahontas, with her attendants, made frequent visits to Jamestown, bringing with her such abundant supplies of provision, that hunger and the dread of starvation was no longer the object of terror among the doubting and the discontent. The visits of Pocahontas are described, at this period, as occurring every four or five days. Female, and childish, and savage curiosity were all no doubt combined in effecting this intimacy, and the provisions were, in all probability, only brought as a pretext for the visit. But other Indians came daily, all bringing something in the shape of food, either as gifts from Powhatan or Pocahontas, or as their own tribute to the superior genius of the man, who, to employ the language of one of the narratives before us, "had so inchanted these poore soules being their prisoner."* The arrival of Captain Newport just about the time when

* Chap. iii., iv. and v. of the "Discoveries and Accidents," ascribed to Walter Russell, Anas Todkill, and Thomas Momford.

Smith had assured them he would come, increased their confidence in his wonderful superiority; and, regarding him as an oracle, he brought them to such a degree of submission that "he might command them at what he listed;" and in this deference they came habitually to acknowledge the God of the Christians, whom they spoke of commonly as the "God of Captaine Smith." To Smith, indeed, and to him only, all their reverence was shown. It was not until he made his appearance that they could be persuaded to approach the fort; but in the cover of the woods they remained, calling him by name, and coming forward as soon as he showed himself at the entrance. Nothing would they sell till they had placed all that they had at his discretion. He affixed the prices to their commodities, and with these they always seemed very well satisfied. This attachment, so confiding and extreme, on the part of those who had always shown themselves so jealous and suspicious in their intercourse with strangers, became a new subject of annoyance to the vain men, the malcontents within the fort, by whom the abilities of Smith were always decried, and his power so frequently resisted. His estimation among the savages was a subject of envy among his Christian brethren in council, some of whom were at the pains to labor diligently in the endeavor to dispossess the Indians of their overweening attachment for their associate. In this labor of love their objects were promoted greatly by the looseness and indulgence which followed upon the arrival of Newport's vessels. New faces from the mother country, with the fresh supplies which they brought, occasioned such general gratification, that the mariners were suffered the freedom of the settlement. They soon ruined the market with the Indians. Smith had prudently rated the wares of the English at the values set upon them by the Indians themselves ; the desires of the purchaser constituting the standard by which the worth of the commodity was to be measured. By this means, maize, beans, and venison, the usual articles brought for sale by the savages, were easily procured with small quantities of European goods. But the profligacy of the seamen soon defeated all the prudent policy of Smith, and rendered it easy to persuade the Indians of the mistake which they had made in so highly esteeming his power. It was soon found that a pound of copper could not now buy the grain which an ounce could formerly procure ; and the greatness of Smith sunk completely out of sight in the vast stature which Captain Newport acquired among the traders of Powhatan. Thus, says our author quaintly, " ambition and sufferance cut the throat of our trade."

Such being the condition of affairs, our hero persuaded Captain Newport that a visit to Powhatan himself, at Werowocomoco, would be a proper and advantageous proceeding. It was desirable to impress that savage chieftain with a high idea of the power of the English people. It was also highly important to confirm the good understanding, and to extend the intercourse which had been established between the parties. Newport concurred with Smith in this policy, and sending certain presents to Powhatan, as from Newport, Smith advised the former of the projected visit. For this, preparations were at once made on both sides. The pinnace was prepared, and Smith and Newport, with some thirty or forty chosen men, as a guard, proceeded towards Worowocomoco, provided with the usual articles of Indian traffic. As they drew nigh to the immediate territories of Powhatan, the good Captain Newport, who had no sort of experience as an Indian fighter, or perhaps as a fighter of any kind, began to entertain some misgivings as to the prudence of the adventure. He had heard a great deal of Indian treachery, and his apprehensions of danger increased with his meditations upon what he had heard. He soon suffered Smith to see that he was exceedingly reluctant at being caught in a predicament, such as that from which the latter had so recently and narrowly escaped. His knight-errantry was not of a sort to be easily reconciled to the peril, by the possible pleasant romance which might attend his rescue from it; and it tasked all the argument of Smith to persuade him to a continuance of the project. There were certain appearances about the shores of Werowocomoco, which, in particular, alarmed his fears. The landing was not a good one, creeks were to be crossed, and over these the Indians had thrown some rude contrivances in the fashion of a bridge, which, to the suspicious eyes of Newport, seemed neither more nor less than traps, in which, when his legs were once fairly entangled, his overthrow and execution were easy. We can very well fancy with what difficulty a veteran like Smith concealed his scorn at this show of imbecility. He, at length, as little troubled by fears of personal danger, or of any sort, as any man, dead or living, volunteered, at the head of twenty men of the party, to go ahead, and "encounter the worst that could happen." To this arrangement Newport consented, and while he remained in the pinnace, with one-half of the force, Smith set out with his "twenty shot armed in Jacks,"* and going ashore, was met by a number of the Indians, among whom was the king's son, Nantaquis, the chief by whom he had been captured, and many other persons of distinction. These accompanied him on his journey, though Smith so contrived to intermingle with

* Mail, or quilted jackets, generally in modern times a merely padded garment, affording partial protection against Indian arrows.

his own men, the king's son and their chiefs, as, in the event of any mischief, to have them sufficiently in his power to enable him to control their followers through their fears. His caution seems to have been unnecessary. Their progress was unembarrassed, and the behavior of the Indians was equally kind and unexceptionable.

Powhatan received our hero with a great show of rejoicing and state. "Sitting upon his bed of mats, his pillow of leather imbrodered (after their rude manner, with pearle and white beads), his attyre a fine robe of skinnes, as large as an Irish mantell; at his head and feete a handsome younge woman; on each side his house sat twentie of his concubines, their heads and shoulders painted red, with a great chaine of white beades about each of their neckes. Before those sat his chiefest men, in like order in his arbour-like house, and more than fortie platters of fine bread stood as a guard in two fyles on each side the doore. Foure or five hundred people made a guard behinde them for our passage, and proclamation was made, none upon paine of death to presume to do us any wrong or discourtesie."

This certainly shows well for the barbaric state of the forest chieftain. It is not difficult to believe that Smith spoke without exaggeration when, describing the noble appearance of this proud savage, he says, "it is of such a majestie as I cannot well expresse, nor yet have often seene, either in Pagan or Christian. With a kind countenance he bade all welcome, and caused a place to bee made by himselfe to sit." Smith presented him with a suit of red cloth, a white greyhound, and a hat. These were welcomed with an address, in which they were kindly accepted, in proof of the perpetual friendship which was to exist between the parties. Water was brought for the ablutions of the guest, and food was set before him.

"But where is your father?" meaning Newport, was the demand of Powhatan. Smith promised that he should see him the next day. The next question was propounded with a merry countenance. "Where are the great guns which you promised me when you went to Paspahegh?" Powhatan was prepared for the answer. He had heard from his trusty messenger Rawhunt, what had been the difficulty in bringing them; and when Smith told him that his guns had proved too great for his people's shoulders, he laughed heartily, but concluded with demanding, in place of them, some of a less burthen. The twenty followers of Smith were then brought before him. They had been well instructed by Smith to maintain a vigilant watch, even while making their obeisance. They received each of them an ample supply of food, and Smith then reminded Powhatan of the corn and land which he had promised him. "He tolde me I should have it, but he expected to have all these men lay their arms at his feete, as did his subjects. I tolde him that was a ceremonie our enemies desired, but never our friends." Smith proceeded to exhort him not to doubt the friendship of the English; that on the ensuing day Captain Newport, his father, would confirm his assurances to this effect, and would bestow upon him a child of his own, in proof of his sincerity; and that whenever he, Powhatan, should be prepared for the enterprise, he should put under his subjection the territories of his worst enemies, the Monacans and Pocoughtronachs. These assurances highly delighted the Emperor, who at once, in a loud oration, created the speaker a Werowance or chief of Powhatan. The conference was much more prolonged, but entirely to the same effect, and, with the warmest assurances of friendship on both sides, the parties separated. But the ebbing of the tide preventing Smith from regaining the pinnace that night; he returned to the hospitalities of Powhatan, who was again delighted to receive him, and their conference was resumed "with many pretty discourses." The day was fairly spent in speeches and feasting, interspersed with sports, with dancing and singing, and such like mirth. "A great house, sufficient to harbor the whole of his men," was assigned to Smith, and a quarter of venison sent him "to stay his stomache." His supper, which was taken at the table of Powhatan, was a much more serious business. "He set before mee meate for twentie men, and seeing I coulde not eate, hee caused it to be given to my men; for this is a general custom, when they give, not to take again, but you must either eate it, give it away, or carry it with you." Two or three hours after supper were "spent in our ancient discourses, which done, I was with a fire sticke (pine torch) lighted to my lodgings." Early the next day, Powhatan conducted Smith to the banks of the river, and made a display to him of his numerous canoes,—a fleet of which the savage king thought quite as proudly, no doubt, as our provincials before the American Revolution thought of that of George the Third. The various uses to which they were put, were detailed particularly to his hearers. Some of them were especially employed in bringing him tribute from the subject tribes along the Chesapeake. Some countries paid him in beads, others in skins, and others again in copper. While engaged in this survey, they descried Captain Newport approaching from the pinnace; upon which, leaving Smith to conduct his coadjutor to his royal presence, Powhatan retired, that he might place himself in his usual state array for a royal reception.

The English captain was no doubt exceedingly anxious about the absence of Smith. How he himself had slept was exceedingly doubtful. In all probability, a confused murmur of Indian song and festivity had been ringing in his ears and through his dreams all night, faint echoes of the merriment which welcomed his comrade in the tents of Powhatan. This, it is possible that he construed into the song of sacrifice over the dismembered carcass of his comrade. That he found him alive and in good spirits when he came ashore, was no doubt a subject of equal satisfaction to both. They approached the royal residence to the sound of trumpets, and with as much state as they could summon for the occasion. Their appearance before the king was hailed, as was that of Smith on the previous day, with shouts and acclamations. Then followed speeches from various chiefs, full of professions of good faith and fellowship. Powhatan, in the language of one of our authors, "strained himself to the utmost of his greatnesse to entertaine his distinguished guests." The proud savage was not to be outdone in bravery by the more courtly Europeans. State and ceremonial were, indeed, much more natural to him than to any of his visitors. He was born "in the purple," and it appears from all testimonies that his ordinary carriage would have done honor to that of any of the oldest houses of Europe. His manner of reception did not differ in any respect from that of the preceding day. He occupied his place of state, and was surrounded, as before, by his chiefs and an imposing array of young women. His reception of Newport was frank and generous. Food and refreshments, the song and the dance, were employed to grace the favor which the Emperor vouchsafed to the strangers; and these civilities were followed by pledges of amity which it would be difficult to persuade modern philanthropy to sanction. A white boy named Thomas Salvage, whom Newport did not hesitate to call his son, was presented to Powhatan; the Indian king, in return, bestowing upon the English captain a native lad named Namontack, "for his trustie servant;" who is described as of "shrewd and subtill capacitie."

In this interchange of courtesies that day passed, the English returning at night to their pinnace. The day following, their conferences were resumed. Powhatan having entertained them with breakfast, reproached them for bringing their arms to the interview. He pointed them to his followers, all of whom appeared without weapons. Was he not their friend? What did they doubt? What fear? Why this distrust? Smith answered, that it was the custom of their country; but to quiet his apprehensions, Newport caused his soldiers to retire to the water side; and, to prevent evil, Smith accompanied them. But this did not satisfy Powhatan. He was not disposed to suffer the absence of Smith from his immediate scrutiny. To please him, Mr. Scrivener, one of the council, and an intelligent gentleman, who had arrived with Newport from England, was sent to take Smith's place. But such an arrangement was scarcely more satisfactory to the wily savage than the other; and the attempt to pacify him by such proceedings was suspended in order to try the effect of a vigorous traffic, and by these means the suspicions of Powhatan, if he really entertained them, were baffled and diverted. Three or four days were consumed, and not unpleasantly, in this sort of intercourse. Songs and speeches, feasting and dancing, with now and then a little traffic, admirably relieved the monotony of this state and diplomatic intercourse. In all this time, says our author, "Powhatan carried himselfe so proudly, yet discreetly (in his salvage manner), as made us all admire his naturall gifts, considering his education." He himself scorned to trade as did his subjects.

"It is not agreeable to my greatness," he said to Newport, " to traffic for trifles in this peddling manner. You, too, I esteem also as a great Werowance.* Therefore, lay me downe all your commodities together. What I like I will take, and in recompense give you what I thinke their fitting value."

Smith was the interpreter between the parties, and it speaks wonderfully for his great facility that so short an acquaintance with the Indians had enabled him to be so. He at once detected the cunning policy of Powhatan, admirably disguised in this majestic carriage, and he warned Newport that his purpose was only to cheat him of his goods. But Newport, not to be outbraved in this ostentation of magnificence, and thinking that he should effectually bewitch the Indian Emperor by his bounty, at once laid his stores before him as he had demanded. The issue was just what had been predicted. Powhatan took what he pleased; and, in bestowing his recompense in turn, valued his maize at such a price as to extort from our Captain the opinion that the article was to be had on better terms, " even in Spaine." Instead of twenty hogsheads, which the same were expected to produce, the stately monarch assigned to the astounded Newport something less than four bushels. Newport could not conceal his chagrin. He had been effectually outwitted. His stores were exhausted, his supplies were yet to be procured, and the savage chieftain was as insatiate in his appetite as ever. The English captain lost his temper, and some unkindness followed between Smith and himself, in consequence, in all probability, of the reproaches of the latter. But our adventurer, who better knew the nature of the savage than Newport, had his revenge upon Powhatan. He contrived, without seeming to design it,

* Prince, or Chief.

to suffer various trifles, which were novelties, to glitter in the eyes of the voracious savage. Among these were certain blue beads, such as had never before been seen at Werowocomoco. These caught the fancy of our forest monarch. But Smith shook his head in denial. These were very precious jewels, "composed of a most rare substance, of the color of the skyes, and not to be worn but by the greatest kings of the world." The pride of Powhatan was piqued; his passions excited; and in due degree with the reluctance of Smith to sell, was the increase of his importunacy to buy. The wary Captain played with his game at his leisure, until it "made him halfe madde to be the owner of such strange jewells;" and he succeeded finally in procuring a pound or two of them, but only at the expense of two or three hundred bushels of corn. Blue beads rose prodigiously in value. Opechancanough, one of the brothers of Powhatan, became the purchaser of a small supply at the same royal prices; and such at length became the estimation in which they were held, "that none durst weare any of them but their greate kings, their wives and children."

CHAPTER II.

Powhatan did not suffer the cupidity of the trader to abridge the hospitalities of the prince. Though Smith had driven a hard bargain with him in the matter of the blue beads, he was yet particularly indulgent to that personage, who sometimes lingered in his tents after nightfall, and long after the more nervous Newport had gone aboard his pinnace. When it so happened that the ebb of the tide required the English to regain their pinnace before the usual dinner hour, the savage monarch sent their feast of bread and venison after them, in quantities equal to the wants of thrice their number. To the last he betrayed an impatience of their weapons. Whether it was that he really distrusted them, or whether, as is more probable, he designed to make himself master of their commodities without being compelled to supply his own, and could only hope to do so in the absence of the murderous instruments of war that the English carried, is matter for conjecture. Smith invariably contrived, without directly showing his apprehensions, to thwart his wishes in this particular. On one occasion, that of the last day of the visit, Powhatan sent his son on board the pinnace at an early hour, to entreat that they would not bring their pieces with them, lest his women should be frightened. But Smith, even against Newport's opinion, contrived to carry with him twenty-five shot. Powhatan took a special dislike to Smith's sword and pistol, and importuned him, in particular, to leave them in the pinnace. "But these," said our hero, significantly, "were the very terms of persuasion employed by those who afterwards betrayed us, and slew my brother." The women do not seem to have been frightened; and the day passed as before. The trade in blue beads was as lively as ever: large quantities —speaking with due regard to the extreme value, and great rareness of the article—changed hands, and the barge of the English was nearly freighted with provisions. The weather became unfavorable; and it was midnight, and after great exposure to wind and rain, besides being nearly swamped in the oozy embraces of a marsh, before Smith, and the parties under his immediate command, could regain the vessel. The next morning was given to their parting interview. At their meeting, Powhatan, "with a solemne discourse," dismissed all his women and the ordinary attendants, suffering none to remain but his principal chiefs. He then referred to what Smith had hinted of their purpose to invade the Monacans, his enemies. He informed them that he was not openly the enemy of this people; that there was peace between them; but that he was not unwilling to do a little towards giving them trouble and discomfort. He would first send out his spies to see in what condition the Monacans stood; what was their strength and ability; and how far prepared against invasion.

Politicians seem to be pretty much the same persons in all countries. Metternich and Talleyrand, Peel or Guizot, could not have declared themselves in more diplomatic language.

"You and I," he said to Captain Newport, "cannot be seen in the business. We are great chiefs, and must stay at home. But Smith and Scrivener on your side, and Opechancanough and my two sons on mine, can manage all this business."—This, if not the language of the old despot, was pretty much what he meant to say. We have quoted in our own terms the very substance of his speech. He added, that the King of Pamaunkeeshould have from him one hundred of his warriors to commence the campaign. They should set forth as upon a hunting expedition, advising the English at what proper time to strike the blow. One hundred, or one hundred and fifty of the white soldiers, he judged would be sufficient for the exploit. For his own part, his desires for the spoils were moderate. He was content to have the women and the young children who were made captives. The men were to be slain.

His fair assurances, and the vague particulars which he gave of great seas in the rear of his immense territories, with other details which Newport linked with a partial knowledge already in his own mind, persuaded that excellent person to believe, that, by this famous scheme for the overthrow of the Monacans, he was destined to penetrate, by a short cut, to the waters of the South Sea; an object, at that time, the great maritime passion of Europe.

From Werowocomoco the English proceeded to the domains of Opechancanough, where they were welcomed with a courtesy like that which had hitherto attended their progress. To this place Powhatan sent to solicit their return. He had received tidings that new supplies had reached them from Jamestown, and he was anxious to make a second princely bargain with his brother Werowance, Newport. But Opechancanough was not willing to give them up. As one likely to have more influence than any other messenger, Powhatan sent a second entreaty by his daughter Pocahontas. Of her nothing has been seen or said in either of our narratives, during the late stay of the English at Werowocomoco. Doubtless she was with the women in immediate attendance upon the king; but her extreme youth might have kept her out of sight. For the same reason she may have been chosen as his messenger. Had she been older, her father would scarcely have perilled her charms, remote from his own protection, in the rude contact with a strange people. As it was, she probably came well attended. Her presence had the desired effect; and after staying two days with Opechancanough they returned to Werowocomoco, exchanged new courtesies with Powhatan—probably made new bargains, but of these we have no mention—and receiving from him a present of another Indian, took their departure, after exchanging many protestations of friendship and fidelity. The Indian thus given by Powhatan was intended to be sent to England. His private instructions from Powhatan were to report the strength in people of that country, and the wealth and magnitude thereof. In attempting this, at a subsequent period, the poor Indian procured himself a stick the moment he arrived in London, and a notch in the stick was made at every new face he met. But he soon gave up the task in despair; assuring Powhatan on his return to Virginia, that the English were as numerous as the leaves on the tree, and the sands on the sea shore.

Some little time was spent on their return, in diving into the bowels of a rock, the appearances about which led them to conjecture that it contained a mineral treasure. Though Smith dug in compliance with Newport's wishes, he yet discouraged the labor as perverse and fruitless. It seems to have been worse than useless. "Our guilded refiners," says one of our narratives, "with their golden promises made all men their slaves, in hope of recompenses; there was no talke, no hope, no worke, but dig gold, wash gold, refine gold, loade gold; such a bruit of gold that one mad fellow desired to be buried in the sands, least they should, by their art, make gold of his bones." "Were it that Captain *Smith* would not applaud all these golden inventions, because they admitted him not to the sight of their trials, nor golden consultations, I know not, but I have heard him oft question with Captaine *Martin*, and tell him except he could show him a more substantiall triall, he was not inamoured with their durty skill, breathing out these and many other passions, never anything did more torment him than to see all necessary busines neglected, to fraught such a drunken ship with so much guilded durt."

To a man of experience and good sense, certainly, nothing could have been more annoying than to witness the fruitless labors of these grown children, prosecuted with so much confidence and zeal, at the expense not only of their own, but of the vital interest of the colony. But he was compelled to groan in secret at this folly. Captain Newport himself was caught and deluded by this insane passion, though, says our author, with a sly sarcasm, "we never accounted Captain Newport a refiner." But this was not the whole of the evil which just then afflicted the colony, and the resolute heart which we have learned to regard as its real founder and support. His trading voyage for corn to Werowocomoco was, soon after his return, shorn of all its fruits by improvidence and accident. The grain thus procured was stored away with the rest in the common granaries. The winter (1607) was one of extreme severity. The ample forests around our colonists made them profligate in the use of fire. The consequence was, that the town, the houses of which were wholly of wood, and thatched with reeds and brush, was set on fire, and the flames raged with such rapidity as to destroy their dwellings. Their granary, with all their provisions, was consumed; the fire even seized upon, and destroyed their palisadoes. Among the sufferers, "Good Master Hunt, our Preacher, lost all his library, and all he had but the cloathes on his backe; yet none never heard him repine at his losse." This worthy clergyman, of whom such good report is made, was the same, who, it will be remembered, exerted himself so worthily to compose and subdue the discontent which prevailed among the colonists on shipboard during the first voyage out. The testimony is uniformly in his favor, as a wise and pious Christian. The loss of his books, in such a region, was one of those trials of the soul which Providence employs for its better strength and purification. That none should ever hear him repine is sufficient proof that the ends of punishment had been obtained.

Smith was a less patient man. His vocation was that of the reformer rather than the preacher. He could better scourge than entreat or expostulate, and his temper was in no respect improved while Newport and his mariners remained in the colony. The wretched passion after gold dust detained the ship fourteen weeks, when she should have been despatched in fourteen days. The consequence was, that the seamen consumed the provisions which were provided for the colony, and required to be supplied besides for the return voyage. Other evils had followed from its presence. "Those persons," says Stith, "who had either money, spare clothes, credit for bills of exchange, gold rings, furs, or any such valuable commodities, were always welcome to this floating tavern. Such was their necessity and misfortune, to be under the lash of those vile commanders, and to buy their own provisions at fifteen times their value; suffering them to feast at their charge, whilst themselves were obliged to fast, and yet dare not repine lest they should incur the censure of being factious and seditious persons. By these means and management the colony was rather burdened than relieved, by the vast charges of the ship; and being reduced to meal and water, and exposed, by the loss of their town, to the most bitter cold and frost, above half of them died. Smith indeed, and Scrivener, endeavored to correct all abuses, and to put things into a better posture; but they could do nothing to effect, being overpowered by the President and his party, who had long before this laid their difference to Smith's judgment and management." It was some consolation to our adventurer that he could send off with the vessel for England, those lawyers whom he had "laid by the heels" for seeking to circumvent and make him liable under the provisions of the Levitical law. "We not having any use of Parliaments, Plaises (pleadings perhaps), Petitions, admiralty Recorders, Interpreters, *Chronologers*, Courts of Pleas, nor Justices of the Peace, sent Martin *Wingfield* and Captain *Archer* home with him, that had ingrossed all these titles, to seeke some better place of imployment."

CHAPTER III.

Newport at length took his departure, to the relief of some and disquiet of other parties. Smith, in his shallop, accompanied him to the mouth of the Chesapeake. A parting gift for the voyager came from Powhatan, in the shape of twenty fat turkeys, for which, however, he claimed as many swords, by way of remembrance and consideration. This demand Newport imprudently complied with. Powhatan soon discovered the superior value of the English weapon to his own, and this knowledge was the source of much evil to the colonists at a later period. Newport fairly at sea, Smith returned to Jamestown, stopping for a brief period on his way at the territories of the king of Nansemond, who had been hitherto hostile, and making a treaty with him. The prospect at Jamestown was little encouraging. The hamlet was in great part in ruins, and the coercive mind of Smith was not in the ascendant. The president, Radcliffe and Captain Martin, supported by a strong and wily faction, carried things after their own fashion. The public stores were withheld from public use, and made the subject of private barter for the benefit of these parties. They used the common stock as if it were so much personal revenue. Doubtless, if there had been any prospect of success in opposition, Smith was the man to have tried his strength against these profligates. We have seen sufficient proof of his resolute will and fierce determination to effect the right, whenever the probabilities were at all favorable to his endeavors. But he had also the admirable judgment which declares the proper time to strike; and yielding the struggle for the present, he contented himself, supported by Mr. Scrivener and others, in amending the evils of the existing government so far as lay in his power. With the approach of spring, he took charge of the corn-fields, prepared them, and set a crop. This done he applied himself to the rebuilding of the town, restoring first the church, the storehouses and the fortifications. While thus engaged, the colony was excited anew by the arrival of the Phœnix, a barque commanded by Captain Nelson, which had been separated from Newport in a storm, driven to the West Indies, and given up for lost. This vessel brought supplies of provisions for six months, and, an acquisition equally important, an addition to the force of the colony of no less than one hundred and twenty persons. It is to be remembered, however, that the disproportion of *gentlemen* to *workingmen*, which had always been a source of discomfort to Smith, was again unprofitably large. "This happy arrival of Maister Nelson in the Phœnix, having been then about three months missing, did so lavish us with exceeding joy, that now we thought ourselves as our harts could wish, both with a competent number of men, as also for all other needful provisions," and it encouraged Smith to plan a journey of exploration into the surrounding country. The Monacans, into whose weakness Powhatan was willing to spy, previous to any attempt upon their territories, were objects of great curiosity to our English, and seventy men being selected for the purpose, Smith proceeded to train them for the adventure; in six or seven days' practice, teaching them "to march, fight and scirmish in the woods, their willing mindes to this action so quickened their understanding in this exercise, as in all judgments wee were able to fight with Powhatan's whole force." Here our hero was at home. His mind resumed its ancient vivacity in this military employ. Already had he prepared his plans of progress—assigned the proper defences to the fort, arranged for his supplies of food on the march, and put all things in order to his purpose, when circumstances, perverse men, and perverse fortune, combined to defeat the scheme. Fears and scruples beset the president and others in council. Such a progress would be an indiscretion, would be an encroachment upon the rights of Newport to whom only the right to prosecute such discoveries belonged. These scruples and objections discouraged Nelson, who was to have assisted in the expedition with certain volunteer marines, and he withdrew from the adventure. The enterprise miscarried in spite of all the hopes and energies of our Captain; and instead of going upon the conquest of Monacan, he was compelled to remain at the fort, contending with the follies of the council on the one hand, and the Indians of Powhatan on the other. Smith was for filling the Phœnix with cedar on her return voyage, while Captain Martin "was opposite to anything, but onely to fraught this ship with his phantasticall gold;" and though the more sensible suggestion prevailed, yet it called for all the resolution and diligence of Smith, seconded by Nelson, Scrivener, and others, to carry their object, and to make the lading of a commodity, which we are told "was a present despatch"—of ready sale—"than either with durt, or the hopes and reports of an uncertaine discovery (the gold mine), which he woulde performe when they hadde less charge and more leisure."

While our Captain was thus busy in freighting the Phœnix, and rebuilding the settlement, a surprising change took place in the behavior of the Indians. This capricious people, late so friendly, began to show themselves troublesome at first, and finally hostile. The first signs of this change took place in consequence of a disappointment of Powhatan. Finding it so easy to procure English swords from Newport in exchange for the fat turkeys of Werowocomoco, he tried Smith in the same manner; sending him twenty of these fowls, and demanding certain weapons for them in exchange. But Smith was not the man to respect the error of Newport. He paid for the turkeys in any coin but that which the savage chief desired. Powhatan had set his heart upon these weapons, and his people, whether positively instructed, or simply anxious to serve their master in a manner that would please him, undertook by twenty characteristic devices to obtain them. First they resorted to simple thieving, a method which seems to have been practised more or less by every primitive people from the beginning of time. They were frequent visitors at Jamestown, and bore away with them whatever they could secrete. Impunity made them bolder. The tools of the workmen disappeared, and the same thief who had been caught one day in the act, was neither afraid nor ashamed to make the same attempt the next. What they steal, says Smith, "their king receiveth." This high sanction increased their audacity. Too closely watched for their wonted sleight of hand, they grew bold to take by violence what they could not obtain by skill. "By ambuscadoes at our very ports, they would take them perforce, surprise us at worke, or any way; which was so long permitted, they became so insolent there was no rule; the command from England was so strait not to offend them, as our authoritie-bearers (keeping their houses*) would rather be anything than peace-breakers. This charitable humor prevailed, till well it chanced they meddled with Captaine *Smith*, who, without farther deliberation, gave them such an encounter" as soon

* In safety themselves.

brought a remedy for the mischief. Two swords having been stolen, he caught the offender and clapt him in the bilboes When let out he disappeared for a time, but soon returned with three others armed with wooden swords. Smith ordered them to depart, but, flourishing their swords in his face, they bade him defiance. Without waiting for them to strike, our ready soldier answered their flourish with a blow. This the others offered to revenge, but Smith fell upon them, and, smiting hip and thigh, drove them from the premises. Then getting together half a dozen soldiers, without asking or waiting for orders, he sallied forth, and drove their lurking parties entirely from the island.

This decision produced for the time an excellent effect. The Indians became modest and conciliatory. The King of Nansemond, who lived thirty miles from the settlement, sent back a hatchet that had been stolen; and such Indians as had been employed upon the wears (fish traps) of the English, but had temporarily abandoned them for the more honorable business of stealing, voluntarily came back, made their submission, and resumed their labors. But the caprice of the savages would not allow them to remain pacific long. They soon put themselves in suspicious attitudes, and renewed their peculations. One of them having stolen a hatchet, and being pursued by Scrivener, drew his arrow to the head upon him; and two of them, well armed and painted for war, made an attempt upon Smith, "circling about mee, as though they would have clubbed me like a hare;" but lacking boldness, they suffered him to reach the fort in safety. Followed by these and several others within the enclosure, and proceeding to offer violence, Smith had the ports closed, and took them into custody. Sixteen or eighteen were seized in this manner. This brought them to a parley. Ambassadors came to treat for the delivery of the prisoners. The answer was, that they should only obtain their freedom upon the restoration of all the swords, spades, shovels, and other tools which they had stolen. Failing in this, the ambassadors were told that the captives should be hung. This, of course, was a threat only. Meanwhile, two of the Englishmen fell into the hands of the natives,* who at once returned in numbers to the gates of Jamestown, and boldly threatened retaliation upon their prisoners if any of their people suffered harm. This threat was answered by a sally from Smith, who, "in lesse than an houre, so hampred their insolencies, they brought then his two men, desiring peace without any further composition for their prisoners."

But peace was not so easily granted. The prisoners were subjected to a searching examination, and, under the terror of death, they revealed the scheme of a conspiracy against the colony, which involved Powhatan and all his tributary kings. This conspiracy had been maturing for some time, and had its birth before Smith himself had been taken prisoner. His arrest had been in consequence of this combination. Their plan had subsequently aimed to surprise them while at work. "Powhatan, and all his, would seeme friends till Captaine Newport's returne," that he might recover his man Namontack in safety. Then he was to invite Newport to a great feast, and take advantage of the occasion to make him prisoner. Like devices were to involve other parties of the whites in a like predicament.

Such was the amount of the confession made by Macanor, the counsellor of Paspahegh; a confession which was

* "Ranging in the woods—which mischiefe no punishment will prevent but hanging."—*Smith.*

confirmed only in part by the statements, similarly extorted,* of other Indians. By these it was learned "that Paspahegh and Chickahammania did hate us, and intended some mischief, and who they were that tooke me, the names of them that stole our tooles and swords, and that Powhatan received them they all agreed"

The tidings of the seizure of his subjects, their detention, their confession, and the constant exercise by Smith of his armed men, reached Powhatan, and rendered it necessary that he should be at some pains to disabuse the English of the unfriendly impressions which they had received of his own hostility. His safety, not his character, was the source of his solicitude. Accordingly, he despatched the boy Thomas Salvage, who had been given him by Newport, with a present of turkeys, especially to Smith and Scrivener, who, the sagacious old savage had already discovered, were the two master spirits of the settlement. The boy thus opportunely placed in his hands, at a moment when there was good ground for suspecting the intentions of the Emperor, Smith resolved to keep, and this increased the anxieties of the former. His next messenger betrayed the extent of his fears and his cunning. This was the young damsel Pocahontas. "Yet he sent his messengers, and his dearest daughter, *Pocahontas*, with presents to excuse him of the injuries done by some rash untoward captaines, his subjects, desiring their liberties for this time, with the assurance of his love for ever."† Smith's own narrative‡ is more explicit, and

* "I bound one in hold to the maine-mast, and presenting six muskets with match in the cockes, forced him," &c. * * * After each examination, "certaine vollies of shot wee caused to be discharged, which caused each other to thinke that their fellowes had been slaine." *Smith.*

† "The true Travels," &c. Richmond ed. Vol. i., p. 171.

‡ "A true Relation," &c. Richmond ed. Page 81.

more ambitious, though to the same effect. "Powhatan understanding we detained certain salvages, sent his daughter, *a child of tenne years old*, which not only for feature, countenance and proportion, much exceedeth any of the rest of his people, but for wit and spirit the only nonpareil of his country: this he sent by his most trustie messenger, called Rawhunt, as much exceeding in deformitie of person, but of a subtill wit and crafty understanding." Through these, the Emperor assured Smith that he greatly loved and respected him—that he must not doubt his affection—in proof of which he had sent his child, whom he most esteemed, to see him. Such was the message borne by Pocahontas. She brought from her father, as a present, a supply of bread and a deer. She entreated that the captives might be spared and set free. She also entreated that the boy might be sent back to her father, as he loved him exceedingly.

Pocahontas might well urge such a prayer to the man whom her own entreaties had saved from death. It was with a happy policy that Powhatan made her his ambassador. If anything could touch the soul of Smith, at any moment, it must have been the presence of such a pleader; and how much must there have been of the pleasing and the tender in the interview between that young Indian child and the stern warrior, whose heart, in frequent trials of the world's strife, had perhaps grown somewhat callous against most human weaknesses! Yet he betrays none of this callosity while he treats with Pocahontas. Her gentle virtues, her eager, earnest interest in his behalf, her extreme youth and wonderful beauty, which made her the nonpareil of her race and country—these seem to have always had their influence over his soul, when she is the subject of consideration. He speaks of her as the dearest daughter, the little daughter of Powhatan; and in such tender diminutives sufficiently declares the feelings of a man who was but too commonly accustomed to conceal them. That he holds her as a thing almost perfect, we gather from his passing and unaffected utterances. He does not speak of her ostentatiously. It is only when it belongs to the absolute business of the narration that he employs her name, and then only in such manner as to make us regret that he does not use it more frequently. A few more passages of this description, and the character of Smith, which must be allowed to have suffered somewhat from a certain harshness and hardness of outline, would have had the requisite softening, and we should then have been at some loss to discover its deficiencies. But Pocahontas has her influence upon him, and it is one of no equivocal character. For the power of the Indian sovereign, her father, his own fierce courage did not allow him to entertain much respect; and, seeing through his faithlessness, he already half despises him. Opechancanough has his entreaties also, for some of the prisoners are his friends and subjects; and sending his presents, seeks an interview himself with Smith, to disarm his suspicions and hostility. But the latter smiles grimly and scornfully, and yields nothing. It is only to Pocahontas that he accords his prisoners. When Opechancanough and his attendants had gone, the prisoners were conducted to the church, and then, after prayer, bestowed upon Pocahontas. It is to her only that they are given; their bows, arrows, and all that they had when taken, are surrendered at the same time without conditions, "to the king's daughter, in regard of her father's kindness in sending her." She herself was presented with certain trifles, which, we are told, contented her. She was probably contented easily. Her actions do not seem to have needed any less noble impulse than the native goodness, gentleness, and benignity of her character.

CHAPTER IV.

In these decisive proceedings Smith had trespassed far beyond the limits of his authority. He had usurped the powers of the President and council in Virginia, and had disobeyed the mild instructions which had been sent out by the proprietors in England. His mind was not of a sort to submit easily to commands which were obviously founded in ignorance of the facts, and to restraints which did not regard their necessity; and just as little was he disposed to yield implicit obedience to a present authority which had always shown itself so impotent, at least, for good. His proceedings, though resulting in advantage to the colony, and though not a life of the Indians was taken, were met with rebuke and dissatisfaction among his brethren. "The patient councell, that nothing would move to warre with the salvages, would gladly have wrangled with *Captaine Smith* for his crueltie;* yet none

* Take a sample of these cruelties, which will at the same time give a lively picture of the life at Jamestown. It is from the "True Relation," by Smith himself: "Two daies after a Paspeheyan came to show us a glistering minerall stone; and with signes demonstrating it to be in great aboundance, like unto rockes; with some dozen more I was sent to seeke to digge some quantitie, and the Indian to conduct mee; but suspecting this some trick to delude us, for to get some copper of us, or with some ambuscado to betray us, seeing him falter in his tale, being two miles on our way, led him ashore, where abusing (misleading) us from place to place, and so seeking either to have drawn us with him into the woods, or to have given us the slippe: I shewed him copper which I promised to have given him, if he had performed his promise, but for his scoffing and abusing us, I gave him twentie lashes with a rope, and his bowes and arrowes, bidding

was slaine [of the savages] to any man's knowledge, but it brought them in such fear and obedience, as his very name would sufficiently affright them; where before, wee had sometime peace and warre twice in a day; and very seldome a weeke but we had some treacherous villainy or other."* It was perhaps fortunate for Smith that the mis-

---

him shoote if he durst, and so let him goe." It was rather dangerous to trifle with our Captain. He was very much the soldier, and the word and blow very frequently went together. But we suspect that such cruelties as this would be practised by Christian soldiery of modern times, under the same provocation, to a still greater extent. At least, we are accustomed to hear of much worse in the wars of Christian Europe.

* Here we lose all farther assistance from the narrative of Th. Watson, *Gent.*, otherwise Smith himself, entitled, "A true relation of such occurrences and accidents of noate as hath happened in Virginia since the first planting of that collony, which is now resident in the south part thereof, till the last return from thence." This narrative, published at the time (1608), brought up the proceedings of the colony to the very moment when it was written. It was probably sent home by the Phœnix, and bears all the marks of being a very hurried performance. The style is very confused and cumbrous—the particulars not always given in due order, and we find—a very remarkable omission—no mention made of the manner in which he was rescued from the executioner Powhattan by the intervention of Pocahontas. Indeed, there appears to be some solicitude that Captain Smith should not become too conspicuous in this narrative, and hence, possibly, the notion of making the publication appear as the work of Tho. Watson—a *nom de plume*, for which we now find it difficult to discover a necessity or motive. All reproaches of his colleagues and associates are spared in this performance. It was the policy to make the settlers appear very well contented in Virginia—as in this way only could others be persuaded to adventure. Hence, at the conclusion, we have a picture of felicity at Jamestown, very far from the truth, which must have brought them to believe in England that Astræa was once more about to make her home on earth—"We, now remaining, being in good health, all our men well contented, free from mutinies, in love one with another, and as we hope in a continuall peace with the Indians, where, we doubt not, but by God's gracious assistance and the adventurers' willing mindes and

conduct of the President himself, in matters which touched more certainly the safety and well-being of the colony, afforded a more legitimate subject for the indignation of their little community. The President who had succeeded upon the deposition of Wingfield, was Captain John Radcliffe. This man was totally unequal to the situation,—is described as being little beloved—of weak judgment in time of danger—and of no industry in time of peace. He was sickly besides, and freely committed the responsible duties of his office to the hands of others. At first, a portion of this trust was given to Smith; but Smith lost favor in his sight, and he then united himself with creatures who hated and dreaded the vigilance of our Captain, and had been his enemies from the outset. Radcliffe himself had been one of these, and only yielded to the influence of Smith when the courage and peculiar energy and ability of our hero were necessary to the common safety. With the disappearance of the danger came a forgetfulness of his worth; and the President sank back into the control of those who were willing to pander to his appetites. We have seen this man, assisted by others, converting the stores of the community into a source of revenue for himself; continuing this practice, as if the stock were wholly his own. So deeply did his rapacity trench upon the resources of the colony, as to force upon Smith and Scrivener the necessity of taking such order with him as to put a stop to his prodigality. Measures were accordingly adopted, by which to limit him and his satellites to a certain allowance, rated proportionally with what was accord-

speedie furtherance to so honorable an action in after times, to see our nation to enjoy a country not only exceeding pleasant for habitation, but also very profitable for commerce in generall, no doubt pleasing Almightie God, honorable to our gracious sovereign and commodious generally to the whole kingdome."

ed to the rest. This difficulty being adjusted, the town rebuilt, the Indians quieted, the corn crop nearly made, and all through the strenuous exertions and manly courage of our Captain, his eager and impatient spirit began to look around him seeking proper employment. He was not the man to rest upon his oars, his cruise being over, but to plan other voyages, and shape out new enterprises, in which his genius could find fitting exercise. Denied to explore the interior, and penetrate to those wondrous territories of which Powhatan had given such glowing descriptions, it was still within the province of the settlers to explore the region contiguous to that in which they had pitched their tents. Accordingly, he meditated the exploration of the Bay of Chesapeake. To this no objection seems to have been made. The President was probably only too well pleased to be relieved from the vigilance of his eye, and the unbending rigor of his justice. His design was less adventurous, less perilous than that which he most eagerly desired. We have seen him training seventy men, with which he felt himself equal to the whole nation of Powhatan. *He* might have made his way with such a force across the Apalachian summits, descending to the waters of the Mississippi. With seventy men Pizarro first penetrated the great empire of Peru. Our Captain was compelled to content himself with a more moderate ambition. His seventy men were reduced to fifteen persons, himself included. One of these was a physician, *six* were *gentlemen*—so *rated*, though we cannot well conceive their uses in such an expedition—and *seven* were soldiers. He left the fort on the second of June (1608), in an open barge of less than three tons burthen, and made his way, in company with the Phœnix, to Cape Henry, at which place he parted with her. Crossing the bay from this point to the eastern shore they made the isles which still bear the name of their first discoverer. Two stout savages at Cape Charles stood armed with lances headed with bone, and seemed prepared to do battle with our explorers, demanding who they were and whence they came. The reply of Smith disarmed them, and they civilly directed him to Accomac, the habitation of their Werowance. Here they were received kindly. This chief is described as one of the most comely and affable savages they had ever met. He told Smith, among other things, of an event which had lately happened, which belongs to that class of wonders of which a superstitious people always make large account. Two children dying, "some extreame passions, or dreaming visions, phantasies, or affection," moved their parents to revisit them at their place of sepulture. To their wonder, the faces of the children "reflected to the eyes of the beholders such delightful countenances, as though they had regained their vitall spirits. This, as a miracle, drew many to behold them." The consequences were fatal to all who did so. A plague seized upon the spectators, and but few escaped the mortality. In this way did the chief of Accomac account to Smith for the sparseness of his population. What effect this superstition had upon his character, in producing that dignity and courtliness which we are told distinguished him, is matter for conjecture. He spoke the language of the Powhatanese, and spoke so agreeably always while describing the country, that Smith acknowledges it gave him exceeding pleasure to hear. The domain of this chief lay within the southwestern part of Northampton county.

From Accomac our Captain proceeded along the coast, "searching every inlet and bay fit for harbours and habitations." He was baffled by a thunderstorm in an attempt to reach certain isles which he discovered in the bay, and had a narrow escape from the "unmercifull raging of that ocean-like water." To isle and headland, names were given in this progress, mostly chosen from the companions of our adventurer. Thus one day was spent. A difficulty in procuring fresh water caused them to turn into the next eastern channel, which brought them into the river Pocomoke, then called Wighcomocco. Here they were at first threatened by the savages with shows of war, but the pacific aspect of the white men, and the judicious management of Smith, converted the fury of their assault into songs and dances, and a reception full of kindness and good feeling. But they got no good water here, turning with loathing from such puddle as was offered them for drink. "But before two daies were expired we would have refused two barricoes of gold for one of that puddle water of Wighcomocco." The next water they found was a pond, which proved to be a natural hot bath, sufficiently fresh, but rather too warm for drinking purposes. This was upon the main, upon a highland, which, in compliment to an honorable house in France, was called Point Ployer. Resuming their progress, they encountered a second thunder-storm, if possible more terrible than the first; lost mast and sails, and were so "overracked" by such "mightie waves," that with great difficulty they kept their barque above the water. They succeeded in making a port among certain uninhabited isles, where they were kept two days by the continuance of the storm. They called this harborage Port Limbo. Repairing their sails with their shirts, they resumed their voyage and fell in with the river which is now called Corghcomocco, but which then bore the name of Cuscarrowack. Here their presence was a novelty and terror. The people ran in troops along the shores as the barque pressed forward, many getting into the tops of trees to see and oppose the strangers. They were not sparing of their arrows, and declared their hostility with the most passionate shows of violence. But, lying at anchor beyond the reach of their darts, our Captain contented himself with making them signs of friendship. These did not appear to produce the desired effect, and the day passed in continued demonstrations of hostility on the part of the natives. The next day they came to the river side unarmed, and bringing with them baskets of corn and dancing in a ring, the wily savages endeavored in this way to beguile the Englishmen ashore. But, detecting an ambush in a neighboring cane-brake, Smith answered their devices with a volley of musket-shot, which sent them tumbling in every direction. Then approaching the shore, after another volley had drilled the place of ambuscade, our Captain penetrated their habitations. Here he left some of the usual trifles, but not a savage was to be seen. The next day four of the Indians who had been fishing in the bay and knew nothing of what had happened, came to him in a canoe and had a conference. They disappeared and soon brought others, the number gradually increasing to two or three thousand, men, women, and children, each bringing a present, and each so gratified with the merest trifle in return, that a friendship was struck up between the parties, of such a zealous nature, that the Indians strove with one another who should fetch water for the pale-faces, become their hostages, guide them through the country, or most content them in whatever they desired. Here dwelt the people of Sarapinagh, Nanse, Arseek, and Nantaquak—tribes of which there now remain no vestiges. Smith describes them as the best merchants among the Indians. They were the manufacturers, and carried on the commerce. They had the finest furs and made large quantities of the best *Roanoke*. This was a sort of white bead wrought from shells, which served with the savages of the whole country as a circulating medium. It was, with copper, their substitute for gold and silver. These people were small of stature. They aroused Smith's curiosity in relation to a people called the Massawomekes, a masculine and valiant race, very numerous, and very powerful; who possessed in large degree the amiable faculty of keeping their neighbors in constant apprehension. These people are supposed to have been those afterwards so famous in English annals as the six nations, and among the French as the Iroquois—the great confederacy of the north, whose claims to conquest—claims which we suspect were only partially founded in the truth—have procured for them the title of the Romans of America. It is very sure that their neighbors gave a formidable account of them. If Powhatan did not absolutely fear, he greatly respected them; and what was said of them, their valor and resources, by the Powhatanese, provoked the curiosity of our Captain, and determined him, very much against the wishes of his companions, to make the discovery of their territories one of the grand objects of his expedition. His adventurous spirit panted to make the acquaintance of a nation sufficiently powerful to make their conquest equally honorable and desirable.

From the eastern shore, which he found broken with uninhabited islands, and for the most part without fresh water, he stood westward across the bay and made the mouth of the Patuxent. For thirty leagues sailing northward no inhabitants were found. In place of these, however, there were wolves, bears, deer, and other wild beasts in abundance, and an ample supply of water. Passing many shallow streams, the first they found navigable was one supposed to be the Patapsco, to which, on account of the appearance of the clay along the cliffs, resembling bol ammonia, they gave the name of Bolus. But that Smith himself has provided us with this derivation, we might have ascribed this infelicitous title to the working of a mutinous spirit among the *gentlemen* of the expedition, which broke out at this place. It was thought, when the voyage was begun, that it would be only too short a one to gratify the eager curiosity of those who were about to embark—that Smith would be in too great a hurry to get back to the colony, supposing his presence to be necessary to the proper management of affairs with such a person as Radcliffe in the presidency. But the notion of these gallants, who were none of them accustomed to hardships, soon began to change when, at the end of twelve or fourteen days, spent in an open barge, weary of the oars, bread soaked with wet and much of it decayed, yet still susceptible of digestion by hungry stomachs—they found him meditating a visit to the Massawomekes, and other tedious and dangerous adventures. Their discontents grew at length to such importunancy, as to provoke our Captain to declare himself in the following manner:

"Gentlemen, if you would remember the memorable history of Sir Ralph Sayre, how his company importuned him to proceed in the discovery of Moratico, alledging they had yet a dog, that being boyled with saxafras leaves would richly feede them in their returnes; then, what a shame would it be for you (that have bin so suspitious of my tendernesse) to force me returne, with so much provision as we have, and scarce able to say where we have beene, nor yet heard of that wee were sent to seeke? You cannot say but I have shared with you in the worst which is past; and for what is to come, of lodging, dyet, or whatsoever, I am contented you allot the worst part to myselfe. As for your feares that I will lose myself in these unknowne large waters, or be swallowed up in some stormie gust, abandon these childish feares, for worse than is past is not likely to happen, and there is as much danger to return as to proceede. Regaine, therefore, your old spirits, for returne I will not (if God please) till I have seene the Massawomekes, found Patawomek, or the head of this water, you conceit to be endlesse."

This firm expression of his resolve silenced the discontents, but circumstances helped their entreaties. Three or four of them fell sick, and this, with a continuance of adverse weather for several days, determined Smith, however unwillingly, to forbear for the present the prosecution of the voyage. He left the bay where it was some nine miles wide, with a draught of nine or ten fathoms, and on the 16th of June fell in with the mouth of the Potomac

The sight of this noble river cheered the drooping spirits of his men, and their health being somewhat restored, it was determined to explore it. For thirty miles no inhabitants were seen. At length they met with two, who conducted them up a little creek towards Onanomanient, and into an ambuscade. Here the English found themselves surrounded by savages to the number of three or four thousand;—"So strangely paynted, grimed and disguised, shouting, yelling and crying, as so many spirits from hell could not have showed more terrible." But Smith cared little for their bravados. Still, it was deemed necessary to scare them a little, and, training his guns so as to allow the stroke of the bullets to be seen by the savages upon the water, he gave them a few volleys, which soon brought them to their senses. Down went bows and arrows, and all was peace between the parties, and wonderment at least with one of them. They surprised Smith with some of their statements. They did not hesitate to declare that they had been commanded to destroy the English by Powhatan, who had heard of this expedition. This was not so much calculated to provoke his astonishment as what they told him farther, to the effect that Powhatan had been advised by certain of the settlers at Jamestown of all Smith's proceedings, and had been encouraged by them to put him to death, as he kept them in the country against their will. The reckless manner in which men were gathered up in England for the purposes of colonization is matter of history. We know very well that the profligate and criminal but too commonly furnished the chief materials for such enterprises. But it is not easy to yield our faith to such desperate wickedness as this, and we should be now inclined to withhold it, and to ascribe it to some imperfect understanding of what was said by the savages, but that subsequent circumstances, absolute facts, and the commission of particular deeds on the part of some of the wretches thus characterized, go fully to confirm the statement.

Their farther progress up the river found the people at all places, with few exceptions, armed and ready in the same spirit and under the same instructions to assail them. The *Moyaones*, *Nacotchtants*, and *Toags* — heathen of whom we have no farther traces—alone received them with hospitality. Having gone as far as they could go in their vessel, they commenced their return, and were fortunate in meeting with numerous savages in canoes well stocked with the flesh of slaughtered bears, deer, and other beasts, of which they received liberal portions. The aspect of the shores, with great rocks towering above the trees, commanded their attention, more particularly as the progress of water down the sides had left "a tinctured spangled skurfe, that made many bare places seeme as guilded." Dreams of gold and gold mountains were ever working in the brains of the voyagers of those days. Smith himself seems to have been superior to the various delusions by which they were mocked. But not so his companions. They clambered up the rocks, and burrowed in the earth among their highest cliffs. The ground was so sprinkled with yellow spangles as to seem "halfe pin dust." Conducted by Japazaws, King of Patawomeke, still under the belief that they were on the tracks of a gold mine, they ascended one of the tributaries of the Potomac as far as the depth of water would suffer the boat to go. Here Smith left her, taking with him six men, and surrounded by divers savages, some of whom, to be sure of their fidelity, he carried in the twofold character of guides and hostages. These he adroitly decorated with chains which, if they conducted him in safety, they were to keep as ornaments. The temptation was too great to suffer them to feel the weight or the restraint of their decorations. They meant him fairly, and conducted him to the foot of a mountain, the substance of which seemed to be antimony. The tribes had burrowed in its bowels before. Their shells and hatchets had long been familiar with its treasures. Washed of its dross "in a fayre brooke of christel-like water," which "runneth hard by it," it is put into little bags, and made an article of trade of ready sale throughout the country. It had no use but as a paint. With this they paint the images of their gods, and their own bodies and faces, "which makee them looke like blackmoores dusted over with silver." Rewarding his guides, and the king to whom they belonged, our Captaine obtained a supply of this precious commodity. This was sent to England; was represented by Newport to be half silver, and new supplies were procured, which proved to be of no value. No minerals were discovered in this search. Some furs were gathered, the best of which were found among the Indians of Cascarawaoke, that merchant tribe which did so much of the manufacturing and trading of the country. Beavers, otters, bears, martens, and minkes, rewarded in some slight degree their search; and fish were in such abundance, "lying so thicke, with their heads above the water, as for want of nets (our barge driving amongst them) we attempted to catch them with a fryingpan!" But this was found, drily remarks our narrative, "a bad instrument to catch fish with." They succeeded better with their swords, following the example of Smith, who, whenever at ebb tide their boat chanced to ground upon the shoals at the entrances of rivers, would amuse "himselfe by nayling them to the ground with his sword." Thus sporting, more fish would be taken in an hour than would suffice the party for a day.

On one occasion this amusement had nearly proved fatal to our hero. Taking from his sword a stingray—a fish the character of which he did not know—"being much of the fashion of a thornback, but a long tayle like a riding rodde, whereon the middest is a most poysoned sting, of two or three inches long, bearded like a saw on each side"—it struck its weapon into his wrist to the depth of nearly an inch and a half. No blood or even wound was perceptible at first, with the exception of a slight blue spot; but the torment was extreme and instantaneous. In four hours such was the swollen state of his arm and shoulder, and such the condition to which the patient was reduced, that his companions concluded he must die. Such was his own conviction, and with that exercise of firmness and will which seemed to distinguish equally all his actions, he chose his place of burial in a neighboring island, and there his comrades, with heavy hearts, proceeded to prepare his grave. But it was not the will of providence that he should perish thus. There was still work for his hands. "It pleased God, by a precious oyle," that Dr. Russell should finally give relief to the agonizing pain of his limb and reduce its swelling, and so far from being buried, he survived to revenge himself upon the fish by partaking heartily of it that night for supper. The island where this occurred, at the north of the Rappahannock, still bears, in the name of the fish, the memory of the event.

CHAPTER V.

THE hurt under which our Captain still suffered in some degree contributed to the return of the voyagers. But for this they might still have loitered along the route for further discoveries. Once fairly under weigh, Smith contrived to extract from his men all the services of which they were capable.

Their arrival at the Indian settlement of Kecoughtan (Hampton) was a subject of surprise to the savages, who "seeing our Captain hurt, and another bloody by breaking his shinne,—our number of bowes, arrowes, swords, mantles and furrs, would needes imagine we had beene at warres." The simple statement of the truth would not satisfy them, and finding them resolved on believing nothing less than they fancied, they were fooled by our voyagers to the top of their bent. "Finding their aptnesse to beleeve, we fayled not (as a great secret) to tell them anything which might affright them,—what spoyle we had got and made of the Massawomeks." In the same spirit, disguising their bark with painted streamers and other devices, our voyagers appeared before the people of Jamestown as a Spanish frigate, and filled them with terror for a season. They reached the colony on the 21st of July, having been absent twenty days.

Smith's return to the colony was always seasonable. As usual he found things in evil condition. The last comers from Europe were all sick; of the rest some were lame and bruised, and all unhappy—all complaining of the President. That weak and vicious person had resumed his evil practices, had riotously consumed the public stores, had been guilty of needless cruelties, and had completed the measure of his follies and offences by tasking the labor of the people in building a sort of pleasure-house in the woods for his personal indulgence. But for Smith's return, the discontents of the country would have summarily revenged themselves upon the offender. Their apprehensions were relieved, but their fury scarcely lessened, by the coming of our Captain. The news he brought, the supplies, and in particular his own presence, which always had the tendency to reassure the timid and desponding, enabled them to forgive the offences of the President. But they insisted upon his deposition, and required Smith to take upon him the government, "as by course it did belong to him." But the mere name of office was not a temptation to one who sought to perform and to achieve, rather than to rule. He preferred the more active toils of exploration; and, resolutely denying their entreaties, substituted Mr. Scrivener, whom he calls his "deare friend," for himself in the Presidency. Then, "in regard of the company, and heate of the yeare, they being unable to worke, he lefte them to live at ease, to recover their healths," and re-embarked on the 24th of July—after a rest of two days only—to finish his discoveries, taking with him nearly the same persons as before. Contrary winds kept them two or three days at Kecoughtan, where the king feasted them with much satisfaction; the more particularly as the Indians persuaded themselves that Smith was going on an expedition against the hateful Massawomeks. A few rockets which he fired in air convinced the terrified savages that their new allies were irresistible, and they saw them depart on the supposed invasion with the happiest hopes and rejoicings. The first night, Smith anchored at Stingray Isle, a place memorable in his late experience. The next day crossing the Potomac, he made for the river Bolus, otherwise Patapsco. This stream, as our voyagers pursued it to its sources, was found to divide itself into four heads. These they separately followed, exploring them as far as their boat could penetrate. Two of these tributaries, the Sasquesahanock (Susquehanna) and the Tockwogh (since called the Sassafras), they found to be inhabited. In crossing the bay, they unexpectedly encountered seven or eight canoes filled with the renowned Massawomeks, so much feared by the Powhatanese, and whom Smith so much desired to see. The bold savages prepared at once for a conflict, and our Captain was no less prompt and decisive. He drew in his oars, and made all sail in pursuit. Some of his men, unaccustomed to the climate, had fallen sick "almost to death," since leaving Kecoughtan. These were "all of the last supply." They were made to lay themselves down in the boat, and were covered with the tarpaulin out of all danger. Their hats only were made use of. Raised on sticks, a hat between every two men, the force of Smith was doubled to the eyes of their enemies. He had need of some such *ruse de guerre* to impress the warlike savages with any respect. His men able to do battle were but five in number. His boldness had its effect. Supposing his hats to be men—and white men, too, of whom probably vague and very terrible accounts had already reached their ears—the formidable Massawomeks took to flight, and made with all possible speed to the shore. Here they drew up, watchful of all the movements of the barge, until she anchored right against them. It was difficult to persuade them of the pacific intentions of the strangers. There were no Indian words known to Smith which they seemed to comprehend. None of theirs could be understood. But perseverance and patience produced their usual effects, and two of the Indians were moved by signs to approach the whites unarmed in a canoe. The rest all followed in their support. A present of a bell to each of the first comers, brought the rest aboard in the most pacific moods and attitudes. They brought venison and bear's flesh to present to the strangers, and even gave them of their bows and arrows, their clubs, targets, and bear skins. Smith requited them with gifts quite as valuable to them or more so. They gave him to understand that they had just been fighting with their enemies the Tockwoghs, and showed him their green wounds in proof of the seriousness of the encounter. The interview was friendly throughout. The night separated the parties, and with the morning the Massawomeks were nowhere to be seen.

The next day the English proceeded to the country of the Tockwoghs. Entering the river of that name, they found themselves environed by the savages in a fleet of canoes. They were all armed, and had prepared themselves, in all probability, for the enemies from whom Smith had just separated. His policy was to conciliate this people, and he did not scruple to shape his story for this purpose. He displayed the weapons obtained from the Massawomeks, and claimed to have taken them in battle. The Tockwoghs recognized the spears and the shields, the bows and arrows of their most formidable opponents, and they welcomed the whites with acclamations. Conducting them to their hamlet, which was palisaded and otherwise strongly fortified, they spread their furs and fruits before the strangers. The women and children hailed them with songs and dances, and all parties strove in every possible way to express the warmth and the extent of their gratification. They saw hatchets, knives, fragments of brass and iron among these people, who said they obtained them from the Sasquesahanocks—a nation of Indians who dwelt at the sources of the river which bore their name. These they described as a very mighty people, and the mortal enemies of the Massawomeks. Smith was curious to see this people. He persuaded his hosts to send a dispatch and invite them to an interview. This was done, and after a few days they came down, sixty in number, bringing with them gifts of venison, tobacco pipes three feet in length, and worthy of a sultan, baskets, targets, bows and arrows—all the specimens of native production which they had to offer. Smith describes them as very noble specimens of humanity. He speaks of them as a race of giants. "Such greate and well proportioned men are seldome seene, for they seemed like giants to the English, yea, and unto their neighbours." He speaks of them as in other respects the "strangest people of all those countries." They were of a simple and confiding temper, and could scarcely be restrained from prostrating themselves in adoration of the white strangers. Their language seemed to correspond with their proportions, "sounding from them as a voyce in a vault." They were clad in bear and wolf skins, wearing the skin as the Mexican his poncho, passing the head through a slit in the centre, and letting the garment drape naturally around from the shoulders. "Some have cassocks made of beares' heads and skinnes, that a man's head goes through the skinne's neck, and the eares of the beare fastened to his shoulders, the nose and teeth hanging down his breast, another beare's face split behind him, and at the end of the nose hung a pawe; the halfe sleeves comming to the elbowes were the necks of the beares, and the armes through the mouth with pawes hanging at their noses. One had the head of a wolfe hanging in a chaine for a jewell, his tobacco pipe three quarters of a yard long, prettily carved with a bird, a deere, or some such devise at the great end, sufficient to beat out one's braines."

Such details will be hereafter valuable to the students of American art. The masquerader, whose ambition it will be to simulate the barbarous fantasticalities of the Sasquesahanocks, need not blunder in his costume. Smith, who was a good draughtsman, the circumstances of his education considered, has given us a spirited sketch of one of these gigantic warriors, "the greatest of them," thus attired:—"The calfe of whose leg was three quarters of a yard about, and all the rest of his limbes so answerable to that proportion, that he seemed the goodliest man we ever beheld. His hayre the one side was long, the other shore close, with a ridge over his crowne like a cock's combe. His arrows were five quarters long, headed with the splinters of a white chrystall-like stone, in forme of a heart, an inche broad, and an inche and a halfe or more long. These he wore in a wolve's skinne at his backe for his quiver, his bow in the one hand and his club in the other, as is described."

It is seldom that we have reason to suspect or accuse Smith of exaggeration. For a traveller he is exceedingly circumspect. We see no reason to question the perfect correctness of this description. In respect to the costume, we have abundant proofs of its singular propriety and truth. His example here is taken from a remarkable instance, even among his people. The Sasquesahanocks are all described as above the ordinary size—a very superior race of men; but this, their chief, is great even among them. He is as Saul among the Israelites—as Goliath among the people of Gath. Pursuing the trade of war, in a climate at once mild and invigorating, fed on the simplest fruits of the earth, enslaved by no intoxicating or enfeebling habits, and constantly exercising in the dangers of the field or the sports of the chase all the muscles of manhood, we must not wonder that the warrior of Virginia towers above the feebler race, whom luxuries circumvent and overthrow, as the lap of Dalilah robs the son of Manoah of all his strength. Individuals may be seen even now, who would compare with our Sasquesahanock giant.

Smith seems never to have neglected the duties of religion. His reverence naturally belonged to, and was in some measure the source of his earnestness of character. His enterprises did not interfere with the daily rites of worship. On the ocean, in the deep forests, his daily order was to have prayer and psalm, such as the Christian manuals have afforded for a thousand years, suited to all the situations and conditions of mankind. This service was not foregone because of the presence of the savages. Perhaps it was more fervently insisted on for this very reason. The Tockwoghs and Sasquesahanocks, much edified and wondering, looked on in respectful silence, then followed up the holy proceedings by something of their own, after a similar fashion. Their hands were lifted in a passionate manner to the sun, the visible source of energy with all barbarous people. Then followed a most "fearefull song." The American Indians are not, like the Africans, a musical race, though it is very possible that our stout Sasquesahanocks sang very nearly as well, though perhaps not in so artistical a manner, as our English. It was the ear of the latter which was not attuned to the "native wood-notes wild" of their tawny companions. In all probability the Tockwogh critics had something disparaging to say of the English music, after the latter had departed. The song of the savages was succeeded by a general embrace of "our Captaine," whom they would have proceeded to worship as a being of superior order but for his decided opposition. Denied to worship, they were yet suffered to apostrophize their guests, and "with a most strange furious action and a hellish voice," they made him an oration, expressive of their friendship. Then followed the symbolical proceedings, by which their sentiments were better conveyed than through their speeches. They seized upon our Captain, covered him "with a great painted beare's skin," hung about his neck "a great chayne of white beads, weighing at least six or seven pounds, and laid eighteen mantels, made of divers sorts of skinnes sowed together," with many other toys, at his feet. Then while their ceremonious hands stroked his neck, they tendered him support and tribute, and implored him to remain their governor and protector. They gave him descriptions of their own and the neighboring countries; "of Atquanachuck, Massawomek, and other people," whom they described as living "upon a great water beyond the mountains, which he understood to be some great lake or the river of Canada."

The Sasquesahanocks were a populous nation, using the standards of tribes equally wandering and sterile. They could muster six hundred fighting men, and dwelt in hamlets which were palisadoed. They were scarcely known to Powhatan,* yet were mortal enemies to the

* And yet, adopting the statements of the Six Nations themselves, the latter are assumed to have been the conquerors of the whole country, and to have swept with their arms the vast Atlantic ranges of the Apalachian chain from Maine to Florida. The pretensions of the Six Nations were greatly misunderstood at first; and they derived their titles (by conquest) from the representations of the whites, to whom they were required to give titles. The Indian tribes have thus repeatedly sold territories on which they themselves had never dared to set a foot.

Massawomekes. From the French of Canada they procured their hatchets and other European commodities. It was with much difficulty that Smith tore himself away from this hospitable and simple people. He left them, promising to visit them again next year.

Returning down the bay to the Rappahannock, our party explored every river and inlet of any consequence along the route, giving English names to stream and headland, boring holes in trees, in which they left notes or memoranda, and raising crosses of wood, and sometimes of brass, to signify that possession had been taken of the country by English authority. In penetrating the Rappahannock they were kindly entertained by a people called the Moraughtacunds, influenced probably by the presence of an Indian named Mosco, whom Smith styles an old friend, and who claimed to be a countryman of the whites. Unlike the savages, Mosco luxuriated in a fine, black, bushy beard, of which he was not a little proud. Upon this peculiarity he built, in ranking himself with the English. Smith supposed him to have been the son of some Frenchman. Mosco took great pride in entertaining his countrymen; brought them wood and water, procured them the services of the Indians, and was himself their guide throughout the neighborhood. At parting he counselled them not to visit the Rappahannocks, whom he described as hostile to the Moraughtacunds, and would be to the English when they knew of their friendship with the latter. Smith, suspecting that this representation sprung from a desire to secure all their trade for his friends, gave it no heed, and crossed the river to the territories of the tabooed people. But Mosco was honest. Some twelve or sixteen Indians along the shore directed the English to the mouth of a creek where there was a good landing. Here they found three or four canoes, in which they had put, as so much bait, certain of the usual commodities which they gave in barter. But Smith was not so easily caught. His custom was, wherever the parties were of doubtful faith, to exchange a man as a hostage—"in sign of love"—and until they complied with this requisition, our Rappahannocks could not persuade him to come within their clutches. At length, after some consultation, some four or five of them darted up to their middles into the creek, bringing with them their hostage. They showed our Captain that they had no weapons, but he was still distrustful, and while detaining their man, sent one of his own, Anas Todkill, ashore to look about for "ambuscadoes." Todkill was not suffered to advance far, nor did he need to do so, for in a stone's throw from the landing he discovered some two or three hundred savages in ambush among the trees. His hasty movement to return to the boat was intercepted. The Rappahannocks, perceiving that their design was discovered, attempted to carry him off perforce; and in the same moment the Indian left as a hostage in the boat sprang overboard, but was slain the next moment in the water. A volley from the barge scattered the savages, and Todkill escaped their clutches. Several of the Indians were hurt, some slain; but though more than a thousand arrows were sped from their bows in an inconceivably short space of time, none of the English were hurt. The targets of the Massawomeks were found eminently useful for their protection. But for the timely employment of these they might have been far less fortunate.

These targets are described as "made of little small sticks woven betwixt strings of their hempe and silke grasse, as is our cloth, but so firmly that no arrow can pierce them." The canoes and arrows captured in this conflict were reserved for Mosco and the Moraughtacunds, by whom the return of the English was hailed with a trumpet. The targets of the Massawomeks had served such an admirable purpose, that Smith fastened them around the sides of the barge, so that they might afford a permanent protection in like dangers hereafter. The conception was a fortunate one. The very next day, in their progress up the river, Mosco being at his own request one of their company, they passed an ambush of thirty or forty Rappahannocks, who, taking advantage of the shelter of a marsh, at a spot where the river was particularly narrow, "had so accommodated themselves with branches as we tooke them for little brushes growing among the sedge." The arrows flew from invisible hands against the Massawomek targets, and but for Mosco our English would have been at a loss to guess whence they issued. Hiding his favorite whiskers in the bottom of the boat, he told them where to look for their subtle enemies, who were again the Rappahannocks. With the discharge of the first volley from the barge, the green bushes fell down among the sedge, and the ambush disappeared. "When we were neare halfe a myle from them they showed themselves, dancing and singing very merrily."

They met with nothing but kind treatment from the several tribes whom they encountered in their farther progress up the river. But their company was lessened by the death of Richard Featherstone, who sunk under the fever of the climate. He was buried, with a volley of shot, on the shores of a small bay, which was called by his name. Smith speaks of him as a worthy person, who had behaved himself "honestly, valiantly, and industriously," while he had been in the country. The other members of the expedition, who had been taken sick after leaving Kecoughtan, had all recovered their health. The toil, exposure, and trouble of such an enterprise as that in which they were engaged at the hottest season of the year, in a close vessel, would seem to be unfavorable to the convalescence of the sufferer, or even to the continuance in health of those not sick; but they suffered far less from disease than those who remained at Jamestown, —as probably would always be the advantage of those who lead an active life, over those who indulge in one of indolence.

There was no indolence where Smith had command. The next day, urging their boat as far up the river as the stream would carry it, he went ashore, set up crosses, and cut their names upon the trees. While thus engaged the sentinel was astonished by an arrow falling beside him. Yet where a savage could hide himself they knew not, for an hour had been spent in examining the spot, groping in the earth, gathering herbs and stores, and seeking for springs of sweet water. But instantly taking the alarm, they found themselves assailed by no less than a hundred savages, who, skipping nimbly from tree to tree, kept up an incessant flight of arrows. The assailants were too timid, and shot too wildly to do much injury; and, after a skirmish of half an hour, they disappeared as suddenly as they came. Mosco played the hero on this occasion, emptying his quiver, flying to the boat for fresh supplies, and gallantly leading off the pursuit against the fugitives. But it was with some difficulty that he could be kept from playing the savage also; for, coming upon one of their enemies who had been wounded by a musket bullet in the knee, "never was dog more furious against a beare, than Mosco was to have beate out his braines." This was not approved of, as scarcely a Christian process. The wounded savage was dressed by the surgeon of the English, and so recovered as to be able to give an account of himself and people. He belonged to the Hassinninga, was a brother of the chief of that tribe, which, with three others, made up the nation of Mannahock. He had heard that the English were a people come from under the world to take their world from them. Some of this was certainly true, and possibly the whole. When asked how many worlds there were, he answered that he knew of none but that which lay under the sky above them, of which he had been taught to believe that the Powhatanese, the Monacans, and the Massawomeks, were the sole inhabitants. The Monacans, he said, were the neighbors and friends of his people. They dwelt in hilly countries, on the banks of small rivers, and lived upon roots and fruits, but chiefly by hunting. The Massawomeks dwelt upon a great water, had many boats, and so many men that they made war with all the world. When asked what was beyond the mountains, he replied, "The sun!" Other questions of the sort he answered in like manner. It was evident he knew little of such unimportant matters. This prisoner was named Amoroleck—not a bad name for a romantic story of the school of Chateaubriand. They persuaded him to go with them, rather than kept him; though he earnestly desired them to remain where they were, that they might make, on better terms than before, the acquaintance of his people.

But all this was opposed by Mosco. He was impatient of the dialogue, which to his ears was no doubt tedious. But he better knew the savage nature than the English, and warned them that their delay would endanger their safety. He described the Mannahocks as a naughty race, as troublesome and treacherous as the Rappahannocks. Still, they lingered until night; then embarked, and took their way down the river. It was not long before the arrows of the Indians were heard rattling upon the Massawomek shields, and dropping into the barge. The stream was narrow, the land on one side high, and but for the darkness, our English might have suffered seriously from this mode of assault. It was in vain that Amoroleck called to his countrymen. The yells of the assailants silenced all other sounds, except that of the musket, which every now and then Smith caused to be discharged against the quarter whence the clamor rose most loudly. So tenacious were they of the conflict, that they followed the course of the boat in this manner for nearly twelve miles. By daylight the English, emerging into a spacious bay, dropped anchor, and fell to breakfast, being only then out of arrow-shot. The savages, four or five hundred in number, crowded the banks, but the party was quite too hungry and too tired to notice them till after breakfast. Then taking down their shields, they showed themselves with their prisoner, between whom and his countrymen followed a long discourse. This led to a proper understanding between the parties. The Indians hung their bows and arrows upon the trees, while two of them, their bows and quivers upon their heads, swam off to the barge, bringing these as tributes and in proof of friendship. Smith promptly went ashore, and bade them summon their kings. These were at no great distance. The word King, as employed by our author, must be understood in the sense of chief. The chiefs were the captains of tens, and hundreds, and thousands, and led the several war parties of the nation under the rule of some one great master like Powhatan.

These soon made their appearance, four in number, according to the requisition of Smith. They received Amoroleck at his hands with great rejoicing. They tendered their bows, arrows, tobacco-pipes, and pouches, refusing nothing that was demanded. They, in turn, asked for nothing but the pistols of the English, which they took to be pipes of a highly improved fashion. But, with less dangerous commodities, Smith left them perfectly happy in their new allies; singing, dancing, and making merry as they went.

The victory of our captain over the Mannahocks, and the subsequent pacification with them, highly delighted the Moraughtacunds; who were a feeble race, of smaller persons, and fewer numbers. They entreated him to endeavor to bring the Rappahannocks to their senses also; a benefit in which, as the allies of the English, they must necessarily share. Smith needed no entreaties to this effect. Though by no means wanton in the exercise of power, by no means blood-thirsty, but, indeed, singularly indulgent and forbearing, though decisive with the savages—he yet felt the necessity of making his power respected by all the tribes in the neighborhood. He summoned the Rappahannocks, accordingly, to a conference, at which several of the Indian kings attended; and giving them a judicious preliminary hint of his power to burn their hamlet, destroy their corn, and prove in other respects a very troublesome enemy to deal with, he demanded that they should bring him—in proof of friendship and by way of tribute—the bow and arrows of their king; should leave their arms on coming into his presence; make a treaty of peace with his allies, the Moraughtacunds; and as a guaranty for the faithful keeping of these pledges, bring him the son of the king as a hostage. Rappahannock—for the name of the people seems to have been that of the king—objected to the last condition. He had but one son and could not live without him; but in lieu of the son, he was not unwilling to give up to the Moraughtacunds certain women of his whom the latter had stolen—a proceeding which had been at the bottom of their recent wars Our Captain was indulgent, and readily accepted the substitute.

Having returned to Moraughtacund, he had the three women brought before him, and put a chain of beads upon the neck of each. Then calling up the king Rappahannock, he bade him choose her whom he most desired; the second choice was accorded to the king of the Moraughtacunds, and the third woman was allotted to Mosco with the whiskers, the suspected Frenchman. The parties were all apparently well satisfied with this mode of distribution. The proceedings finished only with the night. The next day the people of both the tribes, or nations, to the number of six or seven hundred, assembled to celebrate the triple peace which had thus been established by means of the stranger. Not a bow nor arrow was to be seen amongst them: all the shows and images of war were studiously kept from sight. They pledged themselves to perpetual friendship with the English; volunteered to plant corn for them; and were delighted with the promise that, in return, they should receive ample supplies of hatchets, beads, and copper. Mosco, whom these proceedings had greatly distinguished, in the heat of his exultation, repudiated that inexpressive name, and adopted that of *Uttasantough*, which, in his dialect, signifies "*stranger;*" and the supposed son of the Frenchman became the subject of the English Solomon.*

From the Rappahannocks our Captain steered his vessel to the Piankatank, which he explored as far as it was navigable. This river seems to have been sparsely settled. Smith describes it as being able to bring into the field but fifty or sixty serviceable men. At the period of his visit, however, the people were mostly absent on a

* King James the First.

hunt. He saw but a few old men, women, and children, in the cornfields, from whom he obtained a promise of supply whenever he should come for it.

He now took his way home; and on his returning progress was destined to encounter a more narrow peril than any he had yet escaped on the expedition. While in the direction of Point Comfort, he anchored in a bay called Gosnolds, a little to the south of York River. Here, in an instant, a sudden gust changed a fair calm sky into one of night and tempest. So terrible was the storm, with rain and thunder, that our Captain confesses for the party they never more expected to see Jamestown. Running before the wind, they could sometimes see the land by the fiery flashes from heaven; and by this light only were they saved from splitting upon the shores, and finally conducted—the storm and blackness still prevailing—in finding their way to Point Comfort. Verily, it deserved the name in the regards of our voyagers. There, having refreshed themselves, and the skies becoming clear, they once more set out, resolved to finish their adventures by visiting the Chesapeakes and Nasemonds—tribes of which they had only heard, but which, as among their near neighbors, it was deemed more proper they should know than those which were more remote. Steering for the southern shore, they penetrated the river now called the Elizabeth, upon which the town of Norfolk now stands, and sailed some six or seven miles into the territories of the Chesapeake. But they saw none of the inhabitants; nothing more imposing than a few houses and garden-plots, and forests, "overgrowne with the greatest Pyne and Firre trees we ever saw in the country." Returning to the main stream, they coasted the shores to the mouth of the Nansemond, where they came upon half a dozen savages mending their fish-traps. These fled at sight of the strangers. The English landed and left some trifles, as a peace-offering, where the Indians had been working. They had not gone far, when the Indians returned, found the toys, and with great gladness and good humor invited the strangers to come back. They did so, and thus began an intimacy which ended in our voyagers turning their prow into the river, which they penetrated some seven or eight miles, the Indians keeping pace along the shore with the progress of the vessel. One of the savages freely entered the boat, and the rest made an abundant display of good feeling. The sight of large cornfields on the western shore rewarded our explorers with the prospect and promise everywhere of great plenty of provisions. Their Indian companion invited them to his habitation on a little islet in the river, where they saw his wife and children, to whom they gave such presents as greatly contented them. Thus far all things looked smilingly enough. But when their companion had left them, and they had left his islet, and in a farther progress up the stream, they found it became exceedingly narrow, things began to look suspiciously, and our voyagers prepared for the worst. They soon found themselves followed by seven or eight armed canoes, full of people, and this discovery was followed by flights of arrows from the shores on each side of the river, as rapidly shot as two hundred practised bowmen could send them. The canoes opened upon our English at the same moment. Smith addressed most of his muskets to the assailants on the river. It was more immediately necessary to remove them from his path. A volley soon drove them from their canoes—most of them taking to the water and swimming to the shore. A few shot forced those upon the banks into the cover of the woods, and the English took possession of the canoes which they had abandoned. These they drew with them down the river, where it was sufficiently wide to put them out of reach of arrow-shot. Here they proceeded to cut the captured canoes to pieces; at sight of which the Indians—supposed to be the Chesapeakes and Nansemonds together—by whom the shores were crowded, threw down their weapons, making signs of peace and entreaty. To this our Captain had no objections. But he had conditions. He required the bow and arrows of their king, a chain of pearls, and four hundred full bushels of corn; and upon their rejection of these conditions, he threatened not only the destruction of their canoes, but of all their houses and possessions. Their compliance was prompt. "Away went their bows and arrowes, and tagge and ragge came with their baskets." The English took as much as they could carry. They had suffered no injury in the contest, thanks to the targets of the Massawomeks. These were pierced by more than one hundred arrows. Parting with these cunning savages on friendly terms, our Captain now made his way to Jamestown, which he reached on the 7th of September, having been more than six weeks absent.

In these two voyages he had explored the whole Bay of Chesapeake; an excellent map of which he constructed, which still remains to us. Upon his own computation he had traversed more than three thousand miles. He had incurred a thousand perils, and passed through them all in safety; had suffered with his men a thousand hardships and privations, which were all endured with patient courage and uncomplaining fortitude. We must not undervalue these expeditions because they are associated with no event of singular magnitude; the slaughter of no multitudes, and the sacking of no glorious city. In the absence of all those startling catastrophes, which too much make and characterize the renown of conquerors, the achievements of our hero, on these occasions, were not less remarkable. By none but a very remarkable man could they possibly have been done. No disaster marks his progress. He sheds no unnecessary blood; but wins his followers along through all difficulties, among a barbarous people, neither vexing or fatiguing the one, nor provoking the hate and jealousy of the other. The vulgar captain, conscious of the superiority of his muskets over the naked savages, would have tracked his way in slaughter. As prompt in danger as the bravest, Smith rather draws off from the strife, and folds his arms until he finds conflict unavoidable. He prefers the milder course of treaty and expostulation, and gives the ignorant natives time to discover for themselves the superior power which he possesses. His courage and moderation—the skill and ingenuity with which he works himself into the confidence of the simple Indians—the good nature with which he smiles upon and sanctions their sports—the curiosity with which he listens to their histories, and studies their character—and the felicity and great correctness with which he notes all their peculiarities—these proofs alone of the great strength of his natural judgment and genius, and the extent of his experience and resources, shown on this single progress, should sufficiently entitle him to rank among the distinguished men of modern times. No man was ever more successful with the Indians. He admirably understood their character, and treated it with equal firmness and forbearance. To deal with them, as with his own followers, required the happiest discretion. The latter, sick and suffering, strangers in a strange land; sometimes refractory and unwilling, and always inferior to himself in ability and spirit; required equally to be subdued and soothed; to be restrained and goaded; to be upheld by his courage, and stimulated by his enterprise. The successful termination of the adventure is in proof of the excellence of his management; while the details of his daily progress sufficiently show that this success was due, not to mere luck or blind fortune, but to the admirably executive mind by which the whole progress was conceived and counselled.

CHAPTER VI.

THE return of Smith to the colony was always seasonable. The withdrawal of his stern authority and undiscriminating justice, was always sure to result in evil. Nothing had been done in his absence. The crop had been gathered by the diligence of Scrivener, but the provisions in store had been suffered to spoil with rain. Captain Ratcliffe, the late President, had not borne with becoming meekness his exclusion from office, and was now laid up for mutiny. The summer had been a sickly one. Most had been sick, many had recovered, some were still sick, and many were dead. Nothing had been done, except by the small party under Smith.

Three days after his return he was elected to the Presidency, having received the letters patent from the council. He had hitherto refused this office, in the teeth of frequent importunacy on the part of his friends. He could refuse it no longer. His authority was no less necessary to the success of the settlement than his courage and enterprise. This conviction being forced upon him by a succession of proofs, Smith entered upon his duties with becoming resolution. The church and storehouse were repaired; new buildings raised for the supplies momently expected from England; the fort strengthened and altered into "a five square forme;" the watch renewed; and the whole company was drawn out every Saturday and drilled in military exercises, "in the plane by the west bulwarke," which was prepared for that purpose, and called Smithfield. On such occasions the Indians would gather around in great numbers to witness the display, standing "in amazement to behold how a fyle would batter a tree."

Nor did Smith confine his regards wholly to the strengthening and improving of the immediate settlement. He repaired his boats, and sent forth a trading party under Lieutenant Percy, with instructions to seek the country of the Monacans. But Percy had not gone far before he met Captain Newport, just from England, with fresh supplies, and came back with him to the fort. Newport brought with him about seventy individuals; two of whom, Captain Richard Waldo, and Captain Wynne, "two ancient souldiers, and valiant gentlemen, but yet ignorant of the businis," were appointed members of the council. In this ship came also the first Englishwomen that ever were in Virginia, Mrs. Forrest, and Anne Burras, her maid. A few more women had been a more judicious contribution to the wants of the colony than some that were made. But the Company were unwisely counselled, and the new supply, instead of bringing with it comfort to our Captain, brought with it little else than annoyance. The instructions given to Captain Newport were of a sort to offend the common sense of any man having the experience and the knowledge of Smith. They betrayed a singular degree of ignorance as to the nature of the deficiencies, the feebleness, and the true wants of such a colony. A special commission was confided to him, authorizing him, in certain circumstances, to act independently of the council in Virginia. By this commission he was instructed not to return without a lump of gold, a certainty of the South Sea, or one of the lost company sent out by Sir Walter Raleigh.* Requisitions, a rigid

* The lost colony of Captain White, which had been left on the island of Roanoke, had disappeared, leaving no traces, and was probably cut off by the Indians.

endeavor to comply with which might have kept the worthy mariner going to and fro through the territories of Powhatan to the present day. These instructions were probably of his own head. He had obtained the ear of the Company in England, and originated all these inventions. We have heard and seen something of this person before, in his visit to Powhatan. He is described, and seemingly with great justice, as an empty, idle, and selfish adventurer; very great in his own conceit, and swelling in his talk at ordinary seasons, but timorous and suspicious in moments of danger, and totally unequal to its exigencies. "How or why Captaine Newport obtained such private commission, as not to returne without a lumpe of gold, a certaintie of the South Sea, or one of the lost companie sent out by Sir Walter Raleigh, I know not; nor why he brought such a five peeced Barge, not to beare us to that South Sea, *till we had borne her over the mountaines, which how farre they extend is yet unknowne.*" Such, indeed, had been one of the ridiculous projects of Newport and the Company, the absurdity of which our Captain exposes in a single sentence. A barge had been actually constructed and sent out in pieces from England, to be carried upon men's shoulders over the mountains of Virginia, to the waters of the South Sea. The idea was taken from the proceedings of Cortes, in manufacturing his brigantines at Tlascala, and sending them on the backs of *tamanes* to the Mexican lakes. But Cortes, before he did so, knew where to seek for his lakes, and just how far they were distant from his brigantines. But our Virginia Company knew no more of the space between the dominions of Powhatan and the South Sea, than they did of the mountains in the moon. This was not the only absurdity. Some score of foreigners, Poles and Dutchmen, were sent out on wages, for the purpose of manufacturing pitch, tar, glass, milles, and soap-ashes ;—objects, says Smith, which, "when thê country is replenished with people and necessaries, would have done well, but to send them and seaventie more, without victualls, to worke, was not so well advised nor considered of as it should have beene." The folly of the company and their adviser did not stop here; and the next proceeding of which Smith justly complains was one likely to be productive of a great deal of mischief, as tending to elevate the self-esteem of those very persons who were already proud enough, and whom it was the English policy to make subordinate. Certain expensive presents were sent out for Powhatan, and orders were issued for his formal coronation as a Prince, after the European fashion. This was a mischievous, as well as ridiculous mummery, and vexed the good sense and solid understanding of our hero. "As for the coronation of Powhatan," says he, "and his presents of bason and ewer, bed, bedstead, clothes, and such costly novelties, they had much better well spared than so ill spent, for wee had his favour much better onely for a playne peece of copper, till this stately kind of soliciting made him so much overvalue himselfe, that he respected us as much as nothing at all."

But Newport had his commission and his crown, and the coronation and all other follies were to be achieved or attempted. He accordingly summoned the council together, and unfolded his powers and his schemes together. It is needless to say that Smith opposed them as equally unwise and impracticable. He urged his views of the impolicy of all these projects with his wonted force and earnestness. His objections have already in part been given. There were others which he urged before the council. It was sufficiently hard, he argued, to feed two hundred additional mouths, with the provisions obtained with difficulty for one hundred and thirty only; but even this was comparatively a small objection to that which could be urged against the great loss of time consumed in these idle performances. "For wee had the salvages in that *decorum* (their harvest being newly gathered) that wee feared not to get victuals for 500. Now was there no way to make us miserable," he asks, "but to neglect that time to make provision whilst it was to be had, the which was done by the direction from *England*, to performe this strange discovery, but a more strange coronation, to loose that time, spend what victualls wee had, tyre and starve our men, having no meanes to carry victuals, munition, the hurt or sicke, but on their own backs?"

But the arguments of Smith were unavailing. The majority of the council were against him. Scrivener himself desired to see new countries; Waldo and Wynne, the newly arrived, were anxious to carry out the wishes of the Company in England; and even Ratcliffe, who had been laid by the heels for mutiny, was permitted to have a voice on the occasion, which was naturally adverse to the suggestions of Smith. Captain Newport, whom our Captain charged with the conception of all these projects, "so guilded men's hopes with great promises," that his resolutions were adopted. Smith, in language almost borrowed from divine lips, exclaims mournfully, "God doth know they little knew what they did, nor understood their owne estates," to adopt his conclusions. To Smith's objections about waste of time and lack of provisions, Newport pledged himself to freight the pinnace with twenty tons of corn while going on and returning from his discovery, and to procure a similar supply from Powhatan at Werowocomoco. He promised also to divide with them the ship's stores; and when Smith shook his head with doubt at these fair promises, he meanly insinuated that the opposition of our Captain arose only from a selfish wish to undertake the adventure himself to the exclusion of others; and, seizing upon an old charge which had been made against him in the time of Captain Martin, said that nothing, indeed, could prevent the success of the expedition but the desire of the savages to revenge the cruelties which Smith had practised upon them. To this the answer of our Captain was sufficiently conclusive; not only as showing his innocence of this charge in particular, but to prove that he was in every respect willing to facilitate the enterprise, the moment it was fully resolved upon. He was not the man to throw any obstacles in the way of a scheme, which he yet felt himself compelled to disapprove; and exhibited none of that sullen inactivity, by which inferior men passively retard what they can no longer actively oppose. He volunteered to visit Powhatan with only four companions —"where Newport durst not goe with less than 120"— to entreat the Indian monarch to come to Jamestown to receive his presents, and undergo the ceremonial of coronation. His offer was accepted. The small party went over land to Werowocomoco, but Powhatan was some thirty miles distant. He was immediately sent for, and Pocahontas, in the meantime, undertook to entertain the guests of her father.

She did this after a fashion of her own, and which, for a moment, proved rather startling to some of the English. Conducting the party to a "fayre plaine" in the woods, they were placed upon mats around a fire. This done, Pocahontas disappeared, and suddenly a hideous shrieking arose from the woods, which caused the party to leap to their feet, prepare their weapons, and seize upon two or three old men who had remained with them as securities for their safety. They looked momently to see Powhatan and all his power emerge from the woods upon them. In place of these, however, Pocahontas showed herself, to reassure them. She was greatly discomposed that her sports, innocently meant, should have caused alarm, and placing herself among the English, she bade them kill her if any evil was intended. Men, women, and children, flocked around them at the same time, to confirm the assurances of the sweet forest damsel whom they served. Our Captain was soon satisfied that there was nothing to be apprehended. But his companions were mostly fresh from England, and his seizure of the old men as guaranties and hostages was most probably an act meant only to give them confidence. They resumed their places upon the matting, Pocahontas placing herself among them, while a pageant after a primitive fashion—a masque, shall we call it, of the Powhatanese?—took place, sufficiently new to the strangers, but one which did not greatly delight their tastes. We are reminded, as we read, of some of the orgies of nymphs and satyrs, such as the old dramatists used to exhibit in their "daintie devises." The scene was opened by the appearance from the woods of thirty young damsels, who, clad only in green leaves, came boldly forth as from the hands of original nature—with the single exception, that where their skins were visible through the leaves they were decorated with paints of various colors. The style of costume in each, not to fall into an Hibernianism, differed from that of her companions. No two of them were painted alike. "Their leader had a fayre payre of buck's hornes on her head, and an otter's skinne at her girdle, and another at her arme, a quiver of arrowes at her backe, and a bow and arrowes in her hand." How easy to fancy this the Diana of Werowocomoco? Others carried other implements and ornaments, all of which may have been emblematical, but all were alike horned, and, to our English companions, horrible. The language in which our author speaks of their exhibition smacks of the puritan rather than the gallant or the adventurer. He calls them " fiends," and describes their shrieks and shouts as " hellish." They darted headlong from among the trees, cast themselves frantically in a passionate set of antics about the fire, and, according to our narrator, played the part of Bacchantes to perfection. In such maddening manner did the light-heeled and light-handed damsels of Cyprus hail the ascent and approach of their reeling deity. " Singing and dauncing with most excellent ill varietie, oft falling into their infernall passions, and solemnly againe to sing and daunce," they consumed about an hour in their fantastic exhibition, then disappeared among the trees as suddenly and strangely as they had entered. But this scene did not end the " Mascarado." Having invited Smith and the rest to their lodgings, our masquerading dames changed the character of their sports, and from being wild and furious before, they became tender and solicitous. But the proceedings in the latter were not more grateful than in the former character, and our Captain complains that he was now more than ever tormented by their fondling and embraces. They hung upon him, crowding and pressing, as do the nymphs who would tempt Robert le Diable in the opera, crying out—" most tediously," says our hero—" Love you not me ? Love you not me ?"

Poor Pocahontas ! little did she fancy that her primitive forest fancy would have had so unpleasing effect upon her English favorites. Whether our courtly Captain allowed her to see or to suspect his own, and the annoyance of his companions, is not stated. At all events, she continued her efforts, in the absence of her father, to amuse and to delight her guests. The masque being over, the feast was set—"consisting of all the salvage dainties they could devise: some attending, others singing and dauncing about them,"—the whole mirth and festival being ended by their seizing upon blazing firebrands, and conducting them, in a sort of royal state, to the lodgings which had been prepared for them. The scene, making allowances for the ruder tastes of a savage people, was perfectly feminine, and is not without its sweetness and its charm. A little subdued by the hand of art, the poet may yet weave it into some lovely native fabric. Pocahontas does not appear to have engaged in this frolic, except to command it, and she commanded only such pranks as they were no doubt accustomed to practise in the presence of their noblest guests.

Powhatan made his appearance the next morning, and Smith apprised him of the presents and the honors that awaited him at Jamestown, desiring him to return with him, and receive them at the hands of Father Newport. The answer of Powhatan was becoming equally the monarch and the man. It betrayed also something of the sagacity of the politician. A natural and proper caution was no doubt busy with the self-esteem and pride of character of the haughty savage, in prompting his reply.

"If," said he, "your king has sent me presents, I also am a king, and this is my land. Eight days will I stay to receive them. Your father is to come to me, not I to him, nor yet to your fort. I will not bite at such a bait."

To some suggestions which Smith had made, touching a concerted operation between them against the Monacans, and in respect to the meditated journey over the mountains to the South Sea, he answered with equal decision:

"As for the Monacans, I can revenge my own injuries. As for Atquanachuck, where you say your brother was slain, it is a contrary way from those parts you suppose it. For any salt water beyond the mountains, the relations you have had from my people are false!"

Could any answer from any monarch have been more frank and manly, and characterized by more dignity of character? To illustrate the truth of his disclaimer on the subject of the salt water beyond the mountains, he drew upon the ground a rude outline of the countries of which himself and his people had spoken. He was by no means churlish or reserved, though decisive in his answers. On the contrary, the discourse between the parties, which was protracted, was marked throughout by courtesy and kindness on both sides;—both Smith and Powhatan being pretty equally skilled in the arts of diplomacy.

The arguments of our Captain failed to procure any but the one answer from the Virginian Emperor, on the subject of the coronation presents. They were accordingly sent by water, while Smith and Newport, with an escort of fifty men, went across by land to Werowocomoco. Here Powhatan awaited them in all his state, and the next day was appointed for the performance of the ceremony which had been the occasion of the interview. We can readily conceive the importance which such a man as Newport attached to these proceedings, and with what state the guards were arranged, and the several marshals appointed to their places; with what solemn dignity the presents were brought forth; the bason and ewer, the bed and its royal furniture set up, and the scarlet cloak, apparel and crown, got in readiness to invest the tawny limbs and forehead of the forest chieftain. Our authorities afford us but few details, but these give a sufficient clue to the imagination of the reader. Powhatan seemed somewhat suspicious of these presents. The bason and ewer looked innocent enough; so perhaps did the bed and furniture; but the scarlet cloak had something in its aspect which he did not so much relish. He had never heard of the fate of Hercules, but he evidently had some notion of the dangers which might accrue from wearing the cast off clothes of Nessus; and it required all the assurances of Namontack, the faithful Indian whom he had entrusted with Newport to visit England, and who had just returned, to persuade him that there was nothing deadly in the garment. It was with much ado they succeeded in getting the scarlet robe over his shoulders. But as for kneeling to receive the crown, that he could not do. He was not used to such humiliation, and no argument could reconcile him to it. He neither knew "the majesty nor meaning of a crowne," and after "a foule trouble" which they had, and which "tyred them all," they only succeeded in their object at last "by leaning hard upon his shoulders," so that "he a little stooped," and this gave them a moment's opportunity to place the kingly circle over the unwilling brows. When this curious operation in crowning a king had reached this stage of the business, a pistol-shot gave the signal to the boats, which poured forth a volley of musketry in honor of the event. Newport, as we see, had arranged the details with great regard to the solemnity and state of the occasion But Powhatan, suspecting danger at every step in the affair, was prepared to find anything but compliment in this salute, and behaved, when the shot struck upon his ears, in a most unroyal manner—starting to his feet, and, until the matter was explained, showing no small degree of apprehension. Reassured by our Captain, he recovered himself sufficiently to perform an act which, under like circumstances, would have been characteristic of most sovereigns in any part of the world. To show his gratitude, he gave his old shoes and mantle to Captain Newport, who, we may willingly allow, had justly merited them. To this liberal present was added another, just before the parties separated, of seven or eight bushels of corn. The English derived very little farther advantage from this vain and paltry proceeding. For his own reasons, which were no doubt quite satisfactory to himself, Powhatan refused to join with them against the Monacans, whom he had heretofore pronounced his enemies; refused to give them guides to the territories of that people; and earnestly endeavored to dissuade them from their purposes of hostility. Thus ended the expedition. In good hands, what a ludicrous picture might be made of this coronation of Powhatan;—the reluctant savage pressed down by the shoulders, while the three Englishmen, with the crown aloft, standing on tiptoe, seize the lucky moment to drop the shining honor upon his brows!

CHAPTER VII.

The refusal of Powhatan to furnish guides, and his evident reluctance to encourage any further exploration into his territories, did not discourage Captain Newport in his meditated progress in search of the country of the Monacans. Smith in vain strove to divert him from a purpose, the fruits of which, according to his prediction, would be only toil and suffering. But the idea of gold dust and gold mines, which had seized upon the soul of the good sea captain, made him insensible to every argument founded upon reason and experience. To use the verses which Smith employs in this place, and which, for aught we know, may be from his own pen—

"But those that hunger seeke to slake,
Which thus abounding wealth woulde rake,
Not all the gemmes of Ister's shore,
Nor all the gold of Lydia's store,
Can fill their greedie appetite,
It is a thing so infinite."

Leaving behind him eighty or ninety men with Smith, at Jamestown, to load the vessel, Newport, with one hundred and twenty, set forth, soon after his return from the visit to Powhatan, upon his expedition into the wilderness. But his course through the woods proved to be no such pleasant sailing, and a journey of forty miles, which consumed nearly three days, found our adventurers in no humor to proceed further. They made no discoveries, got no gold, saw nothing to recompense their labor. Two Indian towns of the Monacans were discovered, in which they could procure grain for neither love nor money. The savages, anxious to be rid of their presence, yet afraid to be hostile, treated them with sullen indifference, and frightened them with a story of strange ships, which, since their departure, had penetrated to Jamestown with the view to its conquest. They had hidden their corn, and could not be tempted by any offers of trade to betray its hiding-place to the greedy strangers. This treatment, and the fatigue which they suffered from a mode of journey to which they were wholly unaccustomed, soon reconciled our delicate English to the necessity of foregoing those wonderful discoveries upon which Newport had set his heart; and, burdened with some shining earths in which their refiner pretended to discover silver, they turned their faces once more to the settlement. Smith sneers at so sudden an abandonment of a progress through a country equally fair, fertile and well watered; but the result was only what he had predicted. They reached Jamestown, "halfe sicke, all complaining, and tyred with toyle, famine and discontent"—wiser, perhaps, but scarcely grateful for an acquisition so very different from any which their golden hopes had promised.

Smith had little sympathy for the adventurers. They had no sooner reached the town, when he set such of them as were able to labor, each according to his peculiar ability, in procuring the necessary commodities for freighting the vessel. Some were set to the manufacture of glass, others of tar, pitch, and potash, and these were placed under the control of the council; while he himself, with thirty others, leaving Jamestown, proceeded down the river to a proper spot in the forest, where he could teach them the art of felling trees, making clap-boards, and sleeping in the woods. Smith was the proper leader to convert into hardy and enterprising men the puny and effeminate "younger sons" who were sent to him from

England. He himself shrunk from no toil, and no exposure. Neither danger nor labor discouraged his manhood; and, with his example before them—that of grappling always with the worst and most difficult parts of duty—his followers were deprived of all excuse for complaint or discontent. But the employment had its pleasurable excitements. The novelty had its charm, and their tasks soon became familiar. "Strange were these pleasures to their conditions; yet lodging, eating, and drinking, working or playing, they but doing as the President did himselfe. All these things were carried on so pleasantly, as within a weeke they became masters; making it their delight to heare the trees thunder as they fell." And a stirring sound it is: but the delight of our amateur woodcutters had its disagreeables also. "The axes so oft blistered their tender fingers, that many times every third blow had a loud othe to drowne the echo." For this immorality, which our hero seems to have held in considerable dislike, he adopted a novel remedy. Each man's oaths were numbered by his companions, and when the labor of the day was over, for every oath, a can of cold water was poured down the sleeve of the offender. He himself was not exempt from this penalty,—which seems so completely to have had the effect desired, that an oath was scarcely to be heard in a week. "By this," says our author, "let no man thinke that the President and these gentlemen spent their times as common woodhaggers at felling of trees, or such other like labours; or that they were pressed to it as hirelings, or common slaves; for what they did, after they were but once a little inured, it seemed, and some conceited it, only as a pleasure and a recreation: yet thirty or forty of such voluntary gentlemen would doe more in a day than one hundred of the rest, that must be prest to it by compul-

Gentlemen taught to labor. PAGE 240.

sion." We may add that much of this would be due to the skill of him who had the direction of their labors. The hearty zeal with which Smith set the example—his own spirit, promptness and energy—and the excellent humor and judgment with which he planned the penalties of neglect or ill-performance,—these were the essential influences by which to make those work, whom more severity would have only driven into rebellion. Had Smith played the martinet with his volunteers, as the drill sergeant of the regular service is wont to do, he might have had their axes about his ears. Still, though pleased with the spirit and industry of his men, our hero quietly adds, that "twentie good workmen had been better than them all."

Returning to the fort, Smith was vexed to find that the time had been consumed, and no provisions procured. The ship lay idle at a great charge, and her men did nothing. Without wasting more time in unprofitable complaints, his indefatigable spirit at once proceeded to remedy this new evil. Embarking in the discovery barge, and leaving instructions for Lieutenant Percy to follow in another, he set out for the people of Chickahominy. "That dogged nation was too well acquainted with our wants, refusing to trade with as much scorne and insolency as they coulde expresse." But Smith was in no humor to submit to denial or ill-treatment. The exigency at Jamestown was pressing. Besides, he perceived that the countenance of Powhatan was turned away from the colony; that it was his policy to starve them out; and that the time had at length arrived, for making such a display of his power, as would compel a return of that respect, on the part of this savage monarch and his people, as would ensure the future safety of the English. Changing his tone accordingly, he told the Chickahominies that he did not so much come for their corn as for his revenges. He had an old account to settle with them. His own imprisonment had never been atoned for, nor the murder of his people; and it was his humor now to take vengeance upon them for both these occasions of complaint. Landing his men, and making ready to charge the savages, they took to their heels, and sought the cover of the woods; from whence they sent him an embassy, laden with corn, fish, and fowl, as a tribute to the offended strangers. They implored peace and pardon; excused themselves for their refusal to grant supplies, alleging, by way of extenuating themselves, that their harvests that year had been inferior; but concluded with freighting both barges with ample provisions.

Returning to Jamestown with this store, the fruit of his own energy and decision, Smith found himself more likely to suffer from the malice than be honored by the gratitude of his associates. It seems to have been his peculiar fortune in Virginia so to provoke the envy of his colleagues as to make them wholly blind to their dependence upon his abilities. Indeed, these very abilities, which so completely obscured their own, were the subject of their reproach and aversion. Radcliffe, who had proved himself imbecile while President; Newport, who had so recently verified by his own failure the good judgment and the predictions of our hero; would both much rather have hazarded starvation than that "his paines should prove so much more effectuall than theirs." Accordingly, as blind as bitter in their malice, they actually laid their heads together, not only to deprive him of the presidency on the wretched plea that he had left the fort without consent of Council, even though in the common exigency and for the common good, but they made an effort to keep him out of the fort also. But, to use the expressive language of our author, "their hornes were much too short" to effect their object. They themselves narrowly escaped a greater mischief. Our hero was no trifler when his wrath was roused, "and had not Captain Newport cried *peccavi*, the President would have discharged the ship, and caused him to have stayed one yeare in Virginia to learne to speake of his owne experience." We are not told of the manner in which Smith extricated himself from these attempts of his enemies; but the common conviction of his merits, his skill, spirit and invariable successes, set in contrast with the uniform feebleness of those who were envious of his abilities, naturally secured him the support of all the colony. To a certain extent, such an establishment in a foreign land must be influenced by popular feeling and opinion; and, hated by some of his associates, Smith was sustained by all his followers. Besides, he was not wholly alone in the council; and, among the chief persons of the settlement, Scrivener, Percy, Waldo, and others, were his staunch friends and advocates; and it appears to have been easy to baffled the malice of Newport and his more worthless ally, Radcliffe. But, though able to protect himself, and to maintain his authority against their machinations, he was much less successful in preventing the illicit traffic which was carried on between the sailors, the colonists, and the savages. "All this time our olde taverne (the ship) made as much of all of them that had either money or ware as could be desired. By this time they were become so perfect on all sides (I meane the souldiers, saylers and salvages), as there was ten times more care to maintaine their damnable and private trade, than to provide for the colony things that were necessary. Neither was it a small policy in Newport and the marriners to report in England we had such plentie, and bring us so many men without victuals, when they had so many private factors in the fort, that, within six or seaven weekes, of two or three hundred axes, chisels, hows (hoes) and pickaxes, scarce twentie could be found: and for pike-heads, shot, powder, or any thing they could steal from their fellowes was vendible; they knew as well (and as secretly) how to convey them to trade with the salvages for furres, baskets, *mussanaks*, young beasts, or such like commodities, as exchange them with the saylers for butter, cheese, beefe, porke, *aqua vitæ*, beere, bisket, oatmeale, and oyle: and then faine all was sent them from their friends. And though Virginia afforded no furres *for the store* (i. e. for the benefit of the owners), yet our master in one voyage hath got so many by this indirect meanes, as he confessed to have sold in England for thirty pounds."

These extracts give a lively idea of the extent of the peculation which Smith for a time vainly struggled to prevent. As lively an idea of the indignation which he felt may be gathered from another passage, where he seems to indicate his success in putting an end to it; and shows, at the same time, the sort of obstacles which usually serve to impede and baffle all such enterprises. "These," says he, speaking of the peculators, "are the saint-seeming worthies of Virginia, that have, notwithstanding all this, meate, drinke and wages; but now they begin to grow weary (of saint-seeming), their trade being both perceived and prevented; none hath beene in Virginia that hath observed any thing, which knowes not this to be true; and yet the losse, the scorne, the misery and shame, was the poore officers, gentlemen and carelesse Governours, who were all thus bought and sold; the adventurers cousened, and the action overthrowne by their false excuses, informations and directions. By this let all men judge how this businesse could prosper, being thus abused by such pilfring occasions."

The indignant temper which is here displayed is more appropriately shown by our hero in a letter which he addressed to the Treasurer and Council of the Plantation, in England, in the character of President of the settlement. He answers the false reports at the expense of the colony, set afloat by selfish and interested persons, and briefly, but amply, shows what have been and are the true evils and evil influences which have baffled the hopes and efforts of the colonists. His letter speaks for itself, and for the good sense, the clear judgment, and the unselfish manhood of the writer. From the tenor of the answer, the reader will sufficiently gather the sort of reports detrimental to the settlers, which had been circulated in England;—reports, which the disappointments of the council, with regard to the results of their outlay, made them but too ready to believe. It was much easier and far more grateful to suppose that the failure lay rather in the misconduct and disobedience of the agents, than in the errors and absurdity of their own schemes. They complained of the vain hopes with which they had been fed, and of the factions which defeated the performances of the colony; and concluded with threatening, that, unless the proceeds of the return voyage of Newport's ship should defray the expenses of her outfit—some two thousand pounds—they would abandon the settlement to its fate. It was with this threat to stimulate him, that Newport set out seeking mines of gold and silver in the country of the Monacans; while Smith, with more sagacity and industry, proceeded to hew trees, get out clapboards, and freight the vessel with pitch, tar, glass and potash. His letter accompanied the cargo. We furnish it at length:

"*Right Honourable, &c.* I received your letter, wherein you write, that our minds are so set upon faction, and idle conceits in dividing the country without your consents, and that we feed *you* but with ifs and ands, hopes and some few proofes; as if we would keepe the mystery of the businesse to ourselves; and that we must expressly follow your instructions sent by Captain Newport: the charge of whose voyage amounts to neare two thousand pounds, the which, if we cannot defray by the ship's returne, we are alike to remaine as banished men. To these particulars I humbly intreat your pardons if I offend you with my rude answer.

"For our factions, unlesse you would have me run away and leave the country, I cannot prevent them: because *I do make many stay that would els fly any whether.* For the idle letter sent to my Lord of Salisbury, by the President and his confederats, for dividing the country, &c.,—what it was I know not, for you saw no hand of mine to it, nor even dreamt I of any such matter. That we feed you with hopes, &c.—*Though I be no scholar, I am past a schoolboy; and I desire but to know, what either you, and these here doe know, but that I have learned to tell you by the continuall hazard of my life. I have not concealed from you any thing I know; but I feare some cause you to believe much more than is true.*

"Expressly to follow your directions by Captaine Newport, though they be performed, *I was directly against it;* but according to our commission I was content to be overruled by the major part of the councell, I feare to the hazard of us all; which now is generally confessed when it is too late. Onely Captaine Winne and Captain Waldo I have sworne of the councell, and crowned Powhatan according to your instructions.

"*For the charge of this voyage of two or three thousand pounds, we have not received the value of an hundred pounds.* And for the quartred boat to be borne by the souldiers over the falles, Newport had 120 of the best men he could chuse. *If he had burnt her to ashes, one might have carried her in a bag, but as she is, five hundred cannot,* to a navigable place above the falles. And for him at that time to find in the South Sea a mine of gold; or any of them sent by Sir Walter Raleigh: at our consultation I told them was as likely as the rest. But during this great discovery of thirtie myles (which might as well have been done by one man, and much more, for the value of a pound of copper at a seasonable tyme) they had the pinnace and all the boats with them, but one that remained with me to serve the fort. In their absence I followed the new begun works of pitch and tarre, glasse, sope ashes and clapboard, whereof some small quantities we have sent you. But if you rightly consider what an infinite toyle it is in Russia and Swethland, where the woods are proper for naught els, and though there be the helpe both of man and beast in those ancient commonwealths, which many an hundred yeares have used it, yet thousands of those poore people can scarce get necessaries to live, but from hand to mouth. And though your factors there can buy as much in a week as will fraught you a ship, or as much as you please; you must not expect from us any such matter, which are but as many of ignorant miserable soules, that are scarce able to get wherewith to live, and defend ourselves against the inconstant salvages: finding here and there a tree fit for the purpose, and want all things els the Russians have. For the coronation of *Powhatan*,—by whose advice you sent him such presents, I know not; but this give me leave to tell you, I feare they will be the confusion of us all ere we heare from you agane.* At your ship's arrivall the salvages' harvest was newly gathered, and we going to buy it, our owne not being halfe sufficient for so great a number. As for the two ships loading of corne Newport promised to provide us from *Powhatan*, he brought us but fourteen bushels, and from the *Monacans* nothing, but the most of the men sicke and neare famished. From your ship we had not provision in victuals worth twenty pound, and we are more than two hundred to live upon this: the one halfe sicke, the other little better. For the saylers (I confesse) they daily make good cheare; but our diet is a little meale and water, and not sufficient of that. *Though there be fish in the sea, foules in the aire, and beasts in the woods, their bounds are so large, they so wilde, and we so weake and ignorant, we cannot much trouble them.* Captain *Newport* we much suspect to be the author of those inventions. *Now, that you should know, I have made you as great a discovery as he, for lesse charge than he spendeth you every meale; I have sent you this mappe of the bay and rivers, with an annexed relation of the countries and nations that inhabit them, as you may see at large.*† Also two barrels of stones, and such as I take to be good iron ore at the least; so divided, as by their notes you may see in what places I found them. The souldiers say many of your officers maintaine their families out of that you sent

* Already, before the ink was dry on Smith's letter, we find it written—"Master Scrivener was sent with the barges and pinnace to Werowocomoco, where he found the salvages more readie to fight than trade," &c.

† Already referred to. A remarkably well executed chart, singularly correct, considering the difficulties and disadvantages of the explorer; and an admirable proof of the equal zeal, courage and abilities of our adventurer. The accompanying narrative is equally valuable and remarkable.

us: and that *Newport* hath an hundred pounds a yeare for carrying newes. For every master you have yet sent can find the way as well he, so that an hundred pounds might be spared, which is more than we have all, that helps to pay him wages. Capt. Radcliffe is now called Sicklemore, a poore counterfeited imposture. I have sent you him home, least the company should cut his throat What he is now, every one can tell you: if he and Archer returne againe they are sufficient to keepe us alwayes in factions. When you send againe I entreat you rather send but thirty carpenters, husbandmen, gardiners, fishermen, blacksmiths, masons and diggers up of trees' roots, well provided, than a thousand of such as we have; for except we be able both to lodge them and feed them, the most will consume with want of necessaries before they can be made good for any thing. Thus if you please to consider this account, and the unnecessary wages to Captaine Newport, or his ships so long lingering and staying here (for notwithstanding his boasting to leave us victuals for 12 months, though we had 89 by this discovery lame and sicke, and but a pint of corne a day for a man, we were constrained to give him three hogsheads of that to victual him homeward), or yet to send into Germany or Poleland for glasse men and the rest, till we be able to sustain ourselves, and releeve them when they come,—it were better to give five hundred pound a tun for these grosse commodities in Denmarke than send for them hither, 'till more necessary things be provided. For in over toyling our weake and unskilful bodies, to satisfie this desire of present profit, we can scarce even recover ourselves from one supply to another. And I humbly intreat you hereafter, let us know what we should receive, and not stand to the saylers courtesie to leave us what they please, else you may charge us what you will, but we not you with any thing. These are the causes that have kept us in *Virginia* from laying such a foundation, that ere this might have given much better content and satisfaction ; but as yet you must not looke for any profitable returne : So I humbly rest."

CHAPTER VIII.

This bold and manly letter was dictated by a sense of suffering and injustice, and somewhat by a consciousness of exigency. It has devolved upon "our Captaine," as we have seen, on almost all occasions, to procure and to provide, at the hazard of his own repose and life, the greater portion of the food by which the hungry mouths of the colony were satisfied. The ships had brought him consumers, and nothing more. The stores which they furnished were soon exhausted, equally by their own waste, and by the new colonists whom they brought. Seventy persons came with Newport on his last voyage, and were left as burdens to the colonists, who, as Smith states in his letter, was compelled to supply the ship's crew returning home with a portion of their slender store of provision. Of the new comers, *thirty were gentlemen*, *fourteen* were tradesmen, *twelve were laborers*, *two* were boys, *eight* were Dutchmen and Poles, sent out to make potashes; and there were *two* women, "Mistresse *Forrest*, and *Anne Burras*, her maide." The latter was, shortly after her arrival, married to John Laydon, a carpenter, who had been in the colony from the beginning; and this was the first marriage of Europeans that ever took place in Virginia. With this new and numerous supply of gentlemen, added to the already large proportion of the same unproductive sort of population, our Captain might well become affrighted at the new charge upon the feeble resources of the colony. The tone of his letter is enlivened by the sense of wrong done to the really industrious and adventurous portions of the settlement; and he might well be roused at the monstrous expense of two thousand pounds, to be liquidated by the colony, incurred in compliance with the absurd suggestions and dishonest counsels of Newport and Radcliffe—crowns, and robes, and wash-basins, to the dusky potentate of Werowocomoco, and searches after the South Sea in the wigwams and forests of the people of Monacan.

The seventy newly arrived had increased the number of the colony to two hundred persons. It had been found exceedingly difficult to provide for half that number, as the chief supplies of food were drawn from the Indians. These seldom planted more land than would yield provision for their own tribes, and though profligate enough to sell when under great temptation, they were now too familiar with the necessities and with the commodities of the English, not to value their own very highly. Besides, Powhatan was no longer disposed to encourage the growth of a strange people on his soil, whose resources were so great, and whose numbers he saw so constantly increasing. The colonists themselves, mostly dissipated and idle adventurers, unaccustomed to labor, and very soon yielding to the prostrating influences of the summer climate in Virginia, had at no time been able to raise an adequate supply of food for their own consumption. The late season, which had been laboriously employed by Smith in exploring the Chesapeake and the contiguous rivers, had been consumed by Radcliffe, then in the Presidency, in idleness and peculation. We have seen the waste which followed the arrival and the detention of Kenton and his floating tavern. At his departure, the destitute condition of the colony, doubly burdened with its new mouths, distressed and alarmed "our Captaine." "These poore conclusions so affrighted us all with famine," that he determined on an expedition to Nansemond in search of supplies. It will be recollected the fright he gave to this people while on his exploring voyage, threatening to burn their villages in consequence of their treachery, and receiving from them a promise of four hundred bushels of corn whenever he should next visit them. The necessities of the colony moved him to remind them of their promise. But they had entirely forgotten it; treated him very coldly; and not only withheld the required tribute, but positively refused to trade with him on any terms. They excused themselves for this refusal, by alleging that they had no provisions to spare, and that Powhatan had commanded them not only to keep their grain, but not to allow the English to enter their river. Smith, after vainly endeavoring to reason them into a more friendly disposition, brought his muskets to bear upon the argument. This drove them to the thickets, without discharging an arrow. But this brought "our Captaine" no nigher to his objects, and, putting the torch to one of their houses, he signified to them that such should be the fate of all unless the grain was forthcoming. This brought them out of covert. The argument was effectual; and, on condition that he should "make no more spoyle," they loaded the three boats which he brought, before night. "How they collected it," says our author, "I know not." Content with their atonement, and the quantity of grain which they furnished, Smith forbore farther severities, and, on the strength of his forbearance, they promised to plant a crop purposely for the English.

That night, our hero, with his party, dropping a few miles down the river, so as to place his boats and supplies in safety, went ashore, and made their beds at the foot of a hill, in the open woods. The ground was covered with snow, and frozen hard. They dug a space in the snow, and built a fire. When the heat had sufficiently dried the spot, they threw off the fire, swept the ground, and covering it with a mat, slept as warmly and pleasantly as if they had been in a palace. "To keepe us from the winde we made a shade of another mat; as the winde turned we turned our shade; and when the ground grew cold we renewed the fire. And thus many a cold winter night have we laine in this miserable manner; yet those that most commonly went upon those occasions were always in health, lusty and fat." These are encouraging facts, which the luxurious world are slow to understand. We have yet to learn how much the vigor and the elasticity of the human frame depend upon a free and hearty commerce with the air we breathe, and with the elements which enter into our composition.

The toils and perils of such a mode of life, the severities and caprices of the seasons, had no discouragements for "our Captain." Scarcely had he brought these supplies in safety to Jamestown, than he was off on another expedition, having the same object. This time, proceeding up the bay in two barges, he found himself avoided by the jealous savages. They fled on every side at his appearance, until he came to the river and people of Appamattox; with these he traded, with copper, for a small supply of corn, and returned to Jamestown to discover that Scrivener and Percy, who had also gone abroad on a similar quest, had returned with even smaller results than himself; having procured nothing.

These disappointments troubled our hero. The prospects were discouraging. Time was lost unprofitably, the savages were rapidly consuming the provision which was to supply the colony, and the winter, only just begun, promised to be a severe one. Smith's feelings of disquiet assumed a harsher aspect when he beheld the reluctance of the Indians to receive him—when he found them flying at his approach, and heard from their own lips that they were commanded by Powhatan to treat him as an enemy. He resolved to strike at the root of the evil—to single out the one superior offender over all, and, by a striking exhibition of his power, convince the natives that he was no longer to be trifled with. He resolved to surprise Powhatan, and take possession of all his provisions. It does not need that we should argue for the morality and justice of this decision. The discussion would carry us quite too far from our narrative, and beyond our limits. The case seems to have been one of necessity, and Smith was determined not to starve. He consulted with his counsel, but their opinions were divided. Scrivener and Winne, influenced by instructions from England, where, at that time, they were particularly tender of the sacredness of the rights of the royal person, were opposed to the project. Captain Waldo alone sided with him. Smith's reasons were those of Cortes and Pizarro. He felt their importance, the exigency of the necessity, and was not to be driven from his purposes. It happened, just at this time, as if to favor his design, that Powhatan dispatched a messenger to our hero, inviting him to come and see him. The emperor wished for workmen to build him a house after the English fashion. He also desired a grindstone, fifty swords, some guns, and other articles, for which he was willing to give a ship-load of corn. Powhatan had set his heart upon the swords and grindstones. We have already seen the endeavors which he made to procure them from Smith and Newport. With the latter he was successful; but the former was less easily persuaded to provide his treacherous enemy with better weapons of warfare than those to which he was accustomed. It is probable that the instructions given by Powhatan to his people, to refuse all commerce with the English, had no higher motive than so to reduce them by their exigencies as to compel Smith to trade with him on his own terms. Knowing that the several attempts of the colonists to procure grain had been baffled by his instructions, and having learned how eager they were in the pursuit of provisions, he fancied that the time had arrived when he might procure the objects which he desired at his own price; and hence his proposition, and hence his invitation to Smith to visit him. But the latter was disposed to suspect some more profound design at the bottom of this invitation. He well knew the devices and subtlety of the Indian heart, and, regarding only his more obvious policy, such as it would have been in the case of an European potentate, he found in it a full justification for his own project. He complied in part with the request of Powhatan; sent him four Dutch and two Englishmen to build his house, and prepared himself to visit him. But the swords were forgotten. Setting forth with the pinnace, two barges, and forty-six men, all volunteers, he left Jamestown for Werowocomoco some time in December.* His company was victualled for but three or four days, and lodging the first night with the king of Warraskoyack, at a short distance from Jamestown, they received from him ample additional supplies. This chief counselled Smith against visiting Powhatan, whom he described as meditating the most cruel treacheries, sending for the English only to cut their throats and seize their arms. But, though thanking him for his advice, Smith resolved against taking it. From this king he obtained guides to the dominions of another named Chawannock, whose territories lay in the fork of

* The narrative says the 29th, but, as he afterwards tells us of spending Christmas among the Indians of Kecoughtan, this must be an error. The matter is of little moment.

Chowan, between the rivers Nottoway and Meherin. With these he dispatched one Michael Sicklemore, whom he describes as "a very valiant, honest, and painful soldier." His object in sending this gentleman was threefold. He was to conciliate the friendship of the king of the Chowannocks, obtain some specimens of silk grass, and make inquiries after the lost company of Mr. Walter Raleigh. On leaving the king of Wanaskoyack, Smith left with him his page, Samuel Collier, in order that he should learn the Indian language.

From Wanaskoyack Smith next proceeded to Kecoughtan (Hampton). Here they were detained by storms for several days. They kept their Christmas—never more merrily—among the Indians, who feasted them upon oysters, fish, flesh and wild-fowl, in abundance. Better cheer and kinder welcome they never enjoyed. The yule-log had never burned for them more brightly in England, than in the smoky cabins of the Kecoughtan. Departing thence, it was not so agreeable to resume their ancient practice, so productive of health and fat, of lying in any weather by a great fire at the foot of a tree, and with no roof but that of heaven. To afford an idea of the abundance of wild fowl encountered on the route, during this severe season, we are told that the president, with Anthony Bagnall and Serjeant Pising, killed a hundred and forty-eight at three shots. Wild pigeons are probably meant. At Kiskiack, the extreme cold and bad weather, together with a desire to "suppress the insolency of these proud savages," prompted them to delay three or four days longer, and it was not till the 12th of January that they reached Werocomoco. Here winter awaited them with more than usual severity of aspect, as if in alliance with Powhatan. The river was frozen for a space of half a mile from the shore. But Smith's hardihood was not to be discouraged. To lose no time, having broken through the ice with the barge as far as this was possible, he taught his followers by his own example, "to march neare middle deep, a flight shot (an arrow shot), through this muddy, frozen ooze." Thus he gained the shore in safety with his men, and, quartering in the nearest cabins, sent to Powhatan for provisions. The Emperor very promptly supplied him in abundance with bread, turkeys and venison. The next day he received and feasted them after his ordinary manner, which, as we have seen in repeated instances, was not unworthy an Indian sovereign. But, the feast over, to the surprise of Smith, he inquired, with rare inhospitality, when he proposed to depart. The explanation which followed betrayed the duplicity of the savage nature. Powhatan denied that he had ever sent for him. He had no corn to spare, and his people less. Some forty baskets, indeed, might be had, but for these he required forty swords. Smith, in reply to this, coolly confronted him with the men by whom his message had been brought. When asked how he could be so forgetful, he "concluded" the matter with a merry laughter, and asked for his commodities. But none of these suited him. His desires were set only upon guns and swords, and, rejecting the copper with contempt, which was offered for his corn, he said that he could put a value upon his corn, not on the copper.

"Our Captaine" soon saw that the wily savage was trifling with him. He was not much in the mood for trifling, and, with some decision, he gave him to understand that his guns and swords might be bestowed upon him after a different mode from that which he desired. "Powhatan," said he, "though I had many courses to have made my provision, yet, believing your promises to supply my wants, I neglected all to satisfie your desire and to testify my love. I sent you my men for your building, neglecting mine own; what your people had you have engrossed, forbidding them our trade; and now you think by consuming the time, we shall consume for want, not having to fulfil your strange demands. As for swords and guns, I told you long ago, I had none to spare; *and you must know those I have can keep me from want:* yet steale or wrong you I will not, nor dissolve that friendship we have mutually promised, *except you constrain me by your bad usage.*"

Powhatan listened very attentively to this discourse, and promised, in reply, that within two days Smith should have all the corn which it was in his own and the power of his people to bestow. "Yet, Captaine Smith," he added, "some doubt about the motive of your coming hither makes me not so kindly seeke to relieve you as I would, for many doe inform me your coming hither is not for trade, but to possess my country and invade my people. These dare not come to bring you corne, seeing you thus for ever armed. To free us of this feare, leave your weapons aboard your vessel. Here, where we are all friends, they are wholly needless."

The frankness of Powhatan's speech was associated with quite too much wariness of conduct to disarm the caution of "our Captaine," with whom he contrived to confer throughout the day, in the same style and in excellent good humor. They were both politicians equally skilled and subtle,—each having a secret purpose, which he could only execute by first baffling the other's vigilance and circumspection. But the game was rather more intelligible and clear in the hands of the Indian emperor than in that of our hero. The latter little dreamed that he had been betrayed to Powhatan by the very persons whom he had sent to build his palace. Four of these, as we have seen, were Dutchmen. One of them, in particular, in consequence of his great spirit, judgment, and resolution, was so great a favorite of Smith, that he had, in fact, sent him as a sort of spy upon his enemy, to discover and report his secret machinations. Of the man's honesty, Smith had not the slightest doubt, and six months elapsed from the period of these proceedings before he was put in possession of the proofs of his villany. But he, as well as the other foreigners, were bought over by the artifices of Powhatan. The Dutchmen found plenty in the huts of the savage, having left an empty granary behind them at Jamestown. They were soon apprised of Powhatan's preparations to surprise and destroy the English, and became persuaded, knowing little (as late comers) of the prowess of Smith, that the colony must succumb between the joint assaults of the savages and famine. Their social sympathies were not more active in behalf of the English than of the Indians, and they found it little difficult to unite their fortunes with the one, rather than share the seemingly certain fate of the other. Powhatan was accordingly possessed of all the schemes of Smith, while conferring with him on the most amicable footing.

That night, "our Captaine" quartered in the wigwams of the king, and the next day their conferences were resumed. These were enlivened slightly by a languid trade, which Powhatan suffered, most likely, in order to prevent suspicion. In this trade the English succeeded in getting ten measures of corn for a copper kettle which the king seemed greatly to affect. But the people brought no corn, and the gist of Powhatan's discourse seemed chiefly intended to persuade our hero to lay aside his weapons and his caution. The ingenuity and talents of the Indian king are apparent in the following discourse.

"Captain Smith," said he, "I have seen the death of three generations of my people. I am a very old man, and know the difference between peace and war better than any person in my country. I must die ere very long, and would wish to bequeath to my brethren and successors my experience of these things, along with your friendship. But this hint from Nansemond that your purpose is to destroy my people, alarms both them and me. It is for this reason that we dare not visit you. Now, what will it avail you to take by force that which you may quickly have by love, or to destroy the very hands that bring you food? What can you get by war, when it is so easy for us to fly beyond your reach, and hide our provisions in the woods? By wronging us, you only famish yourselves. And why thus jealous of our love? Are we not unarmed among you, and willing still to supply your wants? Think you I am so simple not to know how much better it is to eat good meat, sleep in security with my women and children, laugh and enjoy myself with you, and, being your friend, procure the things I wish, than, as your enemy, be forced to fly from all; to lie cold in the woods, feed upon roots and acorns, and be so hunted by you all the while as to be able to enjoy neither rest, food, nor sleep; with my tired people watching around me, and so anxious and apprehensive, that, if a twig but break, every one crieth out, 'There cometh Captain Smith?' Thus, with a miserable fear, flying, I know not whither, I must soon end a miserable life, leaving my possessions to such youth as yourself; who, through rashness, seeking that which you know not where to find, may also as quickly come to a like miserable end. Let us be wiser. Let these words assure you of my friendship. We shall trade as friends hereafter. Only come to us without your swords and guns as if you looked for an enemy, and we will furnish you with corn."

The excellent reasoning embodied in this speech did not

blind Smith to the old king's subtlety. His answer was couched in the following terms:

"Seeing you will not rightly conceive of our words, we strive to make you know our thoughts by deeds. The vow I made you of my love, both myselfe and my men have kept. As for *your* promise, I find it every day violated by some of your subjects. Yet we, finding your love and kindnesse, our custom is, so far from being ungrateful, that, for your sake onely, we have curbed our thirsty desire of revenge; els had they knowne as well the crueltie we use to our enemies, as our true love and courtesie to our friends. And I thinke your judgment sufficient to conceive, as well by the adventures we have undertaken, as by the advantage we have (by our armes) of yours, that, had we intended you any hurt, long ere this we could have effected it. Your people coming to *Jamestowne* are entertained, with their bowes and arrowes, without any exceptions: we esteeming it with you as it is with us, to wear our armes as our apparell. As for the danger of our enemies, in such warres consist our chiefest pleasures. For your riches we have no use. As for the hiding your provision, or your flying to the woods, *we shall not so unavoidably starve as you conclude.* Your friendly care in that behalfe is needlesse, *for we have a rule to find beyond your knowledge.*"

In this style and spirit their dialogue continued, varied only by a little trade, which Powhatan seemed to permit, the better to beguile his adversary. But the wariness with which Smith maintained his guard baffled the objects of the savage; who, with a deep sigh, at last thus openly reproached our Captain with his strictness and vigilance:

"Captain Smith, I have never treated any Werowance*

* Werowance, or Chief. Smith, it must not be forgotten, was made a Werowance of Virginia by Powhatan.

with so much kindness as yourself; yet from you I have received but little in return. From Newport I had what I wished; swords and copper, bed, towels, any thing that I desired, and he was content to take only what I offered him. I had but to ask, and he sent his guns out of sight. None refuses to do my bidding but yourself. From you I get nothing but what you do not value yourself, yet you will have from me only the thing which you most desire. You call Newport father, and you call me father, yet you are not the son to do for us except what you prefer, and we are both required to submit to you. If your intentions be really friendly, as you say, obey my wishes. Send away your arms, that I may believe you. In the love I bear you, I have stripped myself of every weapon."

Smith was not blind to the fact that the number of Powhatan's followers had greatly increased. He himself had but eighteen men ashore; and but one man, John Russell, immediately in attendance. Seeing that the savage was only solicitous to gain time in order to accumulate sufficient numbers to cut his throat, Smith determined to anticipate the action of his enemy by putting his own schemes into sudden operation. He, accordingly, set the Indians to work to break the ice, that the boat might reach the shore in order to take in himself and the corn which he had bought. He contrived at the same time to convey an order to his men to come ashore, the better to effect the surprise which he designed. Meanwhile, he entertained the Virginian with the following reply—speaking against time, as his adversary had been doing:

"Powhatan, you must know, as I have but one God, I honour but one king. I live not here as your subject, but your friend, to pleasure you with what I can. By the gifts you bestow upon me, you gaine more than by trade;

yet would you visit me as I doe you, you should know it is not our custome to sell our courtesies as a vendible commodity. Bring all your countrey with you for your guard, I will not dislike it as being overjealous. But, to content you, to-morrow I will leave my armes, and trust to your promise. I call you father, indeed, and as a father you shall see, I shall love you; *but the small care you have of such a childe* caused my men perswade me to looke to myselfe."

How Powhatan must have grinned at this shrewd and affecting reproach! It was uttered at a moment when it was full of significance. The conference was going on in one of the houses of the king. While Smith was speaking, the former was apprised of the breaking of the ice, and of the gradual approach of the boat to the shore. The wily savage instantly felt that the time for action on his part had come. It was not his policy to wait until Smith had increased his body-guard with all his force. This body-guard had been stationed at some little distance—at equal distances, probably, between the shore and the place of conference. Smith had but one companion with him in the dwelling, and by this time Powhatan had environed the house with his warriors. Seizing a favorable moment, he left some of his women to keep Smith in conversation, and quietly stole off from the premises. Then it was that "our Captain" was made to comprehend his danger. He became aware of numbers of dusky savages, stalwart and suspicious, who were showing themselves on every hand. He found himself wholly beset with foes, and the chief of them, whose personal presence he had relied on for his safety, had disappeared with the agile dexterity of a serpent, winding away through the distant woods. But Smith possessed in perfection the Alexandrine method of cutting himself out of a difficulty. He did not pause in this predicament. Thought and action grew together in a nature such as his, which needed but the provocation, instantly to receive from his will the impulse requisite to safety. Without a word, closely followed by his companion, Russell, "with his pistols, sword and target, hee made such a passage among the naked divils, that, at his first shoot, they next him tumbled one over another, and the rest quickly fled, some one way, some another." Our Captain was a fierce personage when roused. His aspect was one to inspire terror. His face at ordinary times—sitting for his portrait, when persons most endeavor to appear amiable—wore a fierce gravity; the expression of which, when in his wrathful mood, must have been very imposing and convincing to timid persons. With this countenance, and the auxiliar influence of sword and pistol, he made his way through the discomfited savages, and regained his soldiers without injury.

Roused to anger, and at the head of a stout body of well armed men, Smith was decidedly dangerous, and it was important that Powhatan should explain his conduct, and put such a construction upon his proceedings as should disarm the wrath which he had roused. He sent him, accordingly, an "ancient orator," who, prefacing his discourse with a present of "a great bracelet and a chaine of pearle," spoke as follows:

"Captain Smith, our Werowance, fearing your guns, and knowing when the ice was broken you would bring more men upon him, has fled away for safety. The men whom you see here were only sent to take charge of his corn, and guard it from being stolen—which might happen without your knowledge. Though some of his people have been hurt by your violence, yet Powhatan still remains your friend. Thus will he continue. And now, since the ice is open, he wills that you send away your corn, and, if you would have his company, send away your guns also. They affright his people so that they dare not come to you, as he promised they should."

It was the policy of Smith, baffled in his first object, to maintain appearances. Accordingly, still observing the utmost caution, he yet treated the savages with civility and favor. They had their motives of a like character for like behavior; and their attentions grew sometimes almost too oppressive for the forbearance of our Captain. While one portion of them provided baskets, and conveyed on board the pinnace the corn which he had bought, others were considerate enough to proffer their services in guarding and taking charge of the weapons of the English; a proffer of service which we need scarcely say was gratefully declined. These were all "goodly, well-proportioned fellows, as grim as divils;" in dealing with whom it became necessary occasionally to make such shows of war as to keep them in subordination. They had learned to reverence the implements of death used by the English, so that "the very sight of cocking our matches, and preparing to let fly," would prompt them "to leave their bowes and arrowes to our guard, and beare downe our corn on their backs. We needed not importune them to make dispatch."

The ebb of the tide having left the barges of the English on the ooze, they were compelled to remain till high water, so that they were easily persuaded to return to their old quarters upon the shore; where, agreeably to instructions from their chief, the Indians employed all the merry sports they could devise to pacify the whites, and disarm them of their hostility. The policy was to disarm them of their caution also. The day was consumed in merriment and dancing, and with night came advices of a great feast which Powhatan was preparing to send them. With these agreeable assurances, and with the conviction that he had impressed the enemy with a reasonable feeling of his own inferiority, it might have been that Smith would have somewhat relaxed in that vigilance which had so repeatedly saved him before. But the same guardian angel to whom he already owed so much, the Christian child in a heathen household, Pocahontas, suddenly made her appearance in the wigwam where our Captain found temporary shelter with his party, and opened his eyes to the danger that awaited him. Powhatan had not forgiven him his defeats—had not forgiven him the mortification of that feeling of inferiority which his heart had never felt till Smith penetrated his territories. He burned with a passion to procure the head of our hero, as, indeed, the true head of the colony. This obtained, the rest was easy. This, if his own experience had not taught it him, was the counsel of the traitorous Dutchmen in his employ. It was the design of Powhatan to assail the English while they were gorging at their feast; and while his cooks were preparing the dishes for his victims, his *carvers* were getting ready also. But we must let our author tell his own story, particularly as he always seems to excel—to rise above himself—in those passages where he speaks of Pocahontas.

"The eternal, all-seeing God did prevent him (Powhatan), and by a strange meanes. For Pocahontas, his dearest jewell and daughter, in that darke night came through the irksome woods, and tolde our Captaine great cheare should be sent us by and bye: but that Powhatan, and all the power he could make, would after come and kill us all, if they that brought it could not kill us with oure owne weapons when we were at supper. Therefore, if we would live, shee wished us presently to be gone."

In requital for this information Smith "would have given her such things as she delighted in, but with the teares running downe her cheekes, she said she durst not be seene to have any; for if Powhatan should know it she were but dead; and so she ranne away by herself as she came."

Nothing, of its kind, can well be more touching than this new instance of deep sympathy and attachment on the part of this strangely interesting forest child, for the white strangers and their captain. To him, indeed, she seems to have been devoted with a filial passion much greater than that which she felt for her natural sire. The anecdote affords a melancholy proof of the little hold which power, even when rendered seemingly secure by natural ties, possesses upon the hearts of human beings. Here we find the old monarch, who has just declared himself the survivor of three generations of subjects, betrayed by his own child, and by one of his chiefs,* while in the pursuit of his most cherished objects. *We* have no reproaches for Pocahontas, and her conduct is to be justified. She obeyed laws of nature and humanity, of tenderness and love, which were far superior, in their force and efficacy, in a heart like hers, to any which spring simply from the ties of blood. But, even though his designs be ill, we cannot but regard the savage prince, in his age and infirmities, thus betrayed by child and subject, somewhat as another Lear. He, too, was fond of his Cordelia. She was "the jewel," "the nonpareil," we are told, of his affections. Well might he exclaim, with the ancient Briton, in his hour of destruction—

> "How sharper than a serpent's tooth it is,
> To have a thankless child!"

---

* The Chief of Warraskoyack.

But of her humane treason, for its motive was beyond reproach, Powhatan knew nothing. Smith kept her secret. He was not heedless of her intelligence, the truth of which he had very soon occasion to perceive. In less than an hour after her departure, "eight or ten lusty fellowes, with great platters of venison and other victuall," made their appearance, and invited them to sit and eat. These were very importunate with the English to extinguish their matches, the smoke of which, they pretended, made them sick. But Smith maintained his precautions; and, apprehensive of treachery in the preparation of the food, he made the Indians taste of every dish before he suffered his people to partake of it. He then dismissed them, instructing them to return to Powhatan, and say that "he was conscious of his purposes and ready for his coming. For them, he knew of the bloody task assigned them, but would baulk them in this and all other villainies. They might be gone!" Other messengers from Powhatan followed these, at different periods throughout the night. They came as spies to see how the land lay, and returned disquieted, baffled by the vigilance of Smith, who kept his men to their arms all night. Nothing farther was attempted; and the savages who thronged about them, as with the morning they prepared for their departure, maintained a show of friendliness to the last. Nor was it deemed good policy to leave Powhatan himself, without endeavoring to conciliate his suspicions and his anger. His wishes to this effect being known, it was resolved to leave at Werowocomoco one Edward Brynton, whose occupation was to provide the king's table with wild-fowl.

It may be thought somewhat singular that, after the occurrence of these events, such a measure should have been adopted; but we must not forget that the object was still to maintain appearances . that Smith as yet had no sort of idea of the treachery of the Dutchmen still employed in Powhatan's service ; and that Brynton was really an increase of strength to the armed party which he left behind him, true (as he thought) to his interests, in the very household of his enemy.

CHAPTER IX.

We have not hesitated to express our regret at the design of Captain Smith to seize the person of Powhatan. This proceeding is excused by a regard to the necessities of the colony, the modes of thinking among military men at that period, and the obvious purpose of similar treachery with regard to himself, which was entertained by Powhatan. The excuse is no justification, in any examination upon just principles, of the merits of our hero. It must go for what it is worth. The error must be set down against his qualities of real merit, in proof of those imperfections of character which are found to impair the integrity, and diminish the nobleness of the very purest minds. In a moment of extreme exigency, when evidently nothing short of this degree of violence would suffice for the safety of the endangered party, there could, indeed, be no hesitation in the judgment which would declare in favor of that resolution and promptness by which, even though at another's hurt, the required assurances of safety were to be found. Whether the present was such an exigency, as was that of Cortez in Mexico, is a question which, in our very imperfect knowledge of all the facts in the situation of Smith, we are not exactly prepared to determine. From the details before us, it would not seem to be properly classed among those perilous extremes of circumstance, by which the individual is permitted, at any sacrifice of moral and social law, to regain his securities. But as it is not our desire to urge the perfect purity and integrity of our Captain's character, we shall not undertake the unnecessary labor of proving his freedom from error in the present instance. He was a stout and fearless soldier, of great courage and enterprise, great shrewdness, coolness, and common sense ; full of a rude spirit of chivalry, that was sometimes fantastically virtuous,—but not wiser than his age, and not wholly free from those faults and vices which that age was so frequently found to sanction. It does not appear that public opinion in England found any fault with him for this attempt upon the person of the Indian emperor. If it did, it was rather in consequence of his failure than his attempt. We, at all events, are not sorry that he failed. The character and conduct of Powhatan are such as entitle him to our respect and sympathy; and though we forbear to censure his English adversary, we are not unwilling that the savage chieftain should still exhibit that care of his subjects, that vigilant guardianship of his territory, by which we are made to esteem the sovereign, even though in the dusky leader of a heathen tribe.

Smith had scarcely set sail from Werowocomoco, before Powhatan reappeared. He had timely notice of all his movements, and with his departure, he despatched two of the Dutchmen with all haste to Jamestown. The scheme of these men was probably suggested by themselves, by their knowledge of the habits of the colonists, and of the pretences by which they could be most easily imposed upon. By this scheme, they proposed not only to find favor in the sight of Powhatan, but to gratify their own cupidity. The king had set his affections upon an English armory. Whether this was a mere passion of his taste, or was meant to promote his purposes for the expulsion of the whites, must be left to conjecture. Both motives may be found at work compelling his desires ; in obedience to which our Dutchmen, presenting themselves to Captain Wynne, before Smith could possibly return, assured him that everything was going on well; that Smith having use for their arms had sent them for others; for tools, for clothes, and other commodities, all of which were readily yielded them. Their cunning enabled them to effect an arrangement with six or seven seamen, who became their confederates in the *appropriation* of goods. By these they were soon furnished with everything that could be stolen easily—with swords and pike-heads, guns, shot, powder, and the like—by which the wishes of Powhatan for the English weapons were very tolerably gratified. The number of Indians always prowling about the fort, furnished great facilities for the conveyance to their king of the commodities thus stolen. By these means, and the assistance of one of the Dutchmen, who seems to have been a blacksmith, he soon accumulated eight guns, as many pikes, fifty swords, and three hundred hatchets; such a treasure as few Indian sovereigns of America were ever known to possess. Brynton and Richard Salvage, two of the Englishmen in his employ, observing the readiness with which he accumulated these weapons, and the great diligence which the Dutchmen betrayed in procuring them for him, became alarmed as much for their own as the safety of the colony, and made an effort to escape; but were detected, pursued, brought back, and kept for some time in momentary apprehension of death.

Our Captain, meanwhile, was leisurely pursuing his way, seeking provisions at the different settlements along the river. Having arrived at Pamunkey, the seat of Opechancanough, who was a brother to Powhatan, either by blood or by adoption, they were received and for several days entertained hospitably, with mirth and feasting. A day was set aside for trade, of which the surrounding country was properly apprised. Leaving his boats on this occasion, Smith, with fifteen others, went up to the village of the chief, about a quarter of a mile from the river, which, to their surprise, they found entirely abandoned by the people, and stript of all its goods and furniture. Such a proceeding looked exceedingly suspicious, particularly on a day set apart for trade, when, instead of being abandoned, the settlement should have shown all the life and bustle of a market-town in fairing time. But the strangers had not long been present before the chief arrived, followed by a stout band of warriors. These brought with them bows and arrows in abundance, but such a trifling supply of provisions, and those charged for at such enormous prices, that our Captain readily conceived that they were to be used only as a bait, by which to delude their customers. This extorted from him the following remonstrance:

"Opechancanough, the great love you professe with your tongue, seemes meere deceet by your actions. Last yeare you kindly fraughted our ship; but now you invite me to starve with hunger. You know my want, and I your plenty;—of which, by some meanes, I must have part. Remember, it is fit for kings to keepe their promise. Here are my commodities. Take your choice. What remains I will sell in fair bargains to your people."

Opechancanough took this speech in good part, and the corn which had been brought was disposed of to the whites on terms which they thought reasonable. The Indian chief promised the next day that the supplies should be more satisfactory. Accordingly, at the usual hour, Smith, with his fifteen men, once more proceeded to the dwelling of the chief. Here they found a few persons newly arrived with their baskets. Opechancanough soon made his appearance; but it was observed that his courtesies and cheerfulness seemed straine l and unnatural. He was at some pains to assure them of the trouble he had taken in having supplies brought in; but even while he spoke, news was brought to Smith, by Mr. Russell, that they were betrayed, for that the house was surrounded by no less than seven hundred armed savages. The chief saw that his plot was discovered, and betrayed his intentions by his anxiety and fear. Smith's own followers exhibited signs of dismay, but were encouraged by their leader in the following language:

"My worthy countrymen," said he, "were the mischiefe from my seeming friends no greater than our danger from these enemies, I should not care were they as many more. But it is my torment, that, though I may escape from these, our worthy councill, with their open-mouthed minions, will make me such a peace-breaker in the opinion of those in England, as will breake my necke. I could wish those persons to be here now, that make these seeme saints, and me an oppressor. But this is the worst of all, wherein I pray you to aid me with your opinions. Shoulde we beginne with them and surprise the king, we cannot keepe him well, and at the same time defend ourselves. If we should eache kill our man, and disperse the rest, we should still starve for victuall, getting nothing more than the bodies that are slaine. As for their fury, that is the least danger, for well you know, that, being alone assaulted with two or three hundred of them, I made them, by the helpe of God, compound to save my life. And wee are sixteene, and they *but* seaven hundred at the most; assure yourselves, therefore, that if you dare stand but as I doe, to discharge your peeces, the very smoke will e sufficient to affright them. Yet, howsoever, let us fight like men, not die like sheepe. By such meanes, you know, God hath oft delivered mee, and will, I trust, doe so now. But first let mee deale with them, to bring it to passe. We may fight for something, and draw them to it by conditions. If you like this motion, promise me you will be valiant."

This speech, so cool and confident, reassured his men. They swore to follow him, and do as he commanded. The time did not permit much argument, and we must suppose that they kept the Indian chief in a tacit sort of custody while this discussion proceeded. This over, our Captain turned to him, and said: "I see, Opechancanough, your plot to murder me, but I feare it not. As yet, youre men and mine have done no harme, but by our direction. Take, therefore, your weapons. You see mine. My body shall bee as naked as yours. The island in your river is a fit place, if you be contented. There let us two fight it out, and the survivor shall be lord and master over all our men. If you have not enough, take time to fetch more, and bring what number you will. Only let your men bring, each of them, a basket of corne, against all of which I will stake the value in copper, and the conqueror shall take the whole."

This was in the true spirit of chivalry. It reminds us of our hero before the walls of Regall. It is evident he thought of adding the head of Opechancanough to those of the three Turks already emblazoned on his shield. But to this the Indian chief was no ways inclined. His notions of war implied no such unnecessary personal risks. He preferred the subtler game which he had begun to play, and was evidently disposed to forego none of his advantages. Still, he disclaimed hostility, professed nothing but friendship, and, to prove it, invited Smith to go with him to the entrance of the cabin, where he had a great present in waiting for him. This was a bait to draw him into an ambush of two hundred; thirty others lying concealed behind a fallen tree, each with his arrow ready

Smith seizing Opechancanough PAGE 277

on the string. Commanding one of his men to receive this present, Smith himself refused to go. The rest of his party volunteered to do so. But he would not suffer this. He was in no mood for farther trifling. Satisfied of the treachery of Opechancanough, he resolved to bring the matter to such an issue as would reconcile all the inequalities of numbers. Accordingly, commanding "Lieutenant Percie, Master West, and the rest, to make good the house," he ordered two others to guard the door; then, suddenly seizing upon the long scalp-lock of the Indian chief, who in size was a giant to our Captain, he dragged him from amidst the circle of forty or fifty warriors by whom he was encircled, and clapped a loaded pistol to his breast. This boldness paralyzed the chief and all his captains, and in this manner Smith drew him forth, in the sight of all his people, holding him in a sort of security for the forbearance of his followers. The effect was magical. Accustomed to venerate as sacred the persons of their sovereigns, they regarded with awe the individual who could thus profane them without dread of punishment. They dropped their weapons at the humiliating spectacle. Their chief had already yielded his—"delivering to the Captaine his vambrace, bow and arrowes," and offering his tribute in a sober "sadnesse," which declared his shame and apprehensions, if not his compunction. With his hand still wreathed in his hair, Smith summoned the subjects of his prisoner about him, and gave them a speech after his usual fashion.

"I see, you Pamaunkees," he said, "the great desire you have to kill me; and my long suffering your injuries hath emboldened you to this presumption. The cause which has made me forbear your insolence is the promise I made you, before the God I serve, to be your friend till you give me just cause to be your enemy. If I keepe this vow, my God will keepe me, and you cannot do me hurt. If I break it, *he* will destroy me. But if you shoot but one arrow to shed the blood of any of my men, or steale the least of these beads and copper, which now lie at my feet, I will not cease revenge so long as there is one of your nation to answer to the name of Pamaunkee. I am not now at Rassaweak, half drowned with myre, as when you took me prisoner ; yet for your good usage, and sparing of me then, I so affect you, that your denyals of your trechery doe halfe persuade me to mistake myselfe. But if I be the marke you ayme at, here I stand, shoot he that dare. You promised to fraught my ship ere I departed, and so you shall, or I will load her with your dead carcases. Yet, if as friends you will come and trade with me, I will not trouble you. Your king shall be free, and shall be my friend, for I am not come for the hurt of him, or of any among you."

The condition in which he kept their king made them very placable. They yielded ready obedience to his requisitions, and men, women and children, brought in the supplies, in such abundance, that our Captain, already greatly fatigued, was tired of receiving them. Leaving this duty to two of his men, and having released his captive, he withdrew into one of the cabins for the purpose of repose. Meanwhile, the guard became remiss, and, too soon assured of the docility of the savages, were soon carelessly dispersed among them. The latter resumed their weapons, and Smith, vigilant even in sleep, was awakened to find forty or fifty of their choice warriors pressing into the apartment where he slept, each armed with a heavy war club, or an English sword. The haste with which their entrance was made fortunately awakened him in season. "Halfe amazed with this suddaine sight, he betooke him straight to his sword and target; Mr

Crashaw and some others charged in like manner," and the house was soon cleared of the intruders. The king apologized, in a long speech, for the intrusion; and his people found it advisable to assume the virtue of good humor and good fellowship with the powerful stranger whom they so vainly strove to circumvent, even if they felt it not. Their attempts upon him had invariably resulted in their own defeat and disaster; and our hero had the genuine English shrewdness always to exact a profit for his people from all the failures of their enemies. He knew how to make them pay the expenses of the war.

It was while our Captain was thus exploring the country for supplies, to guard against famine in the colony, that a melancholy event happened at the fort. It seems that Mr. Scrivener, whom Smith had hitherto been always disposed to favor, had somewhat declined in affection towards the President, and under that sinister influence which, in England and the colony, had always stubbornly fought against the influence of our hero, had at length determined to set up in some measure for himself. Accordingly, in order to exercise something like a separate command, he took advantage of Smith's absence to visit a contiguous island; with what object in view is not mentioned. He succeeded in persuading Captain Waldo to join him, though Waldo had been especially charged by Smith not to be absent from the fort, but to be in readiness to second his performances. Scrivener, with Waldo, Gosnold, and eight others, embarked on the enterprise. The weather was extremely cold, the river partly frozen, and the wind violent. The boat was swamped, and all in her were drowned. The bodies were recovered by the savages, from whom came the first intelligence to the fort of the sad disaster. There, nobody could be found to convey the melancholy tidings to the President, then supposed to be still at Werowocomoco, until a brave fellow, named Richard Wyffin, undertook, alone, the performance of this mission. It was one of many difficulties and dangers. He first proceeded to the dwelling of Powhatan, where he lodged that night. Here, not finding the President, and perceiving the great preparations which Powhatan was making for war, his worst fears were aroused for his own and the safety of the persons whom he sought. And the danger seems to have been pressing in his own instance. But for the interference of Pocahontas—who seems to have been always present when the duty of an angel was to be done—he might have fallen a victim to his generous zeal. "Pocahontas hid him for a time, and sent those who pursued him the cleane contrary way to seeke him ; but by her meanes, and extraordinary bribes, and much trouble, in three dayes travell at length he found us in the middest of these turmoyles." Swearing Wyffin to secresy, and dissembling his own grief, so that his company should not be seen to despond while among their enemies, Smith went aboard his vessel, leaving Opechancanough free the night that he received these tidings. That he left this powerful chief at liberty, was only with the view the more successfully to strike at higher game. He felt that, though there was no avowed war between Powhatan and himself, their relations were, nevertheless, sufficiently hostile to justify the prosecution of his first design ; and his experience, before returning to Jamestown, was of a sort to confirm him in this purpose. He was advised that the Indian emperor had issued his commands to his subjects, to procure his death by all means in their power ; and the poor savages, in obedience to these orders, had baited the shores with grain ; which, however, he was not suffered to approach, unless by leaving behind him all his weapons. The first show of his coming, gun in hand, was the signal for carrying their baskets out of sight. They affected to have come unarmed, simply for the purposes of trade, though with such a people and in such a country, it was well known that every bush and tree would afford a sufficient armory of arrows for their Parthian multitudes. Still, they preferred approaching him in a peaceful aspect. Such was their terror of his prowess that, but for the commands of their sovereign, the idea of meeting him in conflict was as "hateful to them as hanging." And thus the parties gazed wistfully upon each other, the one from the shore, the other from the river—they upon Smith's weapons, and he upon their baskets of corn. But when he saw them beginning to depart with their produce, "being unwilling to lose such bootie," he so judiciously disposed the pinnace and barges, as to enable the party on board to form a cover to his men, while he, and three others, armed, took a party ashore, unarmed, to receive the corn they brought. The Indians "flocked before him in heapes, and the banke serving as a trench for retreat, he drew them fayre open to his ambuscadoes." Opechancanough, knowing his party to be mostly unarmed, came down upon him with two or three hundred men, marching in "the forme of two halfe moones," the better to enclose the English. They brought with them some twenty men and several women, bearing painted baskets. As they drew nigh, and when they thought that the bait had taken, and that they had sufficiently environed the whites, the persons, men and women, bearing the grain, threw down their baskets and fled. But the fear of the assailants, even when they thought their purpose sure, was such as scarcely to suffer them to fix their shafts upon the string. Just then, as if in mercy, Smith gave the signal to his party in ambush, and they showed themselves without firing a shot. At this sight the savages took to flight, "esteeming their heeles for their best advantage." We are permitted to suppose that Smith providently gathered up the scattered baskets.

Powhatan had truly described the terrors with which our Captain had inspired the savages, when he said, if a twig was heard to break in the forest, they cried out, "here comes Captain Smith." Fearing to meet him in battle, failing to delude him by their artifices, they attempted his destruction by practices which we have not often been wont to ascribe to our aborigines. Sending down one of his vessels, probably with the supplies he had procured, to Jamestown, he still remained in the neighborhood of Pamunkee, in which there was still an abundance of provision which he hoped to secure by barter. The Indians, under new professions of terror and friendship, came in and expressed a willingness to freight his vessel, in order to disarm his hostility. They believed, or pretended to believe, that he had despatched one of his boats for fresh supplies of men. In this mood, whether sincere or feigned, they employed themselves for five or six days in bringing in grain, through frost and snow, on their naked backs, from all parts of the country. In the meantime, Smith and several of his party found themselves poisoned by some of the dainties with which the savages had supplied them. But their art was not equal to their malice. The poison sickened the whites, but was expelled, without proving fatal in a single instance. *Wecuttanow*, a stout young Indian, finding himself suspected of the crime, and being surrounded by forty or fifty of his companions at a moment when Smith had but a few men about him, braved him with a good deal of insolence. But our Captain, not regarding the inequality of numbers, promptly laid his cudgel over the shoulders of the savage, and kicked him out of sight, "as scorning to doe him any worse mischiefe." This drove his companions into the woods, "thinking they had done a great matter to have so well escaped."

In this tour in search of provisions, our Captain explored the "countries of *Youghtanund* and *Mattapanient*, where the people imparted what little they had with such complaints and tears from the eyes of women and children," as would have moved with compassion any Christian heart. Yet had the search been made in October, November and December, or when Newport was making his idle discovery of the country of the Monacans, there would have been no sort of difficulty in procuring all the provisions they required. "Men may thinke it strange," says our author, in a passage that would seem to be apologetic in its object, "that there should be such a strive for a little corne, but had it been gold with more ease we might have got it; and had it lacked, the whole colony had starved." Such an exigency, which the forethought of the President soon perceived, may well be urged in extenuation of proceedings which might otherwise seem rather harsh than decisive.

CHAPTER X.

It was somewhat with the view of disarming the caution of Powhatan, that our Captain treated the people of Opechancanough with so much indulgence. To seem on friendly terms with them, and to linger with the apparent view to trade, was to lessen the suspicions of the emperor, and keep him still at Werowocomoco. Believing this object to have been attained, Smith, on leaving Pamunkee, suddenly turned his prow up the river, and once more sought the habitation of Powhatan; resolved on effecting, if possible, his original design of surprising him in the midst of his provisions. Approaching the town in secret, he sent two of his party, "Mr. Wyffin, and Mr. Coe," ashore to discover and make way for his intended project. "Those damned Dutchmen," says our indignant author, "had caused Powhatan to abandon his new house and Werowocomoco, and to carry away all his corn and provision." Such also was the ill-feeling for the whites whom he had left behind him, that the two emissaries of Smith were in some doubt whether they should escape with their lives. Baffled in his scheme, and seeing that nothing more was to be obtained in this neighborhood, he returned with all possible speed to Jamestown, carrying with him two hundred pounds of deer suet, and nearly five hundred bushels of corn; all of which was procured at a cost of twenty-five pounds' weight of copper, and fifty of beads and iron.

Here, at the close of this expedition, our author deems it necessary to excuse the gentleness and great forbearance which Smith exhibited in thus dealing with the savages, and thus shows us the difficulty of applying the social and moral standards of the present time to the conduct of that period. "These temporizing proceedings to some may seeme too charitable to such a daily daring, trecherous people: to others not pleasing that we washed not the ground with their blouds, nor showed such strange inventions in mangling, murdering, ransacking and destroying (as did the Spanyards) the simple bodies of such ignorant soules; nor delightful, because not stuffed with relations of heapes and mynes of gold and silver; nor such rare commodities as the Portugals and Spanyards found in the East and West Indies. * * * It was the Spanyards good hap to happen in parts where such was the number of people as to enable them so to improve the earth that it afforded food at all seasons. And time had brought their arts to so much perfection as to give them the free use of gold and silver, together with the most of those commodities which the country was able to afford. What the Spanyard got was chiefly the spoyle and pillage of the people, and not the labours of their owne hands. But had those fruitful countries beene as salvage, as barbarous, as ill-peopled, as little planted, laboured and manured as Virginia, it is likely that their labours would have brought as little profit as our owne. Had Virginia beene so peopled, and so adorned with such store of precious jewells and rich commodities as the Indies, then, indeed, might the world have traduced us and our merits, and have made shame and infamy our reward, had we not gotten and done as much as by their (the Spaniards) examples might properly be expected from us. * * * But we chanced in a land even as God made it, where we found only an idle, improvident and scattered people, ignorant of the knowledge of gold and silver, and carelesse of any thing but from hand to mouth. Nothing was here to encourage us but what nature afforded. And this could not be brought to recompense our paines, defray our charges, and satisfie our adventurers, until we could discover the countrey, subdue the people, bring them to be tractable, civill and industrious, and teach them trades, so that the fruits of their labors might make us some return ; or until we could plant such colonies of our owne, whose first necessity would be to make provision how to live themselves. * * * But to conclude, I onely say this for those that the three first yeares began this plantation ; notwithstanding all their factions, mutinies and miseries, so gently corrected, and well prevented ;" let them peruse the histories of Spanish conquest and discovery, " and tell me how many ever with such small meanes as a barge of 22 tons, sometimes with seaven, eight or nine, or but at most, twelve or sixteene men, did ever discover so many fayre and navigable rivers, subject so many severall kings, people and nations to obedience and contribution, and all with so little bloudshed."

The boast contained in this passage is an equally honorable and becoming one. It is truly astonishing how much was done by the prudence and forethought of this man ; by his coolness and steady courage, and real benevolence ; and how much was forborne of crime and bloodshed, which had been sure to follow, in such a country, and dealing with such a people, had the leader been wanton in the use of power, profligate of human life, and not properly considerate of the feeble and simple savages whom it was his fortune to encounter. And the moral of his progress is to be found in the statement here contained of his general principles : to " discover the countrey, subdue the people, bring them to be tractable, civill and industrious ;" in order that the resources of their own nature, and the virtues of the soil and climate, might at once be brought into just fruition. And this is the highest purpose of human benevolence. We are to judge of a hero's claims, not by this or that single scheme or action—call it crime and error if you please—but by what he has forborne of crime and error, and what he has resisted of temptation. Thus examined, the deeds and enterprises of Smith will honorably compare with those of any hero to be found in the progress of a commercial age and people. To have done so much with so little; in the teeth of discontent and faction; with foes without, and treachery within the settlement; with so much provocation to anger and severity, yet with so great toleration and pity for the offender; so much firmness with so much mercy; and such various resource against such and so many unlooked for annoyances and disasters;—sufficiently establishes to posterity the high and remarkable endowments and merits of our subject. But the facts in his career need no illustrative commentary. They speak for themselves.

Returning to Jamestown, and making a general examination into the affairs of the colony, he found no reason to be satisfied with the doings of those he left behind him. Their tools and weapons were lost or stolen; the provision in store had been suffered to rot, was half destroyed by worms and rats, and in such condition that the hogs would scarcely eat it. Fortunately, it was found, upon due calculation, that the supplies which he had just procured would suffice until the next harvest. With the dread of famine at an end for the present, all care about procuring provision was abandoned, and the whole company was divided into squads of ten or fifteen, and assigned to the necessary duties of the colony. Six hours each day were devoted to their tasks, the rest in pastimes and merry exercises. But such was the untowardness of many among them, to whom labor was equally new and irksome, that our President was compelled to give them sharp counsel after his peculiar fashion.

"Countrymen," he said, "the long experience of our late miseries, I hope, is sufficient to persuade every one to a present correction of himselfe. Thinke not that either my paines, nor the adventurers' purses, will ever maintain you in idlesse and sloathe. I speake not this to you all, for divers of you I know deserve both honor and reward, much better than is here to be had; but the greater part must be more industrious or starve; however you have been heretofore tollerated by the authoritie of the Councell. You see now that power resteth wholly in myselfe. You must obey this now for a law, that he that will not work (except by sicknesse he is disabled) shall not eate. The labours of thirtie or fortie honest and industrious men shall not be consumed to maintain an hundred and fiftie idle loyterers. And though you presume the authoritie here is but a shadow, and that I dare not touch the lives of any lest my owne shoulde answer it, yet will you see by the contents of the Letters Patent, which shall be read to you each week, that the very contrary is the case. I would wish you, therefore, without contempt of my authoritie, to study to observe the orders that I have here set down; for there are now no more councellers to protect you and to curbe my endeavours. He that offendeth, therefore, shall most assuredly meet due punishment."

The members of the Council, if we remember, Scrivener, Waldo, and others, perished in the boat while Smith was at Pamunkee. He, as President of the colony, was left with the sole authority. His speech is to the purpose. It speaks the man of business and of resolution, and was not without its effect, we may suppose. But, to encourage the good, and to spur the sluggish to amendment, he prepared a table or register of each man's name, with a summary notice of his daily conduct. This was placed conspicuously where it could be seen by all, and thus become "a publicke memoriall of every man's deserts." This, too, had its influence. Many became very industrious, though quite as many were only to be goaded to their tasks by punishment. He had so contrived their duties that they found it impossible to deceive him. His eye was everywhere, on all things and persons, and he possessed, in rare degree, that faculty of vision which enables the master to pierce through the secret bosom, and discern all its secrets. But there were some practices which he could not fathom—some offenders who contrived to baffle even his penetration. Still, there was a daily loss of tools and weapons, and common sense naturally led them to conceive that these found their way to the Indians, by whom they were much desired. The thefts were committed by those in the fort, who had become confederates with the Dutchmen sent to Powhatan. At one time, while Smith was at Pamunkee, these confederates, to the number of five, had stolen away from the colony, and were on their way to Powhatan, when they were met by Mr. Crashaw and Mr. Ford, who had been despatched to Jamestown from Pamunkee, by Smith. To these they gave some plausible statement, accounting for their presence on the road, and, the better to baffle their suspicions, they returned with these gentlemen to the settlement, resuming their old business of peculation. Powder and shot, tools and weapons, disappeared with unaccountable rapidity under their agency, leaving no clue by which they could be found or followed. Meantime, the Dutchmen somewhat wondered why their confederates had not followed them as had been promised. They were employed by the savage emperor, not in palace building, but in teaching himself and warriors the proper use of the English weapons. To solve their doubts in relation to the delay of their associates, they sent one of their company, named Francis, disguised like an Indian. This fellow made his way to the glass-house in the forest, about a mile from Jamestown. This was the common place of rendezvous for these conspirators. Here they arranged a scheme for taking or putting Captain Smith to death; forty Indians lying in ambush, for some time, in expectation of his appearance. But his good genius again baffled them, and, in the meantime, tidings of the visit of Francis, and the disguise which he wore, reached his ears. His plans were decisive. The fellow escaped the party that went to the glass-house to apprehend him, but did not escape another party of twenty men, whom Smith despatched to cover the road between Jamestown and the domains of Powhatan. He was captured and brought back; but, before this took place, our Captain experienced an adventure of considerable danger, from which it required all his dexterity and courage to escape. Returning from the glass-house alone, after he had sent off the twenty soldiers in pursuit of the fugitive, he suddenly encountered the King of Paspahegh, a stalwart savage of large stature. To this chief, it appears that the ambush had been entrusted by which Smith was to perish. But Smith's footsteps did not incline in the direction where the Indians were concealed, and, throwing himself in his way, the object of the chief was to beguile his victim in the required direction. But either the art of the savage was too rude, or our Captain had grown cautious and suspicious from a frequent knowledge of his danger, and the attempts of the chief were unavailing. Desperate in his design, and stimulated to the attempt by the urgent wishes of

Smith's Conflict with the King of Paspahegh. PAGE 291.

Powhatan, he conceived the idea, as Smith was alone, and armed only with a falchion, of accomplishing the deed himself. But the attempt to shoot him with his arrow failed in consequence of his having approached too nearly to his enemy. Smith was enabled to close in with him, before the shaft could be dismissed from the string. The grapple now between them was one for life and death, and to prevent the Captain from drawing his falchion, as he had been prevented from using his bow, the stout savage grappled him with equal dexterity and courage. The Indian seems to have been the most powerful man of the two, was large of frame and muscular, though less agile, perhaps, and possibly not so good a wrestler as our Captain. But he succeeded, by main force, in dragging him into the river, where they struggled for some time in the water, neither having the advantage. At length a fortunate movement enabled Smith to get his fingers fairly clutched about the naked throat of his dusky opponent. This he griped with such hearty good will, that the savage, half-strangled, succumbed to his conqueror;—who, drawing his falchion, and about to cut off the head of his captive, was persuaded to spare him by his pitiful entreaties for life. But he made him prisoner, and, under the edge of the uplifted sword, drove him into Jamestown and made him fast in chains.

Here he proved a witness for the conviction of the Dutchman, Francis. This traitor, put upon trial, offered but a lame plea to the charges urged against him. The confession of Paspahegh was conclusive of his guilt; and, to use the phrase of our authority, which leaves us somewhat doubtful of his punishment, "he went by the heeles," accordingly. But his life was spared by Smith, who, as a conqueror, was always merciful;—spared, at this time, to be reserved for a worse fate, equally well deserved, hereafter. Francis, after Smith had left the colony, and its government had fallen into other hands, contrived to escape a second time to Powhatan. To this wily monarch, he promised to play the same game with the new governor, Lord Delaware, which he had played with Smith. But Powhatan had become much more suspicious with increase of experience ; and, telling the traitor that he who had betrayed Smith to him, would be just as likely to betray him to Delaware, he commanded his brains to be beaten out. And thus the miserable wretch rushed only to his doom at last.

Paspahegh was kept some time in prison, Smith proposing to exchange him for the Dutchmen left with Powhatan. But, either they were not willing to return, or Powhatan would not suffer them ; and while the negotiations for this object were in progress, Paspahegh contrived, during a temporary absence of Smith, to escape from prison. He was pursued by Captain Winne, but his faithful subjects covered his flight with such troops of warriors who resolutely braved the combat, freely exchanging shaft for shot, that he succeeded in getting off safely. Returning to the fort, and learning of these events, Smith captured two Indians, Kemps and Tussore—"the two most exact villains in all the country,"—"who would betray both king and kindred for a piece of copper." These he sent with a party of fifty choice men, under Captain Winne and Lieutenant Percy, in pursuit of the fugitive chief. They were to guide the soldiers where he was concealed. But Winne did not follow Smith's counsel, nor the guidance of his Indians, but, trifling away the night when he should have pushed forward with all his strength, he found the savages prepared for him, in all their might, by the dawn of day. They defied him to the combat, and the two parties exchanged shots at a distance so respectful, as to expose nobody to hurt on either side. Winne and his party returned to Jamestown, after burning a few houses and capturing a few canoes.

Smith was dissatisfied with this result, and took the field himself. He feared that the savages would be encouraged by this non-performance of his soldiers, and soon "began himselfe againe to try conclusions" with his warlike neighbors, "whereby six or seven were slaine, and as many made prisoners." He was resolved that their punishment should make them fear him. He burnt their houses, took their boats, removed their fishing weirs to his own waters, and was passing by Paspahegh towards Chickahominy, in order to extend his vengeance to all the deserving, when he was encountered by a large body of the Paspaheghians, who bravely prepared to try his strength. But when, at the first encounter, they discovered our Captain instead of Winne, at the head of the English, they threw down their weapons, and entreated peace. His very name and presence were enough. One of their orators, speaking for the rest, thus addressed him : " Captain Smith, the chief, my master, is here present with this company. It was Captain Winne, and not you, of whom he thought to be avenged. If he hath offended you in escaping from imprisonment, you must remember that fishes swim, fowles fly, and the very beasts strive to escape the snare. Blame him not, therefore, being a man, that he hath done in like manner. He would entreat you to remember your being a prisoner, what paines he took to save your life. If, since that time, he hath injured you, he was compelled to it by another. You, too, have already amply revenged yourself, to our too great losse. Do not destroy us as you now seem to desire. We are here to implore your friendship—to entreat that we be permitted to enjoy our houses and to plant our fields, in whose fruit you shall participate; otherwise, you will be the sufferers if you drive us away to other places. We can plant, but you cannot live lacking our harvests. Proceed in your revenge, and we will abandon the country. Promise us peace, and we will believe you."

This "worthy discourse" which, as our author justly writes, "deserveth to be remembered," had its effect. The chief was forgiven, peace was made between the parties, and they separated good friends; and so continued till Smith left the country. The wonderful influence which our adventurer possessed over the minds of the aborigines, was to be still farther increased by a circumstance which happened soon after his return to the colony. There, it had been discovered that the people of Chickahominy, who had always shown themselves very affectionate and friendly, were yet disposed to be very thievish. A pistol being stolen, and the thief escaping, his two brothers, who were known to be his confederates, were taken into custody. One of them, after a brief imprisonment, was suffered to go free, with a message to the thief that if the pistol was not restored within twelve hours, the brother left in prison would be hung. The message was effectual. The messenger returned before midnight, bringing the pistol, but seemed to have returned too late. The season was one of great severity, and Captain Smith, commiserating the cold and naked condition of the poor wretch left in prison, sent him food, and a supply of charcoal, with which to make a fire. Ignorant of the deadly properties of the burning charcoal in a close apartment, the poor Indian, when his brother was admitted to his prison, was found lifeless. Bitterly did the survivor lament the premature death of his kinsman; and so much did Smith sympathize with him in his cruel sorrow and disappointment, that he confidently promised the wailing savage, if he would be quiet, that he would restore the dead man to life. It was one of those spontaneous, irrepressible impulses of a generous wish, which prompted this promise, for he tells us he had little thought that the victim could be recovered. Yet he went to work with all his industry and skill, and the will to achieve has in itself a virtue which half ensures success to its performances. *Aqua vitæ*, that power, potent as it has proved for evil, has its virtues also; and, with vinegar, proved, on the present occasion, a most fortunate specific. The poor savage, through God's blessing, was restored to consciousness; but the effects of the charcoal promised to be fatal to his intellect. To restore him to his proper senses was another task of difficulty imposed upon him by the entreaties of the anxious kinsman, and this also Smith promised to achieve. Succeeding in this by such simple means as an experienced soldier, or traveller, would naturally have learned to use, our Captain gained the reputation among the Indians of having raised the dead. Another circumstance served to increase the respect in which the English and their Captain were held by the simple natives. An "ingenious savage" of Powhatan's had procured by theft, or barter with the thief, a bag of gunpowder, and the back piece of a suit of armor. To show his superior knowledge, the fellow had gathered several of his companions around him, and proceeded to dry the powder, as he had seen the soldiers practise the operation upon the armor. He dried it a little too long for his credit and his life. The powder exploded, and destroyed the experimenter, and one or two more. Others were so much scorched, as to produce a wholesome distrust in the minds of the whole nation, of the virtues of a commodity so quick to take fire. The result was highly important to our English. "These, and many other such pretty accidents, so amazed and affrighted both Powhatan and all his people, that their conscientiousness returned to them." Numberless things which had been stolen, but which had neither been demanded nor thought of, were suddenly returned; and even the thieves themselves, after this event, were sent back to Jamestown to receive punishment. The stubborn Powhatan was subdued by his superstitious fears, and, with his people, by numerous presents, entreated peace hereafter. The change was so complete, that the country became absolutely as free and safe to the English as to the savages themselves. Fortune thus admirably co-operated with the genius of our Captain to produce all the results to his colony which good government could possibly desire or procure.

CHAPTER XI.

The exclusive control which Captain Smith now possessed over the affairs of the colony, was soon made manifest in its progress. The pacific temper to which he had brought the savages in a short space of time, left him wholly free to administer the internal affairs of the settlement at his pleasure; and the fact that he was no longer embarrassed by the vexing moods and querulous dispositions of his council, rendered his work comparatively easy and agreeable. Accordingly, we find the English making such progress in the useful arts, in the three months which followed the conclusion of peace with Powhatan, as they never exhibited in all their previous history. Tar, pitch, and potash, in considerable quantities, rewarded their exertions; they produced some samples of glass; dug a well of excellent water in the fort, which, till then, had been very much wanting; provided nets and seines for taking fish; built twenty new houses; repaired the church, and, the better to prevent thieving, and to check the incursions of the savages, raised a block-house on the isthmus of Jamestown, which neither Christian nor Heathen was suffered to pass without order or permit from the President. Thirty or forty additional acres of land were also broken up and planted; and such new care taken of pigs and poultry that their increase became marvellous. The former were carried to an islet, which was called Hog Island, and here a block-house was also built, and a garrison established, which should give notice of any approaching shipping. The soldiers here were not, however, left to keep the place in idleness, but for their exercise and amusement were required to fell trees, and split clapboards. A fort was also begun, as a place of retreat—for they had no reason to suppose themselves free from the Spanish rovers—upon a commanding hill near a contiguous river. The plan of this fortress rendered it difficult of assault, and easy of defence; but, before it was quite finished, a more pressing matter arrested the workmen.

It was found that their corn, their entire stock, which had been put up in casks, and probably in a damp condition, was half rotten, and so much injured by the rats—of which reptile, a colony of several thousands had been transferred from the ships to the shore—that it was rendered almost wholly worthless for the future use of the people. This put a stop to all their labors and enterprises, those only excepted which went to supplying them with food; and this last necessity, as our President acknowledges, "drove them to their wits' end." There was nothing to be procured in the country, except that which came from the hands of nature. The Indian women of *Youghtanund* and *Mattapanient*, when sharing with them their last supplies, did it with tears and lamentations, which forbade the idea of ravishing from the poor savages their little remaining store. The two Indians whom Smith had seized as hostages for the return of the chief of Paspahegh, and who were described as the "two most exact villaines in all the country," had refused to leave the settlement even when they recovered their enlargement, but made themselves useful, and were found particularly valuable in teaching the whites how their fields were to be prepared and planted. These "exact villaines" exercised a proper influence over their people, who, in the distress of the colony, brought daily supplies of game—"squirrels, turkies, deere, and other wilde beasts." With common industry and skill, starvation in such a country was impossible; but it became necessary to scatter their forces, that they might more readily procure their game. Accordingly, sixty or eighty, with Ensign Laxson, were sent down the river to feed upon oysters; twenty with Lieut. Percy, to Point Comfort, to live by fishing; "Master West, with as many more, went up the falls, but nothing could be found but a few acornes, of which every man had a fair proportion." The industry of some thirty or forty enabled them, even under these hard conditions, to live tolerably well, and with something of comfort. These had always before been the persons to supply the colony. They now contrived to supply themselves. Sturgeon were in abundance, and these fish dried and pounded, and "mixed with caviare, sorrel, and other wholesome hearbes, would make good bread and meate;" while the *Toghwogh* and other roots would yield bread enough in a day to keep the gatherer a week. But the greater number of the colonists, who had hitherto found their food wholly in the toils of others, were not satisfied to adopt the habits of industry even at a period of such extreme necessity, and "had they not been forced, *nolens volens*, perforce to gather and prepare their victuall, they would all have starved or have eaten one another." It was the painful struggle with our Captain, from the first commencement of the settlement in Virginia, to protect the greater number of his followers from themselves. Their own blindness, and wickedness, and wilfulness; the perversity and malice in their hearts; the profligacy, at once, of moral and understanding with which they suffered, constituted the greater part of the toils and vexations with which he had to contend from the commencement. And now, when, with ordinary painstaking, it was so easy to gather good food and in abundance, these miserable wretches, with idleness, and gluttony, and a pernicious will, thoroughly ingraining their whole nature, preferred infinitely the sacrifice of all that had been done, and all that they possessed, rather than undergo the moderate amount of toils which the necessities of their condition required. They preferred rather to sell their implements of culture, of work and defence, their hoes and kettles, their swords, guns and ordnance, in exchange with the savages for the poor remains of corn they had in store. Powhatan, hearing of their emergency, had, with a rare and noble magnanimity, sent them half his stock; yet were these profligate wretches on the eve of mutinying because Smith would not yield to their clamors, in endeavoring to wrest from him the residue. Failing in this object, their evil humors took another direction; and finding that some of them seriously meditated the abandonment of the colony, he seized upon the ringleader of the faction, one Dyer, "a crafty fellow, and his ancient maligner," and having "worthily punished" him, made a talk to his comrades, in the following form and manner:—

"Fellow-soldiers, I little thought there could be any among you so false to report, or so simple as to believe that I intended to starve you, or that Powhatan, at this season, had any corn for himselfe, much less for you; or that I would not procure it for you, if I knew where it were to be had. Neither did I think any of you so malicious as now I see a great many. Yet this shall not so provoke my passion, but that I will do my best for my worst maligner. But you must dream no longer of any help from Powhatan, nor that I will forbear to force you, if you are idle, and punish you when you wrangle. And if I finde any more runners for Newfoundland with the pinnace, let him assuredly look to arrive at the gallows. You cannot deny but that, by the hazard of my life, many a time I have saved yours, when (might your owne wills have prevailed) you would have starved, and would do so still whether I will or noe. But I protest, by the God that made me, since necessitie hath not power to force you to gather for yourselves those fruites which the earth doth yield, you shall not onely gather for yourselves, but for those also who are sicke. I have shared with the meanest of you in provision, and now my extra allowance shall be distributed among the sicke. They, at least, shall not suffer. You shall help to provide for them. They shall partake of all our labors. As for this savage fare which your mouths so scornfully repine at, your stomaches can digest it. If you would have better you should have bought it. I will take a course which shall make you provide what is to be had. He, therefore, who gathereth not each day as much as I doe, shall be set the next beyond the river, and be banished from the fort as a droan till he mend his condition or starve."

They murmured at his tyranny, but submitted, and thrived accordingly. They did not perish from the famine that was so much feared; but the fishermen to his nets, the fowler to his weirs, the farmer to his fields, all prospered in obeying that imperative will, which saved them in spite of their own. Many were billeted among the Indians, and thus acquired their languages, their modes of life, their forest craft, and the medicinal and culinary virtues of their plants and roots, in the use of which the savages have proverbially great success and skill. And they suffered no injury thus living among their rude and wandering neighbors. Captain Smith was a name of so much power and terror among them, that "they durst not wrong us of a pin." So grateful did this sort of life become to many of the whites, that they afterwards ran away to their forest friends when the necessity for leaving the fort had ceased to exist. But they were soon taught by the Indians that the power was supposed to reside in Captain Smith rather than the race over which he ruled. The simple savages had long learned to distinguish between his endowments and those of his companions; and the treatment of the fugitives, who were always finally brought back by the Indians, was in some cases full of admirable justice. The two savages, Kemps and Tussoree, the "two most exact villaines in all the country," made themselves sport by subjecting the runaway whites to a treatment such as that which Smith had made them endure while in captivity: "feeding them with this law"—a favorite maxim with our Captain—"that he who would not work must not eate," until they nearly starved the spiritless fugitives to death. Nor were they suffered to escape, but were kept closely watched, and under the uplifted club, until opportunity was found for bringing them back to the settlements, with all that they had stolen. Such had been the effect of our hero's training upon these "poore salvages, of whom there was more hope to make better Christians and good subjects than the one halfe of those that counterfeited themselves both."

Among the first public labors which engaged the attention of our President when the emergencies of the colony in regard to food were fairly at an end, was one to recover possession of the Dutchmen who had been left with Powhatan, and another fugitive, named *Bentley*, who had found his way to the same place of harborage. By this time the treachery of those reprobates was well known in the colony, and the desire of Smith to obtain possession of their persons had its origin quite as much in the wish to lessen their influence upon the profligates at Jamestown, as with the view to their own punishment. To effect this object, Smith despatched one William Volday, a

Swiss, who undertook to procure their return to the colony. He was authorized to promise their pardon for past offences, and good treatment hereafter. But Volday himself was no sooner in the tents of Powhatan, than he followed the traitorous example of those whom he had been sent to recover. He had probably been one of their confederates before, but so secretly and adroitly had he played his game that none had ever suspected him. His hypocrisy was of the most odious sort, since he obtained the confidence of Smith chiefly by his openly declared disapprobation and loathing of the Dutchmen—whom our author styles "his cursed countrymen." Volday was a more daring, as well as a more subtle villain than the rest. He proposed to Powhatan and his associates to proceed more vigorously in their objects, and offered to the former that, with his forces, he would undertake, while the English were thus scattered abroad over the face of the country for food, to cut them off, and bring into his service all those whom it was not absolutely necessary to destroy. They were to fire Jamestown, seize the pinnace, slay the hogs, and effectually root out the settlement. Whether Powhatan entertained this plot, to be put in execution at a proper season, or not, we are not advised; but the plan was revealed to Smith in sufficient time to guard against its dangers by two of his own people, Thomas Douse and Thomas Mallard, to whom, as to his confederates, Volday had made it known. Repenting of their connection with this traitor, they betrayed his secret, which Smith caused them still to conceal, while they continued to intrigue with the conspirator. His object was that the plot should ripen, "onely to bring the irreclaimable Dutchmen, and the inconstant salvages, in such a manner, amongst such ambuscados as he had prepared, that not many of them should returne from our Peninsula." But the rumor got abroad among the people, who importuned the President to pursue and destroy the traitors. Lieutenant Percy and Mr. John Cuddrington, "two gentlemen of as bold and resolute spirits as could possibly be found," with many others, volunteered to go and cut the throats of these wretches in the very presence of Powhatan. But Smith had other employments for these. He, nevertheless, gave way to the voice of the multitude, and suffered "Master Wyffin and Sergeant Jeffrey Abbot to goe and stab or shoot them." But this commission came to nothing. Powhatan signified to the messengers of death that the Dutchmen were at their disposal. He did not keep them; nor would he offer to protect them. But when they listened to the representations of the criminals, they began to differ in opinion as to the propriety of executing judgment upon them. Wyffin was for carrying out the purpose on which he came, but Abbot opposed it. The Dutchmen accused Volday, suspecting him of revealing the plot. He, meanwhile, seems to have eluded observation, and probably sought shelter in the forests, from whence he subsequently made his way to England, where he imposed upon sundry merchants with a story of rich mines which he had discovered in Virginia. He was sent out by them with Lord Delaware; but his impostures were soon detected, and he died miserably and in deserved disgrace. Of the other Dutchmen, one remained with the Indians, while the other accepted the pardon which was tendered him by Smith, and returned to the colony. Subsequently, availing himself of a period of confusion in the settlement, he fled again to Powhatan, with Francis, one of his confederates, whose history has already been given,—and shared his fate;—the brains of both of them being beaten out by the Indians, as double traitors, whom no party could trust.

Meanwhile, the return of the several parties, which, in obedience to instructions from England, had been sent out to ascertain the fate of the missing colony of Sir Walter Raleigh, proved the mission to be fruitless. Mr. Sicklemore had explored the Chawwonoke, but found no traces and as few traditions of the lost settlers; and quite as little to reward his toils in the search after "silk-grass," or Pemminaw, as the Indians call it. The soil he found well timbered and exceedingly fertile. "Master *Nathanael Powel* and *Anas Todkill*," who had been sent under guidance of two of the people of Quioughnohanocks, to explore the country of the Mangoags—a tribe not under the sway of Powhatan, but dwelling on the upper branches of the Nottoway—were equally unfortunate. "Three dayes journey they conducted them through the woods, into a high country towards the southwest; where they saw, here and there, a little cornefield, by some little spring or small brooke, but no river could they see." Except in language, they found the savages of this region in manners and appearance to resemble all they had yet seen. They lived upon the wild beasts and roots of the forest, wild fruits, and their slender crops, and carried on a trade with the people along the coasts, exchanging their peltry for fish and other commodities. The Quioughnohanocks were a small nation of Indians, who dwelt on the south side of James River, about ten miles above Jamestown. Their chief was always a fast friend to the English. This "promise-keeping king, of all the rest, did ever best affect us; and though to his false gods he was very zealous, yet he would confesse our God as much exceeded his as our guns did his bow and arrowes; and often sent our President many presents to pray to his God for raine, that his corn might not perish—his own gods being angry."

CHAPTER XII.

While Captain Smith, by his address and energy, was thus retrieving the fortunes of the colony, and laying the solid foundations of a permanent empire, he received letters from England, which were very far from doing justice to his services. These were brought by Captain Argall, a gentleman then engaged in a contraband trade, but who afterwards became a governor in the country. They reproached our hero with the necessities of the colony, with his hard usage of the natives, and with the failure of the ships to return with freights. The accounts of his mode of dealing with the savages came from Newport, and others of his class and calibre. The stern decision of Smith, his knowledge of human nature, his skill in war, his stratagem and adventure,—all these, so far superior to the qualities possessed by his rivals—had inflamed them with an unappeasable hate and envy. To accuse him and to decry his merits and misrepresent his services, was, in fact, to furnish the most obvious mode of justification for their own failures and defeats. Smith, alone, had succeeded,—succeeded in establishing the colony ;—but this was not the sort of success which the proprietors at home desired. They had set out with false notions of the returns which should flow from their expenditure. The history of Spanish conquest, always sounding in the precious metals, was continually present to their thoughts; and their imaginations were too much disturbed by the gorgeous vision of uncounted treasure in the southern parts of America, not to insist, equally in nature's and in reason's spite, that the northern regions of the New World should unfold spoils of equal value and abundance. To conquer a foothold among the furious savages of Apalachia,—to lay deeply and broadly the foundations of a great commercial empire—to maintain himself, in spite of faction and feeble resources, cold, and want, and sickness—with traitors within and unrelenting and unsleeping enemies without,—were not such services as could impress themselves upon a world which had been dazzled by the wondrous good fortune of Cortes in Mexico and Pizarro in Peru, or pacify the demands of those more immediately interested, who, having unwisely trusted their outlay in the hands of incompetent persons, and committed numerous blunders by their own misconception of their proper policy, were now disposed to wreak their indignation upon the only man who had shown himself really responsible. Smith was to be superseded. A new charter, bearing date the 23d May, 1609, was obtained from the Crown, containing larger privileges and more ample powers than the former. The local Presidency and Council were to be abrogated, and the colonists were expressly commanded to yield obedience to those only who should receive their appointment from the Council in England. Under this new system, Lord Delaware was made Captain-general of the colony;—Sir Thomas Gates his Lieutenant; Sir George Somers, Admiral; Capt. Newport, Vice Admiral; Sir Thomas Dale, High-marshal; Sir Ferdinando Wainman, General of the Horse; and other officers were designated, and other appointments made, by which the infant colony of Virginia, which had made no returns, and which had barely maintained itself in an uncertain existence through the vigilance and courage of one man, was to be lifted into an establishment of very imposing exterior. The new charter was granted to the Earls of Salisbury, Suffolk, Southampton, Pembroke, and other Peers, to the number of twenty-one; and to knights and noble gentlemen almost without number. The enterprise became fashionable. So many persons of power and fortune embarking in it, encouraged the more timid capitalists, and enabled the Captain-general and his associates to send off such an armament as never before had floated in the waters of Virginia. Nine ships and five hundred people, were despatched, under the command of Sir Thomas Gates, Sir George Somers and Captain Newport. To each of these gentlemen, a commission was furnished, with which, the first who arrived, was to supersede that by which the colony was held. In this first proceeding, was planted the seed of difficulty and confusion. Unwilling that either should reach the promised land before the other, the three Commissioners concluded to embark together in the same vessel. They sailed from England, accordingly, in the latter part of May, 1609, in a vessel called the Sea-Venture, which was parted from the rest of the fleet in a hurricane, and wrecked upon the Bermudas. Their lives were saved, and, after a long delay and many hardships, they finally reached Virginia; but not until Captain Smith had left it, to return to it no more. One other of the vessels in this expedition shared a worse fate—a small ketch, which foundered in the gale. The seven remaining ships reached their port in safety. Unadvised of their coming, Smith, at their approach, assuming them to be Spaniards, prepared for them as enemies. Putting his men under arms, and his fort in a posture of defence, and strengthened by a large body of Indians, who, glad to conciliate our Captain, came forward promptly with an offer of their services, he little feared the arrival of the supposed Spaniards, nor doubted that he should encounter them successfully. But he was soon relieved of his apprehensions from this quarter, though it is very certain that an invasion of Spaniards would have proved less hurtful to the colony than those who came. Among these were some of whom we already possess some knowledge. These were Captains Martin, Archer and Ratcliffe, or Sicklemore, as we are told he should properly be called—"a poore counterfeited imposture," as Smith describes him in a letter to the Council, "whom I have sent you home lest the company should cut his throat." It is a sufficient proof of the success with which his enemies work d against him in England, that there should have been sent out, on this expedition, and in some command, all the persons with whom he had been compelled to struggle, in maintaining successfully the interests of the colony. These persons, unhappily, succeeded in impressing the new colonists generally with some share of their ill-feeling towards our Captain. They were, accordingly, prepared to dislike and distrust him before they had yet encountered his person. It was easy to influence them in this manner. The greater number among them were profligate youth, whose friends were only too well satisfied to give them ample room in remote countries, where they might escape the worse destinies that threatened them at home. Poor gentlemen, bankrupt tradesmen, rakes and libertines, such as were more apt to ruin than to raise a commonwealth. A small sprinkling of better men among them, a few well-designing persons, of better sense and more experience, were soon disabused of the prejudices which the enemies of Smith had striven to inculcate. They had only to see his proceedings, and to hear the representations of his old soldiers, to arrive at just conclusions; but the wholesome leaven was quite too small for such a lump, and the colony very soon presented a spectacle of most admired uproar and confusion.

Smith, hurt at the injustice of which he had been the victim, was disposed to fold his arms, as a quict and indifferent spectator, while the new-comers ran riot in their abuse of order and authority. His presidency had not yet been superseded. The power to take his place had only been conferred upon those who had been wrecked upon the Bermudas, and his commission was still sovereign against all competitors. But, in his pique, he was not disposed to assert its virtues, nor were his enemies disposed to acknowledge them. He prepared to return to England, and suffered misrule, for some time, to play its fantastic tricks, without offering any obstruction to its progress. Led by Ratcliffe, Martin and Archer, this "lewd rout" passed from one mischievous proceeding to another. They assumed the reins of government, and, on a small scale, were as wanton as the young charioteer whom Phœbus, according to classic fable, entrusted with his steeds. At one moment they chose one governor, who was soon made to give place to another—to-day they were for the old commission, to-morrow for the new, and the third day found them flinging away the restraining influences of all. "Happie," says one of our authorities, "had we beene had they never arrived, and we for ever abandoned; for on earth, for the number, was never more confusion or misery than their factions occasioned." Wanton, indolent and feeble, they presented one of those mournful spectacles of impotence and vanity in power, which the great poet assumes must make angels weep—a spectacle so ridiculous, as well as mournful, that it might well prompt their laughter also. The scorn of Smith seasoned his indignation. He looked on with pity and contempt, until the evil grew too serious to suffer any longer such feelings to prevail. He was too little selfish in his nature—too much the patriot—to hold himself aloof when such dangers threatened the work of his hands, which had already cost him so much risk and labor. The sturdy followers of his past fortunes, most of whom had learned properly to estimate his worth and virtues, were true to the colony, and disposed to sustain him in the due maintenance of its interests. A part of the newly arrived were soon made to see that their hope lay in the energy and will which distinguished his command. Having waited for some time in the hope that the new commission would arrive, upon which he might devolve the legal responsibility, it became necessary for the public good that he should re-assert his own, and he did so with his wonted promptness and resolution. Ratcliffe, Archer, and other factious spirits, were laid by the heels after a long contest, and the strong hand which had so successfully swayed the power of this colony for its good, wielded it once more for its safety. This was not done without a struggle. "It would be too tedious, too strange, and almost incredible," says our authority, "should I particularly relate the infinite dangers, plots and practices, he daily escaped among this factious crew;" but the ringleaders once in prison and awaiting their trial, the restoration of order was comparatively easy. To lessen their power of mischief, and the tendency to it, Smith distributed them in sufficiently large bodies for defence and settlement about the country. Mr. West, with a hundred and twenty chosen men, was sent to make a settlement at the Falls of James River, and Captain Martin, with as many more, to Nansemond. These were furnished with provisions according to their numbers; and, with tools to work with, and weapons in their hands, had it in their power to found and to establish themselves in well-fortified and pleasant abodes.

The disorders of the colony being quelled, and the machine of government and society once more working fairly on its wheels and hinges, Smith evinced the nobleness of his nature by giving up his authority. The year of his

Presidency was nearly expired, and he yielded his seat to Capt. Martin. But Martin had some saving grains of sense and honesty, and had hardly taken possession of the government before the oppressive weight of its responsibility, with a conviction of his personal unpopularity, overcame his ambition, and he resigned it again into the hands of Smith, and hurried back to his establishment at Nansemond. But his rule here was quite as unequal to the exigency as it would have been with the whole colony resting on his shoulders and wisdom. Though kindly treated by the Nansemond Indians, yet, in his anticipations of mischief, or in his wantonness of power, he surprises their chief in the midst of his festivities, and takes possession of the island upon which he lived, with all his houses and treasure. Here he fortified himself, but so feebly, and so bad was the watch which he kept, that the savages took his fortress by assault, killed many of his men, rescued their king, and carried off a thousand bushels of corn. Smith was at the Falls when intelligence reached him of this disaster, together with an entreaty from Martin for thirty soldiers. These were sent him, but he showed himself so little capable of using them, that they abandoned him in disgust, and made their way back to Jamestown, where they were soon followed by Martin himself, who left his people to take care of themselves.

The establishment made by West at the Falls was scarcely more successful. Smith, making him a visit to examine the new settlement, was confounded to find West on his way to Jamestown, already sick of his experiment. The survey which our Captain made of what had been done, proved the competence of the leader to be no greater than that of Martin. The settlement had been fixed on a site which had no single quality to recommend it. The spot was so low as to be liable to the inundations of the river. It was also subject to other and equally serious objections. Smith, as usual, compelled to take the business in hand, determined to abandon the place, and to seek another of more eligible qualities. To effect this, he negotiated with Powhatan for the district of country which went by that chieftain's name. Hither he proceeded to transfer the colony which had been assigned to West, but he was met by resistance and final violence on the part of the infatuated wretches whom he strove to serve. Under the impression that the territory in which West had set them down was one abundant in the precious metal, they refused to abandon it;—refused, indeed, to suffer among them any addition to their numbers, even from among their own people, lest the individual share of spoil to each should be too greatly diminished. Besides, they were not disposed to yield much deference to the tenure by which Smith held the Presidency—looking momently to the arrival of those by whom his commission was to be superseded. Smith, at first, pitying their blindness and folly, endeavored to convince them of the reasons by which he was moved in his selection of a site for their establishment. But they treated his expostulations and authority with equal contempt. He was not the man to submit coolly to such indignities, and, though attended by five men only, he proceeded to take certain of the most factious of their number into custody. But they did not suffer him to proceed. Remote from home, from the restraining and correcting influences of civilized life, and desperate in their resolve to seize the gold which they believed to be growing in the fertile earth around them, and to be had for the gathering, they arrayed themselves in force against the audacious individual, whom they had been taught to hate and to distrust from the beginning, by whom they were to be torn from their Dorado. Five men against one hundred and twenty, suggested a greater inequality of force than it was within the courage even of a spirit so fearless as that of Smith to encounter. He retreated to his boat, accordingly, and with that readiness of resource which seemed never to desert him, he changed his plan of attack by arms, for one which promised less peril and greater success. He surprised the vessel which contained all their stores and provisions, and, after a delay of several days, in which he strove to afford the mutineers time and counsel for return to their obedience, he set sail for Jamestown, leaving these besotted wretches to their deserts.

They did not long elude their proper punishment. With the same wild and reckless spirit with which they had met the attempts of Smith to bring them to order, and put them in safety, they behaved to the simple savages in whose vicinity they had settled themselves. These they robbed and maltreated, dispossessed them of their food and stores, despoiled and drove them from their dwellings, and, when they complained, took them into custody. The Indians, as soon as they perceived the hostile attitude which they took with regard to Smith, whom they had learned equally to venerate and fear, volunteered in numbers to fight his battles. They complained to him, with justice, that he had brought among them, on the plea of protecting them, a far worse enemy than they had ever before had reason to fear; and urged that, since they could not look to him for protection, he must not be surprised or offended if they struggled to protect themselves. Smith, of course, refused them aid, and exhorted them to forbearance. He counselled the refractory whites of their danger from this source; but had the fortune, like Cassandra, to have his predictions laughed at. The mutineers soon paid the penalty of unbelief. The departure of Smith was the signal for the rising of the savages. He had scarcely set sail when a simultaneous attack was made upon the fort, and such of the whites as were straggling in the woods. Many were slain, and the rest so frightened, that it was no longer a difficult matter for Smith to obtain a hearing. His vessel having grounded in the river, within reach of the terrified fugitives, they appealed to him for protection, and at once submitted themselves to his mercy. For once, our Captain found the Indians to be excellent auxiliaries. Taking advantage of their fears, he selected six or seven of the ringleaders for punishment, and having laid them by the heels, conducted the rest of them to the proposed settlement at Powhatan; where he took possession of the fortress, "readie built and prettily fortified with poles and barkes of trees," as it had been raised by that sturdy emperor. The work is described as sufficient to have protected them against all the savages in Virginia; and there were lodging houses ready for use, and more than two hundred acres of land in planting condition. Of so much strength and beauty was the site thus secured to these undeserving runagates, that Smith preferred it to all others he had seen in the country. Accordingly, he called it *Nonsuch*. He had subdued his malcontents for a season; seated them in abodes of pleasantness; and, reconciling them to the Indians, left them to the enjoyment of a peace and security which their merits had scarcely obtained of themselves. Captain West, making his appearance, now that all the troubles of the settlement had been composed, had nearly again revived them by the mistaken efforts which he made for the release of the mutineers who had been selected for an example. He succeeded in prevailing with Smith—who was now completely sickened with the toil of serving men equally against their destiny and will—to give them up. This was done, and our Captain departed for Jamestown. But *Nonsuch*, however desirable and beautiful, could not long content these unhappy people; who, possessed with the dream of finding gold in the country of the Monacans, as soon as they had recovered from the fright which the savages had given them, once more abandoned their settlement, and made their way back to that from which they had been expelled. We need not pursue their history. From this moment the connection ceases between them and our adventurer.

CHAPTER XIII.

Our Captain begins to show a certain degree of weariness and exhaustion, in the protracted struggle which he has been compelled to maintain, as well against, as in behalf of, the oddly assorted community confided to his charge. The elastic spirit of youth with which he rather rejoiced in difficulties, even as the brave swimmer prefers to struggle against the billowy currents, than float without effort on the slumberous lake, no longer buoys him up against all opposition; and the sense of service treated with injustice, and of true and substantial merits denied their due acknowledgment, reconciles him to those irregularities, and that wilful disposition to err and suffer, on the part of the settlers, which he has hitherto encountered with the firm and decisive rule of the patriarch. When, therefore, the people under West "returned againe to the open ayre at West's fort, abandoning Nonsuch"—that delightful, secure, and sheltered spot, which he had been at such trouble to procure for them from Powhatan—he makes no further opposition, and sees them hurrying anew to "the height of their former factions," with an indifference which betrays the exhaustion of his patience, rather than any want of sympathy in the interests of the colony. The proprietors of the establishment seem to have kept pace with the colonists, in weaning him from those attachments to the region and to the enterprise, which naturally grew out of his connection with them; and it needed but a very small immediately impelling motive to cause him to abandon Virginia, as he had just abandoned to their fortunes,

27*

the unstable and obstinate people under West. That impelling circumstance was now at hand. Passing down the river, on his way from Nonsuch to Jamestown, an event occurred which nearly deprived him of life. While he slept, his powder-bag was accidentally fired by one of the crew, and the powder exploding, tore and lacerated his body in a most shocking manner. Roused by the sudden torture from his sleep, he leapt instantly into the river, from which he was extricated with the greatest difficulty, and not before he was almost drowned. In this condition, without the means of comfort or surgical assistance, he had yet nearly a hundred miles to travel in an open boat before he could arrive at either. Suffering thus dreadfully, he was not permitted to forget the cares of his public trust, in his physical disquiets, but found it necessary, on reaching Jamestown, to address his energies and thoughts much more to the troubles of those around him, than to any of his own. There he found everything in disorder from the activity of Ratcliffe, Archer, and the other malcontents whom he had arrested for their mutinies. The time for their trial was approaching, and their guilty consciences counselled them rather to anticipate that period by new commotions, than quietly await its issues. Accordingly, these creatures were busy, and so active and audacious that Captain Smith was compelled, on his return, maimed and mangled as he was, to put the settlement in such trim as would enable it to meet the exigencies of a sudden assault. While thus making his preparations, and particularly striving to increase the store of provisions for the garrison, his miserable condition of body—"unable to stand, and neere bereft of his senses by reason of his torment"—they conceived a more prompt and happy expedient for escaping trial. His feebleness inspired their courage, and emboldened them to try an experiment, which, in his armor, erect, and "ready with his conclusions," their cowardly spirits would never for a moment have entertained. They laid their plans to assassinate him in his bed. But the heart of the base creature who had been chosen to do the deed, failed him at the proper moment. He dared not "give fire to that mercilesse pistoll." We are not told whether the waking eye of Smith encountered the assassin, but, if it did, he was probably quelled and paralyzed, as was the savage Cimbrian who had been sent by the magistracy of Minturnæ to butcher Caius Marius. The voice, the eye, and probably the bare aspect of a man whom even the worst enemies of Smith in Virginia had been wont to fear, must have done, for his safety, that which his own skill and strength could no longer have achieved in this moment of his impotence. The murderer shrunk from the duty assigned him, and other modes became necessary by which the confederate malignants should still elude the justice which they feared. To usurp the government seemed the only process. Smith was advised of their plans in time to baffle them; and, at this period, his old soldiers gave him a new proof of their loyalty and attachment. Gathering around his bed, they importuned him to suffer them at once to take off the heads of the conspirators, and thus, at a single stroke, take away those branches, which had been so fruitful of disease and hurt to the growth of the colony. But Smith, with great magnanimity, refused to avail himself of this short and summary method of revenge. He was sick of the struggle, and saw no reason to persevere in a conflict, for which, whether right or wrong, whether he failed or triumphed, he was still likely to suffer blame. His hurts of body contributed also in great degree to lessen those nervous energies which might have made his mind eager to redress itself—to punish his enemies, and to overcome all the difficulties which they might raise upon his path. But why should he still continue to build for others? Why build for those who, coming after him, might only cast down his fabrics? His labors for several years—the arduous conflict which he had maintained for the establishment of the colony—the firm basis upon which he had founded the little community from Europe, in spite of all savage opposition, in the forests of America—all that he had done, with what recompense, and with what toil, and peril, and annoyance—was about to pass to strangers! What motive for farther exertion, with a frame writhing in agony, with a spirit vexed and wearied by disappointment? His resolves were more pacific and more honorable than his old soldiers would have had them. Contenting himself with taking order for the safety of the colony, by placing the government in the hands of Mr. Percy, he sailed in the autumn of 1609 from Virginia, which he was never again to behold.

Of his services in founding the English colony, the history of which has so far been his own, we have endeavored to afford an account as lively and correct as possible. We cannot doubt that it survived only through his wisdom, his courage, and his great enterprise. He was the master spirit of his little empire; for one year its president; and, during the whole term of his stay in the country—something more than two years—its chief support and security. To those accustomed to measure events by their magnitude alone, the petty details which characterize an infant settlement such as we have described—the small cares of providing food for wandering men, and contending for their lives against bands of naked savages—it will seem something of an extravagance, not to say absurdity, to claim for him, whose life is consumed in such performances, the merits of great heroism. But we are free to express our conviction, that the successful conflict with the minor necessities of life, in strange situations, against active hostility from without, and an antipathy within quite as active, though less overt, and with such inadequate resources as were in the possession of our Captain, require resources of thought, will, courage, energy, and magnanimity, quite as great as are usually exercised by the victorious chieftain; the vastness of whose performance, alone, rather than its value, and the obstacles which have opposed it, constitutes his whole claim to renown and eminence. Smith, in the employment of a company who had but a vague idea of their own objects, and an imperfect notion of the sort of adventure upon which he went, was continually under the check and rebuke of a power which could neither direct his labors nor appreciate his performances. They could find no merit in obtaining a foothold in a foreign and hostile region, from which their extravagant fancies anticipated nothing less than treasure. The vast utility of what he succeeded in doing, in founding his colony, in spite of inadequate numbers, deficient materials, starvation, sickness, and mutiny, was not to be felt or understood, where such insane fancies prevailed in the face of all sober reason and reflection. That he should not have satisfied his employers who sat in silken security at home, is by no means matter of surprise. That he should not have pleased the effeminate and the profligate with whose preservation he was burdened, and whom he made to toil in unwonted labors, when it was their passion to live wholly on the toils and risks of others, is quite as little within the range of expectation; and that his career should have proved grateful to the savage tribes whom he overcame—whom he alone could overcome—whom he subdued to peace—whom he made tributary to his necessities—and upon whose territories he fixed a foot so fast that no improvidence in his successors, however extreme, could enable them to fling it off—was not within the bounds of reason and belief. And yet, in the respect of all these, he secured such a place, that we find the savages volunteering their arms to strengthen his power against the profligate and refractory of his own people;—we find the veterans whom he had trained to successes by his strict and undiscriminating justice, forgetting all their prejudices, and proffering to bring him the heads of his enemies;—and in regard to his general merits in the establishment of the colony, we discover that, surviving all the misrepresentations of that scurvy pack, the Archers, the Newports, and the Ratcliffes, the world of England, very soon after he left Virginia, justly accorded him the credit of being its true founder and sole parent. Time, that great avenger, has ratified the awards of justice, and posterity confirms the decision which even contemporaneous history was disposed to make in the case of our hero. But, unless our narrative has satisfied the reader of his great and superior merits, any summary at this stage in our progress will utterly fail to supply the deficiency. It will be enough here to furnish that which we have at the hands of certain of his followers in Virginia. One of the authorities from which we derive our materials, thus rudely but forcibly accumulates, in one paragraph, and characterizes his performances. "By this you may see for all those crosses, trecheries, and dissentions, how he wrestled and overcame (without bloodshed) all that happened; also what good was done; how few dyed; what food the country naturally affordeth; what small cause there is men should starve, or be murthered by the salvages, that have discretion to manage them, with courage and industrie. The two first yeares, though by his adventures, he had oft brought the salvages to a tractable trade, yet you see how the envious authoritie ever crossed him, and frustrated his best endeavors. But it wrought in him that experience and estimation amongst the salvages as otherwise it had bin impossible he had ever effected what he did. Notwithstanding the many miserable, yet generous and worthy adventures he had oft and long endured in the wide world, yet, in this case, he was againe to learne his lecture by experience. Which, with thus much adoe having obtained, it was his ill chance to end, when he had but onely learned how to begin."

This is well and honestly stated. The writer proceeds to hint what was the contrast between his successes and those of the persons by whom he was succeeded. "And though he left those unknowne difficulties made easy and familiar to his unlawful successors (who onely by living in Jamestowne presumed to know more than all the world could direct them) now,—though they had all his souldiers, with a tripple power, and twice tripple better meanes,—by what they have done in his absence, the world may see what they would have done in his presence had he not prevented their indiscretions: it doth justly prove what cause he had to send them for England, and that he was neither factious, mutinous, nor dishonest. But they have made it more plaine since his return for England, having his absolute authoritie freely in their power, with all the advantages and opportunity that his labours had effected."

It does not belong to our present labors to continue the history of events in Virginia after the departure of our hero, yet, in confirmation of the preceding extract, and to show by relative results what were his real claims upon the admiration of those who appreciated the deeds of a proper manhood, it may be well to mention that his departure from the colony was followed by misery and disaster. The seditious portion of the population got the ascendency; Martin and West abandoned their separate settlements with the loss of half their men; the Indians, as soon as they were sure of the absence of that commanding genius which had always held them in such complete subjection, revolted and murdered all whom they met. Instead of one, the colonists had twenty Presidents, each with his bullies and retainers; the provisions which Smith had gathered with so much care were soon wasted, and West and Ratcliffe, going forth to trade for supplies with the Indians, the former fled to England, and the latter, set upon by the savages, was slain with thirty of his soldiers: but one boy of the number escaped, preserved by the merciful interposition of Pocahontas. It was not long before the worst enemies and maligners of Smith, subdued by suffering and danger to a proper sense of their equal feebleness and undesert, deplored his absence, and, in the bitterness of their hearts, cursed their destinies by which that event had been precipitated.

Such was the distress and suffering of the colonists, from famine and the unremitting hostility of the savages, that, of five hundred persons whom Smith left behind him in the colony, there remained living, at the end of six months, scarcely more than sixty—men, women, and children—and these preserved a wretched existence by living upon roots and herbs, acorns, and wild nuts, and berries of the wood. From the Indians they got little else than scoffs and wounds. They traded away their swords and firelocks for food, and thus fell easier victims to their foes. Famine, in its most horrid forms, assailed them. The very skins of their horses were devoured. A portion among them disinterred an Indian, who had been slain and buried, and, having eaten him, followed up the horrid taste for human food, by preying upon one another. One miserable wretch slew his own wife, and had devoured a portion of the carcass before he was detected. But we gladly turn from a spectacle so wretched, which nothing but the rare conduct, ability and courage of our hero had kept from being seen in the colony before. The day of retribution was not long deferred after his departure, and no more triumphant attestation of his wonderful merits, for such a service, could be found, than in the contrast between the history of Virginia during his administration, and that of the first six months by which it was succeeded. We must now follow him to England.

BOOK FOURTH.

CHAPTER I.

Of "our Captaine," returned to his native land, we hear little or nothing for several years. A period of physical repose seems to have been necessary to his career after so long a conflict with danger and privation. It is probable that he suffered for some time after reaching England from his injuries by gunpowder; for, just before leaving Virginia, we are told, "so grievous were his wounds, and so cruel his torments, that few expected he could live." He did live, but his cure was probably a tedious one; and habits of reading and study, induced by the confinement of his chamber, in all probability opened new resources to his mind, particularly at a period of great physical exhaustion. It is likely that he conceived, while in this situation, those plans of study, and followed out those inquiries in history, which led him subsequently to become a somewhat voluminous writer. In 1612 he published his "map of Virginia, with a description of the countrey, the commodities, people, government and religion." To this work was annexed the history published under the name of William Simmons, "Doctour of Divinitie;" to which the biographers of Smith have been so largely indebted. And we have no doubt that, during the interval between his departure from Virginia, his voyages to, and discovery in New England, about five years, he employed no small portion of his time in a course of study, of which his youth had been neglectful—supplying those deficiencies of his early education, which he might ascribe as much to his own erratic temper as to the indifference and selfishness of his guardians. Smith, indeed, became something of a literary man. He held the pen quite as vigorously as he did the sword; used it with a flourish; and, if frequently rude and incoherent in his style, he sometimes made ample amends for his short-comings by snatching "a grace beyond the reach of art." He was bold in the use of figures; and, where he wrote from his own experience, and without affectations, he was sometimes uncommonly spirited, and even eloquent. His associates seem to have been men of letters. Some of his followers in Virginia were verse makers like himself. The custom of that time was to hail the appearance of the successful author with ode and sonnet, insisting upon his merits and peculiar claims upon the muse. It was a custom that had its beneficial uses, though liable to some objections. His volumes are introduced to the public by epistles from his admirers. R. Brathwait tells him:

> "Two greatest shires of England did thee beare,
> Renowned Yorkshire, Gaunt-stild Lancashire:"

reminds him of his conquests over the affections of Tragabigzanda, the Lady Callamata, Pocahontas, &c., all of whom did for him

> "What love with modesty could doe;"

and concludes, punning upon his name, with the wish that we had

> "Many such *Smiths* in this our Israel."

Anthony Fereby writes in better, and bolder, and truer verses:—

"Thou hast a course most full of honour runne:
Envy may snarle as dogges against the sunne,
May bark, not bite; for what deservedly
With thy life's danger, valour, policy,
Quaint, warlike stratagems, ability
And judgment thou hast got, fame sets so high
Detraction cannot reach: thy worth shall stand
A patterne to succeeding ages, and
Clothed in thine owne lines ever shall add grace
Unto thy native country and thy race."

Edward Jordan writes in a long strain, of which these lines will serve our purpose:

"I know none
That like thyself hast come, and gone, and runne,
To such praiseworthy actions."

Richard James, after enumerating the martial virtues of his subject, thus insists upon his literary as well as military merits:

"Whose sword and pen in bold, ruffe, martial-wise,
Put forth to try and beare away the prize
From Cæsar and *Blaize Monluc.*"

M. Hawkins notices yet other qualities which the lover of military glory does not often insist upon—

"None can truly say thou didst deceive
Thy soldiers, sailors, merchants or thy friends,
But all from thee a true account receive."

He adds—and thus furnishes the proof of what he asserts,

"Yet naught to thee all these thy virtues bring."

Richard Meade gives him that credit of

"Founding a common weale
In faire America,"

the proofs of which are, we humbly think, conclusively embodied in this volume; and so we are furnished with the testimonies of Edward Ingham, M. Cartner, Brian

O'Rourke, S. Tanner and others, all of which prove the esteem if not the poetical endowments of his contemporaries. Some of his followers in Virginia are among these tribute-bringers. J. Coddington signs himself "your sometime souldier, now templar." Raleigh Crashaw writes, "in the deserved honour of my honest and worthy Captain, John Smith and his work." He says, among other things,

"With due descretion and undaunted heart,
I oft so well have seene thee act thy part
In deepest plunge of hard extremitie,
As forct the troops of proudest foes to flee,
Though men of greater *rank* and less desert,
Would *pish*-away thy praise—it cannot start
From the true owner."

"Michael Phettiplace, Will Phettiplace and Richard Wyffin, gentlemen and souldiers under Captain Smith's command," give similar evidence, but in greater detail:

"Thou heldst the King of Paspahegh enchained,
Thou all alone this salvage sterne didst take.
Pamaunkee's king wee saw thee captive make
Among seven hundred of his stoutest men,
To murder thee and us resolved, when
Fast by the haire thou ledst this salvage grim,
Thy pistoll at his breast," &c.

Of Smith's own lines the specimens are few, and they do not impress us with the poetry of his verse, though his prose writings are full of evidence that he possessed a warm and lively fancy. There is, at the opening of his work about New England, a copy of verses entitled the "Sea-marke," which appear as coming from his pen. They possess considerable merit, and are decidedly better than many other samples of this order which have been preserved to us. They remind us of such writers as John Davies and Philip Quarles, and have that peculiar quaintness of tone which marked the verses of the Elizabethan period. It is but fair that we give them to the reader in this connection. They are better lines than those of his eulogists.

THE SEA-MARKE.

Aloofe, aloofe, and come no neare,
The dangers doe appeare,
Which, if my ruine had not beene,
You had not seene:
I only lie upon this shelfe
 To be a marke to all
 Which on the same may fall,
That none may perish but myself.

If in or outward you be bound
Do not forget to sound;
Neglect of that was caused of this
To steer amisse.
The seas were calm, the winde was faire,
 That made me so secure,
 That now I must endure
All weathers, be they foule or faire.

The winter's cold, the summer's heate
Alternatively beat
Upon my bruised sides, that rue,
Because too true,
That no reliefe can ever come;
 But why should I despaire
 Being promised so faire,
That there shall be a day of Dome.

The moral counsel in these verses is not confined to the seaman. The caution was such as Smith practised whether on land or sea. He had, in rare proportion, that "due discretion" for which his admirer gives him praise, along with the merit of "great valiantnesse." Certainly, never was the courage of the soldier more happily coupled with the calm over-ruling judgment of the Captain than in the case of Smith.

Such, then, for five years after he left Virginia seem to have been the exercises—we must not call them amusements—in which our adventurer indulged. But though he read in books, and mixed with literary men, his studies had but one direction. The books which he grappled were those of adventure and discovery. The books he wrote were of war, travel, and colonization; how countries were to be explored and settled; and how men were to be trained for such objects and employments. He was not forgetful of Virginia. His heart was still fondly set upon the fortunes of that colony. After alleging, in the opening of his treatise entitled "The Pathway to Experience to erect a Plantation," that "all our plantations have been so foyled and abused, their best good willes have been for the most part discouraged and disgraced;"—he adds, "but pardon me if I offend in loving that I have cherished truly, by the losse of my prime, fortunes, meanes and youth." This is a melancholy sentiment, which is but too frequently heard to fall from the lips of those who fall the victims to their own enthusiasm, in the service of the selfish. His youth—speaking comparatively—gone, his means exhausted, his successes questioned, and the prospect of future employment small, the forward glance of Smith must have shown him but a gloomy and cheerless pathway. He might well look back upon the history of past struggles in Virginia with mixed feelings of fondness and mortification. He had been successful there; he had done what no other person could have done; and of this neither malice nor envy could despoil his name. His successors were offering daily proof to the nation which tended to the elevation of Smith's abilities and virtues. We have already afforded a glimpse of the ruin and disaster by which his departure had been distinguished. The continued history of the settlement while he lay unemployed in England, conclusively showed how entirely the colony had been indebted to the one man for its preservation in past years. To this history we must return during the period of Smith's sojourn in England; not so much with a view to its details, as with regard to the fortunes of certain individuals in whom our sympathies have been awakened by the previous narrative. The name of Pocahontas is too nearly associated with that of Smith to suffer us to lose her from our sight; nor can we part abruptly with the grim chief, her shrewd and politic old father. These, with the remarkable savage, Opechancanough, will demand just enough of our attention to give a dramatic interest to our biography.

A continual change of governors followed the departure of Smith, and indicated quite as much as anything else the evil administration of the colony. Percy succeeded Smith; was succeeded by Sir Thomas Gates; he by Lord Delaware; Delaware by Percy again; Percy by Sir Thomas Dale; Dale by Gates again; Gates by Dale once more; and Dale by Mr. George Yeardly; and all these changes were made in the short space of six years. In this brief period the colonists were deeply and irretrievably embroiled with the Indians, whom they soon began to massacre, and whose villages they devoted to the flames. They were followed by flames and massacre in turn. The Indians, driven to fury, took courage against their tyrants; and what with their hostility, and the idleness and mutinous dispositions of the colonists, the latter were soon in danger of famine. They were saved only by supplies from England. New towns were established, and old ones taken from the savages. The temper of Powhatan was not improved by these events. The sympathy which Pocahontas expressed for the pale-faces had estranged from her the affections of the vindictive old man. She lived with him no longer, but found her abode in some secresy with her relations, the King and Queen of Potomack. She was no longer able to influence her father's mind in behalf of the English captives, and she fled from exhibitions of cruelty which her entreaties failed to arrest. She thought herself safe in the keeping of her relatives. She was yet to find herself painfully deceived. The English, under Capt. Argall, obtained intelligence of her hiding place, and the cupidity of Japazaws and his wife, with whom she found shelter, was excited by the bribes of Argall. They were prevailed upon to bring her on board the ships of the English. Pocahontas had already seen the great canoes, but the wife of Japazaws had been less fortunate. Her curiosity became a passion which must be gratified, and Pocahontas yielded to her entreaties. Why should she fear evil at the hands of the English? She, who had so frequently interposed to save them—who was even then under the frown of her father, because of her unnatural love for his enemies! Certainly, unless by assuming for them a character of the utmost ingratitude, she had no reason to apprehend treachery from them.

Her confidence was misplaced. Once in the vessel of Argall, she was decoyed into the gun-room, and there informed that she was a prisoner. Her prayers availed her nothing. Her tears were wasted upon the selfish nature of the English captain. Old Japazaws and his treacherous wife were loud in their howlings and entreaties, the better to persuade the unhappy girl of their innocence, but they were quite satisfied when they were put ashore with their copper-kettle, which had been the price of their miserable treachery.

The lesson which Argall thus put in practice was taken out of Spanish books. Failing to compass the capture of the king, his daughter was a prize that promised a goodly ransom. She was the favorite of her sire—had been *the nonpareil* in the days of Captain Smith's administration. It was assumed that Powhatan would pay with liberal hands that she might be restored to his eyes. A messenger was dispatched to him. He was told that his daughter could only be ransomed by a prompt restoration, to the English, of all the men, the guns, tools and weapons, which he had obtained by theft, purchase or conquest from the English. From Smith, Powhatan never succeeded in procuring arms. But the factious and lazy colonists, after his departure, in the loose rule which followed, procured their corn and tobacco from the savages by giving them their swords and matchlocks. Smith says sarcastically, "And the loving salvages, their kinde friends, they trained so well up to shoot in a piece, to hunt and kill their fowle, they became more expert than our owne countrymen."

It was necessary to recover the weapons so improvidently entrusted to their hands, and hence the conditions for the ransom of Pocahontas. They were too stringent for the ambitious nature of Powhatan, though the news of his daughter's capture troubled him much beyond all ordinary cause of grief. He made an effort to obtain her release. He sent back seven English prisoners, with each an unserviceable musket. He promised them, upon the release of his daughter, to make them satisfaction for all injuries, to enter with them into a treaty of peace, and to give them five hundred bushels of corn. But this did not satisfy her captors. They demanded that he should return everything, give up his whole treasure of English arms, upon which he had set his heart from the first moment of his knowledge of their use. The love of the father was not equal to the ambition of the king. He indignantly refused any answer to the demand, and for some time they heard nothing from him. They carried her up to Werowocomo under a strong guard of one hundred and fifty men, apprised him that they came to restore her to his arms, but repeated the original terms of her ransom. He refused to see them, and answered their propositions only with scorn and defiance. Some skirmishes ensued, in which the Indians suffered some injury and had their houses burnt, but the stern old emperor was implacable. The brothers of Pocahontas were permitted to visit her on board of the English vessel, but the concession led to nothing. The whites were compelled to return to Jamestown, leaving the savages more embittered than ever against them.

But a new agent was busy in bringing about a pacification, upon which neither the English nor the Indians had made any calculation. This was love. Pocahontas was now about eighteen years of age. She had, from her earliest knowledge of the English, been impressed with their superiority. She had loved them as a race beyond her own, and had given her entire veneration to their sagacious leader. A tenderer sentiment consoled her in her captivity. Her affections were won by John Rolfe, an Englishman of good family and worth. His addresses were sanctioned by Sir Thomas Dale, the then Governor of Virginia, and finally received the sanction of Powhatan. But he would not risk his person to be present at the marriage. He sent one of her uncles, Opachisco, and two of his sons, to witness the ceremonies, which were solemnized in the spring of 1613. This event softened the asperities between the opposing races. It subdued the hate, if it did not secure the love of Powhatan for the stranger people, and a treaty of peace, followed by a resumption of all friendly relations, was the result of an event which all parties considered auspicious. "Powhatan's daughter," says Sir Thomas Dale, in a letter from Jamestown, dated June 18, 1614, "I caused to be carefully instructed in the Christian religion, who, after she had made such progress therein, renounced publicly her country's idolatry, openly confessed her Christian faith, was, as she desired, baptized, and is since married to an English gentleman of good understanding (as by his letter unto me, containing the reasons of his marriage unto her, you may perceive)—another knot to bind the knot the stronger. Her father and friends gave approbation of it, and her uncle gave her to him in the church. She lives civilly and lovingly with him, and I trust will increase in goodnesse as the knowledge of God increaseth in her. She will goe into England with mee, and were it but the gaining of this one such, I will think my time, toile and present stay well spent."

CHAPTER II.

The resources of Captain Smith were no doubt very much diminished by the life of comparative repose which he led in England, and by the expenses attending his cure. On this subject we are left wholly to conjecture. But, whether he finally obeyed the impulses of his nature, or the necessities of his condition, we find him in 1614 engaging in new perils and adventures, such as he had endured and abandoned in Virginia. It is safe to assume, that a temperament so active and a mind so curious after discovery, could not rest in idleness, whatever might have been his worldly means. His studies were of a sort to keep up in his bosom a passion for adventure ; and his spirit yearned to lay bare the secret resources of that new continent, in the fate of which his sympathies were deeply engaged. He longed to emulate the achievements of the Spaniards in the southern portions of the country, though with a very decided English abhorrence of their faithless and bloody processes for conquest. To seek Virginia a second time, though Virginia really seemed to need his genius for its preservation, was not to be entertained, while a sense of the injustice with which he had been treated by the proprietors of that colony, was still fresh and rankling in his memory. His eyes were fixed, accordingly, on that portion of the English discovery which was then entitled North Virginia. Attempts had been made, probably with his advice, by a company of London merchants, who sent forth one or more expeditions in this quarter. A settlement had actually been made by the Plymouth Company, on the coast of Maine, in 1607, and a small colony had passed a cheerless winter in that region. Their experience was such as to prompt their abandonment of the country, of which they gave a most discouraging account; the effect of which was to prevent other attempts of the same sort, until the peculiar genius of Smith was brought to shape the enterprise. In the month of April, 1614, he set sail from London with two ships. The expenses of the outfit were defrayed by himself and four London merchants. At this time, the land to which his prows were directed, was regarded as a most inhospitable desert—a vast tract of barren waste and rock—which was known in Europe as Nurembega, Canada, Penaquida, North Virginia, &c., precisely as it suited the tastes of those to call it by whom its uninviting coasts were ranged. Nor was it the leading purpose of the present voyage that a settlement should be made in the country. The scheme of the adventurers was partly the whale-fishery, partly a search after mines of gold and copper; and, in the event of their failure in the search after these objects, then "fish and furs were to be their refuge." But "we found this whale-fishing a costly conclusion. We saw many, and spent much time in chasing them, but could not kill any." The search after gold was as little profitable. "It was rather the master's device to get a voyage that projected it, than any knowledge we had of any such matter." Fish and furs next demanded the attention of our voyagers, but here again it was discovered that their quest was likely to be in vain. "By our late arrival and long lingering about the whale, the prime of both these seasons was past ere we perceived it." Some fish were taken, but not enough to defray the charge of the expedition. About sixty thousand cod were the fruit of a month's fishing of eighteen men, while Smith, with eight others, ranging the coast in an open boat, obtained from the savages more than ten thousand beaver, one hundred martin, and as many otter skins. These were procured at small expense. On this progress, Smith amused himself with making a chart of the coast, and writing down all the particulars which he could gather of the country, to which he gave the name of New England, which it now bears, and will probably bear for ever.

Within six months after leaving the Downs, he returned with one of his ships, leaving the other in the command of Captain Thomas Hunt, who was instructed to carry his fish to Spain for a market. The choice of this man was unfortunate. Taking advantage of the absence of Smith, and governed by considerations of the most base and mercenary character, he decoyed twenty-four of the savages on board his vessel, and, in cruel return for the kindness with which the English had been treated by their people, he sold them into slavery at Malaga. The proceeds were a little private perquisite for himself. Smith ascribes to him a more subtle policy—namely, to discourage any settlement of the country by making the English name odious to the natives, "thereby to keepe this abounding country still in obscuritie, that onely he and some few merchants more might enjoy wholly the benefit of the trade." This object is not so apparent. The sufficient motive for the inhuman proceeding of such a wretch is to be found in the petty profits of a trade upon which no return need be made to the owners. It was no atonement to the people he had wronged that he was dismissed with indignation from employment.

Smith presented his map and the record of his proceedings to Prince Charles, afterwards the unfortunate Charles the First, whose sanction he entreated for the adoption of the new nomenclature which he proposed to employ for his discoveries. But, though Charles graciously complied with this request, he has not been successful always in the rejection of the former names. Cape Cod still stubbornly keeps its sturdy epithet, and will not be persuaded into the adoption of the more gentle title of Cape "James." Cape Ann is too easy of utterance to be surrendered for Tragabigzanda, even though in tribute to the Turkish damsel who would have bestowed her charms on our hero. Even the name of Smith himself, conferred modestly on a little group of isles, it better pleased the English lip to convert into the insignificant title of the Isles of Shoals. Surely, we might yield this little verbal tribute to him who was the first Admiral of New England. Numerous other names of places were changed by our explorer, who seems not to have affected the euphony of the Indian syllables. These, with very questionable taste, he repudiates for well-known English words. We cannot regret that the aboriginal words have been found of too sturdy a growth to be eradicated by the will of our adventurer.

Smith, on his return to England, put into Plymouth. He esteems it his ill luck to have done so; for, "imparting his purpose to divers whom he thought his friends," they engaged his services for the Plymouth Company, under a patent which had long lain dormant. They encouraged him with large promises, and thus secured his services which his late associates were quite unwilling to lose. His more recent engagement seems to have given offence to those, whose favoring and friendly opinion he was anxious to retain. But his faith was given, and he was not the man to seek escape, whatever might be his loss, from his engagement.

The effect of this difficulty was to lead to the employment of a master, named Michael Cooper, on the part of the South Virginia Company; and Smith's own facts and suggestions being seized upon, Cooper put to sea with four vessels, long before the Plymouth Company had made any provision for him. The success of his cod-fishery, under all its disadvantages, and the copious particulars which the frank nature of our Captain prompted him but too freely to make public, thus led to the anticipation of his own plans by others, who never would have conceived them. Fifteen hundred pounds had been realized by his first voyage of six months. By knowing the season for furs better than the English, the French, during the same period, had obtained twenty-five thousand beaver skins. These, with other facts, gathered from Smith's relation, together with his unwitting engagement with the Plymouth Company, had given unwonted provocation to their rivals, who had thus taken the start of them in the adventure, to the great detriment of the former. Yet all the advantages, except that of capital, were with the latter. Could the two companies have united, and sent forth a single expedition from Plymouth under our Captain, the results would have amply rewarded all parties. But commercial rivalry forbade the proper wisdom. "Much labor I had taken to bring the Londoners and them to joyne together, because the Londoners have most money and the western men are most proper for fishing; and it is neere as much trouble, but much more danger, to saile from London to Plimouth, than from Plimouth to New England, so that halfe the voyage would thus be saved; yet by no meanes could I prevaile, so desirous were they both to be lords of this fishing."

Smith, on engaging with the Plymouth Company, had been promised four good ships, which were to be ready by Christmas. In January, with two hundred pounds cash, for private adventure, he left London, accompanied by six of his friends, and went to Plymouth. His sanguine expectations were doomed to disappointment. The ships were not ready; and the Company, owing to discouraging reports of disaster to other voyagers, had cooled in their desire for the enterprise. Yet, in behalf of this Company, Smith had declined the command of the London expedition—the four ships sent out under Cooper—which had been first tendered to him. Ordinary men would have desponded under these circumstances. Certainly, fortune warred spitefully against our hero. But he was not discouraged. His soul was always too much in his scheme to yield readily to denials or reverses. He went to work with his wonted energy in beating up supplies and recruits. His friends came forward, he invested all that he himself had, and succeeded in getting furnished one vessel of two hundred and another of fifty tons. Sixteen persons were engaged to go in this expedition, with the view to a permanent settlement of the country. This was a favorite scheme with our adventurer. He says in one of his narratives—"Nor will I spend more time in discovery or fishing till I may goe with a company for a plantation." He had the just notion of what was essential to the permanence of conquest.

The two vessels were soon made ready for the sea, and left Plymouth in March. But the ill luck which had thus far baffled him, was not disposed to forego its hostility. He had sailed little more than a hundred leagues, when the two vessels were separated by a tempest—the ship of Smith was dismasted, and he was compelled to return to Plymouth under jurymast, the crew being kept at the pumps with every watch, with the dread of foundering momently before their eyes. The vessel, probably old and worthless at the outset, and only patched up for the exigency, was not worthy of repairs, and we find our voyager resuming his adventure in a small bark of sixty tons, with but thirty men, instead of the seventy which he had in the former ship. He left Plymouth on the 24th of June. His consort, from whom he had separated, weathered the gale in safety, and, ignorant of the fate of the larger ship, proceeded on her voyage, which was profitable in its results. But the evil eye was still upon our captain, and the adventure, so far as his progress was concerned, was one of mishaps and disappointments. His first danger was from an English pirate, a bark of one hundred and forty tons, manned by eighty men, and armed with thirty-six cannon. The little vessel of Smith was of three score tons only, with thirty seamen and four guns. His master, mate, pilot and others were very importunate with him to yield, and he had more trouble in the contest with their fears than he expected to have with the foe. He was stubborn in his resolution to fight it out with the pirates, and made his preparations accordingly. But, when the enemy drew nigh, and recognized our adventurer, they became pacific. Their leaders recognized him as their former captain. They proffered him the command of their vessel. They were willing that he should lead them at his pleasure. They were prepared to confide in him rather than in themselves. In fact, there was a mutiny among them. They had lately run from Tunis, lacked provisions, and were divided into contending factions.

It was unfortunate that Smith refused their alliance. He afterwards repented that he had not accepted the command which they proffered him. But he was discouraged by their mutinous condition, and had his heart too deeply set upon the leading object of his adventure, to trouble himself with the unnecessary task of reforming these profligates. But his own crew proved even less tractable. Near Fayal he was encountered by two other pirates. But these were Frenchmen. One of them was of two hundred and the other of thirty tons. Here again, his crew were terrified at the disparity of force, and positively refused to go to the guns. But our captain was not to be disgraced in this manner. He had a process of coercion which they learned to fear more than the enemy, and he prepared to fire his magazine, and blow his bark in air, rather than yield while he had any powder left. This brought his mutineers back to their duty. They saw determination in his eye, and the approach of the pirate was welcomed with a cannonade. A running fight followed, in which the English succeeded in making their escape.

But their temporary good fortune was about to leave them. Near Flores they were chased and overtaken by four French men-of-war, all well armed, and each of them superior to the little craft of our Captain. He was made to go aboard of the French admiral and show his papers. These proved him to be neither Spaniard nor pirate, against whom the French vessels were then cruising. But the laws of nations were but little insisted on in those days, where there was no adequate power to enforce them. Though Smith showed the broad seal of England to his commission, it was the policy of the Frenchman to believe him pirate, Spaniard, or what he pleased. They respected neither him nor his papers; detained him a prisoner; rifled his vessel; manned her with Frenchmen; and distributed the English as prisoners among their own ships. After several days' detention they capriciously restored his vessel to our adventurer, restored his men and provisions, and left him to pursue his voyage. This he resolved to do, much against the wishes of his crew; but before he could separate from the French admiral, the latter sent his boat for him, requesting once more to see him. He obeyed the invitation, which was, in other words, a command; and, while on board the admiral, a sail was espied, which sent all the ships forward in pursuit—all but the English vessel. Here, his discontents availing themselves of Smith's absence, the confusion of the chase, and the approach of night, turned their prow for England ; leaving " our Captaine in his cap, bretches, and waistcoat, alone among the Frenchmen." Smith asserts that his detention among the French was intentional, and induced in some degree by the machinations of two of his own seamen, Edward Chambers, the master, and John Miller, the mate, who had been discontents from the beginning of the voyage. They represented that he would " revenge himself upon the *Banke*, or in *Newfoundland*, upon all the French he should there encounter." The mutineers reached Plymouth in safety, having divided Smith's personal property among them. A commission was instituted before the vice-admiral of England to investigate the proceedings, and the particulars thus given were derived from the statements, on oath, of six of the crew. Whether the mutineers were ever punished for this proceeding does not appear. The probabilities are against it. " The greatest losse," says Smith, " being mine," " the sailers did easily excuse themselves to the merchants in England that still provided to follow the fishing : much difference there was betwixt the Londoners and Westerlings to ingrosse it, who now would adventure thousands, that when I first went would not adventure a groat." Indeed, so completely had our Captain shown the way, that he might almost as justly claim to have founded New England as Virginia.

Smith remained during the whole summer a prisoner on board the Frenchman. He soon discovered that his captors were little better than pirates. They certainly sailed under a commission which conferred great privileges. They scrupled at no sort of game. Nothing came amiss that promised to compensate the trouble and the cost of capture; and the cruise was one which promised to be profitable in a high degree. English ships were as frequently plundered as any other; and our Captain was frequently pained to see wrongs done to his countrymen, such as he himself had suffered, which he had not the power to prevent. But the English ships were sometimes hard customers for our French admiral; and Smith indulges in a tone of laudable exultation when he finds the courage of his tribe asserting itself, now and then, triumphant over the cunning and treachery of their enemies. The details of what he witnessed during his captivity will scarce concern us here. Our business is rather with himself. He was not idle during his captivity. Some time was spent by the French admiral in the neighborhood of the Azores. Here, "to keepe his perplexed thoughts from too much meditation of his miserable estate," he employed himself in writing a narrative of his voyages to New England, with an account of that country. His mind was never idle. His eye took in the details of a subject at a glance, and his thoughts compassed all its demands and necessities the moment after. Nor did our Frenchmen leave him unemployed. They were glad to use him whenever they fought with the Spaniards, and he seems to have been no ways unwilling to encounter the national enemy. But when the foe was English, then he was again made a prisoner. His readiness in these cases secured the favor of his captors. The French captain promised to put him ashore at the Azores, but broke his promise, and it was not till the summer was over that he was permitted to approach the land. Reaching Rochelle, the fair promises of the captain were forgotten, and Smith, instead of freedom and reward, was made a close prisoner, and charged with having burnt Port Royal in New France, in 1613 a deed that

Cast ashore. PAGE 347.

was done by Capt. Argall. The object of this accusation was to scare him into giving them a discharge before the Judge of Admiralty.

Our hero was very much in their power. It was not easy to find justice for an Englishman in France, during the feeble foreign administration of any of the Stuart family. Besides, it was a time of great civil commotion among the French—"a time of combustion, the Prince of Condy with his army in the field, and every poor lord or man in authority, as little kings of themselves."

Smith reasoned justly when he concluded that his chief hope must rest upon himself. He determined to escape, if possible. He watched his opportunities accordingly, and, one dark night, at the close of a storm, which had driven the Frenchmen into close cover below, he let himself down into their boat, and with a half pike instead of an oar, he set himself adrift in the hope to reach a contiguous islet. But the current was against him, and carried him out to sea. Here, in a small boat, without even the proper implement by which to work his way, amidst gust, and rain, and darkness, for the space of twelve hours our fearless adventurer, struggling manfully all the while against his fate, looked momentarily to be hurried to the bottom. "But it pleased God that the wind should turn with the tide," and while "many ships were driven ashore and divers split," his boat was drifted upon a marshy islet, where he was picked up the next day by "certaine fowlers, neere drowned and halfe dead with water, cold and hunger." His escape had been a narrow one. In flying from captivity he had also flown from death. The ship of his captors had been driven ashore, and her captain drowned with half of his crew.

CHAPTER III.

Thus preserved by the special mercies of Providence, amidst so many disasters, and even against his own expectations, Smith found the means for getting to Rochelle by pawning the boat which had borne him through his dangers. At this place he preferred his complaint to the Judge of Admiralty, against the Frenchman who had captured him, and was listened to with patience and many promises. Here he first received tidings of the wreck of the vessel in which he had been detained, and the drowning of her commander. Some of the survivors whom he encountered he caused to be arrested, and their story, on examination, confirmed his own. These particulars, properly put on record, he placed in the hands of the English ambassador, then at Bordeaux. But nothing seems to have come of his complaint. The foreign relations of the Government of Great Britain, under the feeble administration of James, were not of a sort to command much respect among the natives of the continent. Smith says—"of the wracke of the rich prize, some three thousand six hundred crownes worth of goods came ashore and were saved, with the caraval, which I did my best to arrest; the Judge promised I should have justice; what will be the conclusion as yet I know not. But, under the colour to take Pirats and the West Indie men (because the Spaniards will not suffer the French to trade in the West Indies), any goods from thence, though they take them upon the coast of Spaine, are lawfull prize, or from any of his territories out of the limits of Europe:—and as they betraied me, though I had the broad seale, so did they rob and pillage twentie saile of English men more, besides them I knew not, of the same yeere."

And there was no redress for the subject, whether from France or England. The feebleness of the latter invited the aggressions of the former. A Cromwell was the only necessary cure for these foreign evils, and his day was approaching. But he came too slowly for the help of Smith. Our adventurer would have been reduced to sad straits in France, wanting means, but that he met good friends. It was his good fortune to meet his "old friend, Master Crampton, that no less grieved at his losse," than willingly, to the extent of his resources, supplied his wants; and "I must confesse," he adds, "I was more beholden to the Frenchmen that escaped drowning, to the lawyers of Bourdeaux," and to another whom we shall name hereafter, than to "all the rest of my countrymen I met in France." This other was of the gentler sex—a Madame Chanoyes, of Rochelle—who, he tells us, "bountifully assisted" him. Smith was always fortunate in finding favor with the ladies. His person was good, his manners easy and dignified. His mind was essentially pure and elevated. His delicacy was distinguished. He had few or no vices; and, stern in battle, rigid in rule, and uncompromising with his foes, he was yet in every sense of the word a gentleman. One of his eulogists, who signs himself "Your true friend, sometimes your souldier, *Tho.* Carlton, writes:

"I never knew a warrior yet, but thee,
From wine, tobacco, debts, dice, oaths, so free."

The line sums up a great many of those vices, from one or other of which, soldiers of fortune are seldom free; and when we regard the trials and vicissitudes, the necessities and the frequent irresponsibility of his career, we must allow that, but for a native delicacy of character, Smith could scarcely have escaped contamination from one or other of the practices here enumerated, and which, vicious mostly in themselves, are but too much regarded as venial because of their common use. One of his poet-eulogists ascribes the favor of Madame Chanoyes to a far tenderer feeling than that of simple humanity:

> "Tragabigzanda, Callamata's love,
> Deare Pocahontas, *Madame Shanois* too,
> *Who did what love* with modesty could doe."

But this is probably an exaggeration of the versemonger. We have nothing in proof of the insinuation. Smith himself affords no countenance to the suggestion, and in no instance suffers himself to speak of either of these ladies, but in terms of proper and respectful gratitude.

"Leaving thus my businesse in France, I returned to Plimoth, to finde them that had thus buried me amongst the French, and not only buried me, but with so much infamy as such treacherous cowards could suggest to excuse their villanies." They pretended, in short, that he was about to convert his vessel into a man-of-war—in other words to become a pirate. "The chieftaines of this mutiny that I could finde, I laid by the heeles; the rest, like themselves, confessed the truth." Our narrative of the second voyage to New England, as far as they were concerned in the events, has been drawn from this confession. But Smith gained nothing for his own, in bringing the mutineers to their deserts. The fisheries, to which he had opened the way, yielded vast profits to the adventurers. The fishers of Iceland and Newfoundland abandoned these places for those of the waters of New England. New England herself was laid open as a rich prize to other colonists, in consequence of Smith's discoveries and representations. He alone pined with denial, while he beheld others grow prosperous and insolent in the wages of his adventure, and the spoils that should have rewarded his genius only. "Now, how I have, or could prevent these accidents, having no more meanes, I rest at your censures; but to proceed to the matter, yet must I sigh and say, 'How oft hath fortune in the world brought slavery freedome, and turned all diversely.'" The disasters all happened to him and not to the enterprises which he set on foot. Two lines, seemingly his own, are made to finish his desponding fancies with a well-known sarcasm:

"Fortune makes provision
For knaves, and fools, and men of base condition."

Denied to seek adventures because of the sad and prolonged hostility of fortune, the indefatigable nature of Smith counselled him to put on record, and in proper circulation, his discoveries. He wrote a book called "New England's Trial." The trial was in fact his own. It embodied all that he had endured in his two voyages, all that he had seen and heard, his comments upon his facts, and a sprinkling of his moral philosophies, drawn from his reading and his experience. Much of the matter of this volume was written while he was a captive with the Frenchman. Much of it appears scattered over his other writings. In the preparation of his pamphlets he was quite desultory, and frequently refers to, and sometimes repeats, the matter which we find in other places. The present work, which was published in 1616, was put forth in quarto form. It gives such sketches of New England as he formerly gave us of Virginia. It describes the shores, and seas, and islands, along the coast, the people of the country, their manners, customs and superstitions. It has its value to this day, and is the source of much of the information of succeeding historians. It was accompanied by a map of

New England, and one edition of the work contained several maps, as well of that region as of Virginia. Colonization in New England was still the object upon which his desires were set. To effect this object he traversed England, distributing his book. Thousands of copies were given to chartered companies of London, in the hope that they might be persuaded to embrace his suggestions. But his time seems to have been thrown away, if not his knowledge. None of it enured to his benefit. The opinion began to spread about that he was unlucky, and to be unlucky is, unhappily, in the vulgar estimate, to be something worse than vicious and unwise. No imputation, indeed, so certainly forfeits for its subject the sympathies of the selfish multitude. Smith answers this imputation of ill luck with a cheerful defiance. "Some fortune-tellers say I am unfortunate. Had they spent their time as I have done, they would rather believe in God than in their calculations." This is very nobly said. His own want of means—his poverty—was urged against him as the only fruit of all his adventures. But this he answers, still as nobly. These profitless adventures which have given him empire and conquest, and which have left him unselfish, have been to him "as children—they have been my wife, my hawks, my hounds, my cards, my dice, and in totall, my best content." He has exercised his own nature in his adventures—he has brought into play the best affections of his soul—his troubles have taught him a knowledge of his resources—his privations and poverty have not brought remorse, regret and repentance in their train. "I would yet begin againe with as small means as at first, not that I have any encouragement more than lamentable experience." Of the discoveries of those who have followed him, he says, coarsely but with natural energy, "they are but pigs of my own sow." "Had men been as forward to adventure their purses, and perform the conditions they promised mee, as to crop the fruits of my labours, thousands ere this had been bettered by these designes." "They dare now adventure a ship, that, when I first went, would not adventure a groat."

Still, though they glean from his suggestions, they cannot do them proper justice. He has learned to feel a manly confidence in his own genius, if not in his fortune. It is Smith, only, that can properly work out the schemes of Smith, to a happy consummation. "For I know my grounds, yet every one to whom I tell them, or that reads this book, cannot put them in practice." He is not illiberal even to those who seek to pilfer from his plans. "Though they endeavor to worke me out of my own designes, I will not much envy their fortunes ; but I would be sorry their intruding ignorance should by their defailments bring these certainties to doubtfulnesse." The eagerness which he feels to continue his career of colonization and discovery, qualified by the mournful results of his own struggle, hitherto, to impress his convictions upon others, declares itself in a highly bold and spirited figure, taken from the *manége* of the days of chivalry. "Thus, betwixt the spur of desire and the bridle of reason, I am near ridden to death in a ring of despaire." His own demands, in the event of success, were moderate enough. He asks only to be rewarded out of the results of the adventure, according to his pains, quality, and condition. If he fails—"If I abuse you with my tongue, take my head for satisfaction."

But he had survived his fortunes. He was a lingerer on the stage. Who keeps the guide when the way is once made clear? Who needs a Columbus to place the egg upright when he has flattened the point already to their hands? The claims of justice are always urged impertinently when it is in the power of men to thrust them from sight with impunity; and great men, having achieved the leading event in their lives, are not willingly believed in any longer, since they always require to be compensated for future services, with some regard to the value of the past. Smith urged his arguments and distributed his books in vain. His mission was at an end with regard to all new discovery. But he could still be of service; and we find him called upon without scruple by those who never knew how to compensate him, when his experience and opinions might be esteemed of importance to the interests which he had already acquired for them. We must once more turn our eyes upon the colony in Virginia.

CHAPTER IV.

While Smith was struggling with misfortune at home, the colony which he had founded in Virginia was rising into greater strength and consequence. Its military characteristics were, however, much more conspicuous than its social. It warred not only upon the Indians but upon the French and Dutch. Early in 1614, Sir Thomas Dale, the governor of the colony, sent Captain Argall with a force against certain settlements which the French had made in Acadia. These were broken up and the colonists dispersed. They subsequently adapted themselves to the habits of the Indians, and were incorporated among the tribes. Hudson's Dutch settlement, now New York, was also made to acknowledge the King of England, and to pay a tribute to the Governor of Virginia; and, waxing insolent with success, and with the gradual increase of power, another demand was made upon Powhatan. Sir Thomas Dale thought it advisable to insist upon other pledges besides Pocahontas, but of a like description. Powhatan had another and a younger daughter. She had become her father's favorite, who now yielded her that place in his affections which had formerly been solely occupied by the former. The attachment of Pocahontas for the English, her marriage with an Englishman, and her entire withdrawal from his sight, had served, in a great degree, to wean from her his regards, and, accordingly, to lessen that influence upon his mind which she had formerly possessed, and which was of so much importance to the colonists. It will scarcely be believed, that the selfishness of the colony was of such a nature as to make its government heedless or blind to the cruelty of the requisition which it made upon the aged Emperor, for the other child of his affections. Mr. Ralph Hamer was sent upon this mission, and the details of his interview with Powhatan have been preserved to us. Hamer was accompanied by Thomas Savage, the interpreter, a youth who had been given by Newport to the king. Powhatan recognized the boy, whom he had restored some years before to the English. "You were my boy," he said, "and I gave you leave, four years ago, to visit your friends; but I have never seen nor heard of you, nor of my own man, Namontack, since; though many ships have gone and returned." Then, turning to Hamer, he demanded the chain of pearl —the string of wampum—which, when a treaty of peace had been made with the English, at the time of his daughter's marriage, he had sent to Sir Thomas Dale. That string of pearl was to be a token between them; and in proof that the messenger came from the English, whenever Dale should send to him hereafter. Failing in this, Powhatan was to take and bind the alleged messenger, and send him back to Dale as a deserter. Hamer had not provided himself with this chain. The requisitions of the Indians were apt to be treated heedlessly. Powhatan looked doubtfully upon his visitor, but Hamer found some ingenious reason for showing that the stipulation could not relate to him, and Powhatan admitted the exception. He inquired after Pocahontas, and his unknown son, and was pleased to hear of their prosperity. When told that his daughter was so well satisfied with her new condition that she would not, upon any account, return to live with him, he laughed heartily, as if his old affections were rejoiced at the happiness of his child.

But when Hamer came to declare his business—to show

the cruel purpose upon which he came—the face of the old chief grew troubled. His countenance fell and darkened. Of course, the application was made in a form of as much mildness as was consistent with the rapacious harshness of the demand. "His brother, Dale, had heard of the fame of his youngest daughter, intended to marry her to some worthy English gentleman, which would be highly pleasing and agreeable to her sister, who was very desirous to see and have her near her; and, as a testimony of his love," the father was desired to send her also to the English.

Powhatan, conscious of the power of the colonists, and unwilling to offend them, endeavored to evade the demand. "He had parted with his daughter—he had already given her in marriage to a chief—had sold her to him, and received his pay." When pressed and driven from these objections, he at length declared himself frankly with the feeling of a father and the dignity of a prince. He desired Hamer to urge him no more upon the subject, but to return to his brother Dale this answer:

"That he held it not a brotherly part to endeavor to bereave him of his two darling children at once: That, for his part, he desired no farther assurance of Dale's friendship than his promise: That, of his own, the English had a sufficient pledge in one of his daughters; which, as long as she lived, would be sufficient; and should she die, then he should have another. Tell him further," said he, "that even were there no pledge, there need be no distrust of me or my people. We have had enough of war. Too many already have been slain on both sides. With my will there shall be no more. I have the power here, and I have given the law to my people. I am now grown old. I would end my days in peace and quietness. My country is large enough for both, and even though you give me cause of quarrel, I will rather go from you than fight with you. Take this answer to my brother."

And the agent in this unworthy mission received no other. He returned to his principal as he went. How far Pocahontas may have been privy to the application is not said. Her name is not otherwise mentioned in the transaction than as it appears in Hamer's report of the message which Dale had sent to Powhatan. It is scarcely possible that she willingly gave her consent to a scheme for depriving her aged sire of the only thing which he had chosen to comfort him after her desertion.

Pocahontas seems really to have been fully satisfied, as Hamer reported to her father, with her English associations and condition. She had been baptized, and had received the Christian name of Rebecca. It was only after this event that the colonists discovered that her real name was Matoaka or Matoax, and that the name of Pocahontas was one only assumed when she was spoken of to English ears. A superstition, which prevailed among the Indians, led them to fear that, with a knowledge of her true name, it was in the power of the Christians to do her hurt. The superstition of the evil mouth, as well as the evil eye, was quite as common among our aborigines as it has ever been among the various people of the East. Her adoption of Christianity seems to have been fervent and sincere. She is described as of quick intelligence, in learning equally the faith and language of her husband; and her career from childhood amply declares the aversion which she felt for the wild exercises and coarse brutalities of her own people. She was with them, but not of them—a creature, as foreign to the sort of world in which she is found, as was that exquisite creation of Goethe—the Mignon of the Wilhelm Meister. Her whole nature was gentleness—there was in her a spiritual craving, which alone seems to have indicated the necessity for the advent, among her tribes, of a superior divinity. The heart which has expelled all other idols, will never be left unoccupied by the true God.

In the spring of 1616, Sir Thomas Dale embarked for England, taking with him Pocahontas and her husband, and several young Indians of both sexes. He enjoyed the triumph which should have belonged to Smith. Powhatan did not see his daughter when she left the country. He never saw her again. The old chief was at this time suffering, not only from the pressure of years, but from the dread of foes at home. He had reason to dread the machinations of Opechancanough—a chief every way to be feared; a favorite with the people; a man of great courage and ability. He aimed at the succession, and finally achieved it. Opitchapan (who is sometimes called Itopatin), the favorite brother of Powhatan, was lame and feeble; and, the latter once removed, could oppose no serious obstacle to the bolder and abler genius of Opechancanough. We shall return to this history again. It is enough here to say, that the reason given for the failure of Powhatan to see his daughter before her final departure, was the necessity which he felt of watching or avoiding the machinations of the former; who was suspected of a plan to deliver him hand and foot into the hands of the English.

Pocahontas arrived in England on the 12th of June. Her fame had long since preceded her, and made her an object of consideration. Respect and curiosity equally brought her the attentions of the great. She was visited by persons of rank and character, whose hospitality spared no pains to make her satisfied with the strange country in which she found herself.

Smith was preparing at this time for a third voyage

to New England. His sanguine temperament seems to have persuaded him, against the fact, that he was in a fair way of obtaining the command of a new expedition. With his heart exulting in new hopes of a favorite character, he was yet not unmindful of his Virginia nonpareil. As soon as he heard of her arrival in England, he penned the following letter "To the most high and virtuous Princess, Queen Anne of Great Britain:

"Most admired Queen,

"The love I beare my God, my King and countrie, hath so oft emboldened mee in the worst of extreme dangers, that now honestie doth constraine mee presume thus farre beyond myselfe to present your majestie this short discourse: if ingratitude be a deadly poyson to all honest vertues, I must bee guiltie of that crime if I should omit any meanes to be thankful.

"So it is, that some ten years agoe, being in Virginia and taken prisoner by the power of Powhatan, their chief king, I received from this great salvage exceeding great courtesies, especially from his son Nantaquuas, the most manliest, comeliest, boldest spirit I ever saw in a salvage, and his sister Pocahontas, the king's most deare and well beloved daughter, being but a childe of twelve or thirteen yeeres of age,* whose compassionate, pitifull heart, of desperate estate, gave me much cause to respect her: I being the first Christian this proud king and his grim

* We have seen in the "True Relation," written at the time, that he describes her as a child of ten years old—a statement more likely to be correct than the present, as his impressions were necessarily more fresh and vivid: he speaks of her only as of a child, sweet and wonderful, but still a child. Had she been marriageable then, she would have found an English husband—nay, in all probability, as soon as she was marriageable, the idea, never before entertained, was suggested of taking her prisoner.

attendants ever saw: and thus inthralled in their barbarous power, I cannot say I felt the least occasion of want that was in the power of those, my mortal foes, to prevent, notwithstanding all their threats. After some six weeks fatting amongst those savage courtiers, at the minute of my execution, she hazarded the beating out of her own braines to save mine; and not onely that, but so prevailed with her father, that I was safely conducted to Jamestowne, where I found about eight and thirtie miserable, poore and sicke creatures, to keepe possession of all those large territories of Virginia: such was the weaknesse of this poor commonwealth, as, had the savages not fed us, we directly had starved.

"And this reliefe, most gracious Queene, was commonly brought us by this Lady Pocahontas; notwithstanding all these passages when inconstant fortune turned our peace to warre, this tender virgin would still not spare to dare to visit us, and by her own faires have been oft appeased, and our wants still supplyed; were it the policie of her father thus to imploy her, or the ordinance of God thus to make her his instrument, or her extraordinarie affection to our nation, I know not: but of this I am sure,—when her father, with the utmost of his policie and power, sought to surprise me, having but eighteen with me, the dark night could not affright her from comming through the irkesome woods, and with watered eyes gave me intelligence, with her best advice to escape his furie: which, had he knowne, he had surely slaine her. Jamestowne, with her wilde traine, she as freely frequented as her father's habitation; and during the time of two or three yeares, she, next under God, was still the instrument to preserve this colonie from death, famine and utter confusion; which, if in those times had once become dissolved, Virginia might have line (lain) as it was at our first arrivall to this day. Since then, this business having beene turned and varied by many accidents from that I left it at: it is most certaine, after a long and troublesome warre after my departure, betwixt her father and our colonie, all which time she was not heard of, about two years after she herselfe was taken prisoner, being so detained neere two years longer, the colonie by that meanes was relieved, peace concluded, and at last, rejecting her barbarous condition, was married to an English gentleman, with whom at this present she is in England; the first Christian ever of that nation, the first Virginian ever spake English, or had a childe in marriage by an Englishman;—a matter, surely, if my meaning bee truly considered and well understood, worthy a Prince's understanding.

"Thus, most gracious lady, I have related to your Majestie, what at your best leasure our approved histories will account you at large, and done in the time of your Majestie's life, and however this might bee presented you from a more worthy pen, it cannot from a more honest heart. As yet I never begged anything of the state, or of any, and it is my want of abilitie and her exceeding desert, your birth, meanes and authoritie, her birth, virtue, want and simplicitie, doth make mee thus bold, humbly to beseeche your Majestie to take this knowledge of her, though it be from one so unworthy to be the reporter as myselfe, her husband's estate not being able to make her fit to attend your majestie: the most and least I can doe, is to tell you this, because none so oft has tried it as myselfe; and the rather, being of so great a spirit, however her stature, if it should not bee well received, seeing this kingdome may rightly have a kingdome by her meanes—her present love to us and Christianitie might turn to such scorn and furie as to direct all this good to the worst of evil —where finding so great a Queene should doe her some honour more than she can imagine, for being so kind to your servants and subjects, would so ravish her with content, as endeare her dearest blood to effect that your Majestie and all the king's honest subjects most earnestly desire. And so I humbly kisse your gracious hands."

This letter, earnest as it is, is not written with the usual eloquence and ease of our adventurer. Big with his subject, and writing to a Queen, he seems to have been struggling with his own conceptions, and to have been overcome by them. His thoughts are clumsily uttered, and never came to their full proportion in delivery. But he evidently wrote from his feelings, and may be believed when he asserts that, though his statement might be presented from "a more worthy pen," it could not come "from a more honest heart." We are not told whether it was to this address that Pocahontas was indebted for those attentions which the Queen of England, as well as her consort, bestowed upon her. She was kindly and honorably entertained at court, though the tradition is that her husband Rolfe was frowned upon for his presumption in intermarrying with royal blood. The Scottish Solomon, whose tenacious sense of legitimacy was probably the one principle to which he more religiously adhered than to any other, is said to have held the proceeding as little less than treason or misdemeanor. It is fortunate that John Rolfe's ears did not pay the penalty of his ambition.

Smith did not content himself with simply writing to the queen in behalf of the Lady Rebecca, for such was the name she bore in England. Though earnestly engaged in his preparations for the voyage to New England, he hurried with several of his friends to see her at Brentford, whither she had been removed from London. At this time Smith was probably at Plymouth. We have the account of the interview from himself. It was highly touching, but unsatisfactory. His salutation was probably reserved and cautious, and she was in a strange land. She expected the warmest signs of attachment from one whom she had regarded with the devotion of a child; and he was governed by those fears of offending the suspicious pedant who sat upon the throne of England, of whose opinion, in this very instance, our captain was probably aware. The untutored damsel of the Virginian forests could not understand his reserve, though the real motive of his caution was that she might not prejudice her claims to the patronage of the crown. She felt his coldness, but not his policy. She cared nothing, perhaps, for any countenance but his. "After a modest salutation," such is Smith's statement, "without any word she turned about, obscured her face, as not seeming well contented." How much spirit was in that silence! What feelings were stirring in that untutored but noble bosom, which could thus move her to shroud and turn away her face! She had calculated largely, no doubt, upon this meeting with the great warrior of the pale-faces, who had first impressed her with the greatness of his people. And to be encountered thus, as if he had never been plucked from death by her embrace—as if she had never wandered through the midnight woods to save him—as if she had not brought him food when he hungered, and taught her maidens to dance about him in strange forest movements, the better to beguile his weariness. In her secret heart she reproached him with want of gratitude—at the very moment when he acknowledged no other feeling.

Smith had told his friends that she spoke the English, and now regretted having done so, for she refused to speak. In this mood they left her for some hours; when they rejoined her, a more indulgent spirit informed her thoughts. She now spoke, and spoke freely. They spoke together of the past, and she thus reminded him of her former love to the English, and what she had done for them.

"You did promise Powhatan," said she, "that what was yours should be his, and he made a like promise unto you. You, being in his land a stranger, called him father, and by the same right I will call you so."

Smith would have objected to this "because she was a king's daughter," and having a fear of King James in his eyes; but, "with a well-set countenance she said, 'Were you not afraid to come into my father's country, and cause fear in him and all his people but myself, and do you fear that I should call you father here? I tell you that I will call you father, and you shall call me child, and so shall it be for ever. They did always tell us that you were dead, and I knew not otherwise until I came to Plymouth. Yet Powhatan believed it not, because your countrymen will lie much, and he commanded Uttomatomakkin* to seek you out and know the truth.'"

* "This salvage, one of Powhatan's counsell, being amongst them held an understanding fellow, the king purposely sent him, as they say, to number the people here, and informe him well what wee were and our state. Arriving at Plymouth, according to his directions he got a long sticke, whereon by notches hee did think to have kept the number of all the men hee could see, but he was quickly wearied of this task."(*a*)—*Smith's Narrative.*

This cunning savage denied to Smith that he had seen the king (James), though it was known that he had. He argued that, as the king had given him nothing, it could not be a king he had seen. "You gave a white dog to Powhatan," said he to Smith, "yet to me, that am better than a white dog, your king has given nothing."

This shrewd savage is sometimes called Tomoccomo, and sometimes Uttomaccomach. His accounts of England were unfriendly, and he was disgraced on his return to Virginia.

(*a*.) When he returned to Virginia, and was asked the number of the people, he answered, "Count the stars in the sky, the leaves of the forest, and the sands of the seashore—such is the number of the people of England."—*Stith.*

Smith frequently visited her, and enjoyed, with a not unbecoming satisfaction, the astonishment of those "divers courtiers and others, my acquaintances," whom she delighted by her natural gifts, and the happy manner in which she received them. "They did thinke God had a great hand in her conversion, and they have seene many English ladies worse favored, proportioned and behaviored."

But the career of the Indian princess was short in England. She sickened and died at Gravesend, early in 1617, as she was preparing to return to Virginia. The event was unexpected, but it did not find her unprepared. She presented to the sorrowing spectators the sweetest example of Christian resignation and fortitude. She left one son, Thomas Rolfe, who was educated by his uncle, Henry Rolfe, in England, and who afterwards became a person of distinction and fortune in Virginia. From an only daughter, whom he left,* some of the first families of Virginia trace their descent, with a just and honorable pride. Among these we may mention a recent and distinguished instance, in the person of John Randolph of Roanoke.

* He left behind him an only daughter, who was married to Col. Robert Bolling, by whom she left an only son, the late Major John Bolling, who was father to the present Col. John Bolling and several daughters, married to Col. Richard Randolph, Col. John Fleming, Dr. William Guy, Mr. Thomas Eldridge and Mr. James Murray. So that the remnant of the imperial family of Virginia, which long ran in a single person, is now increased, and branched out into a very numerous progeny.—*Stith*, 146.

CHAPTER V.

To attempt any analysis of the character of Pocahontas—to offer any eulogy upon her virtues, so equally delicate and decided as they were, would only result in unnecessary declamation. As there is nothing to question in the propriety of her conduct, so there is nothing which needs defence; as there can be no doubt of the extraordinary courage which she brought to the support of a benign humanity, equally extraordinary, so nothing is necessary to the full comprehension of her virtues beyond the actual facts in her history. As these virtues were not of the time or the people among whom she was born and nurtured, so they denote a degree of excellence which lifts her beyond her race and period, and links her name and reputation with those of the few noble spirits, like herself, of whom the universal heart everywhere keeps a tenacious memory. A more incomparable creature never did honor to her sex. A more feminine spirit never was sent to earth for the purposes of humanity.

Powhatan did not long survive his daughter. He lived long enough to lament her. He died in April, 1618, and was succeeded by Itopatin. For a time Opechancanough seems to have submitted to his sway; and a hollow amnesty lulled the colonists of Virginia into full confidence in their treacherous neighbors. They were warned of this impolicy, but treated the warning with contempt—the population of the colony increasing annually, and the adventurers scattering themselves, with few precautions, throughout the forests. But the complete government of the Indians was passing into the hands of Opechancanough. Itopatin was a mere puppet at his will. The former was the leading spirit of his people ; bold, subtle, highly popular, enterprising, and possessed of vast powers of dissimulation. With the gradual acquisition of sway over the popular mind, he prepared for the full assertion of his authority. To supersede Itopatin and to extirpate the English, were his favorite objects, and his schemes rapidly ripened for their gratification. The year 1622 was rendered memorable in Virginia by the massacre of nearly four hundred of the thoughtless and unsuspicious settlers. So well was the plan of the Indians laid, and so general was the combination, that, at the appointed hour, the several assailing parties, however remote from one another, were each of them at the appointed places in which the separate tasks of slaughter were to be done. That the massacre was not complete, was not the fault of the Indians, nor because of the vigilance of the English. Their good fortune saved them from utter extermination.

This terrible event threw the whole country into consternation, and inflicted a most serious blow upon the success of the colony. The excitement was great in England, and our Captain was remembered as one whose experience might be drawn upon with profit to find some remedy for so grievous a disaster. He offered, with a hundred and thirty men, to render the colony perfectly safe against all the power of the tribes. His scheme was one which has been largely adopted in the settlement of our borders in after times. It was to employ bands of Rangers, by whom the frontiers were to be continually traversed. "These I would imploy onely in ranging the countries and tormenting the savages, and that they should be as a running army, till this were effected, and then settle themselves in some such convenient place, that should ever remain a garrison of that strength, ready upon any occasion against the savages, or any other, for the defence of the country." Smith was at some pains to urge this, and some other schemes, for the restoration and safety of the colony, upon the proprietors. He was deeply affected by the fate of the settlement. His affections yearned towards it, and he was prepared to forget and surrender his old grudges upon the altar of patriotism. He frankly proposed to take charge of such a command as that which he counselled, and his opinions were given at considerable detail, involving suggestions of operations by the water courses of the country as well as among the forests. For these services he asked nothing but what he could gather from the country itself. But he addressed ears which were shut by cupidity. The council was divided in opinion. Some favored his project, others were opposed to it; but all consented that he should be permitted to save their colony at his expense and risk, while they were not unwilling to share with him the pillage of the savages, whatever that might be. We need hardly say that their liberality failed to satisfy one who had so largely suffered already by their avarice. He quietly rejected their offer, and yielded the hope, for a moment entertained, of once more triumphing in Virginia. "They supposed," says he, "that I spake only for my own ends!" In truth, it is the most difficult thing for the mere worldling to comprehend the generous nature which lies at the bottom, the vital principle, of an enterprising genius. "It were good," he adds, "if they themselves were sent thither to make trial of their profound wisdomes." "I would not give twenty pound for all the pillage that is to be got among the salvages in twenty years."

The distresses of the colony, and its great expense to the proprietors, finally led to its disparagement. Estimated by its burdens only, it began to be undervalued. Smith answered the aspersions upon the colony "in a brief relation, written to his majesty's commission." He describes the face of the country, its resources, its importance to the crown—the feebleness of the savages if properly managed—and the true causes of all the distresses under which the colony labored;—all of which he insists could have been avoided had his advice been taken. At the close of this relation he tells us that he spent five years, and more than five hundred pounds, "in procuring the letters patent and setting forward, and neere as much more about New England;"—that "these nineteen yeeres I have, here and there, not spared any thing according to my abilitie, nor the best advice I could, to persuade how those strange miracles of misery could have been prevented, which lamentable experience plainly taught me of necessitie must ensue; but few would beleeve me, till now too dearly they have paid for it. Wherefore, hitherto, I have rather left all than undertake impossibilities, or any more such costly tasks at such chargeable rates: *for in neither of these two countries have I one foot of land, nor the very house I builded, nor the ground I digged with my own hands, nor any content or satisfaction at all; and though I see ordinarily those two countries shared before me by them that neither have them nor knowes them, but by my descriptions: yet that doth not so much trouble mee as to heare and see those contentions and divisions which will hazard if not ruine the prosperitie of Virginia, if present remedy be not found, as they have hindred many hundreds who would have been there ere now.*"

The unselfish nature of Smith's, here expressed, could not be denied, with such proofs of his privations and his present readiness still to adventure, even with no better encouragement before him. A commission had been issued by King James, addressed to certain great persons, to examine into the condition of the colony, report the transactions of the company, and devise a scheme for the remedying of evils and abuses. This commission necessarily had resort to Smith. They propounded to him numerous questions, to all of which he answered with his usual sagacity. He was better master of his subject than any other of his successors, knew the country and the Indians more thoroughly, and, indeed, the pathways they had subsequently opened, had been only where he had previously made the *blaze*. To the question, why the colony, left by him in a good state of forwardness, had not better prospered; he answered, that "Idleness and carelessness had brought to nothing in six months, what he had taken three years to do." When asked, "Why the country, if good, should produce nothing but tobacco;" he answered, "that the frequent change of governors makes every man anxious to make the most of his time." As to the cause of the massacres and the use of the English weapons by the Indians, he ascribes it to the want of martial discipline on the part of the English, and their employment of the savages as fowlers and huntsmen; twenty thousand pounds outfit, he thinks, would have put the colony above hazard, if rightly employed; and a good supply of laborers along with the soldiers, at a further cost of five thousand pounds, well managed, would remedy the present disasters. The defects of the government he ascribes to the multitude of councillors, the number and expense of unnecessary officers, the delay of action, and the waste of time in ceremonials and formalities—"the orations, disputations, excuses, hopes"—the "extortion, covetousness and oppression in a few"—and the waste upon governors, deputies, treasurers, marshals, and other unnecessary officers, of the money which should be appropriated only to the necessities of the community. "Thus they spend Michaelmas rent in Midsummer moon, and would gather their harvest before they have planted their corne." Smith concludes with a hint, of which James appears to have availed himself; namely, that the government of the colony might, with as much propriety, be taken into his own hands, as left in those by which it was at present administered. In 1624, the Virginia company was dissolved accordingly, its powers absorbed in those of the crown, and a special commission was issued for the appointment of a governor and twelve councillors, who were to have the whole management of the colony.

But, in all these changes, our captain remained without employment. We have seen him hurrying his interview with Pocahontas, in order that he might revisit New England. But the adventure failed. He never proceeded on this voyage, but lived in a vain struggle with the capitalists, fed for a long time upon hopes, that never yielded any better food. Twenty ships were promised him, and a promise so magnificent was well calculated to dazzle the imagination of one with a faith so sanguine, and a passion for enterprise so deeply entertained and eager. But with his soul ever in America, his body remained in England. If he could not go forth himself, he encouraged all who could do so; and, working to the last in the favorite object of his heart, he seems to have continued to write and to publish until the latest moment of his life. We have already mentioned several of his writings. In 1620, he published a pamphlet, entitled "New England's Trials, declaring the success of twenty-six ships, employed thither within these six yeares." A second edition of this work, with the title somewhat altered, was published two years after. In 1626, he sent forth his "General Historie of

Virginia, New England and the Summer Isles, with the names of the Adventurers, Planters and Governors, from their first beginning, An. 1584, to the present, 1626, &c." To this work, of which we have already spoken, we have been largely indebted in the progress of our biography. In 1630, he published "The true Travels, Adventures and Observations of Captain John Smith in Europe, Asia, Affrica and America, from 1593 to 1629; together with a continuation of his general Historie of Virginia, Summer Isles, New England, and their proceedings since 1624 to the present, 1629; as also of the new Plantations of the great river of the Amazons, the Isles of St. Christopher, Mevis and Barbadoes in the West Indies." In 1631, he put forth his "Advertisements for the unexperienced Planters of New England or anywhere, or the Pathway to Experience, to erect Plantations," &c. The volume is a medley, containing many clever things, sometimes marked by an epigram, at others by a passage or paragraph of force, almost amounting to eloquence, and full, in correspondence with his title, of his various experiences. He was also the writer of a sea grammar, which was highly praised by nautical men of his day, and which was republished several times after his death. Of several of these writings we have American editions. He was engaged upon a work, called "The History of the Sea," when surprised by death in 1631. This production seems not to have been finished, and the fragment has not survived to our day. Smith died at London in the fifty-second year of his age. He probably died in obscurity, for none of the facts attending his demise remain to us. He had survived his uses, at least in the estimation of his patrons and the public. That they erred in this judgment will not be held a matter of doubt by those who have witnessed the proofs, here accumulated, of his good sense, far-reaching sagacity, and great mental activity to the last. Our summary of his career and character has already been made. That a more fiery spirit, more admirably tempered by prudence for the most trying adventure, never lived, will be admitted by all to whom this history becomes familiar. That he shared the fate of merit, to be neglected after the completion of his tasks, will not lessen the value of his performance in the regards of posterity.

Opechancanough, one of the great Virginia opponents of our Captain, survived him for several years, and maintained the same consistent hostility to the whites that he had shown at the beginning. In 1639 he contrived another outbreak of the Indians, to which more than five hundred of the colonists fell victims. His name became more dreaded than that of Powhatan. His resources were greater, and he was fully equal to him in dignity and nobleness of character. His skill in the government of his people at once secured their reverence and affection. He subjected the tribes around him far and near, and extended greatly the domain of his predecessor. But his faculties failed with age. He had become so decrepit that he was no longer able to walk alone, and was carried about in the arms of his people. His flesh was emaciated, the sinews so relaxed, and his eyelids so heavy, that whenever he desired to see, they were lifted by his attendants. In this condition he was surprised by Sir William Berkeley, the then Governor of Virginia. Thus feeble, and in bonds, the proud spirit of the savage king, and his strong intellect, never failed him. Exposed to the rude stare of the multitude, as a public show, he had his eyelids raised on the approach of Berkeley, and fixing his glance sternly upon him, read him a lesson which, if the English governor possessed any remains of noble sentiment, must have made him wince. "Had Sir William Berkeley fallen my prisoner," said he, " I should not thus meanly have exposed him as a show to my people."

Berkeley designed to send him to England, as a royal captive, gracing his government in the eyes of his sovereign; but one of his soldiers, with a scarcely greater degree of cruelty, defeated this purpose by shooting the aged monarch through the back. Thus perished, the victim of a base assassin, one of the bravest and most sagacious of all the forest monarchs of America.

THE END.

APPENDIX.

[PAGE 58.]

SMITH'S PATENT OF NOBILITY,

WITH THE CERTIFICATE OF THE ENGLISH GARTER-KING-AT-ARMS.

SIGISMVNDVS BATHORI, Dei gratia Dux *Transilvaniæ, Wallachiæ, & Vandalorum;* Comes *Anchard, Salford; Growenda;* Cunctis his literis significamus qui eas lecturi aut audituri sunt, concessam licentiam aut facultatem *Iohanni Smith*, natione *Anglo* Generoso, 250. militum Capitaneo sub Illustrissimi & Gravissimi *Henrici Volda*, Comitis de *Meldri, Salmariæ & Peldoiæ* primario, ex 1000. equitibus & 1500. peditibus bello *Vngarico* conductione in Provincias supra scriptas sub Authoritate nostra: cui servituti omni laude, perpetuaq. memoria dignum præbuit sese erga nos, ut virum strenuum pugnantem pro aris & focis decet. Quare favore nostro militario ipsum ordine condonavimus, & in Sigillum illius tria *Turcica* Capita designare & deprimere concessimus, quæ ipso gladio suo ad Vrbem *Regalem* in singulari prælio vicit, mactavit, atq; decollavit in *Transilvaniæ* Provincia: Sed fortuna cum variabilis ancepsq; sit idem forte fortuito in *Wallachia* Provincia Anno Domini 1602. die Mensis Novembris 18. cum multis aliis etiam Nobilibus & aliis quibusdam militibus captus est a Domino *Bascha* electo ex *Cambia* regionis *Tartariæ*, cujus severitate adductus salutem quantam potuit quæsivit, tantumque effecit, Deo omnipotente adjuvante, ut deliberavit se, & ad suos Commilitones revertit; ex quibus ipsum liberavimus, & hæc nobis testimonia habuit ut majori licentia frueretur qua dignus esset, jam tendet in patriam suam dulcissimam: Rogamus ergo omnes nostros charissimos, confinitimos, Duces, Principes, Comites, Barones, Gubernatores Vrbium

& Navium in eadem Regione & cæterarum Provinciarum in quibus ille residere conatus fuerit ut idem permittatur Capitaneus libere sine obstaculo omni versari. Hæc facientes pergratum nobis feceritis. Signatum *Lesprizia* in *Misnia* die Mensis Decembris 9. Anno Domini 1603.

SIGISMVNDVS BATHORI.

Cum Privilegio propriæ Majectatis.

UNIVERSIS, & singulis, cujuscunq. loci, status, gradus, ordinis ac conditionis ad quos hoc præsens scriptum pervenerit, *Guilielmus Segar* Eques auratus alias dictus Garterus Principalis Rex Armorum *Anglicorum*, Salutem. *Sciatis*, quod Ego prædictus Garterus, notum, testatumque facio, quod Patentem suprascriptum, cum manu propria praedicti Ducis *Transilvaniæ* subsignatum, et Sigillo suo affixum, Vidi: & Copiam veram ejusdem (in perpetuam memoriam) transcripsi, & recordavi in Arhivis, & Registris Officii Armorum. Datum *Londini* 19. die Augusti, Anno Domini 1625. Annoque Regni Domini nostri CAROLI Dei gratia Magnae *Britanniæ*, *Franciæ*, *&* *Hiberniæ* Regis, Fidei Defensoris, &c. Primo

GVILIELMVS SEGAR, *Garterus.*

SIGISMVNDVS BATHOR, by the Grace of God, Duke of *Transilvania*, *Wallachia*, and *Moldavia*, Earle of *Anchard*, *Salford* and *Growenda;* to whom this Writing may come or appeare. Know that We have given leave and license to *Iohn Smith* an *English* Gentleman, Captaine of 250 Souldiers, under the most Generous and Honourable *Henry Volda*, Earle of *Meldritch*, *Salmaria*, and *Peldoia*, Colonell of a thousand horse, and fifteene hundred foot, in the warres of *Hungary*, and in the Provinces aforesaid under our authority; whose service doth deserve all praise and perpetuall memory towards us, as a man that did for God and his Country overcome his enemies: Wherefore out of Our love and favour, according to the law of Armes, We have ordained and given him in his shield of Armes, the figure and description of three *Turks* heads, which with his sword before the towne of *Regall*, in single combat he did overcome, kill, and cut off, in the Province of *Transilvania*. But fortune, as she is very variable, so it chanced and happened to him in the province of *Wallachia*, in the yeare of our Lord, 1602, the 18th day of November, with many others, as well Noble men, as also divers other Souldiers, were taken prisoners by the Lord *Bashaw* of *Cambia*, a Country of *Tartaria;* whose cruelty brought him such good fortune, by the helpe and power of Almighty God, that hee delivered himselfe, and returned againe to his company and fellow souldiers, of whom We doe discharge him, and this hee hath in witness thereof, being much more worthy of a better reward; and now intends to returne to his owne sweet Country. We desire therefore all our loving and kinde kinsmen, Dukes, Princes, Earles, Barons, Governours of Townes, Cities, or Ships, in this Kingdome, or any other Provinces he shall come in, that you freely let passe this the aforesaid Captaine, without any hinderance or molestation, and this doing, with all kind nesse we are always ready to doe the like for you. Sealed at *Lipswick* in *Misenland*, the ninth of December, in the yeare of our Lord, 1603.

SIGISMVNDVS BATHOR

With the proper privilege of his Majestie.

To all and singular, in what place, state, degree, order, or condition whatsoever, to whom this present writing shall come: I *William Segar*, Knight, otherwise Garter, and principall King of Armes of *England*, wish health. Know that I the aforesaid Garter, do witnesse and approve, that this aforesaid Patent, I have seene, signed, and sealed, under the proper hand and Seale Manual of the said Duke of *Transilvania*, and a true coppy of the same, as a thing for perpetual memory, I have subscribed and recorded in the Register and office of the Heralds of Armes. Dated at London the nineteenth day of August, in the yeare of our Lord, 1625, and in the first yeare of our Soueraigne Lord *Charles* by the grace of God, King of great *Britaine, France*, and *Ireland:* Defender of the faith, &c.

WILLIAM SEGAR.

www.ingramcontent.com/pod-product-compliance
Lightning Source LLC
LaVergne TN
LVHW040755070826
844660LV00025B/1151
* 9 7 8 1 6 1 1 1 7 6 8 9 6 *